Hope's New Season

Lois Jean Thomas

Seventh Child Publishing, LLC

Saint Joseph, Michigan

This book is a work of fiction. Names, characters, and incidents are the product of the author's imagination or are used fictitiously. Any resemblance between events or persons, living or dead, is coincidental.

Cover design by A. R. Thomas

ISBN: 978-0-9976445-2-4

Library of Congress Control Number: 2017903186
Lois Jean Thomas, Saint Joseph, Michigan

To my parents,
Reverend Charles and Gladys Haarer

CONTENTS

ACKNOWLEDGMENTS

As always, I want to express my deepest appreciation to my husband Allen for his help with research, proofreading, and formatting this book.

I can't possibly express enough gratitude to my dear friend Mary Ruth Fox. She provided invaluable help with editing and proofreading. More than that, she shores up my confidence and offers unending encouragement.

Thank you to the members of Writers Bloc for supplying constructive feedback that helped to make this a better story.

And thank you to Yvonne Lopez of Michigan Rehabilitation Services and Warren Galloway of Warren Galloway and Associates, LLC, who have nudged me forward and helped me see what is possible.

Hope's New Season

Lois Jean Thomas

PART I: SUMMER 1978-SPRING 1979

CHAPTER 1

Only a handful of people, aside from my immediate family, know the true story of my origins. The few loved-ones in whom I've confided live far away from my home community, where the commonly believed version of my story still prevails. None of these loved-ones were part of my childhood, so hearing the truth about my conception ignited no emotional fires in them. None of them raised an eyebrow when they learned that I had three parents.

My mother, Ada Hochstedler Unruh, surrounded her tender soul with a wall of sternness, which made it difficult for me to know her. She was unable to love me without reservation, not until the very end, as the regrettable circumstances of our shared life created a barrier between us. I've always carried sadness about this.

Herman Unruh III, the sweet, humble man who raised me, loved me abundantly despite the fact that I wasn't biologically his. He served as my port in the storm during many difficult times in my life. He has been, and always will be, my dad.

Reverend Harry Hahn, the father who gave me life, was considered by many unknowing people to be a great man. He was, by other estimations, a scoundrel masquerading as a man of God. I've come to realize there was truth in both of these perceptions.

While I'd occasionally seen Reverend Hahn during my growing-up years, I'd been blissfully unaware of his relationship to me, and had never considered the man with more than childish indifference. But just before my seventeenth birthday, he came crashing into my life with the startling intensity of a lightning bolt.

Not that this was his doing. His wife was still living at the time, and he was invested in protecting her from the knowledge of his philandering.

It was my older sister Lucy who was responsible for allowing the carefully guarded secret of my paternity to fly out of Pandora's box and wreak havoc in my life. Lucy suffered from a mental illness, and she and my mother had a tumultuous relationship. One day near the end of my junior year at Conrad Grebel Christian High School, Lucy blurted out the words that sent my orderly little world into a tailspin. "If I had a different father like Tori Grace does," she'd screamed at my mother in a fit of rage, "then maybe you'd love me more."

Alarmed and bewildered by my sister's words, I'd demanded to know what she was talking about. But Lucy immediately thought better of her outburst and refused to say anything more.

When no further information was forthcoming, I assaulted Lucy in an attempt to force the truth out of her. Fortunately, my dad came upon the scene just in time to keep me from doing my sister serious bodily harm. As he unclamped my hands from her throat, he announced the truth that should have been revealed to me years earlier, that Reverend Harry Hahn was my biological father.

This news hit me like a fist in the stomach. Stunned and dazed, I ran away from home for half a day, and was brought back by the police in the early hours of the next morning. Over the following week, my parents provided me with details of the story about how I came to be. How my mother had left our snug little Mennonite community in Goshen, Indiana, to go on a three-month mission trip to Mexico. Her brief affair with the supervisor of the mission project, the dashing and charismatic Reverend Harry Hahn. Her ensuing pregnancy with me at an age when she thought her childbearing years were over. The decision made by Reverend Hahn and my mother to keep my paternity a secret, in order to guard against scandal and to provide their illegitimate child with as normal a life as possible. The noble decision made by my mother's husband, Herman Unruh, to step up and play the part of my father. Reverend Hahn's role as the behind-the-scenes puppet master, exercising irksome control over the way my mother raised me. His going above and beyond his commitment to provide financial support, ensuring that I, his only offspring, had everything he thought I needed.

Although my parents tried to be fair in conveying this information, the story left me with nothing but contempt for the man who had provided half of my genetic endowment.

A year later, when I was about to graduate from Conrad Grebel High, Reverend Harry Hahn and I came face-to-face with each other, to acknowledge for the first time our father-daughter relationship. At that point, he was retired from the ministry and recently widowed. He was well into his sixties by then, as his dalliance with my mother had taken place in his late forties, and he was already in ill-health and confined to a wheelchair. I'd thought then that he was on the verge of death. But he kept a tenacious hold on life, determined to stick around for as long as possible in order to spend time with his only child.

Our first meeting happened at his request. I had wanted to refuse, but somehow couldn't. My birth father seemed to exercise a powerful control over me, just as he'd done with my mother. When I arrived at his small apartment in Goshen's Greencroft senior living community, I was simmering with anger, ready for a showdown. I pummeled him with insults and accusations, but he rebounded from all my attacks, maintaining his dignified demeanor throughout our exchange. I left at the end of the visit with a depleted store of anger and a flicker of warmth in my heart.

But I had no desire to return for a second visit. Although I hated to admit it, my biological father and I shared uncanny similarities, both in physical form and in mind. Looking at him was like staring at an older version of my reflection in the mirror. He seemed to know me as well as he knew himself, and being in his presence sometimes felt eerie. When he gazed at me with the dark, intense eyes that were so much like mine, I'd have to look away.

The months between my senior year of high school and my first year at Goshen College were busy, different from the lethargic summers I'd enjoyed up to that point in my life. Other than the odd babysitting job, I'd had no experience with earning a paycheck. So landing employment at the Taste of Home family restaurant in downtown Goshen seemed like a leap into adulthood. My mother, who worked as a secretary at Goshen College, had her summers off. Thus, I was able to drive her car to work, and did not need to rely on parental transportation. Feeling like a full-fledged grown-up exhilarated me.

I worked as many shifts as I could, trying to accumulate a store of cash to help pay for my upcoming college expenses. The job consumed me, both physically and mentally, distracting me from my uneasy thoughts about my biological father.

Initially hired to wash dishes and bus tables, I quickly found those tasks so repugnant that I didn't think I could stick it out for the entire summer. But within a week of my hiring, Bob, the owner of the restaurant, told me he wanted to try me out as a waitress. He instructed me to come to work the next day dressed in a black skirt and white blouse. When I arrived the following morning, he handed me a little white apron and put me in training with Mindy, one of Taste of Home's long-term waitresses.

Mindy was in her early thirties, a pretty blonde with a sassy personality. She provided constant entertainment for the male customers, who enjoyed bantering with her. "Bob likes me working in the front of the house because he thinks I keep the regulars coming in," she told me. "He put you out here because you're cute and friendly, and you catch on quick."

After shadowing Mindy for several hours, I had the routine down pat: approach the table, greet the customers, introduce myself, and ask, "Can I start you out with something to drink?" Two weeks later, I was also trained in the role of hostess. During the restaurant's busy times, I was often assigned the tasks of seating customers and running the register.

Most of my coworkers were young and remarkably immature, and only the presence of one or two older adults on the shift kept conditions in the restaurant from escalating into mayhem. Two seventeen-year-olds, Allen the dishwasher and Bradley the busboy, were especially prone to disgusting horseplay. They put ice down the girls' backs. They pelted each other with pieces of broccoli and cauliflower left on customers' plates. They had belching contests.

Edna, our head cook, was in her late fifties, an ill-tempered, heavy-set woman with cropped gray hair. She'd worked in food services for four decades, and had the battle scars to prove it. Her burly forearms were pocked with old burns, and she was missing a third of the index finger on her left hand. "It happened when I was running a meat slicer," she told me, almost proudly. "Tore up my finger, and pretty much wrecked that machine, too."

She had no tolerance for the antics of Allen and Bradley, and was constantly yelling at them. "If it was up to me," she'd bellow, "I'd throw your sorry asses outa here."

Skinny, floppy-haired Allen, whose sharp wit compensated for his diminutive stature, dubbed me 'Stretch' because of my five-feet, eleven-inch height. Every time I'd walk into the kitchen, he'd grin, point at something stored on a high shelf, and say, "Would you mind getting that for me, Stretch?"

"I have fantasies about tall women," he'd tell me,

contriving a dreamy-eyed expression.

I'd counter with, "Too bad for you. I don't fantasize about little pipsqueaks."

Bradley, a big teddy-bear of a boy, lumbered through his work, never in a rush to get a table cleared even when the restaurant was at its busiest.

Both of the boys flirted with me incessantly, bombarding me with crude innuendoes. If Edna wasn't in earshot, they'd blatantly proposition me. "In your dreams," I'd quip as I brushed past them.

Whenever I was on break, I'd sit down at a back table to drink a *Coke,* or to eat the one free meal I was allotted during my shift. Inevitably, one of the boys would plunk his bottom down in the chair across from me, trying to chat me up. "Do you mind?" I'd growl at him. "I'm trying to enjoy my food." When I'd refuse to give him any attention, he'd eventually get up and wander away.

Early one morning, as I walked across the parking lot to the back door of the restaurant, I found Allen and Bradley out by the garbage cans sweeping up shards of stoneware.

"What's going on?" I asked them.

"Nothing," they both mumbled, looking chastened.

When I went inside, I found Edna so riled up that I half-expected flames to shoot out when she opened her mouth. "I had a stack of chipped coffee cups and some cracked plates," she fumed at me. "I asked the boys to throw them out. And wouldn't you know it, instead of dumping them straight into the garbage, those little shits took those dishes out to the parking lot and started throwing them up in the air. Just so they could watch them bust into pieces when they hit the ground."

She shook her head slowly, as if she couldn't fathom the ignorance behind such action. "One of the girls came in and told me what they were up to. I stormed out there and told them that if they didn't have that mess cleaned up in two minutes flat, I was gonna make sure their asses got fired.

Those boys think they're such big men, but honestly, they're nothing but snot-nosed brats."

Seconds later, Allen and Bradley came through the back door, brooms in hand. "Idiots," I hissed as they walked past me.

Neither of them bothered me for the rest of the day, as I had witnessed their humiliation. However, the following day, they were back in their usual form.

CHAPTER 2

On the Friday evening of my second week of work, I bounded through the front door of our farmhouse, kicked off my shoes, and flopped down on the shabby sofa, proudly waving my first paycheck.

"Well, what do you know!" my dad exclaimed from his armchair. "My little girl has started earning her own money. Good for you, Vickie."

My mother stepped out of the kitchen, wearing the worried look that was indelibly etched on her face. "Victoria, I need to tell you something." She wiped her hands on her apron, grimacing slightly, as if the words she was about to utter were distasteful in her mouth. "Harry called for you."

Her news pricked the buoyant balloon of my mood, instantly deflating it. "You've got to be kidding me!" I grumbled. "What did he want?"

"He didn't tell me," she replied. "All he said was that he wants you to call him back."

"Do I have to?"

She shrugged. "It's up to you. I can't be the go-between for the two of you anymore. You've got to work things out with him on your own."

"Well, I don't have to jump every time he snaps his fingers," I said defiantly. "I'm just going to blow him off."

My mother laughed bitterly as she headed back into the kitchen. "Don't think you'll get away with that attitude, Victoria. He's not going to leave you alone until he gets what he wants."

Grunting in exasperation, I stretched out on the sofa, burying my face in the crook of my arm. My dad reached over and patted my shoulder with a sympathetic hand. "It'll be okay, Vickie. Just do what you think is right."

Half an hour later, my conscience propelled me to the phone in the kitchen. Reluctantly, I dialed the number my mother had written down for me. Reverend Hahn answered on the first ring, as if he'd been sitting by his phone confidently awaiting the call he expected from me.

"Victoria!" he exclaimed. "How are you? How's your new job going? I bet waitressing is hard work."

I was so startled that I couldn't speak for a few seconds. I'd told my birth father that I was looking for a job, but I hadn't informed him that I'd found one. No doubt, he'd elicited that information from my normally tightlipped mother. But I was rapidly coming to terms with the fact that, whether I liked it or not, Reverend Harry Hahn managed to know almost everything about my life. All those years I hadn't known he was my biological father, he'd been lurking in the background, keeping tabs on me.

"My job's fine," I told him. "I'm working a lot of hours."

"I'd like for us to get together again," he said. "Soon. There's something I need to discuss with you."

"I'm pretty busy ...."

"I'm sure you are," he said, unperturbed by my efforts to brush him off. "But I can adjust my schedule to accommodate any free time you have. When's your next day off?"

And before I knew it, I had agreed to our second visit, on Wednesday afternoon of the following week.

When I arrived at his apartment, Reverend Hahn wheeled his chair to the door to let me in, greeting me enthusiastically. It struck me that he looked even older than he had at my visit a month ago. His once jet-black hair was now almost completely silver. Deep furrows creased the skin around his eyes and mouth. His cheeks were sunken, his jowls sagging, his eyelids droopy.

However, keen intelligence still sparkled in his dark eyes, and he looked as dapper as ever in his dress shirt and trousers. His living quarters were spotless and in perfect order, just as they'd been at my first visit. I noticed a fine china plate, laden with brownies, sitting on the coffee table. An elegant stemware glass containing an unknown chilled beverage stood on a coaster beside the plate.

"Have a seat." Reverend Hahn gestured toward the sofa. "And please help yourself to refreshments."

I didn't want to appear uncouth by immediately diving into the food, so I took a moment to gaze around the apartment. Everything seemed to be the same as at my last visit, except for a vase on the dining table containing an arrangement of giant yellow roses and orange lilies, rounded out with tiny flowers of various colors. I'd never seen anything so lavish. While my mother would occasionally bring in a handful of daisies from her garden and stick them in a jar, never had such an elegant arrangement graced the table in our shabby farmhouse.

"Those are pretty," I said, pointing to the flowers.

Reverend Hahn smiled. "Aren't they, though? I bought them from the Wooden Wagon Floral Shoppe. From time to time, I feel the need to brighten up this little place."

I picked up one of the deluxe paper napkins on the coffee table, then carefully lifted a brownie from the plate and took a bite. It was incredibly rich, with a molten chocolate center. "These are delicious," I said. "Where did you get them?"

"From the little bakery in downtown Goshen," he replied. "I can always trust their goods to be of the highest quality."

I tried to imagine him driving around town doing his own shopping, but given his condition, the idea didn't seem feasible. "So, do you still get out and drive?" I asked. Immediately, I felt embarrassed by my nosy question.

A shadow crossed Reverend Hahn's once-handsome features. "I get out, but I no longer drive. I have friends from church who provide transportation when I need to run errands."

"That's nice," I said. "What church do you go to?"

"College Mennonite. It's not far from here. It's right there on the campus."

I picked up the glass of pale beverage, unsure what I was about to drink. "It's white grape juice," Reverend Hahn said. "I hope you like it."

I took a sip, then nodded. "It's good." Carefully setting the glass back on the coaster, I said, "You don't have to do all this special stuff for me."

"I want to," he replied. "It brings me joy to treat my child well."

I winced at his words. While I'd accepted the fact that Reverend Hahn was biologically my father, I still couldn't think of myself as his child.

"Help yourself to another brownie," he urged.

Chuckling self-consciously, I reached for a second one. "I'll get fat if you keep feeding me like this."

"I doubt it," he said. "You take after me. We both have lean frames that aren't inclined to carry excess weight."

I held out the plate. "Do you want one?"

He shook his head. "No, thank you. Not right now."

I wondered if I'd embarrassed him. Judging by his emaciated condition, I suspected that he had little appetite, or that he didn't want me to witness the difficulty he had with eating.

"If you don't mind me asking ...."

"Ask me anything," he said. "I'll answer if I'm able to."

"What is your ... illness?"

"ALS," he promptly responded. "Amyotrophic lateral sclerosis. I was diagnosed two years ago."

I wasn't prepared for the wave of sadness that washed over me. I looked down, fiddling with the hem of my tee shirt. "What does that mean?"

"It's a disorder that affects the nerves and muscles. It has hit me hardest in my legs. As you might suspect, I can no longer walk without assistance. This past year, I've experienced a slight weakness in my arms and hands, although I still manage pretty well. And eating can be difficult. I have a bit of trouble with swallowing."

"I'm so sorry," I said. "That must be hard."

"It's my cross to bear," he said. "I try to bear it with grace. It could be a lot worse. Many people with the disease have been stricken harder than I have. I'm determined to make the best of each day that I have left."

I couldn't bear to look at the sorrow on his face, so I lowered my eyes again, twisting my napkin in my lap. I wanted to ask him how much time he had left, but I knew that would be terribly insensitive.

He cleared his throat, a task that seemed to require effort. Then he spoke in a lighter tone. "When we talked on the phone, I told you I had something to discuss with you."

I lifted my head to meet his gaze. "What is it?"

"I want to talk with you about living on campus when you go to college this fall."

I stared at him, dumfounded. My parents and I had always assumed that I would commute to college. We lived only seven miles from the Goshen College campus. My mother drove there to her job five days a week, and I could easily hitch a ride with her. The thought of living on campus hadn't even entered my mind.

My parents and I had carefully worked out how we would cover my college expenses. I was entitled to a discount on my tuition because of my mother's employment at the college. I'd been awarded several small scholarships. I was earning money from my summer job, and planned to continue part-time work throughout the school year. My parents would be chipping in what they could, but my mother's secretarial wages and my father's earnings as a mailman didn't provide for a lot of extras. Adding the cost of living in a dormitory was out of the question.

I shook my head. "I don't think my parents can afford to have me living on campus."

Reverend Hahn looked at me from under a furrowed brow, as if to chide me for my silliness. "Don't you know that your college expenses won't impact your parents' finances in any significant way? They'll be receiving a check from me by the end of this week."

I leaned back against the sofa, my mouth hanging open in bewilderment. "Oh," was all I could think to say.

"Would you want to live on campus if you knew that you could?"

"I suppose so," I replied, although I wasn't at all sure I was ready to leave the familiar comforts of my parents' home.

Reverend Hahn smiled in satisfaction. "Then I'll be more than happy to pay the extra to have you live on campus. I want you to enjoy the entire experience of being a college student. If you live at home and commute to the campus, you're bound to miss out on the social life."

As he continued to expound on the merits of living on campus, I knew he was right. My birth father was leading me down a path that would undoubtedly be good for me, even though I wasn't quite ready for it.

"Isn't it too late to put in my reservation for a room?" I asked, hoping for a way to wriggle out of the deal that was about to be sealed.

"I'll make a phone call," he assured me. "I'll let you know."

On my drive home, I suddenly realized that Reverend Hahn's magnanimous gesture had a self-serving underbelly. My living on campus would take me seven miles away from my parents' farmhouse and put me within easy walking distance of his apartment.

Several hours later, I sat down at the supper table with my mom and dad. For the past few years, it had been just the three of us. My two older brothers, Michael and Robert, had been in their late teens when I was born, and they'd left home so long ago that I had no memory of them living in our household. My twenty-seven-year-old sister Lucy, whose mental illness prevented her from being entirely on her own, was living in a small apartment in nearby Elkhart, under the supervision of a case manager.

I had little appetite that evening, because of the three brownies I'd consumed at Reverend Hahn's apartment, and also because I dreaded broaching the topic of me living on campus.

I felt my mother's anxious eyes on me as I picked at my fried chicken and green beans. "How did your meeting go this afternoon?" she finally asked.

"Okay." After a long silence, I added, "He told me something."

My mother bristled. "What?"

"He's pretty sick. He has ..." I paused, trying to recall the official term. "Amyotrophic lateral sclerosis."

"I don't know what that means," my mother said.

"ALS. You've heard of that."

Her eyes widened in recognition. Then she winced and nodded.

My dad still looked puzzled. "It's Lou Gehrig's Disease," I explained to him.

"Oh," he said. "The disease that killed the baseball player. That's a rough thing to go through."

The three of us sat in silence, while the word *killed* lingered ominously in the air.

"So, it's terminal?" my mother asked.

"It will be," I responded. "Eventually."

Something flickered in her eyes, and then my parents exchanged the briefest of glances. I knew their unspoken thoughts. They were imagining the day when Reverend Harry Hahn's overbearing presence would be lifted from their lives.

I was surprised to feel resentment rumbling in the pit of my stomach, and I set down my fork a little too hard. *Don't worry,* I thought. *He'll be out of your hair soon enough.*

"He thinks I should live on campus this fall," I said in a breathless rush. "He says he'll pay for it."

My mother's face reddened with anger. "We had this all figured out," she muttered. "He just can't leave well enough alone."

My dad sighed heavily, his craggy face crestfallen. After he finished eating, he went to sit in his armchair in the living room, resting with his chin on his chest, his eyes closed.

I sat on the floor, leaning against his knee like I'd done as a small child. I could sense his grief. Since my first meeting with Reverend Hahn a month ago, I'd felt my dad pulling back, as if he thought he no longer had the right to be my father.

"I guess I just don't have enough to give you anymore, Vickie," he mumbled. "I guess I need to get that through this thick head of mine."

"You always give me enough, Dad," I protested.

He didn't respond. I sat there at his knee for a long time, until I felt his heavy hand resting on the top of my head, telling me that everything was still okay in the little world we shared.

CHAPTER 3

Two weeks later, on a sweltering mid-summer afternoon, I came home from work to find my mom sitting in the hot kitchen, shelling an enormous bowl of peas from her garden. Wisps of gray hair had come loose from her bun, springing out on each side of her haggard face. I watched a trickle of perspiration run down her chest, disappearing under the bodice of her faded cotton housedress.

She looked miserable, I thought. Suddenly feeling sorry for my joyless, overworked mother, I sat down at the table to engage her in conversation. "Wow, that's a lot of peas. Are we having some for supper?"

She glanced up at me and nodded. "I'm trying to get a few pints in the freezer, too."

When further attempts to discuss the peas fell flat, I got up to leave the kitchen. As I was about to head up the stairs, she said, "Harry called again."

I stopped and turned to face her. "Is this going to be a regular thing?"

She passed a weary forearm over her sweaty brow. "Probably. You might as well get used to it. I had to." She picked up another pea pod, snapped it open, and scooped out the contents with an expert thumb. "I'm sorry, Victoria. I don't mean to sound like I don't care. I know this is hard for you."

Scowling, I headed toward the phone, knowing I couldn't relax that evening until I got the dreaded task over with. When Reverend Hahn answered my call, he plied me with polite questions about my job before saying, "There's something else I need to discuss with you, Victoria. When might you be free to come over?"

I glanced at my mother. I knew she was following the gist of our conversation, as Reverend Hahn's sonorous voice carried through the phone line and across the room. She was shaking her head, a sardonic smile on her face.

"I'm off work Monday," I said reluctantly.

"Good!" came his eager reply. "I'll see you then."

When I arrived at Reverend Hahn's apartment three days later, he greeted me warmly, offering me a tall glass of lemonade and an enormous soft pretzel.

"The first thing I need to tell you," he said, "is that we have a dormitory room lined up for you. You'll need to complete the paperwork. It should come to you in the mail in a day or two."

My anxiety shot sky-high. As I had my mouth full of chewy pretzel that I suddenly couldn't swallow, all I could do was nod.

Then he said, "Let's talk about the courses you'll be taking this fall."

I finally managed to choke down my mouthful of pretzel. Then I took a long drink of the lemonade before responding. "I don't know what I'm taking yet. I thought I was supposed to pick my classes when I meet with my academic advisor."

"Of course." He gazed at me for a long moment, his intense eyes boring into my private thoughts, making me squirm. I was summoning the courage to take another bite of the pretzel when he asked, "Have you decided on your major yet?"

Another bolt of anxiety shot through me, and I set the pretzel down. "I've thought about it," I said in a weak voice. "But I haven't made up my mind yet."

He thinks I'm a clueless dud, I thought. But Reverend Hahn nodded in understanding. "Of course not. I'd actually be worried if you had a decision set in stone. You need to take some time to explore a variety of options."

He shifted his position in his chair, straightening his frail body, and his voice took on an authoritative tone. "So your first year, you should focus on taking your general requirements, the courses you'll need to graduate. By the middle of your sophomore year, you'll have more of an idea of what direction you want to take. When you get focused on your major, you'll be glad you got all those general requirements out of the way."

I'd already had that very conversation with my guidance counselor during my last semester at Conrad Grebel High School. I was irked that Reverend Hahn had lured me to his apartment for such a pointless discussion.

When I arrived back home an hour later, I found my mother on her hands and knees, pulling the weeds from around the hydrangea bushes in our front yard. Her dress was smudged with dirt, her face reddened from her efforts. Clearly agitated, she was yanking out weeds with a fury that couldn't be directed at the true object of her anger. As I approached, she looked up at me, a sour expression on her face.

"I got a check from Harry today," she said. "I put it in the bank. It'll cover the cost of your room and board this fall." She grabbed another weed, yanking so hard that she almost fell back on her bottom.

From then on, whenever Reverend Hahn called me, he made no pretense of having something important to talk about. He simply said, "Victoria, I'd like to see you." As much as I dragged my feet and grumbled to my parents, I always complied with his request.

I never entered the Greencroft community under the guise of my true identity, Reverend Hahn's daughter. If a nurse or housekeeper happened to be in his apartment when I arrived, he'd graciously introduce us, saying, "This is my young friend Victoria Unruh."

Staff members would smile indifferently as they left the room, as if meeting one of Reverend Hahn's visitors was a routine part of their day. I suspected he had a stream of friends coming in and out of his apartment.

No matter how resentful I'd be when I arrived, he'd welcome me with his irresistible charm, gently but surely pulling me into his little world. His dark eyes would sparkle with anticipation, as if he expected our time together to be a momentous event. His coffee table was always laden with delicious refreshments, which I imagined he asked the staff to set out for me.

Reverend Hahn rarely spoke about his illness. He always held his rickety frame with as much dignity as possible in his wheelchair, and was unfailingly well-groomed and well-dressed. I suspected he couldn't manage certain things entirely on his own, like showering, shaving, and dressing, and that the nursing staff assisted him with those tasks. But I never wanted to wound his pride by asking questions about such matters.

While his pompous manner often annoyed me, Reverend Hahn never spoke a harsh word to me. His abundant pride in me, his only progeny, made me uncomfortable. But it was also flattering. Despite the fact that I knew I could never live up to his estimation of me, he always insisted upon my beauty, my brilliance, and my nobility of character.

After an hour or two in his presence, my heart would begin to warm. I'd leave his apartment almost convinced that I liked my birth father.

But when I'd arrive home, I'd see the strain on my parents' faces, and I'd know they'd been worrying about the visit. Then I'd remember that my birth father was manipulative and deceitful, and that he'd caused my family a world of pain. Upstairs in my bedroom, I'd brood on his misdeeds, questioning whether he deserved any positive regard from me.

My last visit with Reverend Hahn that summer was near the end of August. As I sat on his sofa sipping the iced tea he'd provided for me, he plied me with enthusiastic questions about my preparation for college. "Have you started packing yet? What day will you be moving into the dormitory? Who will be helping you?"

Then he said, "There's one thing I want to do yet this summer."

"What's that?" I asked.

"I want to eat at the Taste of Home restaurant during one of your shifts."

I tried in vain to mask my dismay.

"Please don't think I'm checking up on you," he added quickly. "I hope you understand why I want to do this. I've missed out on so much of your life. I didn't have the pleasure of hearing your first words or witnessing your first steps. I wasn't there for your first day of school. Now that we're free to spend time together, I don't want to miss out on any more milestones. I'd like to see my child at work on her job."

He paused, his eyes clouding with sadness. "Most likely, this will be my only opportunity to do such a thing. By next summer, I probably won't be able to get out at all."

I suddenly felt suffocated by the domineering presence that loomed over every aspect of my life. Seeking an escape valve for the immediate moment, I said, "You should have plenty of time to visit me at the restaurant. I'll be working on weekends during the school year."

He shook his head emphatically. "No, Victoria, I don't want you to do that. I don't want you under that kind of pressure. It's too much for a college freshman to juggle the requirements of school and work at the same time. I'm all for you working during the summer. You need that experience. I know you want to do your part in paying for your college education, and I respect that. But during the school year, I want you to enjoy every feature of your college life without the distraction of employment."

I knew what he was really saying: *I want you freed up to spend more time with me.*

"But I need the money," I protested.

Not backing off from his stance, he said, "If you need a little spending money, come to me."

I sat in silence, chewing on my lower lip, trying to wrap my mind around what Reverend Hahn had just said to me. *Well, that really changes my plans. What will my parents think about this?*

"Are you working this weekend?" he asked, breaking into my thoughts.

"Yes," I replied. "Friday evening. Saturday afternoon and evening."

"Good," he said. "I think I can arrange for some friends to bring me to the restaurant Saturday evening."

"Okay." I tried to match his enthusiasm. "I'll see you then."

He looked at me pointedly. "Victoria, I want you to understand something. You and I can have a public relationship as well as a private one. We can have a pleasant and honest interaction in the presence of others without disclosing all the facts about our relationship."

Cringing inwardly, I nodded. I knew exactly where he was coming from. There was a game to be played with our public personas, one we'd already played with the Greencroft staff members who'd seen us together. I was rapidly learning the rules.

At the restaurant on Saturday, I felt nervous and jittery all day, my anxiety increasing as the dinner hour approached. Every few minutes, I'd glance out the window, wondering when my birth father would make his appearance. Around six o'clock, I saw a car pull up to the curb in front of the restaurant. The driver jumped out, opened the trunk, and pulled out a collapsible wheelchair. A woman got out of the back seat. Then the two of them helped their tall, silver-haired passenger out of the front seat and into the wheelchair.

My heart pounded. Pointing to a table in the center of the room, I barked at our indolent busboy. "Bradley, some people are bringing in a man in a wheelchair. Get that table cleaned up so we can seat them."

Moments later, the man wheeled Reverend Hahn through the door. My birth father greeted the hostess on duty with his trademark gentle humor. She led them to the table Bradley was wiping down. "Thank you, young man," Reverend Hahn said to him.

With menus in hand, I approached the table. "Victoria!" Reverend Hahn exclaimed. "How nice to see you!" Then he turned to his companions. "This is my young friend Victoria Unruh."

Turning to me, he said, "This is Dave and Vera Martin. They're friends of mine from College Mennonite Church."

Then, to Dave and Vera, he said, "Victoria attends Westside Mennonite Church. When I was the pastor of First Mennonite in Warsaw, I preached at Westside Mennonite several times a year. So I've known Victoria since she was a little girl."

I was so stunned by the smoothness of his deception that I had to remind myself to close my mouth and stop gawking. Reverend Hahn had gracefully put forward a partial truth while keeping all the unsavory details tucked out of sight.

Dave Martin looked at me with interest. "Who are your parents?"

I felt as if I was teetering on the edge of a precipice, and I struggled to control my panic. Yet, a small part of me enjoyed the treacherous game, the challenge of coming up with my own smooth response. "Herman and Ada Unruh," I replied. "My dad's a mail carrier. My mom works in the Bible and Religion department at the college."

Both of the Martins nodded knowingly. "I work in the admissions office," Vera said. "I've met your Mom. You look a lot like her."

I smiled at her. "A lot of people say that."

"Victoria's going to be a freshman at the college this fall," Reverend Hahn chimed in.

"That's nice," Mrs. Martin said. "Goshen College is a wonderful school. Are you looking forward to it?"

"Yes," I replied. "I'm really excited about it." Then, with a veneer of poise covering my inner agitation, I took their drink orders. I was afraid that, at any moment, Mr. or Mrs. Martin would recognize the striking resemblance between their dinner companion and their waitress. But as I glanced at my biological father, I realized that age and illness had so altered his appearance that such a resemblance would be difficult to detect.

I walked back into the kitchen, biting the inside of my cheek to keep from screaming to discharge my tension. When I returned to the table with a tray loaded with glasses of water and cups of coffee, Reverend Hahn looked up from perusing his menu. "Do you have any suggestions, Victoria?"

"The meatloaf is one of the most popular items on the menu," I said. "It's Edna's secret recipe."

"I've had it before," Vera Martin said. "It's really good."

"Well, I'm going to have to try it." Reverend Hahn's eyes twinkled. "Thank you for the suggestion, Victoria. You provide excellent service."

Thirty minutes later, I breathed a sigh of relief as Mr. and Mrs. Martin wheeled Reverend Hahn out the door of the restaurant. I wasn't a bit surprised when I found a twenty-dollar bill tucked under the edge of my birth father's plate. I quickly pocketed the money, before anyone could ask questions about the disproportionate tip.

Bradley lumbered over to the table to clear off the dishes. "That old fart in the wheelchair barely ate any of his food," he said. "He probably can't eat anything but baby food."

I slapped the back of his head as I walked past him toward the kitchen.

"Ouch!" he yelped. "What was that for?"

"You shouldn't be making fun of people," I scolded. "Someday, you're going to be old and sick."

Bradley followed me into the kitchen and set his tub of dirty dishes on Allen's dishwashing station. Pointing at me, he said, "She's a dangerous woman. She hit me."

Allen grinned lasciviously at me. "Honey, you know Brad can't handle that kind of thing. But you can rough me up any time you want to."

I shook my head in disgust. "You guys are creeps." Picking up a tray of food to deliver to another table, I walked out of the kitchen, wishing I could handle my other problems as easily as I did my obnoxious coworkers.

CHAPTER 4

I'd always thought of myself as a gutsy person. As a child, I'd never been timid, and had loved the stimulation of new challenges. When, at age fourteen, I had left the public school system to attend a private Christian high school, I'd found the change not the least bit daunting.

However, adjusting to college life was harder than I'd ever imagined it would be. Looking back, I can see that the year and a half prior to starting college had been the roughest period of my life. I'd had to recover from hearing the jarring news about my paternity, and then had to piece together a new sense of identity. This had impeded my bold stride into the future, giving me a slight limp as I moved into my young adult years. Truthfully, I needed a little extra time in the security of my parents' nest before heading out to find my own way in life.

And I only had a few weeks to get used to the idea of living on campus before I had to pack up my belongings and move out of the bedroom I'd slept in since I was a toddler.

On a day in early September, my dad and I trudged up the stairs to the second floor of Goshen College's Westlawn dormitory, our arms loaded with bags and boxes. I'd been informed that I would be rooming with a girl from Elkhart named Bonnie Springer. When we walked into my assigned room, I saw a slender girl in blue jeans and a pink tee shirt sitting on one of the two beds. She was looking down, rifling through a handful of greeting cards, her long, silky blonde hair falling like curtains on each side of her face.

Oh my God, I thought, suddenly feeling awkward and ugly. *She's beautiful. She's perfect. All the college girls will probably be like her.*

"Hi," I called out, attempting to mask my insecurity with a friendly demeanor. "You must be Bonnie."

The girl looked up, staring at me with wide blue eyes fringed with mascaraed lashes. "Oh, YOU'RE Victoria," she said, as if disappointed that someone more spectacular hadn't entered the room. "I've seen you before."

"Where?" I asked.

"In the Conrad Grebel choir. You guys sang at my church. Sunnyside Mennonite." She flipped through a few more greeting cards before adding, "Up until two weeks ago, I thought I was going to be rooming alone. Then I heard I was going to have a roommate."

Her tone suggested that she was annoyed by that turn of events. My dad and I glanced at each other. I could tell he felt sorry for me.

"That's your side of the room," she said, pointing to the other bed and the nearby desk. "I've already put my stuff away." Then she stood up, tossed her cards on her desk, and flounced out of the room.

"Not a very friendly welcome, huh?" I said to my dad as we set down our loads and stared around the room.

The bed Bonnie had already claimed was graced with a pink polka-dotted bedspread and decorative pillows. Two of the pillows had scalloped edges, making them look like giant sunflowers. A third one was made of fat, puffy letters that spelled out the word *LOVE*. An oversized stuffed panda sat on her desk chair. His fluffy fur and the crisp red ribbon around his neck suggested that he was newly purchased. On her desk stood a vase containing a floral arrangement with a small card stuck in it. Next to the flowers lay a copy of Dr. Suess's book, *Oh, The Places You'll Go!* A cluster of balloons tied to her desk chair bounced against the ceiling, one of them emblazoned with the words, *Good Luck!* Crumpled wrapping paper had been tossed into the trash can next to her desk.

The scene suggested that well-wishing, gift-bearing guests had just left the room before my dad and I had arrived. My roommate's embarking on her college career had been marked by a grand send-off. In contrast, my last-minute decision to live on campus had resulted in rushed preparations and an unceremonious departure from my parents' home.

After my dad left, I stashed away my belongings, my heart feeling heavy. As I made up my bed, I couldn't help but notice how drab my faded chenille bedspread looked in comparison to the brightly adorned bed on the other side of the room. Somehow, I knew that sharing living quarters with Bonnie Springer was going to be a less than satisfying experience.

While Bonnie was never overtly nasty to me, she seemed to make a point of ignoring me. Whenever I tried initiating conversations with her, she always had someplace to go or someone else to talk to. She was the social butterfly I'd been as a younger teen, before the sobering events of recent years had rendered me more introverted.

Bonnie was bent on getting to know every girl on our floor, and was always in the middle of some giggling conclave. I was never invited to join in her fun. It seemed the only times Bonnie would talk to me was when she'd burst into our room exclaiming some exciting news such as, "Have you met the girl from Texas who lives down the hall? She's such a hoot!" Or, "I was just talking to that girl from Brazil. She lives on the third floor. She's so cool." Apparently, the fact that I was a local girl rendered me uninteresting in her eyes.

In a daze, I stumbled through my first week, the freshman orientation activities, the meeting with my faculty advisor, and registration for classes. At night, the sleep I desperately needed to keep up with my new schedule eluded me. Bonnie and her friends would be yakking away in the lounge across the hall from my room, their loud peals of laughter lasting well past midnight.

When she'd finally come to bed, my dainty roommate would immediately lapse into decidedly unladylike snoring, punctuated by little moans and yelps. Having been the only occupant of my bedroom my entire life, I'd rarely witnessed another person's idiosyncratic sleep behavior. I was sure I wouldn't survive the trimester.

Friday evening found me standing by my mother's secretarial desk in the Bible and Religion department, fighting back my tears. She looked up from her typewriter, surprised. "What do you want, Victoria?"

"Can I ride home with you?" I asked.

She frowned, looking at me over the top of her reading glasses. "I suppose so. Are you already that homesick?"

I waited silently while she wrapped up her work, and then followed her out of the building to the lot where she'd parked her car.

"I don't think I can do this," I told her on the drive home.

She glanced over at me. "Do what?"

"College."

"This is what you wanted," she said sharply. "A couple of weeks ago, you were all gung ho on this. You were completely sure of yourself."

"I didn't know what I was getting into," I mumbled.

My mother sighed in exasperation. "Victoria, you're a capable girl. You've always been able to do anything you set your mind on doing. You're just going to have to tell yourself that you can do this."

Hurt by her lack of sympathy, I turned toward the window, watching the familiar landscape pass by through my blur of tears. Running back home after only a week of college made it seem as if I was going backward in life, not forward. I felt like an abysmal failure.

When I followed my mother through the front door of our house, my dad looked up from his newspaper, startled. "Vickie!" he exclaimed. "I didn't expect to see you."

Of course, my mother hadn't anticipated having me for supper, and the leftover beef stew she put on the table was hardly enough for three people. Out of guilt, I ate very little.

My dad's worried eyes searched my face. "Vickie, you don't look happy."

His gentle concern unleashed the torrent of emotion I'd been holding back for days. "I can't do this," I sobbed. "I'm not ready for college." Pushing away from the table, I ran up the stairs to my old bedroom. The room seemed empty and forlorn, stripped of the possessions that were now housed in my dorm room. My bed wasn't even made up, as my mother had taken off the sheets and blankets in order to launder them. I curled up on the bare mattress, hugging myself, crying like a young child.

Ten minutes later, I heard footsteps on the stairway, too heavy to be those of my petite mother. I knew it was my dad who tapped on the bedroom door. "Come in," I managed to choke out between sobs.

He walked into the room, then lowered his rotund body onto the bed. "Vickie, I've been having a talk with your mom. We know you've had a rough week." He reached out to brush a strand of matted hair off my damp cheek. "But we don't want you to give up on school."

He ran his hand across the top of his bald head, as if trying to collect his thoughts. "I have confidence in you, sweetheart, even though you don't have confidence in yourself right now. I know that, in the long run, things are going to work out for you. Just a minute ago, I said to your Mom, 'Vickie's still so young, and a lot of kids her age aren't ready to be out on their own.'"

I listened quietly to the sound of the voice that had spoken so many comforting words to me over the years, the voice that had never failed to soothe my hurt feelings or smooth my ruffled feathers.

"How about if we make a deal?" he said. "If you stick it out through the weekdays, you can come home with your mom on the weekends. Then you can ride back to school with her on Monday morning. How does that sound?"

"Good," I whispered.

Lois Jean Thomas

He patted my arm before he stood up. "You can do that for as long as you like. For as long as you need to. So get some sheets from the linen closet and get your bed made up again. We'll just keep it made up for a while. Okay, sweetheart?"

When I walked into my dorm room the following Monday morning, my roommate said, "Where have you been? I thought something happened to you."

"I went home," was all I told her.

That week, settling into my routine required every ounce of my concentration. I wrote down my schedule of classes on a note card: World History, Old Testament, Expository Writing, Biology, and Tennis. Even though the campus was small and I kept my trusty card with me at all times, the task of remembering which buildings and rooms my classes were held in seemed overwhelming. I lived in perpetual fear of losing my way and enduring the humiliation of having all eyes on me when I walked into a classroom late.

For some reason, the massive library in the middle of the campus intimidated me. Being a lowly freshman, I felt unworthy to enter it, and for the first several weeks, I did all my studying in my room.

I made sure to attend the required number of morning chapel services held in the College Mennonite Church on the south end of the campus, dutifully turning in my chapel cards at the door. I didn't know what penalty awaited me if I fell short on my attendance, but I imagined a dreadful scene of being called in to face the authorities.

Fortunately for me, the campus cafeteria was located on the ground floor of the Westlawn dormitory. Rather than having to trudge across campus to get my meals, I only had to walk down a flight of stairs. Still, the cafeteria frightened me, with its long lines and the array of food choices. I always had a moment of panic when, tray in hand, I had to

30

face the sea of tables and decide where to sit. At my times of highest anxiety, I skipped meals in order to avoid the cafeteria, satisfying my hunger pangs with snacks from vending machines.

During freshman orientation, I had learned the location of my campus mailbox in the Union Building. But with everything I had on my mind, I kept forgetting about the fact that I needed to check my mail on a daily basis. It was Wednesday of my second week before I remembered that detail. After the morning chapel service, I made my way to the Union Building, elbowing my way through the crowd of students at the mailboxes. I found that my box was stuffed full.

As I sorted through notices about campus events and information about class requirements from my professors, I came upon a pale blue envelope with my name and address typed on it. Immediately curious, I tore open the envelope, pulled out a piece of expensive stationary, and read the typed contents.

My Dear Victoria,

I think about you every day, and am praying that all is going well for you. I would love to hear all about your classes, which I'm sure you are handling with ease. Please come and visit me sometime soon. I'm confident that you are doing well, but it is important to me to hear from you.

Under the typed word, *Love,* was the signature, *Reverend Harry Hahn.* His handwriting was bold and confident, yet slightly shaky. I figured the impairment caused by his illness had made writing by hand a laborious process, and that he'd resorted to using a typewriter for written communication.

I walked into the nearby snack shop and sank down on a chair at an empty table, staring at the note, a mixture of feelings churning inside me. Once again, I felt my birth father's domineering presence looming over me, as if no corner of my life could escape his watchful eye. However, I also felt a bit of comfort in knowing that, in this strange new world of college life, someone who cared about me was standing in the background, cheering me on. I took the note back to my dorm room and stuffed it into my desk drawer.

Thereafter, at least once a week, I received a typewritten note on the same pale blue stationary, with the same bold, but shaky, signature. The notes invariably ended with a request for a visit from me. Sometimes, I smiled when I saw the familiar envelope in my mailbox. On other days, the notes irritated me. Always, I added them to the growing pile in my desk drawer.

CHAPTER 5

Despite my fear of being a social failure, I did make headway in forming new friendships during my first month on campus. While my roommate and her giggling cohorts never invited me into their circle, I told myself they were shallow, and that I wouldn't join in their silliness even if they wanted me to.

But I did get to know some of the quieter girls who lived on my floor. I sat with them in chapel and ate with them in the cafeteria. In my World History class, I found myself sitting next to Laura Zuercher, a girl I'd known at Conrad Grebel High. Laura lived with her parents only a few blocks away from the campus, and walked to her classes every day. Since I was still riding home with my mother on the weekends, I didn't see myself as fully committed to living on campus, and felt I had something in common with Laura.

On a day in early October, I stood in the crowded cafeteria, lunch tray in hand, looking for a place to sit. When I failed to spot any of my friends, I opted to seat myself at a table in the corner of the room, empty except for two young men engaged in earnest conversation. So engrossed were they in their subject matter that they seemed oblivious to the fact that I'd sat down across from them.

I quickly realized they were discussing physics. Having enjoyed my high school physics class, I listened to their conversation with interest.

"Stephen Hawking has established the existence of black holes," one of them said. "He worked out the math to prove it."

"But we can't give him all the credit," his companion countered. "David Finkelstein did a lot of work on the subject, too."

I smiled, recalling the article I'd read on that very topic in a science journal in high school. "The idea of black holes isn't original with Stephen Hawking or David Finkelstein," I interjected. "It's been around for a long time."

The young men stopped talking and stared at me. "Are you a physics major?" one of them asked.

"No," I replied. "Well, I don't know yet. I haven't decided on a major. I'm just a freshman."

"You should think about science," his friend said. "There are hardly any women in our department."

"Maybe I will," I said, even though I knew I wasn't even remotely considering that possibility. Suddenly feeling bold, I added, "I'm Victoria Unruh. From Goshen."

The young men responded by introducing themselves. "Charles Hess," said the taller of the two. "From Eureka, Illinois. I'm a junior. It's nice to meet you."

"Aw, shucks, he's being formal," his grinning companion teased. "Just call him Charlie. I'm Stephen Wenger. Never Steve. I'm a junior from Hesston, Kansas."

We continued our discussion on physics, our conversation sprinkled with witty humor. I soon realized that both young men were brilliant, in possession of the highest IQs I'd ever encountered. And from that point on, every time I spotted the two of them sitting in the corner of the cafeteria at lunchtime, I took my tray to their table. I thoroughly enjoyed matching wits with them, and they seemed delighted to have my company.

I often asked myself why I was pursuing these friendships. My association with Charlie Hess and Stephen Wenger, who seemed to have no friends besides each other, wasn't going to advance my social standing at the college. In contrast to my high school boyfriend Daniel Hooley, whose good looks and athletic build made him the boy that every girl dreamed of dating, Charlie and Stephen were far from the most attractive young men at Goshen College.

In fact, their physical attributes put them in the bottom tier. Tall, gangly Charlie always had a small calculator and several pens in the pocket of his unstylish button-up shirt.

Every shirt I ever saw him wear was marked with ink stains. His black, horn-rimmed glasses looked like relics of the 1950s. He clearly wasn't doing enough to combat the unruly inclinations of his wavy brown hair. I wondered if he ever remembered to comb it after getting out of the shower. He had a habit of running his hand through his hair when formulating a counterpoint to one of his companion's assertions, which caused it to spring out in all directions.

Stephen, who's grooming also took a back seat to his intellectual pursuits, was a head shorter than his friend. He had an unappealing habit of hanging his mouth open when caught up in his brilliant thoughts. The way he smacked his lips when he chewed nearly drove me out of my mind. At first, I thought he was doing it to be funny. I was about to tell him to knock it off when I realized it was his habitual way of chewing. The fact that the scrawny fellow did more talking than eating saved him from being an unbearable lunch companion.

While the two guys might have liked the idea of having girlfriends, I doubted that either of them believed such a development was within the realm of possibility. Thus, neither of them ever flirted with me. They treated me as nothing more than an intellectual sparring buddy, and I found safety in their company.

My friendships with Charlie and Stephen never extended beyond the four walls of the cafeteria, although I often crossed paths with them on campus. In spite of his gangly appearance, Charlie Hess walked with a dignified bearing, never in a rush, but intent on where he was going. His deep-set blue eyes always seemed to be turned skyward, as if he was engaged in intellectual musings that the rest of the population could never hope to understand. But he would always spot me when I approached from the opposite direction, and would give me a cordial nod.

For as short as he was, Stephen Wenger had an unusually long stride, which gave him a distinctive bounce when he walked. Whenever I'd encounter him on campus, he'd flash his goofy grin and raise a hand in greeting.

I'd shone on the academic stage of my high school, taking it for granted that I'd be at the top of my class. But I quickly learned that the competition was much different in college. Even though Goshen College was a small school, I was surrounded by topnotch students from all over the country. I knew that the A's I was determined to earn would not come without considerable effort on my part.

Studying in my dorm room proved to be nearly impossible, as there was always something going on in the lounge across the hall from my room. My roommate Bonnie was invariably the instigator of the commotion. While bemoaning the extra pounds they were rapidly accumulating, Bonnie and her friends partied every evening on calorie-laden food. Whenever one of the girls would run up the stairs carrying a box from Dunkin' Donuts or a package of *Oreos,* Bonnie would say, "Let's go to your room." High on sugar, they'd inevitable migrate to the lounge, where they'd gossip and giggle late into the night.

"Why can't we go to your room?" I once overheard one of Bonnie's friends ask her.

"Victoria wants to study," she replied.

"Oh, pooh!" her friend retorted. "That girl needs to lighten up."

"She's the type that has to make all A's," Bonnie explained. "She'd probably have a nervous breakdown if she ever got a B."

I winced at the accuracy of her description of me before turning back to my biology textbook.

Within three or four weeks, Bonnie's morning routine included ten minutes of wailing about the fact that all her blue jeans were too tight. She'd swear off eating, refusing to go downstairs to the cafeteria for breakfast or lunch. By evening, she'd announce that she was starved, and after an ample dinner, she'd join a friend in devouring an entire bag of barbeque potato chips.

The first paper I had to write was for my Old Testament class. Although I'd plied my professor, Dr. Burkholder, with anxious questions about his expectations for the assignment, I was still unsure of what I was doing when I sat down at my desk to write. At eleven o'clock that night, I was still scribbling away, expounding on a passage from Genesis, sweating as I imagined grim-faced Dr. Burkholder tearing into my work with his red ink pen.

Suddenly, I heard a commotion in the hallway outside my closed door. I paused to listen, recognizing the sound of ropes slapping the tile floor, along with the rhythmic thump-thump of jumping feet. Then a breathless voice exclaimed, "Whew! This is exhausting! How many calories do you think ten minutes of rope jumping burns off?"

I immediately knew what was going on. Bonnie and her friends had decided to burn off the results of their excess eating by vigorous exercise—late at night, and right outside my room.

I knew I was on the verge of blowing up. *Don't lose your cool,* I told myself as I got up from my desk. I poked my head out the door. "Do you mind?" I said through clenched teeth.

Bonnie shot me a dirty look. "There's nothing wrong with having fun once in a while, Victoria," she snapped. Then she and her friends ambled down the hall, their ropes trailing behind them, looking for a friendlier spot for their exercise routine. I made a mental note to inquire about changing my rooming arrangements for the second trimester.

I'd always considered myself to be athletic, and my height had rendered me an invaluable player on my high school volleyball team. So, signing up for a tennis class was the least of my worries.

However, the game of tennis got the better of me. My serves invariably landed out of bounds, I couldn't master the backhand, and I stumbled over my own feet as I raced to return my opponent's drive. One day when I dove to hit the ball, I landed flat on my stomach. I lay there utterly humiliated, my knees and elbows smarting from scraping against the court's hard surface. At that point, I was sure I wouldn't get anything better than a C in the class, and in my mind's eye, I watched my GPA, along with my morale, spiraling slowly downward.

In most regards, my Expository Writing class was my favorite course of the first trimester. My professor Dr. Witmer was a gifted writer, having had several books published, along with pieces in religious and literary magazines. My admiration for him knew no bounds, and I soaked up everything he had to offer his classroom of budding writers.

However, Dr. Witmer utilized one teaching technique that completely unnerved me. Each time we handed in writing assignments, he'd select a few, photocopy them, and pass them out for the class to critique. Invariably, he'd choose mine.

I should have been flattered by the fact that he thought my compositions were worthy of discussion. But having my work passed out for the world to scrutinize and criticize made me feel naked and exposed. Even if the response from the other students was favorable, at the end of the hour, I'd walk out of the classroom shaking from the strain of the ordeal.

After the second time this happened, I hung back at the end of the class so that I could speak with Dr. Witmer in private. "Could you not pass out my essay next time?" I asked him, trying to sound assertive while remaining respectful. "I don't think it's fair to use my work every time. I feel like I'm being picked on."

Dr. Witmer peered at me over the top of his glasses. "I can't make you any such promise, Miss Unruh. Peer review is part of the process in this class. If you want to be a writer, you need to learn to deal with feedback."

I left the classroom feeling chastened, but still hopeful. Maybe, despite what Dr. Witmer had said, he understood what I meant. Certainly, in a class of thirty students, the odds of my essay being chosen for a third time were slim.

Our third writing assignment was an essay on how we viewed our personal identity. My breath caught in my throat as I listened to Dr. Witmer describe what he wanted from us. "This is a creative writing class," he said, "so I don't want a recital of historic facts about your life. Dig deep."

I knew that the details of my personal history would make great fodder for such an essay. How learning about my true paternity had turned my life story on its head, making me reevaluate everything. How both of my fathers had a hand in shaping who I turned out to be, one through genetics, the other through nurturing.

But I was not about to air my family's secret in front of a room full of people I barely knew. So, I danced around the proverbial elephant parked in the middle of my life, sprinkling my essay with clichés about being a child of God. In the end, I found my work quite unremarkable, and I was sure it would be passed over by my professor when he selected essays for distribution.

I was wrong. The following week when Dr. Witmer passed out copies of the three essays he'd chosen for discussion, mine was on the top of the stack, the first to be reviewed. Thomas Yost, a smart-alecky sophomore who had no problem with voicing a negative opinion, said, "I don't dig this essay. I can't even tell what the writer is getting at."

Then he listed everything he thought I'd done wrong. "I mean, what is she saying in the third paragraph? If you ask me, it's pretty lame. Then in the next paragraph, she completely contradicts herself."

I sat there in my seat, sick from humiliation, trying hard not to vomit in front of everyone. I wanted to shrink like Alice in Wonderland so that I could scurry out of the room undetected. Even though other class members jumped to my rescue, saying appreciative things about my work, I felt as if my professor had set me up to be mocked. I hated Thomas Yost. And I hated Dr. Witmer even more.

After class, a girl from my dorm, sweet-natured Hannah Lapp, slid her arm around my waist. "Don't worry about what Tom Yost said," she advised. "He's a bully. He tears up everybody's work. He's just jealous because you're a better writer than he is."

I allowed her to walk me back to the dorm, but as soon as we stepped inside, I extricated myself from her comforting clutch and rushed to the privacy of my own room. Throwing myself on my bed, I cried while I plotted ways to seek revenge on Dr. Witmer.

I'm not doing any more of his stupid assignments, I fumed. *If I don't turn anything in, then he can't use it to humiliate me again.*

I contemplated the prospect of earning an F for refusing to complete an assignment, quite liking the idea at first. But the vision of my downward-spiraling GPA brought me to my senses.

"What's wrong, Victoria?" Bonnie asked as she walked into the room.

I quickly sat up, brushing the hair out of my face. "Nothing."

I went to my desk where I'd thrown down my books, rifling through my notebook to find the next week's assignment for Dr. Witmer's class. It was a piece to be written in the form of a newspaper article. As hateful as I felt about it, I knew I'd end up doing that stupid assignment. But not right away. I'd let my rebellion simmer for at least forty-eight hours.

CHAPTER 6

On a Wednesday afternoon in late October, I sat in my World History class, my stomach in knots, while my professor handed back our first exam. Dr. Stuckey hadn't yet succeeded in matching the names of his students with their faces. One by one, he called out our names, glancing around the room to see who would raise a hand in response.

"Keith Miller?" He handed the young man his graded exam, the pages rolled slightly to protect the privacy of the contents. "Karen Bontrager?" "Carl Shank?" "Marybeth Stutzman?"

After handing back a seemingly bottomless stack of papers, he finally called, "Victoria Unruh?" I raised my hand. With a dispassionate expression on his face, he handed me my discreetly rolled exam, completely unconcerned about the fact that he was about to shatter the fragile emotional structure of a young college freshman.

I looked at my test. On the front was written in red ink, 82%.

Horrified, I scanned through the exam, noting the red X's slashed through multiple choice questions, the scribbled notes in the margins beside the essay questions. Unable to bear a closer look, I stuffed the test into my notebook.

While studying for the exam, I'd talked myself into the idea of accepting something less than 100%. *You don't have to be perfect,* I kept telling myself. But my idea of less-than-perfect was 95%, something still in the A range. Not 82%, a disgraceful B-minus. I couldn't remember having scored so poorly on any test during high school.

At the end of the hour, the students filed out of the classroom, muttering their dissatisfaction over their tests scores. "I'm not surprised," one girl said, waving an exam emblazoned with a red 78%. "Everybody says Dr. Stuckey is a jerk when it comes to grading. Hardly anybody gets an A in his classes."

But the disgruntlement of my fellow students didn't matter to me. My own humiliation was more than I could handle at the moment.

I wanted to go home, to rush up the stairs to my bedroom and crawl under the covers, hiding my shame from the world. But it was two o'clock in the afternoon. My mother was my only ride home, and her work day wouldn't end for another three hours.

With tears blurring my vision, I wandered toward the fountain in front of the library and seated myself on one of the benches. The damp coldness of the concrete chilled my legs and my bottom. Rain began to drizzle from heavy, low-hanging clouds. That morning when I'd opened my dorm room curtains, I'd been greeted by cheerful blue skies, and had believed a light jacket would be sufficient outerwear for the day. I hadn't anticipated the day's turn toward darkness and cold.

I had no way to get to my mom and dad's house seven miles west of town. But my troubled mind lit on another possibility. I had a parent who lived nearby, one who would be delighted to see me. Unable to think clearly about what I was doing, I headed across the campus to College Avenue, then turned east toward the Greencroft complex.

Within minutes, the drizzling rain became a steady downpour. By the time I arrived at Reverend Hahn's apartment, I was soaking wet, my teeth chattering from the cold. My knock on the door was answered by a nurse, who eyed me disapprovingly.

"Now isn't a good time to visit," she informed me. "Reverend Hahn is tired, and I'm getting ready to help him into bed."

Feeling like a first-class fool, I was about to turn away. But then I heard a quavering voice call from inside the apartment, "Who is it, Cynthia?"

The nurse looked at me questioningly. "Victoria," I said.

"It's Victoria," she called back to Reverend Hahn.

"Oh, ask her to come in!" The weariness in his voice had changed to enthusiasm. "You can come back in an hour, Cynthia, and I'll lie down then."

The nurse frowned as she motioned for me to enter the apartment. Then she left, closing the door behind her.

I stood just inside the doorway, my wet clothing dripping on the mat, while Reverend Hahn wheeled his chair into the living room. Clearly, my visit had caught him off guard. I noticed his attire was more casual than on my previous visits. He was wearing a bulky gray cardigan, and slippers instead of his usual dress shoes. No doubt, he would have put on more formal clothing if he'd known I was coming.

"Victoria!" he exclaimed. "I'm so glad you came. It's been ... what, two months since I've seen you?"

I nodded mutely.

"It looks like you've been through a downpour." He glanced toward the back of his small apartment, where the rain was driving against the glass patio door. "Did you walk here?"

I nodded again.

He furrowed his brow, as if wondering why I'd been so foolish as to set out on a mile-long trek in such weather. "Well, we need to get you warm and dry."

He gestured toward the doorway he'd just wheeled through in his chair. "There are clean towels in the bathroom. My bedroom is on the other side of the bathroom. You'll find a blanket on my closet shelf. You can use it to warm yourself." Then he pointed to the small table in his kitchenette. "You can leave your things on the table. Hang your jacket over one of the chairs."

I removed my wet sneakers and left them on the doormat. Then I walked over to the kitchenette and set my books on the table. As I slipped off my wet jacket and draped it over a chair, I realized Reverend Hahn was offering me the hospitality a parent provides for an adult child returning home for a visit. He was making his home my home. I knew he wanted me to feel at ease, to help myself to whatever I needed. It felt strange, but oddly comforting.

I stepped into the bathroom, a room of the apartment I hadn't entered before. In keeping with the rest Reverend Hahn's living quarters, it was sparkling clean. The sight of a shower chair parked inside an oversized shower stall jolted me, reminding me of my birth father's fragile condition.

Hesitantly, I lifted a fluffy white towel from the rack beside the sink and blotted the water from my face and hair. As I stared at my reflection in the mirror, I saw red swollen eyes in a pinched white face, telltale signs of my emotional breakdown. I hoped Reverend Hahn hadn't noticed.

I carefully refolded the towel and hung it back on the rack. Then I walked through the back door of the bathroom into the bedroom, feeling decidedly like a trespasser. Again, the small room was immaculate. The bed was covered with a burgundy spread. The dresser matched the headboard and the nightstand, and all appeared to be expensive and new.

With trepidation, I opened the closet. I told myself not to snoop, but couldn't refrain from surveying the contents. A row of neatly pressed dress shirts, trousers, and suit coats hung on the rod, the signature garments of Reverend Hahn's past. I suspected that the thick navy-blue bathrobe hanging from the hook on the back of the door was getting more than its share of use. On the closet floor, a pair of fleece-lined slippers sat next to three pairs of dress shoes.

The shelf held only one item, a plastic bag that I assumed contained the blanket Reverend Hahn had spoken of. I took down the bag and laid it on the bed. When I pulled out the blanket, I discovered that it was a quilt. It looked like one my mother's sewing group at church might have made, only more elaborate.

I carried the quilt to the living room. "Is this the blanket you mean?" I asked Reverend Hahn.

"Yes," he said.

"It's beautiful."

He smiled. "I bought it at the Mennonite Relief Sale the last time I attended, three or four years ago."

I glanced down at my soaked blue jeans, which were muddy around the ankles. "It's too special. I don't want to ruin it."

"I bought it to be used," he said. "What better occasion than to warm my child when she comes in from the cold?"

I struggled to take in the tenderness of his words. I didn't believe I deserved them, or the special way he was treating me. But I obliged him by wrapping the quilt around my damp clothing and settling onto the sofa.

Reverend Hahn wheeled his chair close to me, then reached out and laid a gnarled hand on my arm. I felt a powerful current pulsating from it, an electric warmth that poured into my arm and spread throughout my body. It felt as if my birth father was intentionally infusing me with his strength.

"What's troubling you, Victoria?" he asked.

I felt my eyes welling with tears again, and I choked on a sob. "I-I'm not doing very well at college."

Reverend Hahn removed his hand from my arm and sat back in his chair, his concerned eyes riveted on my face. "I have a hard time believing that," he said, "although I know it feels that way to you. Tell me what's going on."

I suddenly felt foolish. Nothing was going terribly wrong. I wasn't failing any classes, nor was I on the verge of dropping out. I didn't know how to voice the difficulty I was experiencing. "It's just hard. Everything's hard."

He nodded in understanding. "Tell me more."

"Today, my World History professor handed back our first exam. I didn't do very well."

"What grade did you get?"

Clutching the warm quilt around my body, I got up, walked over to the table, and pulled the troublesome exam from my notebook. The edges were damp from exposure to the rain. Handing the test to Reverend Hahn, I said, "Eighty-two percent. That's a B-minus."

He glanced at the test and then at me, a perplexed look on his face. "That's hardly a poor grade, Victoria. A B-minus is nothing to be ashamed of."

"But I studied hard. I expected to do a lot better."

Reverend Hahn slowly perused the three pages of the exam. "Did you see what your professor wrote at the end of your essay?" he said when he was finished.

"No," I admitted. "After I saw my grade, I was afraid to look."

He held out the test to show me. "Look at this. Most of your points off came from the multiple choice portion of the exam. You have almost a perfect score on your essay questions. That's the most important part. It reflects the development of your own thought. All through the margins, your professor has written positive comments, and at the end, he wrote, 'Excellent work.'"

"Really?" I took the test from his hand and read what Dr. Stuckey had written. Sure enough, the essay portion of my exam had elicited far more positive than negative responses from him.

"I feel stupid," I said. "I should've looked closer before I got upset."

Reverend Hahn gazed at me with compassionate eyes. "I understand. You're a perfectionist. You're a lot like me. We're driven. But life has a way of slowing us down when we get ahead of ourselves."

He lowered his eyes, chuckling, as if remembering events from his own past. Then he looked up at me, a serious expression on his face. "Victoria, you're an excellent student, and you always will be. But don't torture yourself by insisting on making all A's. Allow yourself to be less than perfect. Our most important life lessons often come at times when we've fallen flat on our faces. Learn to forgive yourself for your human shortcomings. If you flagellate yourself for every mistake you make, it will only hold you back in life."

I hadn't expected such a lecture, and for a few seconds, I felt uncomfortable, even a little miffed. I stared down at my feet, noticing that my damp socks had been stained by the inside of my wet sneakers.

Reverend Hahn seemed to sense my discomfort. "I'm sorry, Victoria. I surely didn't mean to scold you. You know how highly I think of you. I am absolutely confident that you will sail through your four years of college in fine form. But there will be ups and downs, and I want you to be prepared for them."

Pointing to the test, he added, "If I were a betting man, I'd bet any amount of money that on your next World History exam, you will earn at least ninety percent."

I stood up, went to the table, and tucked the test, which had lost its foreboding aura, back into my notebook. Then I returned to my seat on the sofa, pulling the quilt around me, unsure what to do next.

"Let's talk about what's going on with you, Victoria," Reverend Hahn said, using a well-practiced counseling tone. "This is about more than the test. This is about you making the transition from childhood to young adulthood. It's bound to be difficult. It's a time of emotional turmoil."

He flashed his charming smile, and his aging visage looked momentarily handsome again. "What you are going through is perfectly normal, my dear. Painful, but normal. Whether you know it or not, every other freshman on that campus is going through the same adjustment period. In fact, if you told me that starting college was easy, I'd think you weren't telling me the truth."

I nodded, listening intently.

"One minute," he continued, "you probably think you're handling things just fine. And the next minute, you want to run home to your parents and be a little child again."

I grinned sheepishly. "That's exactly what I felt today after I got my test back. I wanted to go home and crawl into bed and hide. But I didn't have any way to get there." I hesitated before adding, "So I came here instead."

I didn't anticipate how deeply my last few words would touch my birth father. He sat motionless for almost a minute, as if he could hardly take in what I'd said. "I'm so glad you did, Victoria," he finally responded, his voice thick with emotion. "I'm so pleased that you felt comfortable enough to rely on me in this way. Please know that I'm here for you. I'm always here for you. I'll support you in any way that I possibly can." He reached up an awkward hand to brush a single tear from his cheek.

Hardly aware of what I was doing, I got off the sofa, went to his chair, knelt on the floor, and wrapped my arms around his bony shoulders. "Thank you," he whispered. "Thank you."

After a few moments of that strange intimacy, I returned to my seat, marveling at what I'd just done. Reverend Hahn pulled a large white handkerchief from the pocket of his cardigan, wiped his eyes, and then smiled at me. "Can you stay for a while?" he asked.

"Yes," I said, "I think I can. I don't have any more classes this afternoon."

"Good. If you have time to listen, I'd like to tell you a story. I wish I had some refreshments set out for you. If I'd known you were coming, I would've had something prepared. But you can help yourself to a cup of tea, and there's a tin of cookies on the kitchen counter. A kind woman from my church brought them."

I shook my head. "I'm fine."

"Please," he said. "You can heat some water in the kettle on the stove."

I got up and walked over to the kitchenette, where I filled the tea kettle with water from the tap and put it on the stove to boil. Hesitantly, I opened cupboards and drawers as

Reverend Hahn pointed me to the cups, plates, silverware, and tea bags. I offered to make him a cup of tea as well, but he declined. After pouring boiling water over my tea bag, I carefully arranged the refreshments on the coffee table, in keeping with the formality of our previous visits.

"My child," he said after I'd seated myself again, "I believe today is the right time to tell you something of my history. My history is your history, and it's important for you to know it. I need to do this before it's too late. A year from now, I may not have the breath to tell the story."

I pulled the warm quilt around my shoulders. Then, tea cup in hand, I settled back to listen.

The first thing I must tell you, Victoria, is that I am adopted. I can see by the startled look on your face that you never imagined such a thing. In a way, this is something you and I have in common. Even though it wasn't a legal matter, you were essentially adopted by Herman Unruh.

I know nothing at all about my birth parents. Although I've had a wonderful life, not knowing where I came from has left a void within me. A year ago, you learned that the father who raised you is not your biological father, which created confusion for you. That's why I want to give you as much information about your heritage as possible. I want you to know who you are.

I do know that I was born in Romania. My parents, Willard and Grace Hahn, adopted me from an orphanage in Bucharest when I was just a month old. The orphanage staff told them I'd been left on their doorstep as a newborn, bundled up in a little basket.

You probably wonder what led my parents to Romania. They had traveled there with several other couples from their church to help out a struggling mission near Bucharest. I believe they were helping to found a church and build a school. I'm not sure. They never said much to me about that chapter of their lives.

They didn't stay long in Romania, less than two years. Shortly after my adoption, they returned to the United States, to their hometown of Lancaster, Pennsylvania, where I grew up. Thus, I have no memory of life in the country where I was born.

I've often speculated about the circumstances surrounding my birth, and my biological parents' decision to leave me in the care of the orphanage. Was my mother a young girl with no means to raise a child on her own? A widow with too many children to care for? Was I the product of an illicit affair that had to be kept secret? The mystery intrigues me.

While my birth parents apparently didn't want to risk having their identity known, they must have cared about me. The orphanage staff told my adoptive parents that I'd been delivered to them clean, warm, and well-nourished.

When I was traveling in Europe in the early 1950s, I went to Bucharest, hoping to find that little orphanage, hoping to obtain clues about my biological ancestry. My hopes were dashed when the local people informed me that the establishment was long gone, having been destroyed during World War II.

Being adopted by missionaries is probably where I got my passion for mission work. If Willard and Grace Hahn hadn't adopted me, where would I have ended up? I shudder to think what life would've held for me if I'd spent my growing up years in that Romanian orphanage.

You smiled, Victoria, when I mentioned my mother's name. Yes, you got your middle name from your grandmother. She was a wonderful person, as was my father. They loved me and raised me well. My two sisters, Emma and Rose, were both teenagers when I was adopted. No doubt, I was spoiled, as both of them doted on me.

However, in my youthful eyes, my parents were hopelessly old-fashioned. We lived in a conservative Mennonite community, to which I never felt I belonged. In the midst of these calm, subdued people living their orderly, upright lives, I was restless. My parents often expressed concern about the fact that I was invariably drawn to the sensational and the exciting. Over and over, they warned me about the perils of following worldly pursuits.

While my family lived frugally, we were never poor. My parents were hardworking people who owned a restaurant in Lancaster. Their establishment not only served the local people, it attracted many tourists who wanted to sample traditional Mennonite cuisine.

Under my father's shrewd management, the business thrived and expanded. My parents added a bakery to the restaurant, selling bread, cakes, pies, donuts, and cookies. A few years later, they started a second restaurant, and later on, a third.

My mother did much of the cooking and baking, and my sisters worked as waitresses in the restaurant. They were attractive young women, and the customers enjoyed being served by pretty Mennonite girls in their traditional garb.

My parents never treated me differently than they did their biological children. While my dark complexion stood in contrast to the sandy hair and blue eyes of the rest of the family, my height was not an oddity, as my father and sisters were taller than average. Most people never knew I was adopted. On the rare occasion when the subject came up, people would comment on how well I fit into the family.

When I was still a young child, I started helping in the restaurant, busing tables, washing dishes, and sweeping the floor. By the time I entered my teens, I was working in the bakery. I quickly mastered the art of making pies, cakes, and donuts. To this day, I appreciate fine baked goods.

I knew my parents expected me, their only son, to stay with the family business. At first, I enjoyed the challenge of learning new skills. However, as my teen years passed, I grew increasingly bored and restless. I think some of my appetite for adventure could have been satisfied if I'd been allowed to wait on tables. That would have given me the opportunity to interact with a variety of people from different walks of life.

But I suspect my parents were afraid that such an experience would only fuel my wanderlust. They told me they needed my help in other aspects of the business, doing the work in the kitchen that required a great deal of physical stamina: lifting, carrying, loading and unloading. Work best suited for a young man to do. Work that I found unbearably monotonous. Thankfully, making deliveries in the community afforded me a bit of reprieve from my tedious routine.

I knew that as soon as I found myself in a position where I could chart my own course, I would leave. I had to leave. There was so much more I wanted out of life. So much more of the world I wanted to see.

My parents were fair. They did not take advantage of their children's labor, and each of us earned a wage. We were all encouraged to save our money, so that we would be financially well-established when we entered adult life.

My oldest sister Emma never married. I've often wondered why. She was a beautiful young woman, and certainly could have attracted a husband if she'd wanted to. She stayed with the family business throughout her working years. As she grew older, she was the one who kept the books and managed the financial side of the business. When my elderly parents finally sold the restaurants, Emma was ready to retire.

My sister Rose married when she was nineteen. She left the business to raise her own family. She passed away three years ago, but Emma is still living. She's well into her eighties now, and is quite frail. I call her once a week to check on her, and Rose's children keep an eye on her.

While I felt confined in our Mennonite community, I found ways to satisfy my craving for adventure. I can't say I was a reckless young man. But if I really wanted to do something my parents disapproved of, I'd find a way around their rules.

During my teen years, I was a frequent patron of the picture shows in Lancaster, without my parents' knowledge, of course. They would've been terribly distressed if they'd known what I was doing. In the 1920s, the movies were silent films. I watched all the great stars on the big screen: Charlie Chaplin, Buster Keaton, Laurel and Hardy, Clara Bow, Gloria Swanson. I was enthralled by the world they brought to me.

I don't think I've ever been as thrilled as I was when I watched my first 'talkie' in 1930. I began dreaming about being on a movie set, playing opposite the great leading ladies of the time: Greta Garbo, Myrna Loy, Norma Shearer, Carole Lombard. The more I harbored this fantasy, the stronger it grew.

By the time I was twenty-two, I'd become so restless that I'd get out of bed in the morning thinking I couldn't stay another day in Lancaster, Pennsylvania. At the time when the rest of the country was devastated by the depression, I had $600 dollars of savings stashed in a dresser drawer. Enough to buy me a train ticket to wherever I wanted to go. Enough to get me started in the life I'd been dreaming about.

When I announced to my parents that I was leaving, they begged me not to go. My father pointed out that, at a time when many young men were jobless, homeless, and hungry, I was fortunate. There in Lancaster, I had steady employment, a roof over my head, and plenty to eat.

"Harry," he pleaded, "why don't you stay here a few more years, until this country gets back on its feet?"

But I knew that in the only industry in which I wanted to work, business was booming. While the rest of the country was in decline, Hollywood was moving full steam ahead. In spite of the widespread poverty, people were flocking to the movies, seeking a much-needed escape from the bleakness of their lives.

At a time when tramps were hopping aboard freight cars, I had the means to buy a ticket on a passenger train bound for California. I remember smiling with satisfaction as I gazed out that train window, watching the countryside roll by. I was doing exactly what I wanted to do, going exactly where I wanted to go.

In Los Angeles, I rented a room in a boarding house, keeping a careful eye on my stash of money.

There in Hollywood, I had a young man's cockiness. I knew full well that I possessed striking good looks, keen intelligence, and the ability to win people over with my charm. In spite of the fact that I was initially disoriented in my new surroundings, I was relentless in pursuing what I wanted.

It didn't take me long to land parts as an extra in westerns. Because of my dark complexion, I was often cast in the role of a Mexican or an Indian. Sadly, that work didn't pay much, and I quickly realized I needed to find other employment in order to support myself.

So, I took a job as a bartender. Prohibition had just ended, and people were drinking with gusto. I was drinking my share, but not as much as I could have. I knew that I needed to keep my wits about me if I was going to accomplish what I'd set out to do.

Actors, directors, and producers frequented the bar where I was working. Every time I recognized someone important in the movie industry, I made sure to introduce myself and strike up a conversation. I'd tell them about my interests and inquire about opportunities.

Before long, I was landing small roles in B-grade movies, movies that have long since been lost to posterity. I knew I had to pay my dues before I could move ahead in the business. But I would be satisfied with nothing less than the role of leading man.

To my delight, I quickly found myself surrounded by women who clamored for my attention. I won't repeat the sordid details of that time in my life. I'm sure you can imagine that it was not an environment conducive to maintaining high moral standards. The abundance of female admiration fed my ego, leading me to believe I was on my way to becoming the next Clark Gable or Gary Cooper.

Three years passed in this manner. I thought I was living my dream.

From time to time, fights would break out among the patrons of the bar where I was working. I'd never been a fighter. I'd always been one to use my wits, not my fists, to handle difficult situations, and my employer had schooled me in what to do if things got out of hand in the bar.

One summer night when I was trying to restore order during a fracas, the police arrived on the scene. While I was throwing no punches myself, I was in the middle of the fray, and I landed in jail along with a paddy-wagon full of brawling drunks.

Some young men might consider spending a night in jail after an evening of unruly behavior to be an ordinary event. But having been reared in a God-fearing Mennonite family, I was filled with shame. I sat in a corner of that stinking cell, my head in my hands, surrounded by swearing, scuffling inebriates. "How did it come to this?" I asked myself again and again. Never had I imagined finding myself in such a disgraceful situation. I thought about my parents back in Pennsylvania, knowing how heartbroken they'd be if they knew where I was. I prayed to God that they would never find out.

I couldn't help but think about the Apostle Paul being struck down by God on the road to Damascus. I knew it had taken a dramatic event for God to get my attention.

I sat there for hours, thinking, taking inventory of my life. I realized that, with the way I'd been conducting myself, I'd been tempting fate for quite some time. During my three raucous years in Hollywood, I'd occasionally heard the whisper of God in my mind, telling me that I was headed down the wrong road. But the noise and clamor of the world around me had drowned out that still, small voice.

Of course, my parents had been sending me letters, urging me to reconsider the path I'd chosen. "We love you, son," they'd write, "and God loves you, too. Don't turn your back on Him." They told me about a little Mennonite congregation in Bakersfield, a hundred miles north of Los Angeles. "We've written to Pastor Yoder," they told me. "If you ever need help, go to him."

As you might expect, those letters only served to annoy me. Many a time, I was so aggravated by my parents' admonishing words that I felt like tearing up the letters and throwing them away. But something stopped me from doing that. I stuffed each one of them under my mattress.

That night in the jail, after all my cellmates had fallen asleep, a peaceful stillness settled over me. It must have been around five o'clock in the morning, as dawn was breaking. I looked around at the bodies slumped against the walls and sprawled on the floor. In spite of the stench and squalor, it seemed as if God's holy light was shining on the scene. I was keenly aware of His divine presence in that cell. I knew that even though I'd strayed far from His will, His love had come to seek me out.

A thought came to me in the stillness. It was quiet, but clear, unmistakably the voice of God. "You are destined for a life in the public eye," it whispered to me. "But not on the movie screen. You are meant for a different stage." And then a picture flashed into my mind. I saw myself behind the pulpit, preaching the word of God.

This sense of God's presence was so powerful that it hardly mattered to me where I was. Despite the fact that I was incarcerated, I felt freer than I'd ever felt in my entire life. I must have sat in that state of deep peace for several hours. Suddenly, I was startled out of my reverie by the sound of a guard unlocking the cell door. In the dim light, I saw him beckoning to me. I got up and walked over to him, and he told me that I was being released.

A person could ask why, after having had such a compelling spiritual experience, I went on to make so many mistakes in my life. Why I behaved so scandalously at times. I believe that God's guidance is pure and true. But it gets interpreted imperfectly in our confused human minds, and is manifested imperfectly in our chaotic lives.

While Reverend Hahn had been telling his story, I'd been curled up, wrapped in my warm quilt, my head resting on the arm of the sofa. Although his preacher-like voice had lulled me into state of deep relaxation, I'd been listening intently. I'd pictured his conservative family life in Lancaster, Pennsylvania, similar to my own upbringing. When he'd described his years in Hollywood, I'd felt a little envious, wishing I could have such an adventure.

But his account of the humiliating experience of landing in jail roused me out of my reverie. And when he made the reference to his post-epiphany scandalous behavior, I felt so uneasy that I emerged from the cocoon of my blanket and sat up.

Reverend Hahn paused in his monologue, chuckling. "I thought I'd put you to sleep, Victoria."

"No," I replied. "I heard every word you said."

"Would you like another cup of tea? I could do with a glass of water. My throat is dry from all the talking."

"I'll get it for you," I said.

I stood in the kitchenette, my back to him as I poured fresh water over my teabag. My thoughts churned. *Scandalous behavior. He's referring to his involvement with my mother, of course. And, no doubt, with a string of other women.* I knew Reverend Hahn had never completely given up his Hollywood ways. Old pain welled inside me, as I once again remembered that I'd been the product of a meaningless affair.

Tamping down my turmoil, I forced myself to smile as I carried our drinks back to the living room. Reverend Hahn received the glass of water with a shaking hand and took a few grateful sips. "Thank you, my dear."

"So what happened after you got out of jail?" I asked as I seated myself on the sofa again.

"Good question," he said. "That's where my life took a completely different turn."

Two days after my release from jail, I shot my last scene in the film I'd been working on. When my producer talked about another role he had in mind for me, I told him I wasn't interested. I collected my pay, packed up my belongings, and informed my landlord that I was moving out. Then, single-minded and fully confident in what I was doing, I set out on my trek, hitchhiking north on Highway 99 toward Bakersfield.

Reverend Yoder didn't seem surprised when I knocked on his door. When I introduced myself as the son of Willard and Grace Hahn, he said he'd been expecting me. "The past few days," he told me, "I had a deep sense that the Lord was leading you here."

Just as I stepped through the door, a young woman entered the room. She was small and slender, with wide blue eyes. The innocence in those eyes and the gentleness in her bearing made her seem so different from the women I'd been consorting with in Los Angeles.

Reverend Yoder introduced us. "Mr. Hahn, this is my daughter Myrna." Blushing, Myrna smiled, then turned and left the room. And at that moment, I knew that Reverend Yoder's daughter was going to become my wife.

Reverend Yoder quickly set about making arrangements for my lodging. That night, I took up residence in the spare room of a member of his congregation. The family was on the verge of destitution, and my room and board payment was a godsend to them.

A woman in the church, a mother of five young children, had just lost her husband to a heart attack. He'd owned and managed a grocery store, and she had no idea what to do with the business. I'd arrived in Bakersfield just two days after her husband's death. It turned out that my experience of working in my parents' business made me just the right person to help her out.

Thus, it seemed to the Mennonite congregation in Bakersfield that my arrival in town was as providential for them as it was for me. They welcomed me with open arms.

During my spare time, I met frequently with Reverend Yoder, talking with him about my desire to enter the ministry. He was eager to mentor me. Within six months, I was preaching the occasional sermon at the Bakersfield church, which was always enthusiastically received by the congregation.

A year after I arrived in Bakersfield, Reverend Yoder arranged for me to travel to Indiana, to attend the Mennonite Biblical Seminary on the Goshen College Campus.

Of course, I'd written to my parents about the change in my life, and they were overjoyed. After completing my courses at the seminary, I traveled on to Pennsylvania to visit them. My parents couldn't resist pleading with me to come back to live in Lancaster. But by that time, I felt settled in Bakersfield, and I knew California was now my home.

Besides, there was a young woman waiting for me back in Bakersfield. To the delight of everyone in the congregation, I'd been courting the minister's daughter. I didn't rush things. I took my time. Myrna and I were married two years after my arrival in Bakersfield.

At the time, I truly believed that Myrna was the wife I needed. She was a woman of impeccable character, and I cannot utter a single complaint about her. But in retrospect, I can see that we weren't well-suited for each other.

Myrna needed a quiet, settled life. That was her nature. She wanted nothing more than to be a wife and a mother.

But I couldn't give her the child she longed for, nor the quiet life that she wanted.

Less than three years after our marriage, the United States entered World War II, and I was conscripted for military service. Being a member of one of the peace churches, I registered as a conscientious objector.

My first thought was to serve the military in a noncombatant role, such as a medic. I would have welcomed the adventure. But Reverend Yoder informed me that Mennonites did not support the military in any capacity.

So I agreed to serve my country through the Civilian Public Service program. I ended up working in a mental hospital in Los Angeles. I, along with many other Mennonite conscientious objectors, was appalled at the treatment of the mentally ill, who were often abused and housed in unsanitary environments. I'd like to believe that our letters to the newspaper, reporting on these deplorable conditions and calling for action, helped spur the mental health reform movement that followed.

However, my return to Los Angeles kept Myrna and me apart for long stretches of time. At best, I was able to go home for one weekend a month. She became so lonely that she ended up moving back in with her parents. I knew she was unhappy about our separation, but there was nothing I could do to change the circumstances of our lives.

Shortly after my service ended, Reverend Yoder's health began to decline, and it seemed right that I should take over pastoring the Bakersfield congregation. I felt strongly about that calling, and I stayed with that congregation for almost two decades. Until the day I moved to Warsaw, Indiana, a year after you were born.

However, I often felt restless standing behind just one pulpit. I felt the desire to travel, not only across the United States, but to other countries as well. While I loved my home and my church in California, I saw my life work as embracing the entire world.

So, from time to time, I became a traveling evangelist, scheduling speaking engagements in Mennonite churches from coast to coast. I worked with various mission projects in foreign countries. Early on, Myrna joined me in some of my ventures. But it soon became apparent that the very thing that enlivened me exhausted her. More and more, she chose to stay home while I traveled. Sadly, we drifted apart.

I regret not being able to give my wife what she needed. But I'll never regret my marriage to Myrna. I owe her a great deal of gratitude for being my helpmate all those years, for remaining by my side when things were difficult for her.

Suddenly, Reverend Hahn was overtaken by a spell of coughing, his thin body heaving with the effort to clear his lungs. I jumped off the sofa to hand him the glass of water he'd set on the coffee table. He held up a palm, declining my offer, then reached into the pocket of his cardigan and brought out a box of cough drops.

His fumbling fingers struggled to open the box. I wanted to help, but sensed that his pride insisted that he manage the task on his own. Finally, he popped a drop into his mouth, and his coughing subsided.

"My child," he said when he regained his voice, "there are so many stories I could tell you about my years in the ministry. But today is not the day. My heart and mind still long to do the work I used to do. But my body is worn out, and at the moment, I am exhausted. Cynthia will be back in a few minutes to help me into bed."

I stood up. "I'm sorry. I stayed too long. I should get going."

I walked over to the table and took my jacket off the back of the chair. Thankfully, it had partially dried. I slipped it on, then picked up my books. As I turned to say goodbye to Reverend Hahn, the profound sadness on his face made him look more fragile than ever. I went to his chair and knelt on the floor to give him another hug.

"This last chapter of my life hasn't been easy," he rasped as he returned my embrace. "It has brought challenges I never imagined I would face. But it has also brought me joy. Unspeakable joy. It has brought me you."

I felt exhausted myself, having processed more than my share of intense emotion for the day. I stood up and went to the door to put on my shoes. As I was bending down to tie my laces, Reverend Hahn called out in a voice that was now barely above a whisper, "Victoria, you are the only flesh and blood I have ever known. Having you in my life relieves a deep loneliness that has always been at the core of my being. My dear child, you have no idea what you mean to me."

As I rode home from school with my mother that weekend, she asked the same question she asked every Friday evening: "How was your week, Victoria?"

"Fine," I replied, my tone sounding as distracted as hers.

I thought of telling her about my visit with Reverend Hahn, recounting the story he'd told me, a story that would both interest and agitate her. A story that would jolt her into alertness, setting her mouth in a grim line, making her hands grip the steering wheel so hard that her knuckles turned white. I cleared my throat to speak, but stopped myself.

"What?" she said.

I hesitated. "Nothing."

While my mother prepared the evening meal, I mentally rehearsed how I would tell my parents about my birth father's foreign ancestry, an ancestry that I shared. But as I looked at my parents' weary faces at the supper table, I decided that the episode of my emotional breakdown and the ensuing visit with Reverend Hahn was best left unreported.

I told myself that spouting out the information about my colorful heritage, of which they had no part, would do nothing but set me apart from them. I was afraid I would come across like I thought I was special, better than them.

I especially didn't want to tell my dad. Herman Unruh and I had our own extraordinary history, the story of his unselfish love, his remarkable courage, his going beyond the call of duty in order to provide me with the upbringing I needed. I never wanted to spoil this beautiful story with the account of another father's involvement in my life.

In the end, I decided to keep Reverend Hahn's history in a secret chamber of my mind that neither of my parents would ever enter.

Months later, my mother asked me an unexpected question. "Has Reverend Hahn ever told you about relatives on his side of the family?"

"His parents are dead," I told her. "He had two older sisters. Rose passed away a few years ago. Emma lives in Lancaster, Pennsylvania."

My mother looked at me warily. "Are you planning on meeting Emma?"

I shook my head. "Nope. He hasn't said anything about that."

She seemed satisfied with that interchange, and never brought up the subject of my unknown relatives again.

CHAPTER 7

Going home every weekend helped me make it through the first few months of my freshman year. But I paid a price for indulging my need for security. My roommate capitalized on my absence by holding parties in our room every time I was gone.

Bonnie Springer was anything but tidy. While she had beautiful clothing and top-of-the-line toiletries, pricier than anything I could ever afford, she seemed to care little about her possessions. Bottles of shampoo and tubes of mascara would roll around on the floor, eventually finding permanent lodging among the dust-bunnies under her desk or bed. When she undressed, she let her clothing drop to the floor, and didn't seem to mind trampling designer blue jeans and expensive sweaters underfoot.

On the rare occasion when Bonnie did laundry, she scooped up armloads of the mess and stuffed everything into one load. I shuddered every time I watched her do this. When I was just a young girl, my mother had schooled me in the art of separating laundry: colors in one load, whites in another, sheets and towels in their own separate loads. Certain sweaters and undergarments had to be hand-washed in cold water. I knew Bonnie was ruining countless delicate items by laundering them with her towels and jeans.

In order to keep my sanity, I drew an imaginary line down the middle of our room, allowing mayhem on her side, establishing order on mine. Unfortunately, Bonnie's mess seemed to grow legs, constantly wandering over to my side of the room. Half a dozen times a day, I'd kick a dirty sock, a pair of panties, or a tube of lip gloss back into her realm of squalor.

When I'd come back to campus on Monday morning, I'd find my side of the room overtaken by her weekend party debris: half-empty *Coke* cans on my bookshelves, candy wrappers under my bed, crushed potato chips on the floor.

Time after time, I'd find a stray shirt, a jacket, or a pair of pajama bottoms lying on my bed or draped across my desk chair.

"Oh," Bonnie would say nonchalantly when I'd toss the item onto her side of the room. "That's Sarah's."

Or Linda's. Or Cheryl's. Or Jessica's.

My bedcovers would always be rumpled, the telltale signs of someone lounging on it while I was gone. Sometimes, I'd find my bedspread hastily pulled up over bunched and twisted sheets, and I'd know that one of Bonnie's friends had spent the night in my bed.

One Monday morning, I found a pizza box sitting on my desk. When I opened it, the condition of the cold, slimy slices inside told me they'd been there since Friday night. "What the heck?" I exclaimed to Bonnie.

"Sorry." She snatched the box from my hand, folding it in half and stuffing it into her overflowing trash can. I knew that garbage wouldn't be carried out for another two weeks.

Thus, every Monday morning, I'd feel an overwhelming need to clean my side of the room, to restore order to my college environment before tackling my week's agenda. I'd sweep up the filth and clutter on the floor. Then I'd attack the sticky messes on my desk and shelves with a rag and a bottle of cleaning solution. All the while, I'd boil with righteous indignation, as if channeling Ada Unruh.

Many times, I bit my lip to avoid an ugly argument with my roommate. I knew that if I confronted her about her slovenly ways, she'd mock me for being too uptight, and the interchange would only serve to fuel the steadily rising tension between us.

Surprisingly, in early November, I found a reason to stay on campus for the entire weekend. As I sat at my desk on Friday evening, completing an assignment for my Old Testament class, Bonnie walked into our room carrying a grocery bag. She stopped short when she saw me.

"What are you doing here?" she asked. "Aren't you going home?"

"No." I tried to keep from smirking. I knew I was ruining her plans for the evening, and the thought gave me wicked delight. "I've got things to do."

Bonnie plunked her bag down on her bed. It toppled onto its side, spilling out a package of chocolate chip cookies, two bags of pretzel rods, and a pack of red licorice sticks.

"Oh," she harrumphed. Absentmindedly, she tore open the pack of licorice, pulled out a stick, and chewed on it. Then she abruptly left the room. A few minutes later, she returned, picked up her bag of snacks, and left again. I figured she'd arranged a different venue for her evening food orgy.

I returned to my assignment, smiling to myself. I was determined to get all my work done before Saturday evening, because something special was going to happen then. I was going to my first social event of my freshman year. Laura Zuercher had invited me and three other girls to her home for a pizza party.

I was surprised at how much the invitation had excited me. During my first three years of high school, receiving party invitations had been routine events in my life. I'd been popular back then, surrounded by friends.

Then, at the end of my junior year, I'd been hit with the shocking news about my paternity, which knocked the adolescent silliness right out of me. Robbed of my childish naiveté, I had retreated into a quietness that verged on isolation. I had withdrawn from my friends, because I'd wanted no one close enough to me to detect the secret I was hiding.

So, it seemed like ages since I'd let loose and had some fun, and the prospect made me feel a bit like my old self. In the days preceding the party, I mentally rehearsed how I was going to interact with the other girls. *I can be talkative and outgoing. I can be funny. I can be open without telling everything about myself. I can choose what I reveal to others, and what I keep private.*

As I prepared my strategy, I realized I was adopting the same technique my biological father had practiced over the past two decades. Telling the truth, but only part of it. Allowing others to fill in the gaps with reasonable, albeit incorrect, assumptions. But what other choice did I have?

After the first few awkward moments at Laura's house, I found it surprisingly easy to slough off my worries and move into a party mode. Laura introduced me to her friends, Jeannette, Grace, and Mary. We talked and laughed and stuffed ourselves with pizza. It felt great to once again be a normal teenage girl surrounded by a circle of friends.

Inevitably, the conversation turned to boys. "Are you dating anyone, Victoria?" Jeanette asked.

"No," I replied. Then, selecting a partial truth, I added, "I haven't dated anyone since my junior year of high school."

She shot me a curious look. "Why not? You're so pretty. It would be easy for you to get a date."

I shrugged, and then uttered another partial truth. "I'm just sick of all the problems that come with dating. I decided to wait until I'm sure I've found the right guy. Someone I can really communicate with."

"I've seen you eating lunch with Stephen Wenger and Charlie Hess," Grace chimed in. "I thought maybe you were dating one of them."

"Oh, no," I said. "We're just friends."

"Whew!" Mary exclaimed. "That would be weird. It doesn't seem like either one of them is your type."

"They're cool," I said defensively. "They're both really smart. And funny, too. I enjoy talking with them."

The girls launched into a few minutes of gossip about how weird Stephen and Charlie were, and the things other people said about them. I felt a little bad. I realized that, in a sense, I was using those two social misfits. In keeping company with young men I had no interest in dating, and who were unlikely to pursue me, I was enjoying male companionship without the risks involved with entering a romantic relationship.

"You know who I think is cute?" Jeanette said. "Calvin Zook."

"Who's that?" the rest of us responded in unison.

"He's a sophomore. From Nebraska, I think. Or maybe South Dakota. Somewhere out there on the plains. He's tall, really well-built. I'd love to see that guy with his shirt off."

She shuddered with delight at the prospect. "He's got blonde hair. I sat across from him at lunch the other day. He's got gorgeous, soulful blue eyes, and when he looked at me, I almost stopped breathing. I think he said he's a social work major. He doesn't talk much, but he's really nice."

She glanced around at the rest of us. "Have you girls seen him? He's hard to miss. He really stands out." She ran her tongue lasciviously across her lips. "He's so handsome, just thinking about him makes me drool."

"Does he have a girlfriend?" Mary asked.

"I don't know," Jeannette replied. "I hope not. I'd like to get to know him better." She sighed dramatically. "But he's way out of my league."

As I listened to Jeannette carry on about the magnificent Calvin Zook, I felt my mood darken. The description of the young man sounded uncannily like that of my high school boyfriend Daniel Hooley. A tall, blonde, blue-eyed boy whose striking good looks sent all the girls into a dither. I'd thought Daniel was the love of my life, the boy I'd never break up with. The boy I'd eventually marry.

But Daniel Hooley had belonged to the old Victoria Unruh, the girl who sailed glibly through life, innocently unaware of the dark truth about her family relationships. Learning about my illegitimate birth had changed me into someone who no longer fit with Daniel, and several months later, he'd broken up with me.

I hadn't mustered the nerve to date anyone since then. I knew that if I entered a serious relationship, I'd have to be honest from the start. There could be no holding back of secrets that would later emerge and explode our relationship into smithereens, the fallout landing on the lives of innocent bystanders. The young man to whom I would reveal my true self had to be able to accept all the irregularities in my life. I hadn't yet met such a guy.

Because I stayed up until the early hours of the morning, I slept until noon on Sunday. Missing church was decidedly outside the parameters of my normal behavior. Up to that point in my life, illness had been my only reason for not attending Westside Mennonite with my parents on a Sunday morning.

When I awoke, my roommate was gone. Savoring the peaceful silence, I lay in bed for another twenty minutes, gazing at the rays of light peeking around my drawn curtains. A faint, duty-bound voice in my head whispered that I should feel guilty, but I couldn't muster any remorse. I felt strangely free, liberated from all parental expectations, an adult who could make her own decisions. At that moment, I felt completely emancipated from my mom and dad, which, of course, was not yet the case.

It seemed as if I'd been holding my breath my first two months of college. I'd been fearful, uncharacteristically timid, unable to find my place there on the campus. But the weekend of Laura Zuercher's pizza party represented a mighty exhale. With the renewal of my social confidence, I no longer felt the need to ride home with my mother on Friday evenings. So, aside from going home over the Thanksgiving break, I spent the rest of my weekends on campus that trimester.

I settled more comfortably into the rhythm of my classes, tearlessly earning equal numbers of A's and B's on tests and papers. True to my birth father's prediction, I earned a 94% on my next world history exam. But I failed to prepare for a biology quiz, and earned a C-minus. When I bragged to Reverend Hahn that I hadn't cried over my low grade, he laughed, but suggested that studying for the next test would be a good idea.

I hung out every weekend with Laura, Jeannette, Grace, and Mary. Several times, Laura borrowed her parents' car to drive us downtown to the Goshen Theatre on Main Street, where we watched *Grease* and *Heaven Can Wait.* Sometimes, the five of us would walk the short distance to the Southside Soda Shop, a popular hangout for Goshen College students. On week nights, I occasionally hosted my own gathering of friends in my room, forcing my disgruntled roommate to do her rowdy socializing elsewhere.

I slept late two Sunday mornings in a row, exercising my right to choose whether or not to attend church. But this made me feel uneasy. Despite cherishing my newly claimed freedom, I knew that, deep down, I wasn't ready to turn my back on my religious upbringing. So, instead of having my parents drive all the way to the campus to pick me up to attend Westside Mennonite, I decided to try out the College Mennonite Church.

That first Sunday at College Mennonite, I attempted to steal into the church without anyone noticing me. The sanctuary was packed, housing a congregation three or four times the size of Westside Mennonite. Looking around at the sea of people made me feel a little dizzy.

With trepidation, I climbed the steps to the balcony and slipped into a pew. Immediately, smiling faces turned toward me. Introductions were made and welcoming hands were extended. Then the singing started, and as I joined in the familiar hymns that swelled around me, I knew it wouldn't be hard to consider this congregation my home away from home.

At the end of the service, I watched from the balcony as the congregants on the main floor slowly made their way out of the sanctuary. Suddenly, I saw Reverend Hahn in his wheelchair, escorted by his friends Dave and Vera Martin. He was shaking hands and chatting with the people around him. Then he looked up, and his eyes widened with pleasure when he spotted me. Lifting a hand in greeting, he flashed me a dazzling smile.

From the distance, I could not detect all the tell-tale signs of aging and illness. Instead, I saw the handsome and charming man of his youth. The Hollywood actor, the ladies' man. The dashing young minister who traveled across the country and around the world. In that moment, the story of his early years seemed more real to me than the day he'd told it.

It struck me that, despite my quest for independence, I was still attending church with a parent. It seemed like the right thing to do. For now, anyway.

CHAPTER 8

After my unplanned trek to Reverend Hahn's apartment in late October, I began a pattern of visiting him once a week, usually on a Wednesday afternoon.

I knew my biological father's time was running out, and that more than anything, he craved time with his only child. I knew he wanted to make up for what he'd missed out on during my growing-up years. I told myself that by granting him this opportunity, I was being kind and honorable.

But I also had to admit that I was beginning to enjoy our visits, even to look forward to them. While getting ready for class on a Wednesday morning, I'd smile to myself, knowing that in the afternoon, I'd take a break from my college routine and enter a different world. Ordinary little Victoria Unruh would step into a realm no one else knew about, a fairytale life in which she played the role of the princess whose every word and action charmed her father the king.

Much as I did with Charlie Hess and Stephen Wenger, I took pleasure in my birth father's keen intelligence, his quick wit, his humor. However, Reverend Hahn's polished demeanor was very different from my friends' social awkwardness.

At every visit, we'd talk at length about my classes. He was always eager to hear about what I was learning, and would add his own input to my growing store of knowledge. Sometimes, he'd make a counterpoint to something my Old Testament professor said, offering an idea that would invariably end up in the next paper I wrote.

He'd hang onto every world I said about my World History class. "I'm not much of a history scholar," he admitted. "You have a lot to teach me on this subject."

He'd insist on reading my assignments for my Expository Writing class. I formed the habit of bringing the first draft of an essay for his inspection, incorporating his suggestions into my final product.

After a particularly stimulating conversation one day, I suddenly understood what it was that had drawn my mother into Reverend Hahn's world. His charisma, coupled with his good looks and keen intelligence, would have been irresistible to her. To any woman. Being around him would have lifted her spirit out of the deadening routine of her mundane life. Talking with this brilliant man would have brought out a matching brightness in her, a brightness she'd long ago buried under layers of duty and obligation.

As Reverend Hahn's daughter, I had the privilege of enjoying his charming personality without reservation. But his ability to light up my mother's life had posed a danger to her. It had turned her world upside down.

In that moment, I felt something shift inside me. In my mind's eye, I watched all my lingering resentments about my mother's affair soften, dissolve, and then vanish. I was no longer a child who could naively point fingers and cast blame without knowing another's reality. I had moved into a woman-to-woman understanding of my mother.

I pondered this new awareness as I walked back to the campus, cherishing how tender it felt in my heart.

Admittedly, not every visit with Reverend Hahn was entirely scintillating. There were times when I grew bored and restless sitting with the sick, aging man in his tiny apartment. When he'd embark upon a lengthy story about his evangelistic work in some remote part of the United States, or his month-long stay at a mission in Africa, my mind would start to wander. My eyes would roam over the titles of the endless volumes on his bookshelves. Or I'd find myself staring out the patio door, watching a Greencroft grounds worker raking leaves or mulching the flowerbeds.

But Reverend Hahn would notice when this happened, and would apologize for his long-windedness. Then he'd turn the tables by insisting that I tell him a story, usually about my childhood.

"Tell me about first grade," he said one day. "What was it like for you?"

I paused, thinking back. "I did fine in first grade. I'd get done with my work so quickly that my teacher would have to find other activities to keep me busy."

Reverend Hahn smiled proudly. "I can believe that. School was always easy for you, wasn't it?"

I nodded. "But I was naughty sometimes. When I got bored, I had trouble staying in my seat, and I'd bother the other kids. Mostly, though, I got in trouble on the school bus. My neighbor was my bus driver. He'd tell me to keep my hands to myself, but I wouldn't listen to him. He ended up having to talk with my dad about my behavior."

Reverend Hahn tossed back his head, laughing so heartily that I was afraid his frail body couldn't bear the strain of it. "Normal childhood experiences, I'd say. A bright, creative child often has trouble following the rules."

Right then, I realized there would be hardly anything I could do to disappoint my birth father. He would invariably shine a positive light on my failures or lapses in judgment.

"Tell me about your relationships with boys," Reverend Hahn said during a visit in mid-November.

I detected fatherly concern in his voice, and knew this was more than an idle question. His all-seeing eyes were ready to probe into another private area of my life. Feeling defensive, I chose my words carefully. "I liked playing with boys when I was little. I was a tomboy. I liked to compete with them. But I didn't like them as boyfriends."

I hoped we could leave that uneasy topic, but Reverend Hahn nodded and said, "Tell me more."

"In junior high," I reluctantly continued, "I started liking boys in a different way. During my first two years of high school, I had a few boyfriends. But I wasn't allowed to date them. I just walked around with them at school. Sometimes, I'd talk with them on the telephone, but not for too long. My mom was strict about things like that. She didn't allow me to go on any real dates until I was sixteen."

"That's good," Reverend Hahn said. "I'm glad she was protective of you. I would've been protective, too. You probably would've gotten a few lectures from me."

His affirmation of my mother's stance on dating surprised me, actually pleased me. It was nice to have my biological parents in agreement on some aspect of my life.

"I've only dated one guy," I confided, my defensive wall crumbling. "That was Daniel Hooley."

"Is he that tall, blonde-haired fellow I saw you with when your choir sang at First Mennonite Church in Warsaw a couple of years ago?"

I was surprised that he'd remembered that detail. "Yes, that was Daniel. We were together for about two years. We broke up the summer after my junior year."

Once again, the memory of losing Daniel hit me hard. I bit my lip to keep from tearing up.

Reverend Hahn suddenly seemed ill at ease. He reached out a long arm to straighten a magazine on the coffee table. "Why did you break up?" he asked, not looking at me.

Against my will, tears spilled from my eyes. I didn't want to tell my birth father that his presence in my life was the reason Daniel and I could never have a future together.

"Did the breakup happen after you found out I was your father?" Reverend Hahn's voice sounded weak and strained, as if his disease had suddenly reared up and gotten the best of him.

"Yes."

"Did you tell him about me?"

"No. I couldn't. I knew he wouldn't be able to handle it. His family has been our neighbors all my life. I couldn't tell Daniel something that would upset everyone. That would ruin my parents' relationships with their best friends."

I fiddled with the strings of my hooded sweatshirt, twisting them together in a coil, avoiding Reverend Hahn's gaze. "Daniel knew I was holding something back from him. That created a lot of tension between us, and he lost trust in me."

A deafening silence permeated the small apartment, so thick and heavy that I thought I was going to choke on it. I wanted to jump up and run out of Reverend Hahn's apartment and never come back. But I remained on the sofa, my body too wooden to move.

When I finally summoned the courage to look up, I saw the strain on my birth father's face. His eyes were lowered, and he seemed to be struggling to breathe.

"I hope you know, Victoria," he rasped, "that I deeply regret any difficulty I've brought into your life. Any pain I've created for you causes me great sorrow."

"It's okay," I quickly replied. I burrowed into the corner of the sofa, then picked up a throw pillow and hugged it to my chest. "I loved Daniel. In a way, I still do. But he and I wouldn't have worked out in the long run. Daniel's future is going to be wrapped up in farming. When he gets out of college, he'll come back here to Goshen, and he'll probably stay here all his life. I think it's best that we broke up when we did. I don't think I would've been happy being a farmer's wife."

"Your thoughts show maturity." The confidence had returned to Reverend Hahn's voice. "You are able to accurately assess your own needs."

His response nudged me into a territory I hadn't planned on entering. "My mother hasn't been happy with her life. Even when I was little girl, I knew that. She always seemed angry and frustrated. I think she felt trapped. She wanted something more." I took a long breath, exhaling deeply. "I never want to end up like that."

Reverend Hahn shifted his posture in his chair, then straightened his tie and fingered the buttons on the cuffs of his shirt. "Yes," he said emphatically. "Your mother had an adventurous spirit that her mundane life nearly extinguished.

I never want you to consign yourself to being trapped in such misery."

Another long silence ensued. I had no desire to speak what was on my mind. *That my mother's adventurous spirit had led her into the arms of the brilliant and dashing man who now sat across from me in this tiny apartment. That if she'd never strayed into forbidden territory, I never would have been born.*

The silence was broken by Reverend Hahn's laborious clearing of his throat. "So, you're not interested in anyone now?"

I shook my head. "No. I'm not ready to date anyone else." I was pretty sure he knew the reason why.

"There's nothing wrong with not dating," he said. "It's probably best that you don't get distracted by a serious relationship your first year of college. I don't want you to close down any options for your future. You have plenty of time to find the young man who's right for you."

Then his voice lightened as he steered the conversation in a different direction. "Are you going home for Thanksgiving next week?"

"Yes," I replied.

"Good. You'll probably enjoy the long break from your classes."

I chuckled. "That's for sure. I'm looking forward to sleeping in. And to Mom's cooking."

And then, my birth father caught me off guard when he asked, "Victoria, would you consent to celebrating Thanksgiving with me, too?"

I stared at him, bewildered. "What do you mean?"

The smooth flow of his response told me this wasn't a spur-of-the-moment idea. He'd had his plan worked out before I'd arrived that afternoon. "Come here next Wednesday," he said. "After your one o'clock class, as you usually do. I'll arrange for food services to deliver a turkey dinner to the apartment. Would you be willing to do that?"

"I suppose so." I took a few moments to think. "I'll skip lunch that day so that I can eat here. But I'll have to leave in time to get back to my mom's office by five o'clock. I'll be going home with her for the weekend."

Reverend Hahn flashed a beatific smile. "That's fine. That will give us several hours of holiday time together."

The Wednesday before Thanksgiving was windy and overcast. As I made the mile-long trek between the campus and the Greencroft complex, icy flurries swirled around me, nipping at my face. I pulled up the hood of my heavy parka, tying it tightly to protect myself from the cold.

When I stepped into Reverend Hahn's apartment, the welcoming warmth immediately began to melt the ice in my bones, making me feel cozy and deeply relaxed.

"Your cheeks are as red as apples," my birth father commented, concern in his voice. "I wish I could've sent a car around for you. I hardly wanted you to walk here in such bitter weather."

"It didn't hurt me," I replied. "It was an adventure."

I noted that the lights had been turned off in the back half of the apartment. The small dining table was graced by a fine linen tablecloth and an elegant autumn centerpiece. The flickering flames of the orange and gold taper candles bathed the room in a soft glow. The effect was homey, inviting, festive.

I peeled off my coat, gloves, and boots, staring in wonder at the candle flames, thinking about the fact that I'd never once seen a centerpiece on our kitchen table at home. Not as much as a single candle. The table was for utilitarian purposes only. If not laden with food, it was used as my mother's sewing station, or for doing homework, paying bills, or folding laundry.

I told myself that I shouldn't have expected anything less from Reverend Hahn. Everything he did was in the finest style. I wondered whether he was trying to teach me something about elegant living, something I'd completely missed out on during my childhood.

Just as I was seating myself on the sofa, I heard a knock on the apartment door. "Should I get it?" I asked Reverend Hahn.

He nodded. "Please."

I jumped up to open the door, and a young man from food services wheeled in a cart bearing a covered plate of food and several side dishes. He set the food on the dining table, along with a napkin and some silverware. As he wheeled his cart out the door, he lifted a hand and said, "Have a good afternoon, Reverend."

"Thank you so much, Keith." Reverend Hahn's warm response made it sound as if he and the young man were the best of friends. Then he wheeled his chair over to the table, carefully arranging the dishes and silverware in the proper configuration.

"Aren't you eating?" I asked him.

He shook his head. "I've had my lunch."

I sat down at the table, then waited as he wheeled his chair to the other side. "Shall we say grace?" he asked.

"Sure." I bowed my head and closed my eyes.

"Dear Lord," he intoned, his voice thick with emotion. "I thank you for your faithfulness, which is greater than our human minds can comprehend. For your boundless mercy, which you bestow upon us even when we fall short of doing your will. Most of all, I thank you for the wonderful blessing of sharing this time with my precious child. May the food she is about to eat nourish and strengthen her. Amen."

I opened my eyes, waiting for Reverend Hahn's cue for what to do next. He smiled. "Help yourself."

Lifting the cover off the plate, I found a delectable dinner before me: turkey, mashed potatoes, stuffing, and green beans. There was also a side dish of cranberry salad and a dessert plate bearing a generous slice of pumpkin pie with whipped cream.

"Wow!" I exclaimed. My cold walk had rendered me ravenous, and I was eager to dive into the feast set in front of me. But I forced myself not to eat too quickly, so as not to appear uncouth.

While I enjoyed the delicious food, Reverend Hahn sipped from a glass of water with a straw. "Tell me about Thanksgivings growing up," he said.

"There's not a lot to tell," I replied between bites. "Mom and the other women from church would make up food baskets to give to poor people and shut-ins. Usually, we went to services on Wednesday evening. On Thanksgiving Day, we always had lots of good food. But it would be just Mom, Dad, Lucy and me."

A shadow crossed Reverend Hahn's face. "Didn't your brothers ever come for the holiday?"

"No. They were never there on Thanksgiving. Never on Christmas, either. They hardly ever came around. If they did, it was just for a couple of days during the summer."

"That's too bad." Reverend Hahn averted his gaze, looking out the patio door at the falling snow. I could almost hear him thinking, regretting his role in ruining relationships in the Unruh family.

Then he pulled his cheerful demeanor back into place, smiling at me again. "I wished you'd had more festive holidays. But I suppose my own childhood holidays weren't much different. Throwing lavish celebrations wasn't the Mennonite way of doing things."

Feeling stuffed from eating every bite of the sumptuous meal, I chatted idly with Reverend Hahn about my classes and what I'd been doing with my friends. When I glanced up at the clock above his bookshelves, I saw that it was already 4:00 P.M. "I should be going now," I said. "I need to pack my things, and then meet my mother at her office."

At the announcement of my departure, Reverend Hahn's face sagged. "I didn't realize it was getting so late."

I got up from the table and walked over to the door. As I was pulling on my boots, he said, "Might I persuade you to join me in a little Christmas celebration next month?"

Suddenly, I understood what my birth father was trying to do. He wanted to capture something that he'd missed out on the first eighteen years of my life. From this point on, he wanted holiday time with his child.

At first, the idea seemed burdensome to me, a heavy obligation. I was used to the simple holiday traditions in my household. My parents never made much of a fuss over any special event. But Reverend Hahn had more elaborate tastes. I wasn't sure I could pull off what he expected from me, to make each holiday something special for him.

But I forced myself to smile and say, "Sure!"

The minute I made the commitment, my mind began racing frantically, wondering what my part in the Christmas celebration needed to be.

As if reading my thoughts, Reverend Hahn said, "Don't worry about buying me a gift. I have everything I need." With a sweep of his arm, he indicated the entirety of the small apartment. "Anyway, I don't have space for anything else."

Then, his emotions bursting out of their proper containment, he spoke with eagerness. "I'd much rather have you make me something. Draw me a picture. Write me a story. I missed out on all those things when you were growing up."

I grinned, thinking about all the childish artwork my mother had dutifully affixed to our refrigerator with magnets. "You mean like something to hang on your refrigerator?"

Reverend Hahn beamed. "Exactly."

I walked over to his chair, allowing him to clutch my gloved hand before I headed out the door. As I trudged back to the campus through the rapidly accumulating snow, an idea began brewing in my mind.

CHAPTER 9

When I followed my mother through the front door that evening, my dad's craggy face broke into a wide smile. "There's my little girl!" he exclaimed.

Heaving himself out of his ragged armchair, he wrapped his big arms around me, holding me to his heart. I nestled into the embrace, resting in the comfort for a few moments.

"It seems like you're doing better, Vickie," he observed. "I miss having you here, but I'm glad you're getting along okay at college."

"I'm doing fine, Dad," I said, even though I felt riddled with guilt. I'd gone nearly a month without a single word to him, while devoting my attention to my other father. *I might as well get used to guilt,* I told myself with a bit of grim humor. *I seem to run into it every which way I turn.*

I wasn't hungry for supper that evening, after having eaten the huge Thanksgiving meal at Reverend Hahn's apartment. When my mother commented on my lack of appetite, I told her that I'd had a big lunch.

I felt as if I was living a double life, like a bigamist surreptitiously moving back and forth between two families. Still, I decided it would be easier on everyone if I continued to practice a little duplicity. My parents didn't need to know about my visits with Reverend Hahn. And it wouldn't be fair to drag his contentious presence into the middle of the holiday weekend, setting everyone's nerves on edge.

So, as life with my birth father receded into the background, I eased back into the persona of Herman and Ada Unruh's youngest child.

That night, I snuggled under the covers of a bed I hadn't slept in for almost four weeks. Had I not been so guilt-ridden, I would've allowed myself to sleep until noon the next day. But I made myself get up early to help my mother with preparations for our holiday meal.

I forced myself to show interest in what she was doing, trying to make up for the fact that I'd been spending time with the man she despised more than anyone in the world.

"So what all goes into the cranberry sauce?" I asked her.

She shot me a funny look. "Cranberries, sugar, orange zest, walnuts."

A few minutes later, as she was preparing to put a sweet potato casserole into the oven, I said, "I didn't know you use marshmallows with the sweet potatoes. Wow, that's cool!"

My mother shook her head in disbelief. "Victoria, I've done that for years. I'm surprised you haven't noticed."

"What can I do next?" I asked after I'd peeled a bowlful of potatoes for her.

She shrugged indifferently. "I guess you can set the table."

I went to the cupboard to pull out the plates. All my growing up years, I'd been used to our family eating off mismatched plates, the remnants of old sets. Remembering my elegant meal at Reverend Hahn's apartment, I was determined to bring a bit of graciousness to this family dinner. So I picked through the stack of plates until I found four that matched.

"Do you have a tablecloth or placemats?" I asked my mother.

She shot me another questioning look. "There should be a couple of tablecloths in the linen closet. They'll need to be ironed."

I set up the ironing board in my parents' bedroom. As I tried in vain to press the creases out of a tablecloth that hadn't been used in years, I thought about my idea for Reverend Hahn's Christmas gift, a plan that was gradually taking form in my mind. A plan that would distress my mother to no end if she knew what I was up to.

Mid-morning, my dad wandered into the kitchen. "When should I go pick up Lucy?" he asked.

My mother grimaced. "Go get her just before we eat. Otherwise, she'll be pacing around the kitchen and getting in my way."

The reminder of the lifelong tension between my mother and my mentally ill sister saddened me. Still, it was a part of the family life I'd always known.

During the meal, Lucy's loud, rambling talk dominated the conversation. Time and again, my mother's face reddened when my ill-mannered sister reached across the table for a dish of food, or helped herself to one-too-many servings. I knew that, as always, my mother was struggling to keep from lashing out at her oldest daughter.

I was back in the heart of my real family, a million miles away from the charmed little world I shared with my birth father. My flawed, wounded family that kept limping along in spite of the beating it had taken over the years.

"How've you been, Tori Grace?" Lucy asked between mouthfuls of food. "You never come see me anymore."

Once again, the all-too-familiar guilt sickened my stomach. I'd been so busy with my own life that I hadn't visited my sister for more than six months. Worse, I'd hardly even thought about her.

When I woke up around noon on Friday morning, I went downstairs to find my mother puttering around the kitchen. "Where's Dad?" I asked as I poured myself a cup of coffee.

"He's at work," she said, sounding impatient with my ignorance. "Mailmen don't get a long holiday weekend like the rest of us do."

After serving me a turkey sandwich for lunch, she announced that she was going out to do some shopping. My mental wheels began to turn. With both parents out of the house, I'd have the opportunity I'd been waiting for.

"Do you need me to pick up anything while I'm out, Victoria?" my mother asked. I shook my head.

She began clearing the dishes from the table and stacking them on the counter by the sink, along with the unwashed breakfast dishes.

"I'll take care of those," I told her. "You better go if you want to get ahead of the rush. It's Black Friday, and there's going to be a lot of holiday shoppers out there."

My mother looked at me with something I'd never before seen in her tired eyes: gratitude. I smiled at her, then averted my gaze as I gave myself a mental strapping. *She thinks you're being a good daughter. She thinks you're being helpful because you care about her, when all you want is to get her out of the house so you can do some snooping.*

I stood by the front window in the living room, watching my mother's car pull out of the driveway and head down our county road. Then, praying that she wouldn't backtrack because she'd forgotten something, I headed straight to her bedroom. Even though I was the only one in the house, I closed the door behind me to hide my surreptitious activity from any prying eyes.

With every movement choreographed to a tune of guilt, I opened my parents' closet door. The closet looked as if it had been recently cleaned out and organized. My mother's prim dresses hung on one side, while my dad's flannel shirts and work pants hung on the other. There was a sizable gap between the two sparse wardrobes, as if the two sides were never meant to come into contact with each other. The metaphor was not lost on me.

I wasn't a bit surprised about the order in the closet, as I knew my mother had a penchant for cleaning and sorting. She'd had more time for such activities since her youngest child had left the nest.

I looked up at the closet shelf, expecting to find something that had been there since my earliest memories: the familiar tattered shoebox containing our family photos.

As a young child, I had often asked my mother for permission to look at the photos. She'd always made me sit at the kitchen table to look at them, where she could keep an eye on me, making sure I didn't mistreat her old treasures.

From time to time, a few new photos would be added to the box, such as school pictures of Lucy and me. My old school photos were at the heart of my surreptitious plan that day. I intended to sort them out, take them to the camera shop in downtown Goshen to get them copied, and then return the originals to the shoebox without my mother noticing. The duplicates would be my Christmas gift to my birth father, a gift I knew he'd cherish.

But the old shoebox wasn't there. I couldn't believe it. Had my mother moved it? Where could she have put it?

I was about to engage in a more serious invasion of privacy by rifling through the drawers in my parents' ancient dresser, something I'd never done even as a young child. Then my gaze returned to the closet shelf, falling on a neat stack of manila envelopes sitting there. I lifted them down.

Each envelope was labeled with my mother's careful handwriting: *Michael, Robert, Lucy,* and *Victoria.* I opened the one marked *Victoria* and peered inside, seeing a stack of photographs. And I realized that, for the first time in my memory, my mother's organizing penchant had extended to the collection of family photos. The old box had been thrown out, the tidy envelopes taking its place.

Right away, I noticed something. The envelopes marked *Michael* and *Robert* were thick, stuffed full of pictures. As I was growing up, I'd seen very few childhood photos of my brothers. I'd always assumed that my much-older siblings, who were teenagers when I was born, had grown up in some remote era where people barely even had cameras.

Had my mother lost these photos, and only recently found them? Had she held them back, as something too precious to be pawed through by the grubby little hands of her youngest child? Or were they intentionally kept for her eyes only?

Lucy's envelope was considerably thinner than those of my brothers. But even compared to hers, mine was decidedly underweight. For a moment, pain knotted my stomach. *I'm the one who doesn't belong with the rest,* came the old familiar thought.

But I tried to persuade myself not to take the situation personally. Of course, my mother wouldn't have been inclined to collect an abundance of pictures of her illegitimate child. I knew her well enough to know that she would not be enthusiastic about photographing the results of her entanglement with Reverend Hahn. Capturing my image on camera would have seemed like celebrating her wrongdoing.

I sat down on my parents' quilt-covered bed to examine the contents of the envelopes. First, I dumped out the photos in my own envelope. Most of my school pictures were there. I laid them out in order, first grade to my senior year, and saw that nine of the twelve were present. There was a newborn picture of me taken in the hospital, and one of me as an infant curled up on my dad's broad chest. A photo of me as a toddler had been taken at my Aunt Myrtle's house in Ohio. Finally, there was one taken when I was around six, with a group of children whom I presumed were my Sunday-School classmates.

Exactly thirteen photos in all. Because there were so few, each one seemed rare and precious to me, and I decided to have copies made of all of them. I set the envelope aside and turned to my siblings' envelopes.

I dumped out the contents of Lucy's envelope, realizing they were all photos I'd seen many times when I'd rifled through the old shoebox. There were almost a dozen pictures of the chubby baby girl with the curly red hair and big blue eyes. *She was so cute back then,* I thought sadly.

As I lined up her school photos, I noticed how her scowl had increased with each passing year. I felt sorry for the progressive toll life had taken on her.

Finally, I dumped out the contents of my brothers' photos, first Michael's and then Robert's. Each made a sizable pile on the bed. When I saw how extensively their childhoods had been captured on film, I felt decidedly shortchanged.

I browsed through countless photos of dark-eyed babies dressed in little outfits that looked old-fashioned to me. I realized those photos had been taken in the 1940s, an era that seemed worlds away from what I'd known as a child. I looked at photos of two little boys, preschoolers, standing next to each other, looking very much alike. The taller one always had his arm around his brother's shoulders.

There were photos of the same little boys with their very young, very pretty mother, who was smiling in a way I'd never known her to smile. There were photos of the boys cuddled on the laps of my Grandma Hochstedler and my Aunt Myrtle. I found one photo of the boys standing with their other grandparents, the ones I'd never met. Apparently, in the early years of their marriage, my parents had made trips to Kansas to visit relatives on the Unruh side of the family.

There were pictures of the boys as toddlers, playing in the same backyard I'd played in as a child. School-age boys standing in front of the barn, holding kittens. Preteen boys making silly faces as they posed with their arms around the necks of the goats. Teenage boys shooting baskets in the hoop that was still affixed to the front of our garage.

There were photos of the boys with groups of Sunday-School and Bible-School children, taken in front of Westside Mennonite Church. Photos taken on their first day of Bible Memory Camp.

I carefully laid out my brothers' school pictures, a complete set for each of them, noting the changes in their appearances over the years. While the two of them looked quite a bit alike with their dark hair and eyes, their differences became more pronounced as they grew older.

Michael, who had a thin build, resembled my mother, except for the fact that his hair was curly like my dad's. Robert appeared to have inherited my dad's sturdier frame.

As I studied the photos of the brothers I'd never really known, I felt as if I was catching a glimpse of an era I'd not been part of, a sweeter chapter of my family's life. My arrival on the scene had changed everything.

The sound of my dad's car tires crunching on the gravel driveway jolted me back into the here and now, and I realized I'd lost track of time. Quickly, I stuffed my siblings' photos back into their envelopes, which I returned to the closet shelf. Then, slipping my own envelope under my sweatshirt, I ran out of my parents' bedroom and up the stairs to my own room.

Seconds later, I heard the sound of the front door opening and my dad's heavy footsteps trudging across the living room floor. "Vickie, are you home?" he called out.

"Yes, dad," I called from my room, hoping he'd think I'd been there all afternoon. Then I headed down the stairs, coat in hand, the envelope still tucked under my shirt. "Can I borrow your car for a little bit? I need to run an errand."

"I suppose so," he said. "Where are you going?"

"I want to run down to Hook's Drugstore to pick up some shampoo." I told myself that wasn't a lie. On the way back from the camera store, I planned to pick up the shampoo, which I didn't need, in order to show my parents that I had a legitimate reason for my outing.

Grabbing the keys from my dad's outstretched hand, I walked out of the house and to the car. As I slid the envelope from under my shirt and laid it on the car seat beside me, I felt another surge of guilt. I was getting way too good at deception. Entering the world of my birth father had pulled me into the pattern of pretense and half-truths that he'd practiced for years.

When I presented my photos at the camera store and explained my request, the man behind the counter informed me he could have the duplicates ready in a week. I was dismayed. I'd somehow thought the task could be completed in a few minutes, so that I could go home, slip the envelope back into the stack on my mother's closet shelf, and be done with the whole sneaky ordeal.

"I'll call you when your order is ready," the man said. "Can I have your phone number?"

I shook my head, shuddering at the thought of my mother taking such a call at the house. "I'll just stop by in a week to see if they're ready." At the moment, I had no idea how I'd make that happen, but I told myself I'd figure out a way.

Before I headed home, I stopped by the drugstore to get the bottle of shampoo that would serve to ward off any suspicion on my mother's part. When I pulled into our driveway, I was dismayed to see that her car was already there. I had hoped her shopping would keep her away from the house much longer.

I walked into the kitchen to find her up to her elbows in sudsy water, tackling the dishes I'd promised to wash. When she looked up at me, I saw a hurt expression in her eyes. I knew she'd been thinking that her youngest daughter had finally become a grownup who could consider the feelings of others. But I'd proven that I still wasn't mature enough to keep my word, that I was the same thoughtless child I'd always been.

"Where have you been?" she asked. "I thought you said you were going to wash these."

"I went to Hook's Drugstore to get shampoo," I replied, plunking the bag down on the table as evidence of my truthfulness.

"I asked you if you needed anything," she scolded.

"I know," I said. "But I wanted to get out of the house. I'd been cooped up all day." I was edging perilously close to the brink of a bold-faced lie, and felt decidedly uncomfortable. I placed my hands on my mother's shoulders and gently edged her away from the sink. I noticed how thin and frail she was.

"I said I'd wash these dishes," I told her, "and I will."

She smiled bleakly at me, then dried her hands on a dishtowel. As she walked off to her bedroom, I breathed a prayer that she wouldn't open her closet, check the shelf, and notice that someone had stolen one of the envelopes from her neat stack.

CHAPTER 10

As I rode back to school with my mother the following Monday morning, I began to ponder the next phase of my problem with Reverend Hahn's Christmas gift. How was I going to get back to the camera store to pick up my duplicated photos? Then, how was I going to get my mother's envelope back to the house and on the closet shelf when neither of my parents were at home?

The only solution I could come up with was to ask my mother if I could borrow her car during the middle of her work day. Of course, she would demand to know why I needed it, and I'd have to make up a plausible story.

But I didn't have the stomach for any more lying. And I knew that if I kept pushing the limits with my deceptive behavior, I would raise my mother's suspicion. Shrewd detective that she was, she would inevitably find out what I was up to.

My only other alternative was to solicit the help of a student who had a car on campus. I wracked my brain, but could come up with no candidate for my partner in crime.

At lunch that day, I sat across the table from Charlie Hess and Stephen Wenger. "Do either of you happen to know anyone with a car on campus?" I asked.

Stephen pointed his fork at Charlie. "My buddy here has a car. It's a heap of junk, but it's got four wheels and it runs."

My eyes widened with excitement. "Really?"

Charlie nodded. "Yes, I have a car."

Both boys eyed me curiously. I swallowed hard, knowing I was about to impose upon a friendship that, up to that point, had been limited to the confines of the college cafeteria. While I was unsure about the implications of taking the friendship into a broader arena, my desperation propelled me forward. "Charlie, can I ask a favor of you?"

He looked bewildered. "I suppose so."

"I need someone to run me to the camera store in downtown Goshen. I have to pick up something. Then I need to run it to my house. The whole thing shouldn't take more than half an hour."

"When do you need to do this?" he asked.

"Friday. It has to be sometime during the day. Like early afternoon, before my parents get home."

Charlie looked dubious. He glanced at Stephen.

"Oh, help the girl out, Charles," Stephen scolded.

Charlie furrowed his brow, as if carefully thinking through the commitment he was about to make. Then he smiled. "I'm free between two and three on Friday."

I sighed with relief. "That's perfect."

At five minutes past two on Friday afternoon, I met Charlie Hess in the student parking lot on the east side of the campus. He was standing next to a battered red Volkswagen Beetle. Nodding in greeting, he opened the passenger door for me. I ducked down to get into the tiny vehicle.

"Cool car," I said as he climbed into the driver's seat. "I've never ridden in one of these before."

He shrugged. "This bug's falling apart, but as long as it keeps running, I'll hang onto it. So, where is it you need to go?"

"First, to the camera store on Main Street."

"Okay," he said. "I know where that is."

We headed toward downtown Goshen, and he pulled the Beetle up to the curb in front of the store. I hopped out, rushed inside, picked up my order, and was back in the car in five minutes.

"Now, to my parents' house," I said breathlessly.

As Charlie drove, I provided directions while at the same time rifling through my order and making sure the contents of my mother's envelope were intact. Charlie glanced over at me curiously, but asked no questions.

Seven minutes later, we pulled into my parents' driveway. I felt enormously grateful that the previous day's light snowfall had already melted. Otherwise, Charlie's car would have left tire tracks on the gravel driveway, and I would have left footprints leading to the front door. It seemed as if God was watching over my surreptitious plan.

"So, this is where you live." Charlie glanced around, taking in the details of the house and yard.

"Yup," I replied. "I grew up here." I was too preoccupied with my plan to worry about what he thought of the rundown property.

With my mother's envelope in hand, I jumped out of the car, sprinted to the house, and bounded up onto the porch. During my growing up years, my parents had rarely locked our house, and had never given me a house key to carry. Our neighborhood was safe, virtually crime-free. Furthermore, my family owned no valuables that would be of interest to a thief. So, while formulating my secretive scheme, I had counted on the front door being unlocked.

But when I attempted to open the door, the knob was unmoving. I tried again, to no avail. *Think, Victoria,* I coached myself. *I know Mom has a spare key out here somewhere.*

I stared around the porch, trying to imagine where she could have hidden it. I decided to look under the three large terracotta pots that held the dried remains of the geraniums she'd planted last spring. I laid the envelope on the porch swing, then got down on my hands and knees, tilting up each of the pots and peering underneath. There was no key.

Oh my God! I thought. *Did Charlie run me out here for nothing?*

I rose to my knees, glancing at Charlie in his waiting car. Shrugging my shoulders, I lifted my hands in a gesture of helplessness. He looked puzzled, but slightly amused.

Frantic, I looked around again, trying to imagine where else the key might be hidden. I looked under the doormat, knowing my mom would never keep it in such an obvious place. Then my gaze fell on a plastic pot on the other side of the porch, this one containing a shriveled tomato plant.

Not bothering to stand up, I crawled across the porch on my hands and knees to look under the tomato pot. In my clumsy haste, I knocked the pot completely over, spilling out half its dirt. But there lay the spare key, sparkling in a ray of sunlight, the holy grail of my quest.

With a whoop of excitement, I snatched up the key. Holding it between my teeth, I righted the pot and scooped up as much dirt as I could, patting it back into place. I brushed the remaining dirt off the side of the porch.

Then I jumped to my feet, brushing my dirty hands on my jeans. Triumphant, I turned toward the car, waving the key in the air. Charlie was shaking with laughter.

Grabbing my envelope off the porch swing, I tucked it under my arm while I unlocked the door. I was so unnerved that my hands were trembling, and it took repeated attempts to get the door open. When I stepped into the living room, I coached myself to move with care in order to avoid another mishap.

Heading straight to my parents' bedroom, I opened the closet door, lifted the large envelopes, and slid the one I'd stolen into the bottom of the stack.

In my rush to get out of the room, I stumbled over a pair of my dad's shoes, knocking one of them askew. I stopped, bending down to straighten it. Then I had a moment of panic, wondering whether the bedroom door had been open or closed before I entered. Carefully, I retraced my steps in my mind, concluding that the door had been open. *Anyway,* I reasoned, *I've never known Mom to keep the bedroom door closed, except for when she's secluding herself inside.*

With a sigh of relief, I headed out the front door, stopping to lock it behind me. Then I raced toward Charlie's car. Halfway there, I realized I still had the spare key in hand. I spun around so quickly that I almost lost my balance, then bounded back onto the porch, dropped to my knees, and shoved the key under the tomato pot. Breathless, I ran back to the car, yanked open the door, and plopped down in the passenger seat.

"Let's get out of here," I panted. "Hurry, before somebody sees us."

"Breaking and entering," Charlie said, grinning at me. "So that's what you do."

"I wasn't committing a crime," I snapped. "I live here."

"So you say," he quipped as he pulled out of the driveway.

"Stop laughing at me," I demanded, even though I was laughing myself. Playfully, I bumped his arm with my fist.

"I'm not laughing," he protested, still grinning. "I'm sure this is serious business."

Looking at his profile, I noted his chiseled features, and it suddenly occurred to me that Charlie Hess wasn't a bad-looking young man. If he wore more stylish clothing, got up-to-date glasses, and did something to tame his unruly hair, he would actually be quite handsome. I quickly put that thought out of my mind and went back to worrying about whether my mother would find any tell-tale signs of my clandestine visit.

Before I climbed out the Beetle in the student parking lot, I pulled a crumpled five-dollar-bill from the pocket of my jeans. "This is for the gas," I told Charlie.

He shook his head, holding up a protesting palm. "We're good."

At lunch the next day, I was still so embarrassed by my strange outing with Charlie that I thought about avoiding him and Stephen. But when I glanced toward where they were sitting, Stephen caught my eye and grinned knowingly. He beckoned me over, and I immediately knew that Charlie had told him every detail of the previous day's weird adventure. Sighing, I figured I might as well get the inevitable harassment over with, and I headed in their direction.

"Breaking and entering," Stephen said as I deposited my tray on the table. "Home invasion." He jerked a thumb in Charlie's direction. "And you corrupted an upstanding citizen by putting him behind the wheel of the getaway car."

Glancing at Charlie, he said, "I always suspected young Miss Unruh had a shady side. What else do you suppose we don't know about her?"

Stephen's comment struck me so funny that I almost lost a mouthful of milk I hadn't yet swallowed. As I laughed along with the guys, I thought, *There's a lot you don't know about Victoria Unruh.*

CHAPTER 11

One week before Christmas, I knocked on Reverend Hahn's apartment door, carrying the gift I'd made for him. I'd placed my duplicated photos in a small album, which I'd purchased from a drugstore near the campus. I'd taken pains to wrap the photo album in shiny foil paper and top it with a giant bow. The gift looked more elegant than anything that had ever appeared in my household at Christmastime.

Reverend Hahn welcomed me warmly, looking festive in a dapper charcoal gray cardigan, white shirt, and red necktie. I was not surprised to see a small tree, strung with colorful lights, standing in the corner of his living room. Boxes of ornaments sat next to it on the floor.

A large poinsettia sat in front of the patio door, and the dining table held yet another centerpiece, consisting of sprigs of evergreen, gold and silver ornaments, and flickering red candles.

I gazed at the collection of expensive-looking holiday music boxes and snow globes displayed on the bookshelves. Like a small child, I wanted to pick them up and turn them over in my hands, but felt afraid to do so.

"It's all so beautiful," I said. Never in all my childhood Christmases had my parents decorated the house like this. I knelt down in front of the crèche sitting on the end table beside the sofa, captivated by the rustic stable and the hand-carved wooden figures. I couldn't help but contrast it with the pitiful cardboard nativity scene my mother always set out.

"Where did you get this?" I asked.

"I purchased that crèche when I was traveling in Germany," he said. "About twenty years ago, I believe. I've set it out for every Christmas since then. It's become a precious keepsake."

Tentatively, I picked up the figure of Mary, admiring her serene face and her purple gold-trimmed robe.

"Perhaps that lovely crèche will be yours someday," Reverend Hahn said.

Startled by his words, I swung around to look at him. His eyes conveyed a message that I couldn't read, that I didn't want to read. Leaving the crèche, I stood up and walked over to gaze at the tree.

"I wanted my daughter to help decorate the tree." Reverend Hahn gestured toward the boxes of ornaments on the floor. "Why don't we get started while we wait for the meal to arrive?"

He wheeled over to a cassette player sitting on the kitchen counter and pressed a button. The sweet sounds of a Christmas carol filled the room.

Then he came back to the living room, and at his request, I set a box of ornaments on his lap. One by one, he picked up the ornaments, which I took from his awkward hands and hung on the tree. Some of them looked old and exotic, as if they came from foreign countries. Others appeared brand new, purchased for our special occasion.

My mother had never allowed a Christmas tree in our house, as she considered it to be a worldly distraction from the true meaning of the holiday. As I hung the ornaments on my birth father's tree, I realized that, at the age of eighteen, I was going through the childhood ritual of decorating my first Christmas tree. The thought brought tears to my eyes. When one trickled down my cheek, I wiped it away with the back of my hand.

Reverend Hahn noticed the tear, just as he noticed my every mood, my every expression. "Is something troubling you, Victoria?"

I shook my head. "It's just that I've never decorated a tree before. This is my first time."

His face darkened. I knew what he was thinking, that he was judging my parents for never providing me with such an experience. But the dark look was quickly replaced by an expression of tenderness. "I'm so delighted that I can be the one to share this experience with you," he said.

After the last ornament was hung, I sat down on the floor in front of the tree, staring at it with the wonder of a six-year-old. Then I scrambled up to get the gift I'd brought. With great care, I placed it under the tree.

Reverend Hahn chuckled fondly. "Excuse me for a minute." Then he wheeled his chair through the bathroom and into his bedroom. Moments later, he returned with a beautifully wrapped gift on his lap.

"Would you put this under the tree?" he asked. "We'll open gifts after the meal."

I was amazed at how precisely Reverend Hahn had choreographed the afternoon's activities. Seconds after I set his gift under the tree, there was a knock on the door. When I answered it, Keith from food services wheeled his cart into the room. Just as we'd done at Thanksgiving, my birth father sat across from me while I ate a sumptuous meal of ham, mashed potatoes, and Brussels sprouts, along with an array of Christmas cookies for dessert.

As I ate, I suddenly realized that while I'd be with my family on Christmas Day, my birth father would be alone. "What will you be doing over the holidays?" I asked him.

He must have caught the note of concern in my voice. "Don't worry about me," he said. "I'll have visitors, probably more than I can handle. People from church will stop by. And my sister Emma plans on driving out here for a visit. I worry about her traveling, but she's determined to make the trip. I believe one of Rose's daughters will be coming with her, doing the driving. That puts my mind at ease."

After I finished eating, Reverend Hahn said, "Shall we open gifts?" We moved from the table into the living room. He gestured for me to take my package from under the tree.

I unwrapped the small box and found that it contained an expensive leather wallet, the likes of which I'd never owned. "Oh!" I gasped. "It's beautiful!"

"Open it," Reverend Hahn instructed. And when I did, I found five crisp one-hundred-dollar bills.

"This is too much!" I exclaimed, feeling decidedly unworthy of such a gift.

"Not at all," he said. "This is petty cash for next trimester's expenses." His eyes twinkled as he added, "And I hope you'll treat yourself to something special. Not something practical. Something you really like."

"I'll go shopping for clothes," I promised him. I got up, wrapped my arms around his shoulders, and kissed his cheek. "You spoil me."

"I love spoiling you," he replied, his voice husky.

Then I fetched his gift from under the tree, and he unwrapped it with clumsy hands. Tears rolled down his cheeks as he gazed at the pictures of me at various stages of my childhood.

In that moment, I knew that all the convoluted efforts I'd gone through to create my birth father's gift had been worth it. Because whatever misdeeds Reverend Harry Hahn had committed in his younger years, he still deserved a relationship with his child. And I deserved to know him, to embrace the best of him while forgiving the worst.

CHAPTER 12

On the first Friday evening of my second trimester, I was sitting in the Westlawn lounge watching TV when my roommate plopped down on the couch next to me and whispered in my ear. "Victoria, I need to talk to you."

Her announcement caught me off guard, as she and I had never had any talks as important as the one she seemed ready to initiate. "Okay," I said.

I followed her across the hall to our room, where I sat down on my bed, ready to hear what she had to say. She sat on the other end of the bed, crossing her legs, assuming the pose of a best friend about to confide an intimate secret. "Do you know Darlene Glick?" she asked.

I shook my head. "I don't think so."

"She lives here in Westlawn, on the third floor."

She stopped talking, as if afraid to proceed with what she had to tell me. I nudged her on. "Well, what about Darlene Glick?"

"Her roommate Sarah didn't come back this trimester. She's sick, I think. Mononucleosis, or something like that."

"And?" I prompted.

Then Bonnie spoke in a breathless rush, trying to mask her eagerness with a pretense of concern for my feelings. "Darlene wants me to room with her. She doesn't like being alone. I told her I'd talk with you, to see if you were okay with me moving out. I told her I wouldn't do it if it was going to hurt your feelings." Her eyes searched my face. "Do you mind?"

Attempting to hide my own eagerness, I forced myself to hesitate before responding. "No, I don't mind if you want to room with Darlene. I'm okay with being alone."

Abandoning her pretense, Bonnie jumped off the bed, clapping her hands in excitement. "Oh, good! I can't wait to tell her."

She rushed out of the room, then returned a minute later

with a girl whom I assumed was Darlene. They each grabbed an armload of clothing from Bonnie's closet and hurried off, giggling like twelve-year-olds. And I realized that the moving process was to take place that very evening.

Within twenty minutes, the bulk of Bonnie's belongings had been carted up to the third floor. All the while, I remained sitting on my bed, watching the process in amusement.

As they were about to carry their last load upstairs, Bonnie looked down at the dust and clutter on the floor of her side of the room, which not been cleaned a single time during the previous trimester. "Maybe we should sweep this floor," she said to Darlene. She shot me a guilty look. "Victoria, where do you get your cleaning supplies?"

"In the closet down the hall," I informed her.

She and Darlene left, returning with a broom, a dustpan, and a trash bag. Then my roommate began using the broom with unwieldy strokes, unmindful of what she was sweeping up. I cringed as I watched perfectly good items—ink pens, hair barrettes, socks, and an almost full tube of toothpaste—being dumped into the trash bag.

When the girls left after their haphazard sweeping job, I sighed with relief, promising myself to give the room a thorough cleaning in the morning.

After her move, I saw very little of Bonnie Springer. She and I would essentially have nothing to do with each other, not until much later.

Throughout my second trimester, I enjoyed sublime solitude in my clean, tidy room. Instead of cramming all my clothing into one tiny closet, I made use of the second closet in the room. I spread out projects for my art history class on the extra desk. I closed my door and studied for psychology exams, without fear of interruption. At night, I turned off the light any time I wanted to, drifting off to sleep without the unpleasant distraction of Bonnie's snoring.

The entire floor seemed quieter after Bonnie moved upstairs. One morning as I headed down to breakfast, I encountered two girls from the third floor on the stairway. They were complaining to each other about the girls who'd been carrying on in the lounge until the early hours of the morning. I smiled to myself, knowing that the third floor had inherited the second floor's old problem.

I continued my weekly visits with Reverend Hahn throughout the rest of that school year. We celebrated Easter together. Several days before my birthday in May, he presented me with a beautifully decorated cake, purchased from his favorite bakery in downtown Goshen. He took great pains to light the nineteen candles. Even though he struggled with the task, I refrained from wounding his pride by offering to help.

As we sat gazing at the flickering candles, he said, "When you were born nineteen years ago, it was one of the best days of my life."

I tried to imagine that day, and what it would have been like for him to hear the news of my birth. "How did you find out?" I asked.

"Herman called me," he replied. "Under the circumstances, that was generous of him. No matter how he felt about me, he still believed I had the right to know my child had just been born. The minute I heard the news, I arranged a flight to Indiana, and several days later, I was there in your mother's hospital room, holding you."

"Really?" I was astounded. In telling me the story of how I came to be, my parents had never divulged the fact that Reverend Hahn had visited me as a newborn. When I'd first learned about my true paternity, I'd pictured my birth father as cold and calculating, entirely self-serving as he arranged to cover up the fact that he'd fathered an illegitimate child. Knowing that he'd cared about me that much was hard to take in. I felt a bit lightheaded.

After a few moments, I asked a question that I'd never even ventured to ask my mother. "What was I like?"

Tenderness shone in Reverend Hahn's eyes. "You were the most beautiful baby I'd ever seen. Perfectly formed, nicely filled out, with fat little cheeks. You were sleeping all the while I held you. But your eyes did flicker open once, and I could see that they were dark. And I could also tell from your black hair and dark skin tone that you'd inherited some of my traits. That pleased me. It made me feel as if part of me would continue on in the world after I was gone."

He paused, a faraway look on his face. "I'll never forget how you felt in my arms. You were a warm little bundle of pure love. You amazed me. You took my breath away. It was almost more than I could do to let you go."

His eyes pleaded for my understanding. "But at the time, I felt I had no other choice."

"I know," I said.

"Your parents and I made the best decision that we could. But there were many times over the years when I second-guessed that decision. There were times when I wished I'd confessed everything to Myrna and to the church, and then done what I needed to do to bring you into my home and raise you myself."

Again, his words stunned me. I closed my eyes for a moment, picturing how different my life would have been if Reverend Hahn had made such a decision. I knew full well that when my mother had brought me home from the hospital, she'd done so out of obligation rather than joy. She hadn't been eager to raise another child, especially the child of the man who'd misled and seduced her. Had circumstances been different, my birth father would have been overjoyed at the prospect of bringing up his only child.

"But I always knew," he added, "that someday, you and I would have the chance to be together. And here we are. I thank God every day for the opportunity to spend time with you."

I never told my parents about holiday and birthday celebrations with Reverend Hahn. I'm sure my mother suspected that I visited him from time to time. But she didn't want to know the details any more than I wanted to tell her about them.

PART II: SUMMER 1979-SPRING 1980

CHAPTER 13

When I'd left my waitressing job at the end of the previous summer, my boss told me he was sorry to see me go. "You're a good worker," he said. "I hope you come back next year."

So, in early June, I showed up for my second summer of work at the Taste of Home family restaurant. It felt good to walk in already knowing how to do the job.

Nothing much had changed in the restaurant while I was gone, other than the fact that the old hardwood floor in the dining area had been refinished. My waitress friend Mindy was still there, sassy as ever, bantering with the same regular customers. Allen and Bradley, one year closer to manhood, spouted out their disgusting innuendoes with more bravado.

When I went to the kitchen to greet Edna, she looked up from the meatloaf she was mixing with her gloved hands. "Well, look who's here," she chortled. "Doggone it, honey, I'm glad to see you back. We need somebody around here who can behave herself long enough to get the job done."

She shook her head woefully, lapsing into the grousing I'd grown used to the previous summer. "I don't know what Bob's thinking with some of the kids he brings in here. Pretty near every day, I go home telling my old man I've had my fill of this nonsense. I keep telling Bob I'm ready to hang up my apron and walk out of here, but he keeps talking me into staying. Says he needs me. I don't know why I keep falling for that crap."

"We all need you," I said, patting her plump shoulder. "This place wouldn't be the same without you."

Snorting, she returned to mixing the meatloaf, squeezing it furiously. But I saw a hint of a smile on her hardened face.

On the Monday of my second week at the restaurant, I stopped short when I walked through the back door. There was a new face among the kitchen staff, an extraordinarily handsome face, with chisled features, a strong, square jaw, and breathtaking blue eyes. This striking visage belonged to a tall, blonde, powerfully built man who appeared to be around my age.

Edna cackled when she saw the expression on my face. "That's Calvin," she said. "Ain't he something?"

Calvin was trailing around the kitchen after Allen, who was providing the newcomer with an orientation to the dishwashing process. The diminutive Allen appeared to enjoy his power over the man who towered over him, keeping his trainee in place with all the disdain he could muster.

"No, dummy," he said with an exaggerated sigh of frustration. "You've got to scrape the dishes off, and then rinse them. You can't just throw them into the dishwasher."

Calvin fumbled through his task, while Allen continued to point out his errors. "What the hell are you thinking? You can't put that pan in there. You need to soak it first, and then wash it by hand. Sorry, buddy, you're going to have to get those dainty hands dirty."

But the handsome Calvin seemed unscathed by the bombardment of criticism. He was soft-spoken and rather slow-moving, but he willingly completed all his assigned tasks.

Every time I entered the kitchen, I couldn't help but sneak a peek at the newcomer working in the dishwashing station. Edna caught me watching him.

"Keep some sense in your head, sister," she scolded. "All of us are going to enjoy looking at that fine specimen of a man, but that's all the farther it can go. He's going to be looking at you, too, because you're easy on the eye yourself. I've seen him watching your little behind when you go swingin' out of here. Just remember, Bob doesn't allow any hanky-panky going on between co-workers when they're on the clock."

Soon, everyone in the restaurant was talking about Calvin. "How old do you think he is?" Mindy whispered to me.

"Maybe twenty or twenty-one," I whispered back.

She sighed. "Way too young for me. But maybe ten or twelve years isn't that big of an age difference."

"What are you aiming to be, a cougar?" I teased.

"Why not?" she retorted. "He seems kind of naïve. Maybe he'd appreciate a woman with little experience."

Allen and Bradley made it clear in every possible way that they resented Calvin's presence in the restaurant. Every time he asked a question about his work, they'd look at each other and roll their eyes. Then, when he was barely out of earshot, they'd complain that he didn't know what he was doing.

"Don't mind the boys," I said to Calvin one afternoon as I walked past him with a tray of food. "They're little jerks. You've got to learn to blow them off."

He turned his handsome face toward me, flashing a knowing grin. "I'm not worried," he said. And I knew that all the harassment was simply rolling off his broad back. I sensed solidness in him, a steadiness that was not easily shaken.

At the end of my shift, I was not at all displeased when Calvin walked out the back door of the restaurant behind me. I stopped in the parking lot beside my mother's car, hoping to chat with him for a minute.

"I'm Victoria Unruh," I said. "I live here in Goshen."

He surprised me by extending his hand for a proper handshake. "Calvin Zook. From Nebraska."

"Wow!" I said. "I've never met anybody from Nebraska. What brings you all the way out here to Indiana?"

"I'm a student at Goshen College. I decided to stick around here for the summer."

My mind raced back half a year, to the conversation with the girls at Laura Zuercher's pizza party. One of them had carried on about the magnificent Calvin Zook. And here he was, standing right in front of me.

As I gazed at his handsome face, I suddenly felt jittery, unable to believe my good fortune. I'd be working closely with this guy for the remainder of the summer. Calvin was at least four inches taller than me, something I wasn't used to in a man, and I enjoyed the experience of smiling up at him. "I'm a Goshen College student, too," I said, hoping I didn't sound too coy. "I'll be a sophomore next year. How about you?"

"I'll be a junior." He smiled, almost sheepishly. It struck me that Calvin Zook was oblivious to his stunning good looks, that he was indifferent about his impact on the female gender. There was no posturing on his part, no strutting in his manner. Being around him felt easy and comfortable, like wearing a favorite old sweatshirt.

At that moment, I felt my self-imposed ban on dating lifting off me and floating away. It wasn't a conscious decision on my part. Something was happening outside my volition. Whether or not I was ready, Calvin Zook was going to be in my life.

CHAPTER 14

For the next two weeks, Calvin and I did little more than exchange smiles during our workday, or a friendly word in passing.

"How's it going?" I'd say as I rushed past him with a tray of food.

He'd look up from the pot he was scrubbing, grinning at me. "Good."

Sometimes, we'd chat a minute or two in the parking lot after our shifts, standing beside Calvin's blue Ford Falcon or my mother's green Chevy Nova. I was disappointed to discover that Calvin wasn't much of a talker. Most of our conversations consisted of me initiating a topic, and him grinning and nodding in response to what I was saying. At most, he offered one or two sentence replies to my probing questions.

"What dorm will you be living in this fall?" I asked him one evening.

"I'll be living off campus this year," he said.

"Oh? Where?"

"On Sixth Street. Same place I'm living now."

"Do you live alone?"

"Nope, I'm living with three other guys."

I waited to see if he'd reciprocate and ask something about me, but he just stood there looking at me. So I offered information I thought he might like to know. "I lived in Westlawn last year, and I'll be living there again this fall. My parents' house isn't that far from the college, seven miles or so. I could live at home and commute if I wanted to. But my parents think it's good for me to have the experience of living on campus."

Calvin grinned and nodded.

"What are you majoring in?" I asked during another one of our parking lot conversations.

"Social work," Calvin replied.

I thought about the social workers who'd taken care of my sister Lucy the past few years. Somehow, I couldn't picture Calvin in such a role.

"What do you plan on doing with your degree?" I asked him.

"Probably something in the schools. I like working with kids." He gestured toward the back door of the restaurant. "That's why those guys don't bother me. They're just being teenagers."

"Yeah," I said, "they're little brats."

Again, I waited for him to reciprocate the question, to ask me something about my career plans. When he didn't, I plunged ahead. "I haven't decided on my major yet. I'm a little nervous about that. I need to get focused on what I want to do this year."

My mind wandered for a few seconds, imagining the conversations I'd be having with my birth father about choosing a major. I realized how fortunate I was to have at least one parent who could help me think through such matters.

"I'm kind of nervous about that making that decision," I repeated to Calvin. "You know what I mean?"

He nodded. "It's a big decision." He lifted a hand before opening his car door. "See you tomorrow."

"Do you play sports?" I asked Calvin the following evening. "You look like you would." Then I realized my eyes had just traveled down the length of his magnificent physique, from his broad shoulders and heavily muscled arms to his taut stomach and narrow hips. I felt profoundly embarrassed, and hoped he didn't think I was coming on to him.

"I play basketball," he replied. "I played in high school and my first two years here at Goshen College."

"Will you be playing this year?"

He nodded. "Yup."

"What position do you play?"

"Forward."

I hadn't attended any of Goshen College's basketball games during my freshman year. But I knew for certain that I'd be sitting in the bleachers my sophomore year, cheering for Calvin.

I didn't bother to wait for a reciprocal question. "I played volleyball during high school. My height came in handy. I was good at spiking the ball."

He smiled and nodded. "Yeah. I could see that."

Our coworkers quickly picked up on the spark of interest between Calvin and me, assuming there was more going on than what was actually happening.

"Have you gone out with him yet?" Mindy asked me time and again. She seemed disappointed that I had no titillating stories to share with her.

"Watch your step, girlie," Edna would say if she saw me glance in Calvin's direction when I entered the kitchen.

Of course, Allen and Bradley's dirty talk now focused on the subject of what was happening during all the supposed dates I was having with Calvin. I stopped trying to set the record straight and simply ignored them. But Edna was constantly hollering at them to keep their filthy mouths shut.

One day, Allen said something so crude that Edna's face reddened in fury. She grabbed a large spoon from her cooking station and lunged at him, chasing him several laps around the kitchen before she caught him. Holding him by the arm, she smacked his bottom with the spoon half a dozen times before turning him loose. Then she returned to her station, huffing from the exertion. Pointing at the bewildered Allen with her spoon, she barked, "If you value your worthless little life, you'll never talk such filth in my kitchen again!"

"Okay, okay," Allen muttered.

During a slow time that afternoon, Bob ushered Allen and Bradley to a table in the dining area. The boys sat with downcast eyes while Bob lectured them. I could see from the grim expression on his face that he meant business with them. As I moved back and forth between the tables, I strained to hear what he was saying. I caught bits and pieces about 'respecting coworkers' and 'standards of conduct in the workplace.'

"What's going on out there?" I asked Edna when I returned to the kitchen.

I could tell she was still in a sour mood. "I told Bob what happened this morning," she said, angrily whipping a bowl of cream with her whisk. "I told him that if he didn't get a handle on what was going on in his business, I'd walk out that minute. He promised to have a talk with the boys."

She grinned evilly. "He said I wasn't allowed to get physical with those little brats. But, I swear to God, I'm not going to be able to stop myself if those smart alecks get out of hand again. I'll beat them to a pulp. Bob can go ahead and fire me. I don't care."

For the next two weeks, Allen and Bradley were quiet and sullen. They seemed to make a point of not talking to me, and the only time they spoke to Calvin was when they accused him of screwing something up.

All the uproar in the restaurant caused by my supposed relationship with Calvin unnerved me, temporarily snuffing out any fantasies I had about dating him. Our conversations in the parking lot dwindled. After a month, our coworkers seemed to lose interest in our imaginary affair.

But as I walked out of the restaurant one Friday night in July, the starry summer sky put a little romance back in my mood. Calvin was standing by his car, as if waiting for me to come over and talk with him. I wanted to say something to him. More than that, I wanted him to say something to me, to give me an indication that he was interested in me.

"Busy night, huh?" I said as I walked toward him.

"Yup," he said. "It sure was."

We stood in silence, staring at each other. Suddenly, I blurted out, "Do you like movies?"

He nodded. "Yup."

"What kind of movies do you watch?"

"Comedies. Action."

"*The Jerk* is playing at the Concord Cinema," I said. "With Steve Martin and Bernadette Peters. I've heard it's really funny."

Then I stopped, reigning in all the other words that threatened to pop out of my mouth. I was determined not to take the actual step of asking Calvin out on a date. *If this guy is interested in me,* I told myself, *then he's going to have to show some initiative.*

But Calvin said nothing. I turned abruptly and walked the few steps to my car, humiliated, berating myself for acting like a fool. Just as I was putting my key in the ignition, Calvin's face appeared in my open car window.

"Would you like to go see the movie with me?" he asked.

"Sure," I said.

"How about the late show Sunday night?"

"Sounds good to me."

"Want me to pick you up at your house?"

I thought about my parents, and knew I wasn't ready to have them meet a guy I was dating. "How about if I meet you at the cinema?" I suggested.

The next morning, as I was leaving the house for my lunch shift at the restaurant, I found my mother sitting at the kitchen table in her shabby bathrobe. She had not yet attended to her hair for the day, and her limp, gray-streaked locks trailed down her back. Her small, bony hands were wrapped around a mug of coffee. She looked as if every ounce of strength had been drained from her body.

I halted my steps. "What's wrong, Mom? You look tired. Didn't you sleep well last night?"

She shook her head. "I slept okay. I just don't seem to have any pep these days."

Fear shot through me like a jolt of electricity. I sat down at the table across from her. "Maybe you should see a doctor."

She shook her head again. "This is part of getting older, Victoria. I guess I'm just wearing down."

"Don't say things like that, Mom," I protested. "Just try to take it easy for a while. You always work too hard."

She shrugged, staring down at the table.

We sat in silence for a minute before I changed the subject. "Mom, I have a date tomorrow night."

She lifted her haggard face to look at mine. "Oh? You haven't dated anyone for a couple of years. Who is it?"

"Calvin Zook. He's a guy at work."

My mother mustered the energy to shoot me a stern look. "You're dating one of your coworkers? Do you think that's a good idea?"

"Well, he's actually a student at Goshen College. We've talked a little bit at work. I think we have some things in common."

"Okay," she sighed, still sounding dubious. Then she added an obligatory, "Just be careful, Victoria."

CHAPTER 15

The Jerk was hilarious. As I sat in the theater next to Calvin, the two of us laughing together at Steve Martin's antics, I congratulated myself on picking a great first-date movie. *This guy is so easy to be with,* I thought.

At one point in the movie, I laughed so hard that I rocked back and forth in my seat, clutching my stomach. In the middle of the hilarity, I unthinkingly slapped Calvin on the knee. He looked over at me and grinned. Then he slid his arm over the back of my seat, encircling my shoulders, caressing my upper arm with his fingertips. I immediately wondered whether I'd been out of line with the knee slap, whether I'd given him a signal I didn't intend to send.

As we left the theater after the movie, I felt Calvin's hand on my back, guiding me through the crowd. "Want to go for a drive?" he asked as we walked toward our cars.

"Sure," I said.

It was after 11:00 PM by then, but I didn't care about the time. It felt wonderful to be a normal nineteen-year-old spending the evening with a guy, staying out late, doing whatever I wanted to do. Enjoying teenage activities that I'd cut myself off from the past two years.

We got into Calvin's car, and he drove us around aimlessly for a few minutes, passing the Concord Mall, Concord Elementary School, and Concord High School. In keeping with our typical pattern of conversation, I chatted lightheartedly while Calvin responded in monosyllables.

"I need to get some gas," he said as he pulled up to a convenience store. I waited in the car while he filled the tank. Then he stuck his head through my open window and asked, "Do you want anything to drink?"

"No, I'm fine," I replied. As I watched him walk into the store, I realized how tired I was, and I wished I would have opted to go straight home from the theatre. But a minute later, Calvin emerged from the store with a definite bounce in his step. He had a soft drink in hand, as if fueling up for further nighttime activity. Humming under his breath, he got into the car and started driving again.

I soon realized we were heading down County Road 45 toward Goshen, driving farther and farther away from my car in the Cinema parking lot. "Where are we going?" I asked.

"Oxbow Park," he said. "Is that okay with you?"

Bewildered, I said, "I suppose so." I couldn't imagine what he had in mind to do. Surely, he didn't think we'd hike any trails that late at night.

Minutes later, he pulled into a parking lot near the park entrance. He switched off the ignition, carelessly tossing his empty paper cup out the car window. Then he turned to look at me. In the darkness, I couldn't make out the expression on his face. I suddenly felt afraid.

He reached for me, pulling me toward him, kissing me roughly. Before I knew it, his hand was up my shirt, fondling my breasts, fumbling with the hooks of my bra. "Let's get in the back seat," he whispered hoarsely in my ear.

Panicked, I fought off the strong, determined hands that roamed over my body and pulled at my clothing. "Stop it!" I screamed. "Stop it!" When I finally succeeded in pushing him away, I pulled down my shirt and fastened my jeans. Then I sat with my back against the passenger door, my body trembling, my heart pounding. "What the heck are you doing, Calvin?" I asked in a shaky voice.

"Isn't this what you wanted?" He sounded confused.

"No," I said. "I mean, not now. Not so soon."

"When?"

"After we get to know each other a little better. After we get a little closer."

He sighed, sounding exasperated.

"I'm sorry, Calvin," I said, trying to rescue a date that had suddenly taken a turn for the worst. "If I gave you the wrong impression, I'm sorry."

He said nothing. I pressed my back against the door, berating myself for having been so naïve and stupid. *You should've known what he was up to. You shouldn't have agreed to ride around with him.*

"Are you a virgin?" he asked after a few minutes.

"Yes," I replied.

In the darkness, I watched his handsome profile nodding slowly, as if he suddenly understood my panicky response to his advances. I did not need to ask him the same question. I knew full well that Calvin Zook was not a virgin. Despite his apparent shyness, his initial reticence in approaching me, he was obviously sexually experienced. I wondered whether his shyness was a front, whether he purposely held back and waited for women to chase him, knowing it wouldn't take long for some female to lose her head over his irresistible good looks.

"Sorry I got out of line," he said. "I don't want you to think I'm a rapist, or anything. I know how to behave myself."

He turned the key in the ignition and pulled out onto the county road, heading back toward Elkhart. I stared straight ahead, my mind racing, wondering how this unfortunate incident was going to impact my working relationship with Calvin. *You can't tell anybody about this*, I cautioned myself. *Don't even tell anyone you went out with him. Not even Mindy. If word gets out, all hell will break loose in the restaurant.*

When Calvin pulled up next to my car in the empty cinema parking lot, he turned to me and said, "I didn't mean to ruin your evening."

Pulling my composure around me, I was determined to say something that would end the evening on a positive note. "You didn't ruin it. I thought we had a good time together watching the movie. You just took me by surprise out there at Oxbow. Let's not have this be something awkward between us."

"Okay." In the dimly lit parking lot, I could see him smiling at me. Then he caught me off guard by asking, "Wanna do this again sometime? If I promise to control myself?"

"Really?" I said. "You want to go out with me again?"

"Yeah. You're a cool girl. I like you a lot."

His words warmed me, reassured me. My body relaxed, releasing the fearful tension I'd been holding. "Thanks. I like you, too, Calvin."

He reached over and squeezed my hand. "I'll wait until you're ready to do something. I promise. I'll let you take the lead."

"Okay." On impulse, I leaned toward him and gave him a peck on the cheek. Then I opened the car door. "Thanks, and have a good night."

As I drove home, I thought about the last words Calvin had said to me. I wondered whether he was taking it for granted that I would eventually give in and have sex with him. Was he willing to be patient, knowing he'd inevitably get what he wanted? Was he enticed by the idea of me losing my virginity to him?

I'd responded with, "Okay." Had my one-word assent given him the impression that I was on board with his plan?

But why not? I thought. *I'm nineteen years old. What's the point of waiting any longer? Most people my age have been sexually active for several years. It's time for me to get some experience.*

"Why not?" I whispered aloud. Then I threw back my head and laughed. "Why the hell not?"

Three days later, as I sat with Reverend Hahn in his apartment, he broached the subject I'd been expecting him to bring up. "Victoria, have you given any more thought to what major you're going to choose?"

"Yes," I replied. "I have. I'm still not entirely sure. I've thought about a lot of things: psychology, communications, elementary education. Sometimes, I even think about math or science. But for some reason, I keep coming back to English."

Reverend Hahn nodded, his eyes bright with interest. "And why is that?"

"I love literature. I'm good at writing. And I think I'd be good at teaching English. English was always my favorite subject in high school."

"You know, I like that option for you," Reverend Hahn mused. "You could teach English here in the states, or anywhere in the world. And there are all kinds of opportunities for writers."

"That's kind of what I was thinking," I said.

Reverend Hahn sat back in his chair, his breathing a bit ragged, as if our brief conversation had worn him out. Such episodes were now familiar to me. While the evidence of my birth father's progressing illness made me sad, I no longer panicked when the incidents occurred, as I knew he'd rally again. He often looked as if he was teetering on the edge of a complete collapse. But he'd pull himself together, regaining his sure footing. His determination amazed me.

"Can I get you anything?" I asked him.

"A glass of water would be nice," he replied.

I went to the kitchenette, opened the cupboard, took out a glass, and filled it with water from the special faucet on the sink. By this time, I was quite familiar with the tiny apartment. I knew where to find all my birth father's little necessities: the drinking straws in the top left-hand drawer in the kitchen cabinet, the clean handkerchiefs in his dresser drawer, the cough drops in his night stand.

Since my last visit, the furniture in the living room had been slightly rearranged, disrupting the perfectly balanced order. One of the end tables had been moved across the room, beside the spot where Reverend Hahn usually sat in his wheelchair. It now served as a table for holding his cup of coffee, or the book or magazine he was reading.

I set the glass on the table, mindful to put it on the coaster placed there for that purpose. Despite his own physical decline, Reverend Hahn insisted on keeping his furniture in pristine condition.

"Thank you, my child," he said to me. "Now, help yourself to something. There's a carafe of iced tea in the refrigerator."

After pouring myself a glass of tea, I settled onto the sofa again. "How's work going this summer?" Reverend Hahn asked.

"It's fine," I said. "Pretty much the same as last year." *Except for one thing,* I thought. *Except for Calvin.*

As I contemplated whether I wanted to tell my birth father about my new dating relationship, he said, "You looked like you were about to say something."

I shook my head, chuckling. "You always pick up on everything. Okay, I'll tell you. I'm dating someone. A guy from work."

Reverend Hahn cleared his throat. "A guy from work?" He sounded dubious.

"Well, that's where I met him. But he's also a student at Goshen College."

My birth father's steady gaze told me he expected me to continue. I bought a little time by taking a sip of tea. Setting down the glass, I said, "His name is Calvin Zook. He's from Nebraska. He's a social work major, and he plays basketball. That's all I can say about him."

I saw a flicker of fear in Reverend Hahn's eyes. Then, with perfect composure, he asked, "Have you told him much about yourself?"

"Not really," I said. "Not anything important."

"Why not?"

"Because ..." I chewed on my lip, trying to come up with a response to a question that I'd already asked myself, one that I'd been unable to answer. "I guess he isn't the kind of guy who asks about personal things."

"What kind of a guy is he, then?" Reverend Hahn's gaze penetrated through all the defenses I'd built around my new relationship. Whether or not I wanted to, he was going to make me think deeply about the man I was dating.

"He's quiet," I said, "and very good-looking." I immediately knew I'd made myself sound superficial.

Reverend Hahn slowly reached for his glass, took a sip of water, then carefully set the drink back on the coaster. "What is it that attracts you to Mr. Zook?" he asked, his words deliberate. "Besides his good looks?"

My face flushed with embarrassment. "I guess ... I guess he's easy to be with. I feel comfortable around him."

My birth father's features took on a mask-like appearance. I knew he was trying to keep from conveying his disapproval. Folding his hands in his lap, he said, "Let me offer one piece of advice, Victoria. Don't allow this young man to take you somewhere you don't want to go. Make sure you stay in the driver's seat."

Anger rumbled inside me. I averted my gaze to stare out the patio door. *You hypocrite!* I wanted to shout at the crippled old man sitting across from me. *When it comes to women, you're the biggest con artist of all. You lured my mother into a situation that completely turned her life upside down. How dare you give me dating advice!*

Once again, he read me with uncanny accuracy. "I know you think I have no right to give you such advice. Such a cautionary note must sound absurd coming from me. But I know men. We're scoundrels, the whole lot of us." His voice softened, taking on a pleading tone. "I don't want my daughter to get hurt. Please, Victoria. Be careful. Make sure you're the one who stays in charge."

I thought of Calvin's words: *I'll wait till you're ready.* "I AM in charge," I said, more sharply than I intended to.

CHAPTER 16

My second date with Calvin was at the Maple City Bowling Alley. I wasn't at all surprised to discover that he was a highly skilled bowler. I hadn't had much experience with that particular sport, and we laughed over my mishaps with the bowling ball. When Calvin instructed me on improving my form, his touch sent a shiver of electricity through me.

Afterwards, we drove to The Chief, a popular ice cream stand on the west side of Goshen. "Let's not tell anyone at the restaurant about us," I said as we sat at the picnic table eating our tin roof sundaes. "If they find out, they'll never stop hassling us." Calvin nodded in agreement.

On our third date, we went miniature golfing at a course in Dunlap. Once again, Calvin proved himself to be a skillful player. Our fourth date involved watching Calvin's roommate play in a city league softball game at Roger's Park. As I sat in the stands that warm summer evening, holding hands with my new boyfriend, my life seemed perfect. I wondered why I'd held myself back from dating for so long.

Calvin had begun picking me up at the house for our dates, although I wasn't yet ready for him to come inside. I'd watch out my bedroom window until I'd see his blue car coming down our county road. Then I'd fly down the stairs and out the front door, meeting him just as he pulled into our driveway.

True to his word, Calvin behaved himself on our dates, letting me take the lead with any physical contact. He didn't even hold my hand without my consent. When he drove me home at the end of the date, we went no farther than a goodnight kiss before I got out of the car.

My mother raised her eyebrows about this sudden flurry of dating activity. "When are we going to meet this fellow?" she asked me time and again.

"Soon," I'd say. In my mind, things were moving along nicely between Calvin and me, rapidly approaching the point where it would be appropriate for my boyfriend to meet my parents.

Toward the end of August, when my mother once again asked about meeting Calvin, I said, "Why don't we have him over for dinner Sunday night?"

She winced, and I knew my worn-out mother was thinking about the effort involved in making dinner for a guest. "Don't worry," I reassured her. "I'll help. I'll do most of the work."

"My folks want to meet you," I said to Calvin as we sat in his car at the end of our next date.

"That's cool," he said. "I figured they would."

"How about coming for dinner this Sunday evening?"

"Sure. I'll be glad to do that."

I exhaled forcefully, trying to dispel the nervous energy that was already building at the thought of such an event. "I need to tell you about my family before you meet them."

"Okay."

"My parents are pretty old. Older than you'd expect, with me being only nineteen. My dad's a down-to-earth kind of guy. Real sweet. Everybody likes him. You'll feel comfortable around him."

"That's good," Calvin said.

"My mom's kind of uptight," I continued. "Nervous. She doesn't smile much, and she isn't all that friendly. You shouldn't take that personally."

"No problem." Then, with uncharacteristic curiosity, he asked, "Do you have brothers and sisters?"

I hesitated, mentally preparing myself for venturing into that sticky territory. "Yes. I have two brothers. They're a whole lot older than I am. Both of them live in Virginia, so we don't see much of them. And then there's my sister Lucy."

"Does she live around here?"

"Yes, she lives in Elkhart." I turned in my seat to face Calvin more fully. "Lucy's a little bit weird. She's mentally ill. She lives alone, but she has to be closely supervised. Otherwise, she ends up going off the deep end."

I watched him closely, trying to read his reaction. He sat motionless for a few seconds, then shrugged. "That doesn't bother me. I'm okay with weird people."

"Actually, she's fine most of the time," I explained. "But you never know when she's going to do or say something that's out of line."

Calvin chuckled. "Don't worry. I can deal with that. So who all am I going to meet?"

"Just my parents," I said.

"Not your sister?"

His question surprised me. "Do you want to meet her?"

"I don't care. It's up to you." He smiled at my disconcerted expression. "Sure. I'll meet her. Might as well get all the awkward stuff over with, huh?"

The following Sunday afternoon found me bustling around the kitchen, helping my mother with dinner preparations. I peeled and chopped the potatoes, carrots, and onions for the roast beef she was fixing. Then I attempted to ice a chocolate layer cake I'd just taken out of the oven.

"You should've let that cool down," my mother scolded when I ended up with dark cake crumbs in the white frosting. She grabbed the knife from me, and with a few deft strokes, rescued the cake from near disaster.

As I set the table with five place settings, my mom shook her head, muttering, "I can't believe you want to bring Lucy over for this. You know how she is."

"I might as well get it over with," I said, echoing Calvin's words. "He has to meet her sometime."

My mother whipped her head around to stare at me. "Are you that serious about this guy, Victoria?"

I cringed at her judgmental gaze. "Maybe. I don't know. It's too soon to tell."

Shortly before Calvin was due to arrive, my dad came home with Lucy in tow. She walked into the house yawning. "I'm tired," she announced. "I'm going to lie down." As she tromped noisily up the stairs to her former bedroom, my mother shook her head in disgust. "Why does she always do this?"

"She feels at home here," my dad said. "That's a good thing, isn't it?"

My mother's jaw tightened. "I suppose so. But she always messes up that room, and I have to clean it after she's gone."

When Calvin arrived, I introduced him to my parents, then left him in the living room with my dad while I helped my mother get the meal on the table.

"So you're from Nebraska," I heard my dad say. "I grew up in Kansas."

"Yup," Calvin replied.

"What do your folks do out there?"

"Farming. Corn, mostly."

"My folks raised wheat," my dad said. "But we ended up losing the family farm during the depression."

"That's rough," Calvin said, genuine concern in his voice.

"Does your dad raise any animals?"

"Dairy cattle."

"Oh, really?" I could hear the excitement in my dad's voice. "What breed?"

"Holstein."

"I worked on my uncle's dairy farm here in Goshen when I was a young man. We raised Jerseys. I imagine your dad runs things a whole lot different than we did back in my day."

Then Calvin launched into a description of his father's

milking operation. I was stunned. I'd never heard him speak so fluently, and at such length, on any subject.

Before I knew it, the living room conversation had turned to a discussion of our barnyard animals. "Ada, do I have time to take Calvin out to see the goats?" my dad called.

"Make it quick," my mother called back. "Dinner will be ready in ten minutes."

As the men trudged through the kitchen and out the back door, my mother shot me a perplexed look. "So you decided to date another farm boy," she said. "Are you sure that's what you want?"

"I didn't say I was going to marry him," I snapped.

Just as my dad and Calvin stepped back inside, Lucy came down the stairs. She looked disheveled, her short red hair sticking up on one side after having lain on it during her nap. She grinned widely when she saw Calvin. "You must be my sister's new boyfriend."

During the meal, Calvin ate heartily, complimenting my mother and me on the food. "I miss my mom's cooking," he said. "It's been a while since I've had a good home-cooked meal."

My mother's lips stretched into a grim smile.

Calvin and my dad continued their discussion of corn crops and dairy cattle for so long that I was beginning to get irritated. To my relief, Lucy was so intent on eating that she said nothing.

But suddenly, she pointed at Calvin with her fork and blurted out, "You know who you remind me of?"

Calvin looked startled by my sister' rude interjection. He stared at her for half a minute before saying, "Who?"

"That kid that lives down the road from us. That Hooley kid." Turning to me, she said, "Tori Grace, what was the name of that boy you dated in high school? Daniel?"

She turned back to Calvin. "You look a lot like him."

"Lucy …," my mother cautioned.

But Lucy wasn't ready to stop. "Tall, blonde hair, blue eyes. Really cute. I guess that's my sister's type." She took a huge bite of roast beef, waving her fork at Calvin while she chewed. "I mean that as a compliment, you know."

"Lucy!" my mother said firmly. "That's enough."

"Okay, okay! I'll shut up now." Lucy made a motion of zipping her lips, then returned her attention to her food.

The rest of us continued eating in an awkward silence, until my dad jump-started the conversation by asking Calvin another farming question. "Has your dad ever raised any hogs?"

After Calvin left, I helped my mother clear the table and stack the dishes on the counter. She seemed too tired to ask me any more questions. "Let's wash these in the morning," she said.

As I headed up the stairs, my dad called, "Vickie, you've got a nice boyfriend."

I flung myself across my bed, allowing myself to fully consider Lucy's ill-mannered comments. The resemblance between Calvin and my former boyfriend Daniel was indeed uncanny. They were both tall, handsome, soft-spoken farm boys. Was I interested in Calvin only because he reminded me so much of my beloved Daniel? The boyfriend I was forced to give up because I couldn't divulge the truth about my paternity? Was dating Calvin my way of hanging onto the past?

"That's just silly," I whispered to myself.

CHAPTER 17

All through my teen years, whenever my mother and I were getting ready to go somewhere together, we enacted a predictable little drama. She'd stand at the foot of the stairs, jingling her car keys impatiently. "Victoria," she'd bark up at me, "We need to get going. We're running late."

"I'll be down in a minute," I'd call back as I scrambled to put on my shoes, check my hair, and grab whatever I needed to take with me. Then I'd bound down the stairs and follow her out the front door.

"That was more like ten minutes," she'd inevitably grouse. "I don't know why you don't start getting up earlier. There's no point to this last-minute rushing around."

However, on the first morning of my sophomore year of college, something different happened. My dad and I had moved most of my belongings to my dorm room on Saturday, and then I'd come back home for the weekend. On Monday morning, I'd gotten up early to load the car with the rest of my things. And I was the one who ended up waiting impatiently, standing outside my mother's closed bedroom door calling, "Hurry up, Mom. It's time to go."

Several minutes later, she emerged from her room, looking tired, pale, and a bit disoriented. "You got the keys?" I asked her.

She hesitated, shook her head, then walked into the kitchen to get them from the hook by the telephone. And I sensed that something was wrong.

"Mom," I chided as we drove the familiar route to the campus. "When are you going to retire? I think work is getting to be too much for you."

"I'm nowhere near retirement age," she replied. "I haven't even turned sixty." She glanced sideways at me, forcing a smile. "Don't worry, Victoria. I just need to get back into the swing of things."

I began my second year at Goshen College with considerably more self-assurance than I'd had at the start of my freshman year. I declared myself as an English major, and met with an academic advisor from that department. When I signed up for my classes—philosophy, sociology, world literature, and a writing course—I felt a little daunted. But I convinced myself that I was fully capable of mastering all my coursework.

Confident from my success with the sport in high school, I joined the women's volleyball team. Then I did something I hadn't mustered the nerve to do a year earlier: I tried out for a spot in Goshen College's fifty-voice chorale. After singing in front of the director, music professor Dr. Metzler, I was assigned a place in the alto section. Afterwards, I felt so elated that I could hardly contain myself. I wanted to run up and down the hallway of my dorm, shouting out my good news. Instead, I secluded myself in my room, cherishing my joy in solitude. I lay there on my bed, thinking that I'd finally arrived, that I'd finally grabbed the world by its elusive tail.

I've got the hang of being a college student now, I told myself, feeling self-satisfied. *I'm not the insecure kid that started here a year ago. I'm going to do just fine. There aren't going to be any emotional breakdowns this year. I'll have to work hard, but I'm also going to have fun. I'll have a blast playing volleyball. I'll travel with the chorale. Calvin and I will go out on weekends. I'll be so proud to watch him play basketball. This is going to be the best year of my life.*

I was initially disappointed when I learned that I would not be allowed the luxury of rooming alone during my sophomore year. The college assigned me a new roommate, Rhonda Yost, a transfer from Hesston College in Kansas. She proved herself to be a quiet, studious girl who minded her own business, kept her possessions in order, and organized her daily routine down to the last detail. In my mind, these traits rendered her the ideal roommate. We got along well, although we never became particularly close.

At first, it felt strange to take my relationship with Calvin into the college setting. But having a good-looking boyfriend only added to my confidence. When the girls in my dorm caught on to the fact that we were a couple, they flocked to my room, eager to know the details of how we'd gotten together.

Even though Calvin lived off campus, he took most of his meals in the college cafeteria. At lunch, I sat with him instead of with Stephen Wenger and Charlie Hess. Sometimes, I'd glance at my old friends still sitting at the corner table I'd shared with them, and I'd feel guilty and a bit nostalgic. I missed their keen intelligence and their witty humor. But at that time, Calvin claimed a higher spot on my list of priorities.

On an evening in late September, I came down the stairs for dinner to find Calvin standing in the crowded lobby, waiting for me as he usually did. But he wasn't watching for my arrival. He was deeply engrossed in a conversation with a girl.

As the girl had her back to me, I couldn't tell who she was at first. All I saw was a willowy figure and long blonde hair. Calvin spotted me walking toward them. He shifted his gaze to meet mine, looking guilty. Then the girl turned around, and to my dismay, I saw that it was Bonnie Springer.

Anger darkened my mood. I knew that almost every girl on campus would be delighted to have a moment of attention from Calvin Zook. I knew I couldn't prevent him from talking to other women, and I'd already cautioned myself not to act jealous when this happened. But I couldn't handle the sight of him happily chatting with my former roommate.

Anyone but her, I thought. *I don't care who else he talks to. I don't care who he flirts with. Just not Bonnie Springer.*

It seemed that over the summer, Bonnie had lost all the pudginess she'd accumulated from her party nights in the Westlawn dormitory. She looked fabulous: more self-possessed, more womanly. And dangerously alluring.

"Hi, Bonnie," I said, determined not to let her shake my confidence.

"Sorry, Victoria," she said as she flounced away. "I didn't mean to monopolize your boyfriend."

"Wow, she sure was thrilled to be talking to you," I said to Calvin as we moved into the cafeteria line. Then, pulling my dignity around me, I lightened my tone. "But any girl would be excited to talk to you. You're hot stuff around here."

Calvin shrugged, grinning.

I'm not sure why I made the decision to do what I did next. Perhaps with all my newfound confidence, I believed I was mature enough to take the step of being intimate with a man. Or maybe after witnessing Bonnie Springer cozying up to my boyfriend, I thought I needed to do something to mark him as mine. The next day before we parted ways after lunch, I whispered to Calvin, "I'm ready to do it."

His eyes lit up. "Really?"

"Really."

"You sure about this?"

"Absolutely," I said, even though I was quaking inside.

He looked thoughtful, as if calculating how such a feat could be accomplished. "You can come to my apartment Saturday night. We'll have the upstairs to ourselves." He smiled down at me. "Okay?"

I nodded. He gave me a kiss on the cheek, then strolled away, looking as if he was walking on air.

I knew full well that going to Calvin's apartment for a sexual rendezvous was against college rules. While not official campus housing, the residence where Calvin and his roommates lived was associated with the college, as off-campus students had lived there for years. Goshen College took a firm stance against sex outside of marriage, and I was not prone to breaking rules.

So that Saturday evening, I walked to Calvin's house filled with trepidation. He met me at the door, grinning widely.

I glance around the apartment. To the left was the living room, with a ragged sofa and matted carpeting in dire need of vacuuming. To the right was the kitchen, the table laden with pizza boxes and other fast food wrappings. The pile of dirty dishes in the sink spilled over onto the countertop. Feeling slightly sick to my stomach, I followed Calvin up the creaky wooden stairs, to a room in no better shape than the ones downstairs.

Had the sex been wonderful, I probably wouldn't have walked out of that house so filled with regret. But it wasn't.

I was undressed by Calvin's eager, fumbling hands, in a room that smelled like gym shoes. He pushed aside the covers of his unmade bed, and we lay down on sheets that needed washing. Then came the rough kissing, the uncomfortable penetration, and the complete lack of any pleasurable sensation on my part. When Calvin rolled his sweaty body off mine, he left me feeling more alone than I'd ever felt in my entire life.

"I'm going downstairs to get something to drink," he announced.

When he returned a few minutes later with two cans of *Pepsi,* I was already dressed. "So how did you like it?" he asked.

"Fine," I lied.

He offered me a can of *Pepsi,* but I shook my head. "I have to get going."

"See you tomorrow," he called after me as I rushed down the stairs.

I walked back to my dorm feeling disconnected from myself, as if the body I was inhabiting wasn't mine. I tried to sort out what had just happened to me, but I couldn't formulate any coherent thoughts. As soon as I got back to my room, I grabbed my towel, soap, and shampoo, and went down the hallway to the bathroom. In the shower, I tried to scrub away the experience I'd just had.

I lost my virginity, I wailed inwardly. *It wasn't supposed to be like this.*

When I got back to my room, I crawled into bed, even though my hair was still soaking wet. My roommate glanced up from the book she was reading. "Is something wrong?" she asked.

Making no response, I turned my face to the wall. Rhonda wisely left me alone.

The next morning, I couldn't bring myself to go to the College Mennonite Church, as I felt too dirty to enter the house of God. I couldn't imagine ever going to church again. I couldn't imagine going back home, either. My mother would know what I'd done just by glancing at me. And I especially didn't want to see Reverend Hahn, as he would end up forcing the entire story out of me.

I lay in bed until noon, brooding. *Why wasn't the sex good?* I'd heard so many stories about how wonderful the experience was supposed to be. Sex was something that people desired more than anything in the world. People lost their minds over sex, making all kinds of disastrous life choices just to get it. Why hadn't it been good for me?

Was it just because I hadn't known what I was doing? Or was I one of those women afflicted with the unfortunate condition known as frigidity? Did I have no capacity to enjoy sex?

When I dared to shift the blame away from myself, I wondered whether Calvin wasn't a good lover. Then came another sobering thought: maybe I simply wasn't in love with Calvin. Maybe I didn't feel close enough to my boyfriend to enjoy intimacy with him.

My guilt felt overwhelming. I'd put myself in a situation where I'd risked becoming pregnant with an illegitimate baby. *You should've known better,* I berated myself. *Of all people, you should've known better. You know what being an illegitimate child feels like. You know about the pain it causes a family. You cannot afford to repeat your mother's mistake. You cannot pass this family legacy down to another generation.*

I knew I had to talk to Calvin. He'd be down in the lobby, waiting for me to join him for lunch. Reluctantly, I threw back my covers, pulled on a pair of jeans and an old sweatshirt, and ran a brush through my tangled hair. I didn't bother to put on makeup. I had no desire to look attractive.

Calvin met me with a huge grin on his face. He gave me a kiss on the lips, something he'd never done before in the presence of others. With a protective hand on my back, he steered me into the lunch line.

While we ate, I tried to mask my inner turmoil, making myself laugh at the lighthearted conversations going on around us. But after Calvin and I left the cafeteria, I said, "I need to talk to you."

I watched his smiling features realign themselves into a guarded expression. "What about?" he asked, rather testily.

The sharpness of his tone angered me, giving me the steam power to blurt out the announcement that was sure to rile him. "I don't think I can do this anymore."

"Do what?"

"Sex. I can't have sex with you anymore."

His face reddened with anger. "If you weren't ready, you shouldn't have led me on. You lied to me."

"I didn't mean to lead you on," I said defensively. "I thought I was ready." I cast about for an explanation for my change of heart. "I can't take the risk getting pregnant. Right now, I'm scared I might be pregnant."

"What the hell?" The words exploded out of Calvin's mouth. "I used protection. Didn't you notice? I always do."

"Protection doesn't work one hundred percent of the time," I snapped.

"You need to trust me, Victoria. I know what I'm doing. I've never gotten a girl pregnant before."

The mention of his past sexual activity only served to fuel my anger. I wanted to reach out and slap his face, marring his handsome features with a bright red handprint.

"I'm not going to fight with you about this," he said petulantly. "If you don't want to do it, then we won't do it." Abruptly, he turned away from me, heading in the direction of his apartment.

I watched him for a few seconds, then ran to catch up with him. Grabbing his arm, I said, "Just give me some time to think about it."

He glanced at me, a flicker of hope in his eyes. But I knew I'd promised him nothing.

When my period arrived on time three days later, I offered up a fervent prayer of thanksgiving and vowed never again to tempt fate in such a way. Spitefully, I decided not to alleviate any fears I'd planted in Calvin's mind by telling him the good news. Over the next week, the two of us went about our usual routine, eating meals together, trying to act as if nothing had happened to shake our relationship.

But exactly ten days after that fateful Saturday night with Calvin, something happened that swept the thorny issue of sex off the center stage of my life, replacing it with a drama of much greater import.

It was a Tuesday evening in mid-October. I was in my dorm room studying for a philosophy exam. I'd just closed my textbook and was running a brush through my hair before heading downstairs for dinner. One of my dorm-mates, Ellen, called to me from the doorway. "Victoria, there's a guy down in the lobby looking for you."

"Calvin?" I asked, knowing he'd planned on meeting me there.

"No," she said. "It's an older man."

It's probably Reverend Hahn, I thought with a twinge of irritation. *He's drummed up some ridiculous reason for seeing me here on campus.*

"Is it a gray-haired man in a wheelchair?" I asked Ellen.

"No," she said. "He's not in a wheelchair. He's bald, kind of heavyset."

Startled, I swung around to face her. "My dad?"

She shrugged. "I don't know. I've never seen your dad."

Other than helping me move my belongings in and out of my dorm room, my dad never set foot on the Goshen College campus. I knew the college intimidated him, that he felt out of place here. If he was here now, it had to be for a compelling reason. I brushed past Ellen and rushed down the stairs.

Calvin was at the foot of the stairs waiting for me. "What's wrong?" he asked when he saw the anxiety on my face.

"I think my dad's here," I said breathlessly as I scanned the sea of faces in the lobby. "I've got to find him."

Calvin pointed toward the front entry doors. "Over there."

And there stood my dad in his flannel shirt and work jacket, feed cap in hand, looking decidedly forlorn. I made my way toward him.

"What's going on, Dad?" I asked.

He stood there staring at me, wordless, fear in his eyes. Then he took a deep breath and spoke, his voice catching. "You're mom's sick, Vickie. She's real sick. I think you'd better come home with me."

CHAPTER 18

I followed my dad out to his car, which he'd parked in the circular drive in front of the lobby. "What's wrong with Mom?" I pressed him as we pulled out onto the highway.

He opened his mouth to speak, then shook his head, as if he couldn't manage to get the words out.

"Is it really bad?"

He nodded.

"Like cancer?"

He nodded again.

"Oh Dad, no!" I wailed. "No! No!"

Without taking his eyes off the road, he reached over to hold my hand.

"What kind of cancer?"

An awkward, noisy sob escaped his throat before he forced out the words. "I don't exactly know, Vickie. I was pretty shook up when the doctor was telling us what was going on, and I couldn't follow what he was saying. Your mom will need to tell you. All I know is that it's in her female parts. It's spread too far for them to do much of anything about it."

It felt as if someone had slammed a sledge hammer into my midsection, knocking the breath completely out of me. "Is she going to die?" I gasped.

"I think we might have to face that possibility, Vickie." He whispered the words so softly that I could hardly hear them.

I turned my head to look out the window, staring at nothing while tears streamed down my face. All I could see was the image of my mother over the past few months, quietly fading, losing her strength. Why hadn't I paid closer attention? Why hadn't I made her do something?

"These last three or four weeks, she was feeling so poorly that she could hardly put one foot in front of the other," my dad said. "But she kept on trying to go to work.

Finally, I convinced her to take a day off and go to the doctor. From there, it seemed like all we were doing was going to one doctor after another, getting all kinds of tests done.

"Yesterday, she went back to work. She was so weak, and I was so worried about her. But you know how she is. She insisted that there were things at the office that needed to be taken care of. She came home feeling lightheaded and sick to her stomach. I told her to go straight to bed.

"A couple of hours later, when she tried to get out of bed, she fell down on the floor and couldn't get up. I picked her up and carried her to the car and drove her to the emergency room. She didn't want to go, but I took her anyway. The ER doc checked her over. She was running a fever. He said her belly was swollen, but he couldn't tell us the reason why. He said we'd have to get the results of all the tests she'd had done. This afternoon, I took her to her doctor, and that's when he told us what's going on."

He glanced over at me. "Vickie, I've known for some time that she wasn't feeling well. She just wasn't herself. Over and over, I said to her, 'Ada, I think you need to see a doctor.' But she wouldn't have any part of it. She kept making excuses as to why she was run down and worn out. It took a lot of convincing to get her to do anything."

I knew he was blaming himself. "You did your best, Dad," I said. "You know how stubborn she can be."

He nodded. "Yup. But I should've pushed harder."

I pictured my mother running from one medical appointment to another, absent from her secretarial desk in the Bible and Religion department. All the while, I'd been carrying on with my life on the same college campus, caught up in my self-centered thinking, ignorant of the crisis in her life. "Why didn't you tell me what was going on?" I asked.

"We didn't want to upset anyone unnecessarily," my dad said. "Just in case it was something not too serious. Like a bad case of the flu. We both decided it was best to wait to tell you kids until we knew exactly what was going on."

We rode in silence the rest of the way home, joined in our shock and grief. As we pulled into the driveway, I asked, "How's Mom taking the news?"

My dad turned off the ignition and turned to face me. "She's pretty calm, actually. To tell you the truth, Vickie, I think your mother started giving up on life a while back. She acts like she's ready to go."

I sat glued to the car seat, not wanting to go into the house. I didn't have the courage to face the heart-wrenching sight I knew was waiting for me. But I forced myself to open the car door and get out.

"Your mom's in bed," my dad said as I followed him through the front door and into the living room. "I told her to stay there until I got back. I'm afraid that if she tries to walk around on her own, she's going to fall again."

The door to my parents' bedroom was cracked open a few inches. Taking a deep breath, I pushed it open and walked in. My mother was lying on the bed, fully clothed. The worn patchwork quilt my parents used as a bedspread was drawn over to partially cover her. She opened her eyes and smiled bleakly as I approached.

"Hi, Mom," I said softly. I sat down on the edge of the bed and took one of her hands in mine, caressing it gently. Her hand seemed tinier than ever, with large blue veins showing prominently through her translucent skin. Tears spilled from my eyes.

"It's okay, Victoria," she murmured.

"No, Mom," I said. "It's not okay. I don't want you to be sick like this."

She closed her eyes, as if she had no more strength for speaking. I noticed that lying in bed had pushed her bun to one side, pulling hard on the other side of her hair. It looked uncomfortable.

Gently, I lifted her head, pulling out the hairpins and unwinding the bun to release the tension. Then I reached for the hairbrush on her dresser top. She rolled her head to one side so I could brush out her hair. As I ran the brush through her long locks, I remembered all the years of her brushing my hair when I was a child.

My dad appeared in the bedroom doorway. "Let's get her undressed and under the covers," I said to him.

While I slipped off her black, low-heeled pumps, he went over to the dresser and pulled out a clean flannel nightgown. I helped her sit up, and supported her in that position while he peeled off her dress and slip. He unhooked her bra, but waited to remove it until he'd pulled her nightgown over her upper body. His concern for her modesty touched me.

Carefully, we worked together to straighten the nightgown and pull the covers over her. She fell asleep almost immediately.

"She's had a hard day," my dad told me as we stood beside her bed. "She's all tuckered out now. But she'll rally a little bit tomorrow."

I linked my arm through his, leaning my head against his shoulder. "I hope so."

"Every night when I climb into bed next to her," he said, "I take her in my arms and hold her. It's something I've always wanted to do, but she would never allow it. She always kept a wall around herself. But since she's been sick, she seems to welcome my comfort. I just want to hold her and hold her." His voice caught on a sob. "While I still can."

Silently, we walked out of the bedroom, down the hallway, and into the kitchen. A glance at the clock told me it was nearly 7:00 PM. "Have you had supper?" I asked him.

He shook his head. "I can't even think about eating anything right now." Wearily, he lowered himself into his chair at the head of the table. I filled a glass with water at the sink and brought it to him, then sat down to join him. I watched his anguished eyes roam around the kitchen, and my gaze followed his. My mother's domain, usually kept in pristine condition, was now in disarray. Dirty dishes filled the sink. An empty can of *Campbell's* tomato soup and an open pack of saltines stood on the stove next to a pot with dried soup spatters trailing down its sides. I imagined my mother rousing herself and coming into the kitchen, muttering about the mess, pushing up her sleeves as she prepared to restore cleanliness and order. But I knew I'd never again see her elbow-deep in sudsy dishwater, diligently scrubbing pots and wiping down her countertops.

"I've been trying to get her to eat a little something," my dad said, gesturing toward the pot on the stove. "But it seems like I'm losing that battle."

"Do the boys know about Mom?" I asked.

He took a sip of his water, then set his glass down. "I called Michael just before I came to get you. He'll be talking to Robert tonight. I imagine they'll both be coming out to see her in a week or so."

"How about Lucy?"

My dad winced. "I was thinking that maybe the two of us could tell her together. This is going to be awfully hard on her, and it might take both of us to keep her calm." He exhaled deeply, running a big hand over the top of his bald head. "But that's not something I can take on tonight. How about this weekend?"

"Sounds good," I said. Then I asked him a question that had been playing on my mind since the moment he'd told me about my mother's illness. "Dad, do you want me to drop out of school and move back home to help take care of Mom?"

"Oh, no, Vickie," he quickly replied. "I want you to keep carrying on as normal as you can. I've been thinking about how to handle the situation. I've got a lot of vacation days piled up at work. Three or four weeks' worth, I'd say. This would be the time to use them. And I'm sure some of the ladies at the church will help out."

He gestured toward my mother's car keys hanging on the hook by the telephone. "How about if you take her car back to the campus? She won't be driving it anymore. That way, you can come home anytime you need to."

I pictured my petite mother in the driver's seat of her green Chevy Nova, her tiny hands gripping the wheel, her face stern, her dark, vigilant eyes glued to the road. She'd never be behind the wheel of that car again.

"Yes," I whispered. "I'll do that."

"Matter of fact, you can drive it back this evening."

"No," I said. "I'll stay here tonight. I'll drive it back in the morning."

CHAPTER 19

When I left the house the next morning, my mother was still sleeping. My dad had taken the day off work. "Don't worry, Vickie," he said cheerfully. "I'll take good care of her."

As I drove back to the campus in my mother's old car, my insides felt numb and hollow. I'd borrowed that car countless times, for running errands and driving to work at the restaurant. But this time, I was behind the wheel for a different reason. I knew that, for all practical purposes, the car was now mine. And yet, I couldn't fathom the circumstances that had brought about this reality.

It was a beautiful autumn day, with bright blue skies, crisp air, and temperature in the fifties. The leaves were beginning to show tinges of red and gold, promising a season of glorious color. The perfection of the day stood in sharp contrast with the tragedy unfolding in my personal life. It amazed me that the world kept on turning, day following night, autumn following summer in perfect order, while my life was in the process of falling apart. It seemed as if the shattering was happening in slow motion, one piece breaking off at time and falling to the ground with a sickening thud.

0II knew all along my mother was sick, I told myself. *I saw the changes.* Yet, in my wildest imagination, I couldn't have paired her weakness and fatigue with this dreadful disease. With impending death.

It occurred to me that I hadn't yet obtained the specifics of her condition. My dad wasn't the best person for understanding and conveying such details. I'd have to get them from my mother herself, when I went home that weekend.

I tried to picture what my life was going to be like over the next months. Certainly, I'd go home to help my dad every weekend. I'd take advantage of any time I had left with my mother.

I sat through my morning classes, too dazed to take any coherent notes. As usual, Calvin met me for lunch. We hadn't spoken since I'd abruptly left the campus with my dad the previous evening. My boyfriend searched my face with questioning eyes. I responded with a flat, "My mother's sick. She has cancer." He slipped an awkward arm around my shoulders, for which I was grateful.

After my early afternoon class, I was walking back to my dorm room, head down, deep in thought, when it suddenly occurred to me that it was Wednesday. My day to visit my birth father.

Changing my course, I headed toward College Avenue. As I turned east toward the Greencroft complex, I thought about the fact that I could have shortened my trip by driving my mother's car. But the mile-long trek had become part of my weekly routine, and I wasn't ready to change another part of my life.

When I stepped into Reverend Hahn's apartment, the concern on his face told me that he'd instantly perceived my state of shock and grief. He waited in respectful silence while I removed my jacket and sat down on the sofa. Then he asked, "What is it, Victoria?"

"My mom's sick," I said.

The news caused his frail body to lurch, as if I'd hit him with words made of concrete. For a few moments, he steadied himself by breathing deeply, deliberately. Then he said, "I'm afraid to ask, but is it something serious?"

I nodded. "Cancer."

His face whitened with shock, and it took another few moments of deliberate breathing before he responded with, "I'm so sorry, Victoria. I'm so sorry." He hesitated before asking, "What kind of cancer?"

"I don't know all the facts yet," I replied. Then I recounted the story of my dad coming to get me at the college, and my mother's condition when I arrived home. "My dad isn't good at understanding details like that. I'll be going home this weekend. My mother will have to tell me herself."

"Is it something treatable?" Reverend Hahn asked.

Suddenly, I was the one who was having difficulty breathing. My chest and throat felt so tight that I could barely whisper. "I don't think so. She's going downhill very quickly. The way my dad was talking yesterday, I got the impression that she's dying."

Speaking those facts aloud dispelled some of my numbness, enabling the agonizing reality to sink a little deeper into my consciousness. Reverend Hahn appeared stunned. He reached a trembling hand into the pocket of his cardigan, pulling out a handkerchief to wipe the tear that trickled from one eye.

"I don't know what to do," I blurted out. "I thought maybe I should drop out this trimester and move back home to help with Mom's care. But my dad doesn't want me to do that. He said I should carry on as normally as possible."

Reverend Hahn nodded slowly, looking thoughtful. "I agree with your dad, Victoria. You're almost halfway through your trimester. It would be a shame to lose what you've already invested in your classes. Maybe there's a middle ground here. Maybe you can stick with your coursework, but drop everything else and devote the rest of your time to your mother."

I thought about my volleyball practice, and the chorale rehearsals I'd already attended. My birth father had been so proud of me when I'd told him about my extracurricular activities. But I knew that as the holiday season approached, chorale rehearsals and performances would take up more and more of my time.

As if reading my thoughts, Reverend Hahn said, "Perhaps you could postpone your involvement with volleyball and the chorale. Those activities might be more than you can handle at this point in time."

"Yes," I said, "you're probably right."

He dabbed at his eyes again. Then, with a long forefinger, he adjusted his glasses by pushing them a little higher on the bridge of his aquiline nose. "I'm so sorry that you have to go through this, Victoria. Right now, I feel so sad for you that I hardly know what to say. I wish I could spare you this pain, but I know that I can't. Just remember that I'm here for you. Any time you need to talk, I'll be here. And please keep me updated on your mother's condition."

He suddenly looked very tired, as if my tragic news had been too much for him to handle. An ironic thought struck me. *I always figured he'd be the first one to go. I've been preparing myself for that. But here he is, offering me support while another parent is dying.*

I went to his wheelchair and got down on my knees to give him a hug. "Let's pray together, Victoria," he said.

Obligingly, I closed my eyes. Then I felt his hand on the top of my head. As he prayed, I felt power streaming out of that hand, infusing my depleted body. "Oh Lord," he intoned, "my precious child is facing one of the most difficult trials of her young life. Only you can carry her through this time. I ask that you strengthen and comfort her, and provide the guidance she needs as she prepares to minister to her mother. And I pray that Ada will feel the comfort of your loving presence throughout the remainder of her days."

I lingered there at his side for a few minutes before standing up to leave. "I may not be able to come here every week," I said apologetically.

Reverend Hahn reached out to grasp my hand. "I understand that. I understand completely. Come see me when you can. If nothing else, give me a phone call."

CHAPTER 20

That evening, I called my dad from the phone in my dorm. He seemed to be in good spirits. "Your mother's feeling a little better today," he said. "She's up and sitting on the couch." He gave a similar report when I called the next evening.

After my last class on Friday, I packed a bag to go home for the weekend. I thought about things I could take along to leave there—pajamas, underwear, shampoo, and a toothbrush—as I knew I'd be spending many nights at home over the coming weeks.

When I arrived at the house, my mother was in bed. But when she heard me come in, she called for my dad to help her up. Holding onto his arm, she shuffled out to the sofa.

"I'm glad you're here, Vickie," my dad said. "You can keep your mom company while I run out to the barn to take care of the animals."

I was relieved to see that my mother looked bright-eyed and alert. *Maybe it's not that bad,* I thought. *Maybe she isn't dying after all.* "Tell me exactly what's going on, Mom," I said as I settled into my dad's armchair.

"I have ovarian cancer," she replied calmly. "Stage four. It has metastasized to other organs in my abdomen."

My heart sank as denial took wing and flew away. "Are you in pain?"

"Not too much," she said. "My back hurts sometimes. Mostly, I just feel uncomfortable and bloated." She laid a hand on her abdomen, which looked markedly distended in her emaciated frame. "I feel nauseated most of the time, and I don't have much of an appetite."

"Are you planning on any treatment?"

She shook her head. "The doctor talked with your dad and me about treatment options. He said chemotherapy might buy me a few more months of life. But at the same time, it would take a toll on me."

For a moment, she met my gaze. Then she looked down, fingering the buttons on her housecoat. "Victoria, I don't want to put my family through that kind of stress. And I don't want to put myself through the misery."

I couldn't bring myself to ask how much time she had left. Leaving things open-ended seemed more acceptable than facing a terrible finality. "Are you absolutely sure you don't want to try treatment?" I asked her.

"Yes, Victoria." Her dark eyes looked at me with a gentleness I'd never before seen in them. "Your dad and I have discussed this. Treatment would mean a lot of discomfort for me, along with endless trips to appointments. The thought of that exhausts me. I'd rather die in peace in my own home."

Don't say die! I screamed inwardly. *I can't hear you say that word yet!*

"I'm ready to go home, Victoria," she murmured. Then a shadow crossed her face. "If God will have me."

"Of course God will have you," I said. "But not yet. You're not going anywhere for a while, Mom. You're going to stay here with us for as long as you can."

Saturday morning, our neighbor Marilyn Hooley came to stay with Mom while my dad and I went to visit Lucy. For as far back as I could remember, Marilyn had been my mother's best friend. She was unable to hold back her tears as my dad updated her on my mother's condition. "Ada will probably sleep most of the time while we're gone," he told her. "If she wakes up, you can offer her a little bit of *Seven-Up* or some peppermint tea. Sometimes, she likes to munch on a few saltine crackers."

"Don't you worry, Herman," Marilyn said. "I'll take good care of her." She tiptoed to my parents' bedroom, peering through the open door to assure herself that her charge was sleeping comfortably.

Twenty minutes later, my dad and I pulled into the parking lot of Lucy's apartment complex. "I don't know how this will go," I fretted.

"That's why I'm glad we're doing this together," he said.

Lucy opened her door when we knocked, looking startled and tousle-haired. Then she glanced over her shoulder at the mess in her living quarters. "I didn't know you guys were coming."

"Lucy," my dad said, "we have something to tell you."

"What?" Lucy's eyes widened in alarm. "Did I do something wrong? Am I in trouble?"

"No," he said. "Let's sit down."

Lucy hurriedly straightened the covers on her daybed. Then she sat down, and I sat beside her. The only other seating option in the room was the folding chair she used at her makeshift kitchen table. My dad pulled it out, turning it to face us.

"Lucy, your mom is sick," he said.

Lucy searched his face suspiciously, as if trying to discern what he wasn't telling her. "What do you mean?"

Suddenly, my dad seemed to be at a loss for words, and I knew I needed to jump in. I scooted close to my sister and placed my arm around her shoulders. "Lucy, Mom has cancer."

Lucy threw her head back, emitting an ear-piercing wail. "No, no, no!" she screamed as she pounded the daybed with her fist.

I glanced at my dad. His heavy body had sagged, as if Lucy's reaction had drained the last ounce of energy from him. I scrambled to my knees on the daybed and wrapped both of my arms tightly around my sister's body. "Lucy! Stop!" I commanded. "You need to stop this!"

As her cries subsided, I gradually lowered my voice, until I was whispering in her ear. "Lucy, you need to be strong. I need you to be strong. Dad needs you to be strong.

It's going to take all of us pulling together to get through this. Dad and I need your help."

"I can't be strong," Lucy whimpered.

"Yes, you can," I said. "I'll help you be strong, and you'll help me be strong. We'll do it together."

Suddenly, Lucy seemed calm. Wiping her eyes on the sleeve of her shirt, she asked, "What am I supposed to do?"

"You'll need to come visit your mother," my dad said from across the room.

"She won't like that," Lucy protested. "She hates me. She won't want me there."

"It's different now, Lucy," I said. "Everything's different. I'll come get you tomorrow. You'll need to be ready."

When I arrived at my sister's apartment the following afternoon, I was dismayed to find her in the same soiled clothing she'd been wearing the day before. "I'm ready to go," she said brightly, attempting to smooth down her unruly red hair.

"No, you're not," I said. "Not looking like that. You need to go clean up."

Lucy opened her mouth to protest, then seemed to think better of it. I stood there quietly with my arms folded over my chest, letting her know I wasn't going to budge until she complied with my request. Grumbling, she headed off to the bathroom. Moments later, I heard the shower running.

I searched through the mess in her apartment for a suitable outfit for her to wear. Thankfully, I found a basket of freshly laundered and folded clothing beside the daybed. I figured one of her workers had taken her out to do laundry a few days earlier. Rummaging through the basket, I pulled out a pair of blue jeans and an unstained sweatshirt.

When Lucy emerged from the shower, she put on the clothing I handed her, but not without protest. "Why do I have to do all this? Mom knows how I look."

"It's different now," I said. "It's important that you try not to aggravate her anymore. You need to try very hard to respect her."

As she was bending down to tie her tennis shoes, she suddenly looked up at me and said, "Mom's dying, isn't she, Tori Grace?"

"Yes, Lucy. I think she is." I braced myself for another outburst, but none came.

On the drive back to Goshen, Lucy asked, "So what am I supposed to do when we get there?"

I blew my breath forcefully through my lips, thinking about how to choreograph an event that was bound to be fraught with tension. "Well, you'll need to speak quietly. Mom is very weak, and she can't stand a lot of commotion."

"Okay," Lucy said. "I'll try to keep my trap shut."

"It'll be okay to talk," I said. "But quietly."

"What am I supposed to say to her?"

"Ask her how she is. Tell her that you love her."

Lucy grimaced. "I don't know if I can do that."

"I'll be right there with you," I promised. "I'll help."

Fifteen minutes later, Lucy followed me into the house. My dad was sitting at the kitchen table eating a slice of the pie one of the church women had brought over. "Your mother's in bed," he told us. "She's resting, but I think she's awake."

I took Lucy's hand, and we tiptoed to the bedroom. The door was open a crack. "Mom?" I whispered as I opened it a little wider.

With difficulty, she rolled from her side onto her back and made a move to sit up. I rushed into the room to stop her. "That's okay, Mom," I said. With a pat on her shoulder, I urged her to lie down again. "You don't need to get up."

Lucy remained in the doorway, her face white with shock and fear. *God, please help Lucy stay calm,* I prayed silently. Then I said, "Mom, Lucy came to see you."

I beckoned to my sister, who took a few hesitant steps toward the bed. Putting my arm around Lucy's ample middle, I guided her forward. As Lucy gazed down at our mother, I watched her face soften, tears of sympathy pooling in her eyes. "Mom," she whispered.

And then something astonishing happened. My mother's eyes searched Lucy's face, and I saw something new register in them. She was looking at Lucy, not as a person she could barely tolerate, but as a beloved daughter. A smile crept over her face. With considerable effort, she pulled her hand from under the covers and extended it.

I nudged my sister, gently pushing her forward. Lucy took the fragile, bony hand in her plump one, tears spilling out of her blue eyes and flowing down her cheeks. Without my prompting, she whispered, "I love you, Mom."

"I love you, too, Lucy," my mother whispered back.

"I'm sorry," Lucy blurted out.

"So am I," my mother said.

Overcome with emotion, Lucy turned and rushed from the room. I placed my mother's arm back under the covers, kissed her forehead, and then joined Lucy in the living room.

"I need to go home, Tori Grace," she choked out between sobs.

"Okay," I said. "I'll take you."

I drove my weeping sister back to Elkhart, allowing her to cry until she regained her composure. "I've been so bad," she said when she could finally get the words out of her mouth. "I've been a terrible daughter."

"Lucy, that's all in the past," I said. "Today, you and Mom forgave each other. That was beautiful. The important thing is where you go from here."

Lucy nodded, sniffling.

We pulled into her parking lot, got out of the car, and went into her apartment. Emotionally exhausted, she flung herself across her daybed and buried her face in her pillow.

I sat down on the folding chair. "I need to talk to you for a minute, Lucy." She turned her face to look at me.

"This is going to be a rough time for all of us. For Mom, Dad, you and me. Even the boys. We've got to hang together. It's really, really important that you take care of yourself and try to keep yourself stable. You have to take your medication on time, every single day. If you get worried, call Dad or me. It's best to call the house in the evening. If you try to call me at my dorm, chances are I won't be there to answer."

Lucy nodded. "I understand."

"Every weekend, I'll come get you so you can visit with Mom for a few minutes. Okay?"

"Okay," she replied.

"Have you told your social workers about Mom being sick?"

"Not yet."

"You need to. They need to know important things like this. Maybe they'll look in on you more often."

She sat up on the daybed. "Okay, Tori Grace. I'll do that." When I hugged her goodbye, she kissed my cheek and said, "You're a good sister, Tori Grace."

CHAPTER 21

The next weeks flew by, the days passing so quickly that I could hardly keep track of time. I went home every weekend and several times during the week, to help my dad with my mother's care. Together, we'd ease her into the tub, helping her bathe, gently washing her long hair. Afterwards, I'd dry her hair with my blow-dryer. Then I'd fix it in a loose braid that would allow her to lie comfortably in bed.

We'd offer her food, hoping to stimulate her appetite. She'd smile gratefully, but could never tolerate more than a few bites. We'd bring her out to the sofa to watch a favorite television show. After ten or fifteen minutes, she'd become exhausted and would ask to return to bed. Sometimes, I'd take a kitchen chair into her room and sit by her bed, reading to her from the Bible. The sound of the familiar passages would lull her to sleep.

My dad cut his work hours by half, using up the vacation days he had accumulated. On the days when he went to work, one of the ladies from the church would come to stay with my mother. Marilyn Hooley came as often as she could, alternating with Irene Nussbaum, Carolyn Shank, Thelma Kauffman, and our pastor's wife Lydia Schrock. As my mother slept most of the day, her caretakers would pass the time by cleaning the house, doing laundry, and washing dishes. Other church women brought in meals: meatloaf, fried chicken, casseroles, macaroni and cheese. Our refrigerator was always overflowing with more food than my dad and I could possibly eat.

Church member John Nussbaum, who worked as an electrician, helped my dad install a phone line in the bedroom. This enabled my mother to take calls without getting out of bed. My brothers took turns calling her from Virginia, and she talked with at least one of them every day. I could tell how much it brightened her spirits to hear from her sons. They both promised to come see her soon.

One evening, my old friend Judy Prentiss and her mother Barbara arrived at the house, bringing a card and a small bouquet of flowers. The beleaguered Prentiss family had been on my dad's mail route for years, and had often been the recipient of his abundant kindness. Judy and Barbara filed quietly into my mother's bedroom, and I allowed them privacy while they visited her. I could hear their soft murmurs as they offered their love and support.

A few minutes later, they came out, teary-eyed. "I'm so sorry for what you're going through," Barbara said as she hugged my dad. "Good people like you and Ada don't deserve something like this."

As they headed toward the door, Barbara stopped and turned back to my dad, clutching his hand. "You've always been so kind to us, Herman. If there's anything we can do for you, please let us know."

"I will," my dad said, smiling at her.

Every weekend, I drove over to my sister's apartment and brought her home for a brief visit with our mother. Lucy could never tolerate a lengthy stay. But she no longer needed my prompting to maintain quiet, solicitous behavior in my mother's presence. Between visits, I fielded anxious calls from her, patiently answering questions I'd answered many times before.

"How long did the doctor say Mom has to live?" she'd ask.

"Not more than a few months, Lucy," I'd tell her. "We have to make the best of the time she has left."

Calvin and I saw little of each other during those weeks, other than meeting for lunch in the college cafeteria. "How's your mom doing?" he'd ask. I'd give him a brief account of any changes in her condition.

He and I had no further discussions about sex. Calvin seemed to understand that my family crisis took precedence over his sexual frustration, and I was deeply relieved that the subject was off the table for now.

I'd told my roommate about my mother's illness, explaining my frequent nights away from the dorm. She spread the word among the other girls on our floor, who asked me concerned questions and offered comforting hugs.

As my mother had been employed at the college, my professors all knew about her illness. They inquired about her on a regular basis, and kindly did not dock my grade on the occasion when I turned in a late assignment.

On an evening in early November, my dad and I sat at the kitchen table eating the tuna casserole our pastor's wife had dropped off for us. "Vickie," he said to me, his voice tentative, "I signed your mother up for hospice care today."

I set my fork down, feeling heavy-hearted. "What's that?" I asked, even though I knew full well what hospice care was all about.

He lowered his voice to make sure my mother couldn't hear from the bedroom. "It's something they do for dying patients. Nurses will be coming to the house to help take care of your mom. That way, when she gets really bad ..." His voice caught. "When she gets really bad off, she won't need to go to the hospital. She can stay right here at home where she's comfortable."

I pictured our quiet home bustling with strangers, and the idea repelled me. "Don't you think you and I can take care of her? We've done pretty well so far."

He shook his head. "She's going downhill so fast, Vickie. The two of us are getting in over our heads. Her doctor says this is the best thing to do, and I trust he knows what he's talking about."

Two days later, the first of the hospice workers arrived at the house. I came to understand the benefits of that service, as the ministrations of the nurses and aids took a great deal of strain off my dad and me. The nurses were able to answer our questions about my mother's condition. They explained the significance of the changes we were observing, letting us know what to expect next. When her skin took on a baffling yellow hue, they informed us that the cancer had spread to her liver.

One of the nurses told us that my mother could be kept more comfortable in a hospital bed, and she arranged to have one delivered to the house. But my mom refused to have it set up in the living room, as the nurse had suggested.

"I don't want to be out there on display," she protested.

So, my parents' bed was moved to one side of their room, and the hospital bed was squeezed in beside it. My dad wept when the new bed arrived.

"I've shared a bed with my wife for almost forty years," he told the nurse. "I can't stand the thought of not having her lying beside me."

He turned abruptly and walked out of the room, then out of the house to the barn. I stood at the back door, watching him fill the goat's drinking bucket with water from the pump. I was glad that he still had the comforting ritual of caring for his animals.

CHAPTER 22

A Wednesday afternoon in mid-November found me sitting on Reverend Hahn's sofa with a cup of tea I'd prepared in his kitchenette. I'd called him the previous evening, telling him I was coming. I hadn't seen him in a month, not since the day I'd told him about my mother's illness.

It felt good to relax and catch my breath in his quiet, perfectly ordered apartment, away from the chaos of visitors and hospice nurses coming and going in my parents' house. Away from the scene of cancer and death. But, of course, those topics were close at hand.

Reverend Hahn, wearing a striped dress shirt, black tie, and blue sweater, looked more dapper than I'd seen him in a while. His carefully combed silver hair was freshly trimmed. *He did all this for me,* I thought. *Since I'm dealing with my mom's decline, he wants to appear as vibrant and healthy as he possibly can.*

He looked at me intently, deep pools of compassion in his dark eyes. "Tell me how your mother is doing, Victoria."

I sighed heavily, running my finger around the rim of the fine china cup I was holding. "As good as can be expected, I guess. She's getting weaker every day. She's in a hospital bed now, and that's where she stays most of the time. Every once in a while, my dad carries her out to the living room so she can sit on the couch for a few minutes. But I don't think that's going to happen much longer."

"And how are her spirits?"

"She seems calm," I said. "She doesn't talk much, because it wears her out. So, I don't exactly know what's going on in her mind. I think she's accepted the fact that she's ...." I forced myself to speak the difficult words. "That she's dying."

Taking the last sip of my tea, I set my cup back in its saucer. I suddenly realized how exhausted I was.

Instinctively, I made a move to curl up on the sofa like I would have done at home. But I caught myself, hesitating to put my stockinged feet on Reverend Hahn's fine furniture.

As always, he assessed the situation with uncanny accuracy. "My child," he said, "you're worn out from all the strain you've been under." Wheeling his chair closer to me, he laid a hand on my knee. "Why don't you lie down for a bit? I'll sit here and read while you nap."

Ready to comply with his suggestion, I started to lie down. But then I thought of something else I wanted to say, something that had been troubling me for weeks. I sat up again.

"Mostly, Mom seems okay. But there are times where it seems as if she's brooding on something. And every now and then, she makes a comment that sounds like she doesn't think God will let her into Heaven. I always tell her that's not true, but it doesn't seem to make any difference. That makes me so sad."

Reverend Hahn's jaw dropped in dismay. Then he lowered his head, shaking it sorrowfully. I was certain he knew what my mother was brooding about, the transgression for which she had never forgiven herself.

The two of us sat together in a weighty silence, recognizing ourselves as key players in her painful drama. Him, the instigator of her wrongdoing. Me, the result of it.

"I just hate it," I burst out. "I can't stand to think she's worrying like that. She's a good person. I want her to be at peace."

Reverend Hahn turned his head, gazing out his patio window at the fluffy snowflakes settling on the shrubs in the courtyard garden. Then his somber words broke the stillness. "Victoria, ever since I learned of your mother's illness, something has been heavy on my heart. I've been praying about it, asking for guidance. And what you've just told me makes me realize what I need to do."

He turned back to me. "I'd like to visit your mother."

I stared at him, dumfounded.

"Maybe that seems strange to you," he said. "But your mother and I never made peace with each other after what happened between us in Mexico. It has weighed on my soul all these years. And I'm quite certain it has weighed on hers. I want to do anything I can to take that burden off her."

Stunned, I leaned back on the sofa, trying to take in the magnitude of Reverend Hahn's proposal. In previous conversations, he'd tried to convince me of his remorse over his wrongful behavior. But while I'd come to appreciate other aspects of his character, I'd never stopped thinking of him as the cad who'd failed to take responsibility for what he'd done to my mother.

I tried to imagine what it had been like for him to carry this unfinished business for two decades. And what it was like now to feel compelled to make amends at the last hour. I closed my eyes, searching inwardly for what I truly felt. His intention seemed noble, and I hoped it held the power to ease the distress of my dying mother.

My mom had never verbalized hatred for another person. Doing so would have violated the rigid standards she'd set for herself as a Christian woman. But in the past few years, I'd come to realize that simmering inside of her was a well of hatred for one specific person: the man who'd seduced her and then spurned her, leaving her to spend the rest of her life feeling like a fallen woman.

"What if my mom doesn't want to see you?" I ventured.

"Then I'll respect that." Reverend Hahn looked at me pointedly. "Victoria, would you ask her for me?"

"Okay," I whispered. Wearily, I laid my head on the arm of the sofa.

"Rest, now," he murmured as drowsiness overtook me.

As I drifted off to sleep, I heard the sound of his wheelchair leaving the room. Moments later, I heard him return. Then I felt the weight of a warm blanket being spread over my body.

After a quick dinner in the cafeteria that evening, I drove to my parents' house. "How did she do today?" I asked my dad as I walked through the front door."

"Pretty much the same as the last few days," he replied. "She had three different visitors this afternoon, but she slept through most of that time. I checked on her a minute ago, and she was starting to wake up. She asked if you were coming home, and I told her I thought you were. I was just getting ready to fix her a little bit of the soup Marilyn Hooley brought for her today."

I walked into my mother's room and found her with her eyes open. She smiled slightly when she saw me.

One of our kitchen chairs had become a permanent fixture beside my mother's bed, so that visitors could sit and talk with her for a few minutes. "Mom, I have a question for you," I said as I sat down. "There's someone who wants to come see you, and I need to find out if it's okay with you."

She mouthed the word, "Who?"

I held my breath, afraid to deliver news that was bound to upset her. "Reverend Hahn."

She looked startled. Then she closed her eyes and whispered, "Okay."

"Are you sure, Mom? Because if it's going to hurt you in any way, he won't come. He'll respect your wishes."

"It's okay," she repeated.

I smoothed the wisps of hair away from her sunken cheeks, then bent down and kissed her forehead before leaving the room. My dad was in the kitchen, heating Marilyn's soup on the stove. I spoke to him in hushed tones.

"I need to let you know what's happening, Dad. When I was talking to Reverend Hahn this afternoon ...."

My dad winced, but said nothing, so I continued. "When I was telling him about how Mom was doing, he said he wanted to come see her. What do you think about that?"

"Why does he want to do this?" he asked.

"I think he wants to make things right with her."

Slowly, my dad stirred the wooden spoon around and around in the pot of soup. After a few moments, he said, "That might be a good idea, Vickie. I think your Mom is working on letting go of all the burdens she's been carrying. It seems to me that's what a person would want to do when they face the end. Her past with Reverend Hahn has been a dark cloud that's hung over her all these years. If they can talk things out, then that's fine with me. Let him come over. I'm willing to do whatever I can to help her find peace."

Saturday afternoon, I drove over to Reverend Hahn's apartment. When I knocked on the door, his nurse Cynthia opened it. Reverend Hahn was waiting for me in his portable wheelchair, wearing a gray wool overcoat and a red scarf around his neck.

He smiled at me. "Ready?"

Cynthia wheeled him out of the building to my waiting car, and helped him transfer from the wheelchair to my passenger seat. Then she folded the wheelchair and placed it in the back seat.

When we pulled up at my parents' house, my dad walked out the front door and down the porch steps, ready to help. I saw that he'd fashioned a ramp from pieces of scrap lumber he'd found in the garage.

I got out of the car and lifted the wheelchair from the back seat. In a moment of panic, I tried to recall Cynthia's instructions on how to help Reverend Hahn transfer from the car seat to the wheelchair. But my dad was there, ready to assist.

"Put your arm around my shoulder," he said to the man who'd inflicted such pain and turmoil on his life. Using his robust strength, he situated the frail invalid in the wheelchair. Then he eased the chair up the makeshift ramp and through the front door.

I followed the two of them into the house. As I watched Reverend Hahn's eyes dart around our shabby living room,

I experienced a moment of embarrassment. But I pushed those feelings away, reminding myself of why he was there in our home.

"Let me make sure Mom is ready," I said. When I entered her bedroom, I saw that she was sleeping. I placed my hand on her shoulder and shook it gently. "Reverend Hahn is here," I said when she opened her eyes.

I took a minute to brush out her hair. Then I brought a damp washcloth from the bathroom to wipe her face, and gave her a few sips of water to moisten her dry mouth. I straightened her twisted nightgown and pulled the covers neatly around her.

"She's ready," I announced when I returned to the living room. As I wheeled Reverend Hahn into the bedroom, my stomach fluttered with nervousness. I moved aside the kitchen chair to make room for the wheelchair.

I had intended to leave the bedroom, to allow the two of them to have a private conversation. I made it as far as the doorway, but then I stopped, my feet refusing to go any farther. *I need to make sure Mom is okay,* I told myself, all the while knowing it was my curiosity, not my concern, that held me there.

"How are you, Ada?" Reverend Hahn's voice was tender.

A smile spread slowly across my mother's face. I was surprised that she'd let her guard down so quickly. It struck me that she no longer had the strength to keep her protective wall in place. She was allowing herself to take in the genuine regard her former lover was offering her. I suspected it was something she'd wanted years ago, but had never received.

"I won't stay long," he said. "I know you're tired."

I knew he was tired himself. I could tell the exertion of the trip had exhausted him, and that he was using every ounce of his will to hold himself with grace and dignity. But he would not let her know that. The moment was about her, and he was not going to burden her with his own hardship.

"There's something I want to say to you." Clumsily, he reached for her frail hand and held it in his own afflicted hand. His voice softened to a near whisper, and I strained to hear what he was saying.

"Ada, if you feel any remorse about what you and I have done, allow me to take that guilt off your soul. Allow me to take the responsibility." He cleared his throat with difficulty. "Because the responsibility was mine. Entirely mine. You were not to blame."

My mother lay perfectly still, her eyes closed, her breathing quiet.

"When you came to Mexico to work at the mission," he continued, "you came with a pure heart. You came to serve God. You never intended to be unfaithful to your marriage. You trusted my leadership, and I took advantage of that. I betrayed your trust."

His voice was thick with emotion. "Please, Ada. Let go of the guilt. Let me carry it."

A hush fell across the room. I could see the uncertainty in Reverend Hahn's eyes as he waited for a response. I held my breath, wondering where the moment would carry us.

Then came a faint whisper from the bed. "Thank you, Harry. Thank you."

Those whispered words seem to run through Reverend Hahn like a current of energy, and his body shuddered slightly. "Thank you, Ada," he said. "I owe you so much gratitude for taking good care of our daughter all these years. You've done a wonderful job." He glanced over at me and smiled. "She's grown into a remarkable young woman. I am so proud of her."

It felt so strange to see my biological parents together for the first time in my memory, engaging in such an intimate conversation. I stood there in the doorway, feeling like an intruder, yet an inextricable part of the scene.

"Come here, Victoria," Reverend Hahn said.

I walked over and sat down on the edge of my mother's

bed. My birth father held out his hand, and I took it. Then I reached for my mother's hand, connecting the three of us in a small circle. For a fleeting moment, we were a family joined in perfect harmony, as if we'd never been anything other than that.

Suddenly, my mother coughed. Reverend Hahn and I simultaneously released her hands. "I'll let you rest now, Ada," he said. He looked at me and nodded, signaling to me that it was time to go. I saw that tears had dampened the deep creases in his cheeks.

As I wheeled my birth father through the living room toward the front door, my dad looked up from his armchair. I wondered how much of the conversation in the bedroom he'd overheard. He looked sad and lost. I knew that, as always, he was doing what he thought to be right, in spite of the pain that it caused him.

He helped me get Reverend Hahn down the porch steps and back into the car. Before climbing into the driver's seat, I wrapped my arms around him. "Thanks for being so wonderful, Dad," I whispered in his ear.

"It's okay, Vickie," he said, patting my back with his big hand.

When I came downstairs the following morning, my dad was sitting at the kitchen table. He raised his face to greet me, and I saw joy shining in his eyes, joy that erased all signs of grief and weariness.

"Dad!" I exclaimed. "What is it?"

"I'm so happy." He choked back a sob. "And so thankful."

"Why?"

"Early this morning, I woke up to the sound of your mother singing *Nearer My God to Thee*. I don't think I'd ever heard her sing in her entire life, other than in church. I got out of bed and went over to her. 'Ada, what is it?' I asked her.

"And she said, 'Herman, I had a vision.' Then she told me about it."

"Wow," I breathed. "What did she see?"

He opened his mouth to speak, then hesitated. "I think I should let her tell you. I'm afraid I won't get it right."

I tiptoed to my mother's room. She was sleeping, her tiny, shrunken body barely making a mound under the bedcovers. Her skin was pale, translucent. In the moment, it seemed as if she was more spirit than flesh and blood.

She opened her eyes when she heard my footsteps, and smiled blissfully. "I had a vision, Victoria," she said, repeating her words to my dad.

I sat down on the chair beside her bed. "Tell me about it, Mom."

Suddenly, she seemed to have the strength to speak fluently. "Early this morning, I woke up. Around four o'clock or so. It was dark outside, but there was a white glow in the room. I knew it was the presence of God. Then I heard a voice singing. It was a tenor voice, so beautiful and pure. Like nothing you would ever hear on this earth."

"What was it singing?" I asked.

Her face lit up with joy. "The voice sang out the words, 'All of my transgressions have been pardoned.' And right at that moment, I felt everything lifting off me. I felt free, Victoria."

"Oh Mom!" I exclaimed. "That's wonderful!"

Slowly, she raised a hand, and I felt the brush of her dry fingers on my cheek. "I love you, Victoria," she said. "You've been such a blessing to me." Then the hand collapsed onto the bed.

I sat there holding that tiny hand for moments that stretched into timelessness, realizing that my mother had just taken the most important journey of her life. She had moved past the rigid rules and self-recrimination that had held her prisoner for so long, and had been carried into a realm of pure love.

I walked back into the kitchen, my body light and airy, my mind feeling as if it had been expanded into infinity. "You know what, Vickie?" my dad said. "This morning, for the first time since I can remember, your mom told me she loved me. A man can't ask for anything better than that. I'd count this as one of the best days of my life."

CHAPTER 23

My brothers came to visit my mother the day after Thanksgiving. They'd left Virginia after Thanksgiving dinner with their families, and had driven all night.

My mother was overjoyed to see them. Their presence seemed to energize her, and at first, I was afraid my brothers wouldn't understand how ill she really was. While they visited with her, I took the opportunity to leave the house for a while, to run a few errands.

By the time I came back home, my mother was worn out from visiting and was sleeping again. I fixed a pot of coffee for my brothers, who were bleary-eyed from their all-night drive, and served them slices of pie left over from the Thanksgiving dinner church members had brought for us.

It had been more than two years since I'd seen either of my brothers. While they ate, I studied their faces. Up to that point in my life, I'd only known my brothers from a distance, their personalities making vague impressions on my mind. Now, they had become crucial players in a family crisis, and I needed to know who they really were.

Both boys were now in their late thirties, fathers of children entering their teens. Both were losing their youthful appearance, and were taking on the attributes of middle age. Michael, the oldest, was slight of build like my mother, although he'd clearly put on weight since I'd last seen him. He'd lost much of his dark curly hair.

Robert, endowed with my dad's sturdier build, had a broad chest and ample belly. His full head of dark hair was streaked with gray.

While they discussed my mother's condition, her prognosis, and the hospice care she was receiving, Michael leaned forward, his dark eyes intense, bombarding my dad with pointed questions. Robert sat back in his chair listening, occasionally interjecting a thoughtful comment. All the while, I refilled coffee cups and collected dirty plates, feeling invisible to my brothers. Anything I attempted to add to the conversation seemed to fall upon deaf ears.

To my surprise, Michael informed my dad that he was taking a leave of absence from his employment as a middle-school teacher, and that he would be staying in our home for the remainder of Mom's life. Robert explained that he needed to fly back to Virginia on Monday morning, as he was unable to leave his electrical business unattended. However, he promised to return when Mom's end was near.

After they ate, Michael and Robert carried their luggage upstairs to Lucy's old bedroom. I'd been so distracted by my mom's care that I'd given little thought to preparing for my brothers' arrival. Fortunately, Mom had always kept Lucy's former bed made up with clean linens and blankets, ready for any overnight guest. As the boys trudged up the stairs, it occurred to me that they were the original occupants of those two bedrooms, and that their claim on that space was more authentic than mine had ever been.

The weekend flew by, and Robert was soon gone. For the next month, whenever I spent the night at home, I had the strange experience of sleeping in the room across the hallway from Michael, my much-older sibling who'd left our household when I was still a baby.

After a few days of having my brother in the house, I began to resent him. Edging me aside, Michael stepped up and took over as primary coordinator of our mother's care. Every time a hospice nurse came to the house, he'd corner her, engaging her in a long discussion about Mom's condition, demanding to know the rationale for the type of care the agency was providing. I could tell he was trying the nurses' patience. But I also sensed he felt the need to be a diligent advocate for his mother, to make up for the years of being absent from her life.

The more time I spent around Michael, the more I disliked him. Whatever I did or said didn't seem to count for anything in his mind. Several days after he arrived, I overheard him confronting my dad about not giving my mother enough to eat.

"Son," my dad mumbled, clearly hurt by Michael's accusation. "I try my best to give her whatever she'll take. She just doesn't have any interest in food."

Anger boiled inside me, and I couldn't refrain from jumping in to rescue my dad. Walking into the room, I said, "We've talked to the hospice nurses about Mom's nutrition. They told us not to force her to eat. They said that because her body is shutting down, making her eat puts a strain on her system and creates discomfort for her."

Michael shot me a dismissive glance, then muttered, "I'll have a talk with the nurse when she comes tomorrow." The following day, I smiled to myself when I overheard the nurse telling my brother exactly the same thing she'd told my dad and me a week earlier.

The second weekend Michael was at the house, the weather was unseasonably warm, with temperatures climbing into the low fifties. On Sunday, visitors from church came and went all afternoon. The house felt stuffy, permeated by the smell of grief and death. I went out to the porch to catch a breath of fresh air.

I sat on the swing, staring at the patches of bare ground exposed by the melting snow, watching the sparrows, cardinals, and blue jays pecking at the corn kernels and sunflower seeds my dad had scattered for them. Suddenly, the front door opened, and the alarmed birds fluttered away. I looked up and saw my brother stepping out onto the porch. Without a word, he sat down on the swing beside me.

His nearness made me nervous. Never in my life had I spent time alone with this stranger of a brother. I had no idea how to carry on a private conversation with him.

Glanced sideways at his profile, I noticed the well-formed features so like those of my mother. I saw pain etched in the lines of his face, something beyond mere grief. Something that looked like deep suffering.

"What's going on?" I asked him.

"Mom," he murmured, closing his eyes and shaking his head.

"Yeah," I said. "It's really hard to see her like this."

"She shouldn't have to suffer like this. She doesn't deserve it."

"I know."

Michael ran a hand through his thinning hair, staring out into the yard. "She asked me to forgive her." His words seemed like an eruption of pain from his soul, not intended for my ears.

But I decided to respond anyway, knowing that the next words I spoke would carry us into uncomfortable territory. "Forgive her for what?"

Michael responded without hesitation, not to me, but to some anonymous listener. "She thinks she drove me away. It's true that I was angry with her. But it was my decision to go. My choice to keep myself at a distance."

He turned slightly, as if my presence beside him on the swing suddenly meant something to him. "And, Victoria, that's ...."

The sound of Michael speaking my name startled me. I realized that I'd never before heard him address me in a personal manner.

"Victoria, that's a decision I deeply regret."

I nodded. He looked away, staring out into space again.

I felt my insides quivering as I contemplated the question I was about to ask him, a question that could break down the walls of silence that had separated family members for two decades. "Why did you go, Michael?"

He jumped as if I'd poked him, his head snapping around, his dark eyes searching my face. I could almost hear his thought: *How much does she know?*

I decided to help him out by yanking the lid off the can of worms. "You know," I said to him. "You've known all along that Dad isn't my real father."

His jaw dropped, and he stared at me, wide-eyed. Then he nodded slowly. "Yes. I knew from the beginning. I knew what she'd done, and I couldn't get over it. I coped by running. I ran as far away from home as I could. I blamed her. I thought of her with contempt. I couldn't see her as I see her now, a good woman who made a mistake."

He turned his body on the swing, angling to face me more fully, looking as if he was settling in for a long talk.

Victoria, I wish you could've known the mother I knew when I was a little boy. Those were wonderful years, the best years of my life. Back when it was just Mom, Dad, Robert, and me, life seemed perfect.

I don't remember life without Robert. He's just a year younger than me. He and I were the best of buddies, an inseparable pair, almost like twins. People even said we looked alike. We both knew that Mom loved us, and that she was proud of us. She lit up when we were around. She was happy back then. I remember her smile, her laughter.

My earliest memory is of a time when I was three years old. We were sitting in a pew at Westside Mennonite Church. Mom was holding Robert on her lap, and I was snuggled up next to her. She looked down at me and smiled, and I remember thinking that she was the most beautiful mother in the world. Then she put her arm around me and drew me closer. Life couldn't have been any better.

Mom included Robert and me in everything she did. When she washed dishes, we'd dry them. When she baked cookies, we'd have our fingers in the dough. When she was fixing supper, we'd set the table. When she hung laundry on the line, we'd hand her the clothespins. She taught us about the plants in her vegetable garden, and when she picked the green beans and strawberries, we'd be out there helping her.

I remember her sitting here on the front porch, watching us while we played in the yard. I remember her smiling when we showed off for her.

Robert and I slept in the upstairs bedrooms. Up to the point when Lucy was born, we each had our own room. Every evening at bedtime, Mom would read us stories. One evening, we'd be in Robert's room, and the next evening, we'd be in mine. Mom would sit on the bed, and Robert and I would snuggle up on either side of her.

She'd read to us out of a set of Bible story books. Earlier today, when I was looking at the bookshelves in the living room, I saw that those Bible story books are still there. I took one down and leafed through it. It brought back a lot of old memories.

We also had books of missionary stories, which Mom seemed to like even more than the Bible story books. After reading us a story, she'd talk with us about how courageous the missionaries were, and then she'd have us imagine what we would do if we were serving God in a faraway country like that.

She'd talk with us about what we wanted to be when we grew up. Usually, we'd tell her we wanted to be preachers or missionaries, as we knew that made her happy. She'd talk with us about growing up to be good Christian men. Looking back, it seems that some of those discussions should have been Dad's province. But I don't think Mom trusted him with that kind of thing.

Before we went to sleep, she'd have Robert and me kneel beside our beds, and she'd help us with our prayers. I knew that the evening ritual with her sons was the most important part of Mom's day.

When we started school, she was on top of everything Robert and I did. She was proud of the fact that we were good students. Over and over, she'd tell us that doing well in school was the first step toward a successful life. She'd supervise us while we did our homework, although neither of us had problems in that area. She wanted to make sure that everything we did was on target.

We did things with Dad, too. We helped him in the barn, taking care of the animals. But in most regards, we were Mom's sons. We knew our loyalty belonged to her.

Looking back, I can see that Robert and I filled an emptiness in her life. She derived little satisfaction from her relationship with Dad. She counted on her sons to bring meaning to her life. As a young child, that was fine, but as I grew older, her attention began to feel burdensome to me. I knew that if I wasn't who she wanted me to be, I'd be letting her down in a way that would devastate her.

By the time I reached my teens, I began feeling sorry for Dad. It was as if, for Mom, he barely existed. I thought he deserved more respect from her. Even though he was on the edge of family life, he worked hard to support all of us. That should've counted for something.

When I was eight, Lucy was born. That's when Mom started to change. I saw anger in her that I'd never seen before. I didn't know why.

I suspect now that Mom hadn't wanted another child. Or that she hadn't wanted a girl. And you know how difficult Lucy can be. Even back then, she was a handful. She was a cranky baby, and her constant crying got on everybody's nerves.

Mom would get to the end of her rope, and then Dad would take over with Lucy. He was better at calming her than Mom was.

I resented Lucy myself. Her arrival disrupted our perfect family life. But I also felt sorry for her. She got a pretty raw deal. I always knew Mom didn't love her daughter like she loved her sons.

Lucy didn't do well in school. She wasn't the quick learner Robert and I were, and she had problems getting along with the other children. Mom was always getting notes from her teachers. If she was in a bad mood, I'd know it was because of the latest thing Lucy had done. She yelled at Lucy constantly, but it never did any good.

Dad seemed to understand Lucy. He was gentle with her. It was good that he showed his daughter affection, because she got very little from Mom. I don't mean to speak disparagingly of Dad when I say that Lucy was more like him.

Toward the end of my junior year of high school, Mom made a surprising announcement. At the supper table one evening, she told us three kids that she was going to Mexico for the summer, to help with the Mennonite mission there. I'd never known a life without having Mom around to keep the household running. But after I got over my initial shock, I felt relieved at the idea of having her gone for a while. A teenage boy needs space from his mother, and I'd come to think of her as overbearing.

But I didn't understand why she wanted to go. So, one day I asked her.

It took her a little while to answer me. Finally, she said, "Michael, do you have any idea what it's like to long for something you don't think you can ever have? For more than twenty years, I've felt the Lord speaking to my heart, calling me to serve in the mission field. I've never had a way to answer that call. But now, I have the opportunity, and I'm going to take it."

She was strangely determined about going to Mexico, and I knew she wasn't going to let anyone talk her out of her plan. I remember walking out of the house thinking that she was being selfish. I thought she was putting herself ahead of her family.

But we did fine while she was gone. Robert and I were old enough to take care of ourselves. Dad looked after Lucy, and she behaved better with Mom out of the home. Dad didn't care about the rules the way Mom did, which was nice for a change. Even though the house was a mess and the laundry piled up, none of us minded.

I fully expected that when Mom came home at the end of the summer, she'd crack down on everyone and get the house back in order again. But when dad brought her home from the airport, I could tell right away that something was wrong. She was sad and distant, as if she was worried about something. She seemed indifferent to Robert and me. She paid no attention to Lucy, even when she was acting up. She barely spoke to any of us.

At first, Dad was excited to have her home, but then something changed in him, too. Every evening after supper, he'd sit in his chair, deep in thought, not talking to anyone.

Mom never told us that she was going to have another baby. She kept to herself so much that I didn't even notice she was pregnant until she was almost full term.

Robert and I picked up on it at about the same time. One evening when we were out in the barn doing the chores, he said to me, "Can you believe it? Mom's going to have another kid. I thought she was too old for that."

"I know," I said. "It's weird, isn't it?"

There was so much tension in the house during that time. Mom and Dad barely spoke to each other. I knew that something about Mom being in Mexico had changed the entire family.

I hated being home, living under that cloud of gloom. So, I went out with my friends every evening. Mom didn't seem to care, or even notice, if I stayed out late.

One evening when I came in, I was about to go upstairs when I heard Mom and Dad talking in their bedroom. I stopped to listen. And I overheard the conversation that would change my life.

Dad said, "Ada, I want you to know that I forgive you. I wish you'd accept that."

And Mom said, "How can I accept your forgiveness when I can't forgive myself?"

Then it hit me what the problem was. It hit me like a ton of bricks.

The next evening when we were out doing chores, I said to Robert, "That baby isn't Dad's."

Robert's face went white. He ran out of the barn, and I could hear him vomiting outside. When he came back in, he didn't argue with my idea. I suspected he'd already known the truth.

"What did she do?" he asked. "Have an affair with some guy down in Mexico?"

"That's what I'm thinking," I said.

Being teenage boys, Robert and I weren't inclined to talk about our feelings. We didn't discuss the matter after that. Not until after you were born.

When Lucy was born, she had blue eyes and curly red hair. We all knew she was the kid who was going to look like Dad. But when you came along, you had black hair, dark eyes, and a dark complexion. You didn't look like anyone in the family. It was like you came from somewhere else.

"Looks like Mom got herself knocked up by some Mexican man," Robert said to me. And I agreed with him.

Neither of us had any proof, of course. We couldn't go around telling everyone that the baby wasn't Dad's. But we knew what we knew.

I'm sure I can speak for Robert as well as myself when I say this: Mom's betrayal of us was beyond anything I'd ever experienced. I can't even put into words what that was like.

She'd so diligently taught her sons about morality and what it means to be a Christian. And then she'd done the worst thing a woman could possibly do, cheating on her husband and getting pregnant by another man.

I couldn't stand to look at Mom. I felt sick to my stomach every time she walked into the room. As soon as I was able, I ran as far away as I could. I went off to college in Virginia.

A year later, Robert joined me. He and I have made a life for ourselves in Virginia, separate from the rest of the family. I know now that it hurt Mom terribly when we pulled away like that.

Victoria, I'm not saying what we did was right. But Robert and I were kids when this all happened. Mom and Dad never talked to us about what was going on, and Robert and I had no idea how to bring the subject up. Back then, people didn't communicate about family problems. They tended to sweep things under the rug.

This whole business has left its mark on me. I've had difficulty trusting women. I've been unreasonably suspicious of my wife, which has taken its toll on our marriage. It got to the point where we either had to get help, or she was going to leave me. We ended up going to marriage counseling.

I hadn't told my wife about what Mom had done. I'd never told anyone. Robert and I had kept that secret between us. But during our marriage counseling, it all came out.

My wife was glad that I told her. She said she'd always sensed there was something from my childhood that I hadn't dealt with. She'd always known I was reluctant to go back home for visits.

She gave me some things to think about. "What if it wasn't your mom's fault?" she said. "What if someone took advantage of her?"

When I thought about that, I felt bad. I realized I'd wasted half of my life being angry with her.

Now, I wish I would've dealt with the problem head on. I wish I would've confronted Mom and Dad and demanded to know the truth. I wish I would've worked through it and not allowed one mistake to make me lose sight of everything good about Mom. But as the years went by, I felt less and less inclined to stir that old pot.

So, Victoria, you grew up as the little sister that I never learned to know. I hate to admit this, but I tried not to think about you. I put you out of my mind, because you were a reminder of what Mom had done. But seeing you sitting here as a young adult, I realize that treating you that way wasn't fair to you. No matter how you got here, you're still my sister, and you deserve to be treated like a sister.

I'd been sitting with my eyes downcast, listening intently to what Michael was saying. When he paused, I looked up and met his gaze. "Thanks," I said. "Thanks for telling me all this. It helps me make sense of things."

"Good." He glanced around the front yard, as if taking in all the reminders of his childhood. A car drove by on our county road. "Never was much traffic out here," he commented offhandedly. "This was a dirt road when Robert and I were growing up. We would've been safe playing ball in the street, but of course Mom would've never let us do that."

He stood up. "It's getting a little nippy out here. I'm going in to check on Mom."

Michael thinks this is the end of the story, I thought. *He believes my real father is some anonymous man down in Mexico, someone none of us will ever need to deal with. Case closed.*

"Michael," I said, ready to correct his misinformation.

He turned to look at me, his hand on the doorknob. "What?"

I hesitated. *No. Now isn't the time. Michael has made his peace with Mom. I don't want to complicate things for him. He doesn't need to contend with the messy reality of my biological father living nearby, and that fact that I am now involved with him. The rest of the story can wait.*

"Thanks," I said.

"No problem," he replied.

CHAPTER 24

Around the middle of December, my mother's condition declined markedly. Her breathing changed, becoming more labored. She stopped talking with us and slipped into an interminable sleep. From time to time, we'd moisten her parched lips or succeed in rousing her enough to take a sip of water through a straw.

As I stood at her bedside, watching her frail, emaciated body heaving pitifully with each breath, I knew she was existing in a world somewhere between life and death. She had left us, but was not yet gone.

On the morning after I finished my final exams, I moved back home for the three-week holiday break. Shortly after I walked into the house, one of the hospice nurses sat down with my dad, Michael, and me. "Ada is at a point where she could go at any time," she told us. "She won't last longer than another week. So you should plan accordingly." She gave us instructions about what to do when my mother passed, reminding us to call hospice immediately.

Then the nurse left. The rest of us sat in a heavy silence, trying to take in what we'd already known but had been afraid to acknowledge. My dad sat in his armchair, slumped forward with his elbows on his knees, staring at the floor. "We won't be celebrating Christmas this year," he said, his voice thick with unshed tears.

"Of course not," I murmured. "None of us have the heart for that."

"I'll call Robert," Michael said. "He'll want to get here as soon as possible."

"I'll talk to Lucy," I said. "I'll explain things to her."

My dad looked at me gratefully. "That would be good of you, Vickie. She won't take this very well, and I don't think I can ...."

"I know, Dad," I interrupted. "I'll take care of her."

That afternoon, I drove to Elkhart. Lucy answered my knock on her apartment door, looking sleepy-eyed and disheveled. Within seconds of seeing me, her face contorted into a mask of horror. "Oh no, Tori Grace! Something happened to Mom. She's dead, isn't she?"

"No, Lucy," I said. "She's still alive. But we need to talk."

We both sat down on her daybed. "It's going to be soon," I told her. "Probably in a few days. I just wanted to make sure you're ready for this."

"How do you know she's dying?"

"She's going through all the changes people go through when they're close to death," I explained. "Her body is shutting down. The hospice nurse told us this morning that she can't last more than a week."

"Maybe she's wrong."

"No, Lucy."

My sister stared at me, her round blue eyes large and frightened in her pale, freckled face.

"We have to accept this," I said. "There's nothing else we can do."

Lucy stood up abruptly. With considerable effort, she bent her plump body over, picking up a dirty shirt and stray sock and tossing them into the laundry basket beside the daybed. Then she picked up a dirty plate and fork and carried them to her kitchen counter. "I've got to get this place cleaned up," she mumbled.

The past few years, I'd heard Lucy make a hundred empty promises about cleaning up her apartment, and I'd long ago given up any attempt to motivate her. But I knew this time was different. She wanted to make one last effort to step up her game, for Mom's sake. One last effort to meet Mom's standards, before Mom was no longer there to set those standards.

"Good idea," I said as I stood up to join my sister at the kitchen sink. "I'll help you."

As I scrubbed a pot Lucy had used to heat up a can of spaghetti, I asked, "Do you want to be there at the house when Mom passes?"

Lucy grimaced, shaking her head vigorously. Then she stopped, and a thoughtful look crossed her face. "Yes. I need to be a grown-up about this, don't I, Tori Grace? Yes, I want to be there."

"We'll be there together," I reminded her.

On Sunday night, two days before Christmas, I made my bed on the living room sofa. Robert had arrived two days earlier, and was once again sharing the upstairs bedroom with Michael. That afternoon, I'd gone to Elkhart to pick up Lucy, and she was sleeping in my room.

I slept fitfully on the lumpy, broken-down sofa, sinking briefly into light sleep, then rising back to the surface of the fully awakened state, listening to the sound of the winter wind in the trees, the creaking of our old farmhouse, and my mother's labored breathing coming from the next room.

The night felt interminably long. It seemed as if my mother's slow descent into death had gone on for years, rather than weeks, and I didn't think I could live through another day of witnessing that heartrending journey. *Please, God,* I prayed. *Take her home with you. Soon.*

Around four o'clock in the morning, I felt a hand on my shoulder, and was instantly wide awake. I opened my eyes and saw my dad's stout body outlined in the darkness.

"She's gone, Vickie," he whispered. "She's gone."

I quickly sat up. My dad sat down beside me.

"I couldn't get to sleep tonight," he said. "Somehow, I knew this would be the last night I'd ever hear my wife draw a breath. I just lay there listening. Her breathing was kind of irregular. Sometimes, she'd stop breathing altogether, and I'd think, *this is it.* But then she'd start up again.

"I must have finally drifted off. When I woke up about ten minutes ago, I couldn't hear her breathing. I lay there two or three minutes, waiting for her to start up again, but she didn't. So I got up and went over to her bed. I touched her cheek. It was still warm, and I knew she hadn't been gone long."

He stood up, and I followed him into the bedroom. My mother's body lay still on the bed, her chest no longer heaving with her struggle to breathe. As my dad had done, I touched her cheek. It was now cold, devoid of her life. I bent down to kiss her forehead. "Goodbye, Mom," I whispered as I stroked her wispy hair away from her face.

"We're supposed to call hospice," I reminded my dad.

"I know," he replied. "But let's have a little family time first. Before all the commotion starts."

"Okay," I said. "I'll go get Lucy and the boys."

When I knocked on my brothers' bedroom door, Michael immediately called out, "What is it?" I knew he hadn't been sleeping. Like my dad and me, he'd been keeping vigil.

I cracked the bedroom door open, calling softly, "She's gone." When I heard the rustle of bedcovers and the sound of my brothers' feet shuffling on the floor, I moved across the hall to where my sister was sleeping.

I opened her bedroom door and walked to the side of the bed. Under the influence of her psychiatric medication, Lucy was the only one in the house who'd been sleeping deeply. I worried that I might have difficulty rousing her. Placing a hand on her shoulder, I shook it gently. She cracked one eye open, then closed it again, and I thought I might have a battle on my hands. But then she opened both eyes and struggled to sit up.

"What's wrong, Tori Grace?" she mumbled.

"Mom's gone," I whispered. "Let's go downstairs."

Minutes later, the five of us surrounded Mom's bed. The two boys stood at the foot of the bed, while Lucy stood between my dad and me along the side. The early morning was dark and quiet, the atmosphere hazy and other-worldly, the spirit of God almost palpable in the room.

In the stillness, my dad began to hum the last song he'd heard my mother sing when she'd had her middle-of-the-night epiphany several weeks earlier: *Nearer My God to Thee.* His voice faltered and wandered off-key.

Then I heard a soprano voice join him, as if to strengthen him and keep him on track. It was Lucy's. I was surprised that she knew the tune, as it had been many years since she'd set foot in a church. Her tone was sweet and clear, and I realized that, if she'd been so inclined, she would have fit right in with the tradition of sublime Mennonite singing.

I began humming the alto line of the hymn. Then Michael's voice found the tenor line, and Robert took up the bass.

CHAPTER 25

Soon, the intimacy of the family circle gave way to taking care of business. In prompt response to my dad's call, the hospice nurse came and officially pronounced my mother's death. Then the men from the mortuary arrived, and my mother's body was carried away to be prepared for her viewing and funeral.

Several hours later, a van from the medical supply company came to retrieve the hospital bed and other medical equipment we'd rented for my mother. My brothers helped my dad rearrange his room, putting his bed back into the position it had been in before the hospital bed entered the house.

All evidence of my mother's last journey was wiped away so quickly that I could hardly fathom the change in our lives.

That afternoon, our pastor, Reverend Delbert Schrock, came to our home to arrange the final details of my mother's funeral. He sat at the kitchen table with my dad, my brothers, Lucy, and me. "I always like to offer family members the opportunity to say a few words at the service," he said.

When his words were met with silence, he added, "If you'd like to." His kind eyes searched one face after another, as if wondering which of us would step forward to take on that responsibility.

"Not me," Lucy piped up.

"I'm not one to speak in front of a crowd," my dad said.

Reverend Schrock closed the notebook he'd been writing in, as if closing the door on the subject. "I don't want anyone to feel uncomfortable about doing this. You've gone through enough already." He glanced at my brothers one more time, offering them one last chance to step up.

They sat unmoving, their faces devoid of emotion. But I knew what was hiding behind those unreadable masks: shame and remorse. After having removed themselves from my mother's life two decades ago, neither of them felt worthy to eulogize her.

My dad broke the awkward silence that had descended over the room. "How about Vickie? She's good at making speeches."

My brothers' gazes shifted toward me, and I saw the surprise in their eyes. Reverend Schrock smiled at me and said, "Are you interested in doing this, Victoria?"

Me? I thought. *The child who was never supposed to be born? The child whose very existence caused the rift in this family? The sister my brothers have never been willing to acknowledge? I'm the one chosen to speak on my mother's behalf?*

But I knew that in the eyes of all the unsuspecting people who would attend my mother's funeral, I would be the logical choice to present her eulogy. My brothers had long ago moved away from the community, and had rarely returned to visit. Lucy had left the church as soon as she could wriggle out from under my mother's control. I was the only one of my mother's children who was still in touch with the life of Westside Mennonite Church, who was still known by members of the congregation.

"I'll do it," I said to Reverend Schrock.

Lucy gave a big sigh. "Well, that's all taken care of."

Three days later, my mother's viewing was held at the Yoder-Culp Funeral Home, located across the street from Goshen College. It seemed fitting that she should be memorialized near the place where she'd put in so many years of service.

My dad and I had talked with Lucy about what would happen at the viewing. The three of us had agreed that the long hours of standing by my mother's casket and greeting an endless stream of visitors might be too much for my sister's fragile nerves. "Why don't you plan on saving your energy for the funeral?" my dad suggested to her.

However, we did arrange for Lucy's caseworker to bring her to Yoder-Culp before visiting hours, so that she could view our mother's body prior to the funeral.

I held Lucy's hand while we stood together at the casket. Mom was wearing one of her plain dark dresses, a garment that had become too large on her as her body wasted away. Her small hands were folded primly over the coverlet. I had grown accustomed to the look of death that had overtaken her in the last weeks of her life. Now, the embalmer's expertly applied makeup made her look healthier than she'd been in months.

Lucy reached out and touched our mother's cheek with a plump forefinger. "She was kind of pretty, wasn't she?"

"Yes," I agreed. "Mom was very pretty. Even though she didn't try to fix herself up, she was still a beautiful woman."

"Yeah .... I remember how pretty she was when I was a little kid." Lucy looked wistful. "I always wished I could be like her."

The sorrow in my sister's eyes touched my heart. I knew that for the rest of her life, she'd carry the baggage of believing that she'd never been the pretty, smart, and capable daughter her mother had wanted her to be. No one would ever be able to relieve her of that burden.

After Lucy left with her caseworker, Michael, Robert, and I stood with my dad to receive the long line of people coming in to pay their respects.

It seemed that every member of Westside Mennonite Church came to the viewing. I received so many hugs that my body began to ache from being squeezed so often. Unsurprisingly, waves of faculty and staff from the college poured into the room, including some of my own professors. While most of the college students had gone home for the Christmas break, some of my friends who lived locally showed up to offer their support.

My communication with Calvin had dwindled during the last weeks of my mother's life. He'd had little to say when I provided him with updates, and it came to the point where I felt too exhausted to bother filling him in on what was happening.

However, he did show up at the funeral home halfway through visiting hours. He hovered around me for a few minutes, his hands in his pockets, shifting his weight from one foot to the other, an awkward Adonis ill-at-ease in his surroundings.

My dad recognized Calvin and thanked him for coming. I introduced him to my brothers as 'my friend Calvin,' and nothing further was said of our relationship.

Frankly, I was as uncomfortable having my boyfriend at the viewing as he was being there. When he mumbled that he had to get going, I hugged him and sent him on his way.

Soon after Calvin left, my boss from Taste of Home arrived, accompanied by members of his crew. Allen and Brad both managed to maintain their decorum while hugging me. With tears in her eyes, Edna wrapped me in a sympathetic embrace that told me she'd known her own share of life's sorrows.

Then my old friend Judy Prentiss came in, along with her mother Barbara. They followed a group of dark-suited college professors in the receiving line, and I could tell this made the two shabbily dressed women feel self-conscious. Yet, they offered their bountiful heart-felt support. "If there's anything I can do for you, Herman," Barbara said, "let me know."

Judy hugged me, murmuring in my ear, "If you ever need to talk, Victoria, you know where to find me."

As I watched Judy and Barbara leave the room, I realized how exhausted I was. I checked my watch, noting that visiting hours wouldn't be over for another thirty minutes. But then I saw a tall young man entering the room, and I felt a surge of excitement. It was my neighbor and former boyfriend, Daniel Hooley. His parents, Wendell and Marilyn, had come to pay their respects an hour earlier, and I'd been sad to see that their son hadn't come with them.

"Daniel!" I exclaimed as he walked toward me. "Thank you so much for coming." He responded by giving me a big hug. I nestled into his embrace for as long as I could without appearing inappropriate.

"We've been neighbors all our lives," he said as he held me. "I can't wrap my head around the idea that your mom is gone. I don't know how I'd ever deal with losing one of my parents."

"Thanks, Daniel," I said.

He released his embrace and stepped back. He seemed to have grown even taller since I'd last seen him. He'd also filled out a bit, which gave him a massive appearance. As I looked up into his eyes, I saw his sincerity, and realized once again what a nice guy he was.

Old pain wrenched my heart. If I'd been able to continue my relationship with Daniel, I would have had a loyal partner for life. We would have been like his parents, stable and prosperous, a salt-of-the-earth couple living our entire lives in Goshen. I never would have feared him betraying or abandoning me.

"Vickie," he said, using his old nickname for me, "when I heard about your mother's death, I felt so bad for you. Then I started thinking about us, and I knew I wanted to apologize to you."

His words caught me off guard. "Why? You haven't done anything wrong to me."

He glanced over at the sofa sitting along one wall of the room. "Want to talk? Just for a few minutes. I know I shouldn't keep you from the others."

I was glad for the chance to get off my feet, to escape from the never-ending stream of people who'd come to offer condolences. I glanced at my dad, who seemed to sense what was going on.

"Why don't you take a break, Vickie," he said.

I followed Daniel to the sofa, and we sat side-by-side, our shoulders barely touching. Old memories came rushing back to me. Sitting with Daniel in Sunday-School class, touching just enough to maintain contact, but not enough to create a scene. Sitting with him in the back seat of our high school choir bus, struggling to keep my hands off him so as not to risk the displeasure our choir director. In that moment, I wanted to reach over and take his hand, to intertwine my fingers through his as I'd done so many times before. But I didn't.

"When we were dating," Daniel said, "I was an immature jerk. I harassed you because I thought you were keeping secrets from me. Back then, I didn't realize that people in relationships have the right to some privacy. And because of my stupid behavior, I ruined things between us."

My mind reeled back to the fateful day when I learned of my true paternity. I remembered the shock, the sensation of my world spinning, turning inside out and upside down, and then falling to pieces. I recalled the effort it took to put my life back into a semblance of order, realizing that I had to go on living while hiding an enormous secret. A secret that I could divulge only to the right people, at the right time.

And those people did not include Daniel Hooley and his parents. Not that they weren't trustworthy. But I had never doubted that sparing our neighbors, my parents' closest friends, the sordid details of our family life was the right thing to do.

"You were just a kid, Daniel," I said. "We were both kids, and kids do stupid things. I wasn't very mature about the matter, either."

I held my breath, half-expecting him to question me again about the issue that had torn us apart three years earlier. But he didn't. I sensed he had put the matter to rest.

"The truth," he said after a few moments of silence, "is that it never would've been right for you to be tied down to my lifestyle." He glanced over at me, grinning. "Vickie, you aren't cut out to be a farmer's wife. You still have a lot of miles to travel in life—places to go and people to meet. While I'm looking to settle down in a year or two, you're just getting started. Someday, you'll be famous, and I'll tell people, 'I knew that girl.'"

I chuckled, shaking my head. "I sincerely doubt that."

He made a move to stand up, but didn't. "Just wanted to clear the air. I'd like to think that we're friends again."

"Of course," I said. "As far as I'm concerned, we're friends for life."

He smiled his fantastic smile, his deep blue eyes twinkling. I thought again what a handsome man he'd turned out to be, and how lucky some woman would be to have him as a husband. On impulse, I said, "Are you dating someone now?"

He looked sheepish. "Yes, I am. As a matter of fact, I'm thinking about proposing to her. Of course, we wouldn't get married until after I graduate."

His announcement triggered a surge of jealousy in me. I'd never stopped thinking about my old boyfriend, and from time to time, I'd have erotic dreams about him and me. Clearly, my subconscious mind had not caught up with the fact that Daniel Hooley and I were no longer a couple.

"Who is she?" I asked.

He winced, as if knowing his response would upset me. "Deanna Yordy. For the past few years, we've been seeing each other when I come home from school."

Deanna Yordy. My old high school nemesis. Although I was truly happy for Daniel, my insides growled with anger.

Deanna Yordy was among the minority of my class who hadn't gone on to college. Upon graduating from Conrad Grebel High, she'd started working at Mennonite Mutual Aid, the insurance company on the north side of Goshen. Apparently, she had no interest in leaving town, and would be all too happy to settle down on a farm with Daniel Hooley.

Suppressing my flood of childish emotions, I smiled and said, "I wish you all the best."

"And you?" he asked. "Are you with anyone?"

The image of Calvin popped into my mind, accompanied by a feeling of irritation. If, as my mother and my sister had suggested, I'd indeed chosen Calvin as a replacement for Daniel, he certainly hadn't filled Daniel's shoes.

"Sort of," I admitted. "But it isn't anything serious. I think I'm a long way off from being serious about anyone."

"Take your time," Daniel said, sounding fatherly. "Don't settle for anyone who isn't right for you."

"I'll always love you, Daniel," I blurted out. I immediately regretted my loss of control, and my face burned with embarrassment.

Daniel reached over and took my hand, intertwining his fingers with mine. I knew it was the last time we would ever indulge in such an intimate act. "You're my first love, Vickie," he said. "We'll always have that."

He released my hand, then stood up. "I need to get going."

"Thanks for coming," I said. Together, we walked back to the receiving line, where he shook hands with my dad and brothers and offered his condolences. I stood beside my mother's casket as I watched him leave, my heart aching from both old and recent losses.

CHAPTER 26

My brothers' wives and children drove out from Virginia on Friday, the day before the funeral, arriving late in the evening. Because there were too many of them to stay comfortably in our small home, Robert, along with his wife and two sons, went to spend the night in the home of a church member who had offered to host them. Michael, his wife, and their two daughters slept in our upstairs bedrooms, while I once again made my bed on the sofa.

Throughout the twenty-four hours they were with us, my brothers' wives and children huddled together, as if they were strangers among us. Michael's teenage daughters, Mallory and Laramie, were unyielding little blocks of ice who refused to warm to my friendly overtures. Thus, it felt awkward to encounter them in the house as we got ready for the funeral on Saturday morning, fixing our hair in the bathroom or helping ourselves to the fruit and coffee cake Marilyn Hooley had brought for our breakfast.

My nieces' behavior toward me was so stand-offish that it bordered on rudeness, almost as if they'd been poisoned against their extended family. I quickly realized that trying to win them over was pointless. It was Michael's job to address the problems that harboring resentment had created.

My mother's younger sister Myrtle drove from Ohio for the funeral, making the round trip in one day. My dad and I expected her to arrive at the house, but she didn't. When we first spotted her at the church, we greeted the tiny, nervous woman who looked so much like my mother, attempting to draw her into our family circle. But she seemed to prefer keeping to herself, dabbing at her tears in solitude.

During the service, Lucy sat between my dad and me in the front pew, with Michael and Robert sitting on the other side of me. My brothers' wives and children occupied the pew directly behind us. We tried to persuade Aunt Myrtle to join us, but she disappeared somewhere in the crowd in the back of the church. She went home immediately after the funeral, without taking part in the fellowship meal that followed.

As Reverend Schrock fumbled his way through the service, I had to bite the inside of my cheek to keep from smiling. In spite of the fact that Delbert Schrock was beloved by all his congregants, no one could give him accolades for his public speaking abilities. My mother had complained about his inept preaching for years. I wondered if she would forgive him for staying true to form at her funeral.

While I was indulging in this humorous reverie, I heard Reverend Schrock saying, "And now, Ada's daughter Victoria will share a few words with us."

Lucy nudged me. "It's your time, Tori Grace," she whispered. "Don't worry. You'll do okay."

I stood up. Carrying a copy of the speech on which I'd worked so diligently the past few days, I made my way to the podium. As I looked out over the sea of familiar faces, I saw that all their eyes were trained on me. They were waiting to hear what I had to say about the woman they'd all known and loved. At that moment, I desperately wanted to do my mother justice. I wanted to give the woman who felt so unworthy the honor she truly deserved. I opened my mouth and began my short speech.

Being the youngest in the family, I didn't have the privilege of knowing my mother as long as my father, my brothers, and my sister did. I count it as a misfortune to have shared only nineteen years of my life with her.

My mother was the most devout Christian I have ever known. She took her walk with God seriously, and it hurt her deeply when she thought she let Him down. In her mind, she was never good enough, and she was always striving to be better. When she made mistakes, she was hard on herself.

But in her last days, she came to realize that God loved her unconditionally, just as she was.

Sobs welled up inside me, choking out my words. I stopped speaking to calm myself. Then, deviating off script for a moment, I continued.

I am so thankful for that. It means the world to me to know that, in the end, my mother knew she was worthy of God's love.

I glanced at my dad. He was nodding in response to what I was saying, tears running down his face. Lucy's eyes were closed, her head resting on my dad's shoulder. My brothers were once again wearing their pain-concealing masks. I looked down at my paper and continued to read.

My mom was a wonderful role model for me. She taught me by example to face my responsibilities. No matter how tired she was, she always did what needed to be done. Even when she became so sick that she could hardly put one foot in front of the other, she was still cooking and cleaning and going to her job. She didn't want to let anyone down.

My mother was an intelligent woman. She loved to learn. In her fifties, she decided that it wasn't too late to start taking college classes. She wanted to expand her mind. I hope I take after her in that regard.

My mother had amazing courage. Even when life brought her devastating disappointment, she picked herself up and kept on going. She did the best she could in difficult circumstances. I will always admire her for that.

I set down my speech and looked out over the audience.

I don't need to say anything more. You all knew who Ada Hochstedler Unruh was. You all have your special memories of her. You loved her, and she loved you. She was my devoted mother. She was your loyal friend. And she lives on in all our hearts.

I made my way back to my seat, completely spent, my heart thumping, my legs feeling like rubber. In an unprecedented big-sisterly act, Lucy put her arm around my shoulders and drew me close. "You did good, baby girl," she whispered as she stroked my hair. "Mom would be proud of you."

CHAPTER 27

After my brothers and their families left for Virginia and Lucy was tucked back into her apartment in Elkhart, my dad and I found ourselves alone in a dreadfully quiet house. He had one more day off work before he needed to return to his mail delivery routine on Monday morning. I had another week before I was scheduled to start the second trimester of my sophomore year.

Around ten o'clock that night, we sat together in the living room, him in his ancient armchair, me on the sofa. He looked dazed, his tired eyes rimmed in red, his craggy face sagging heavily. "I guess it's all over then," he said.

"Yeah," I replied. "Everything seems surreal."

He nodded slowly. "I suppose that's a good way to put it, Vickie. Life's been turned upside down, and I don't know how to set it right again. I don't know what to do tonight or tomorrow or the day after that. Other than go back to work."

I chose that moment to venture a question that had been playing on my mind the last few weeks. "Dad, do you want me to drop out of school for a while? I could stay home and take care of things for you."

My offer seemed to jolt him back into focus. "Oh no, Vickie! I don't want you to stop your life. You're doing so well, and I want you to keep on going."

"I could live at home," I suggested. "I could stay here with you and commute to my classes."

He shook his head. "No, sweetheart, I'm afraid that rattling around this empty old house would just drag you down. Don't you be worrying about me. Knowing that you're carrying on with what you need to do will take a load off my mind."

"I'll come home on weekends," I promised him.

The week following my mom's funeral, I was so tired that I could hardly move. I slept at least ten hours a night and took naps in the afternoon. I knew there were chores around the house to take care of. Even though the women in our church had done what they could to help, once my mom had become too weak to perform her regular regimen of cleaning, the house had grown a layer of grunge.

I mustered the energy to clean the bathroom, mop the kitchen floor, and vacuum the living room carpet. When I went into my parents' bedroom to run the dust mop over the hardwood floor, it occurred to me that someone would have to go through Mom's things and decide what to do with them.

"Well, I can't do it now," I said aloud. I retreated from the room and closed the door behind me.

When I returned to school a week later, I felt like a wooden puppet, hollow in the center where my spirit should have been. Every morning, a feeble flame of motivation did battle with the lethargy that had taken over my life. It took every ounce of my will to get myself out of bed, down the hall to the shower, and across campus to my classes.

The girls in my dorm were kind to me, but when they asked how I was doing, I found little to say in response. I managed to meet Calvin for at least one meal a day. However, I skipped quite a few meals, opting to sleep rather than make the effort to go downstairs to the cafeteria.

The first weekend of the trimester, Calvin suggested that we go off campus to see a movie. I sensed he was looking for a way to heat up our physical intimacy again, but the thought of contending with the issue of sex was more than I could handle.

"I'm sorry," I said to him. "I'm not up for going out."

"Why not?" he asked.

His cluelessness infuriated me. *My mom just died, stupid,* I wanted to tell him. Instead, I said, "I'm dead tired. It feels like the life has been sucked out of me. Besides, I need to go home this weekend to check on my dad."

"No problem," he said. But his strained smile told me he was growing impatient with having his needs take second place to my family crisis.

On the Tuesday evening of my second week at school, I sat at my dorm room desk, trying in vain to read an assignment for my Women's Studies class. Suddenly, I remembered that four years earlier, my mother had taken the same class. Overcome with grief, I pushed my book aside and buried my face in my folded arms.

As I sat there engulfed in sadness, I recalled an evening at home when my mother had been reading an assignment for that class in her bedroom. She'd come out to get a drink of water, and in response to my dad's innocent inquiry about what she was studying, she'd blurted out a diatribe about the world's long history of mistreating women.

I knew that while my mother had begun to explore the concept of women's liberation, she hadn't succeeded in finding her own freedom. "She'd want more for me," I whispered to myself, desperately wishing I could discuss the course content with her.

Then I remembered how, during my freshman year, Reverend Hahn had been eager to discuss my class assignments with me. And I realized I hadn't seen my birth father in almost two months, not since the November day when I'd brought him to the house to visit my mother. I hadn't even thought to call him to inform him of her death. Overcome by the raw emotions surrounding my mother's last days, I'd simply forgotten about my birth father.

I pushed back my chair, forcing my wooden body to trudge down the hallway to the phone. When Reverend Hahn answered my call, I said, "I wondered if you'd like me to come over tomorrow."

"Of course, Victoria," he said. "I'd love to see you."

Then, embarrassed, I admitted my shortcoming. "You know my mom died, don't you? I'm so sorry I didn't call."

"I saw her obituary in *The Goshen News.*" His voice sounded calm and controlled, as if he was determined not to reveal hurt feelings. "I'd been watching for it."

When I entered Reverend Hahn's apartment the next afternoon, I was taken aback by the sight of a Christmas tree, the lights twinkling cheerily in the dimly lit room. The nativity scene and music boxes were set out on display. And under the tree lay an enormous gift wrapped in red paper.

The opulent holiday scene collided with my inner desolation, and rage exploded inside of me. *That son-of-a-bitch! One way or the other, he's going to make sure he celebrates Christmas with me. He doesn't care if I'm not in the mood. He doesn't care that I've just lost my mother. He just wants his way.*

I sat down on his sofa, forcing myself to breathe deeply and evenly, hoping that the fumes of my anger weren't escaping through my nostrils and ears. I desperately wanted to leave. But I also realized that I'd come to a point in my relationship with my birth father where I couldn't excuse myself for neglecting him.

"I knew you and your family weren't able to celebrate Christmas this year," Reverend Hahn said, reading my mind in his uncanny way. "With everything you've been through, I'm sure the holidays have been the farthest thing from your mind."

When I didn't respond, he looked apologetic. "Perhaps I should've let the matter slide. But I didn't want the season to pass without doing something special for my child."

I forced myself to nod.

"Are you hungry?" he asked. "Obviously, I can't offer you a holiday meal. But I do have cookies, and we could fix some hot chocolate."

"Maybe later." I hoped my voice didn't sound too snippy. "I'm not hungry right now. I don't have much of an appetite these days."

"Of course not." He searched my face, tenderness in his dark eyes. "How are you, Victoria? Tell me how you've been coping with your mother's death."

I slumped forward, hugging my body with my arms, rocking slightly. "I don't know what to say. I feel numb. I don't feel like doing anything." I raised my head to look at him. "I feel like I'm dead myself."

"I understand," he said. "That's how we feel when we lose someone close to us." He reached out a trembling hand to pat my knee, then pulled back, as if sensing that my sorrow kept me insulated from any deeper connection with him. "It will take time before you feel like your old self again. But someday, you will."

"I hope so," I whispered.

"I know you're not up for much of a visit," he said. "Don't worry about talking. Don't think you need to please me. Be any way you need to be."

Relieved by knowing he expected nothing from me, I huddled in the corner of the sofa, drawing into myself, my birth father in his wheelchair a hazy figure on the edge of my awareness.

I hadn't noticed the white taper candle on the coffee table until Reverend Hahn picked up the box of matches sitting next to it. With awkward hands, he made multiple attempts to strike a match before it finally burst into flame.

"This is for your mother," he said softly as he touched the match to the candle wick. "I feel the need to memorialize her in some way. As you know, I didn't attend the funeral. The last thing I wanted to do was to cause your family any further distress."

While I knew he was speaking sincerely, I also knew there was another reason he hadn't attended my mom's funeral. I'd been well aware of the fact that his outing to visit with her had been almost more than he could physically handle. I couldn't imagine him leaving his apartment for much of anything these days. In the dim recesses of my mind, it occurred to me that I could lose two parents in quick succession. *Not yet,* I beseeched God. *Wait a little while. I can't go through another death right now.*

"When I saw your mother's obituary," Reverend Hahn said, "I felt sad for you. But I also felt sad about Ada passing from my life. That surprised me, actually. I was forced to search my mind, to ask myself what she'd meant to me.

"I know I told you some time ago that my relationship with your mother never progressed to the point where we developed strong feelings for each other. But after her death, I realized that, if circumstances had been different, I could have grown to love her deeply."

His words astonished me, rousing me to full awareness. I sat up straight, listening intently as he continued.

"Not only was I attracted by your mother's physical beauty, I enjoyed her keen intelligence. When Ada was young, women were expected be little more than wives and mothers. But something in her drove her to seek more than that. She wanted to expand her mind. She wanted to learn, to grow, to explore. I picked up on that very quickly when we were together in Mexico. I suspect that all her life, your mother was frustrated by the fact that she had no outlet for expressing who she really was.

"Had circumstances been different, Victoria, your mother would have been the ideal life partner for me." He shook his head sadly. "But life never provides us with perfect circumstances."

I stared at the flickering candle flame, allowing his validation of my mother to sink deep into my heart. For the rest of my life, I would hold that validation close to me, carrying it for her. I hoped that, somehow, Reverend Hahn's words had reached her. Tears streamed from my eyes, and I took a tissue from the box on the end table beside me.

"But at least she gave me you," Reverend Hahn said. "It pleases me that you are so much like her." He gestured toward the candle. "Here's to Ada. May she have every opportunity in Heaven to be the brilliant spirit she was meant to be. May she shine like she never had the opportunity to shine here on earth."

After the impromptu memorial for my mother, I felt ready for a belated Christmas celebration. I ate my fill of fancy cookies and delectable chocolates, and then opened my gift. It was a set of expensive luggage, the smaller pieces stored inside the larger ones like nesting dolls. Unsurprisingly, I found a stash of one-hundred-dollar bills inside the smallest piece of luggage.

When I thanked Reverend Hahn profusely for his extravagant gift, he said, "My child, you are going places in life. I want you to be prepared."

Shamefacedly, I said, "I brought nothing for you."

"Having you here," he replied, "is the greatest gift I could ever have."

CHAPTER 28

On a Thursday morning in early February, my English professor handed back a paper I'd written a week earlier. I had fumbled my way through the assignment, feeling as if I was working with only a fraction of my brain. So, seeing a big red A on the top of the front page surprised me. As I read through my professor's comments, I felt my old confidence flowing back into me. For the first time in four months, it seemed possible that I could find myself again.

I need to do something normal, I told myself. *Like a normal nineteen-year-old. It's been so long since I've seen a movie, or gone out for pizza, or watched a ballgame.*

It occurred to me that since I'd started dating Calvin, I hadn't seen him play in a single basketball game. My mother had gotten sick before the season started. Although Calvin had asked me several times to come to his games, family obligations had always taken precedence.

I'm going to surprise him, I thought. I smiled to myself, picturing his eyes light up at the sight of his girlfriend in the stands. As I waited to meet him for lunch in the cafeteria, I checked the schedule of basketball games posted in the lobby. There was a home game that night, and I resolved to be there at the gym in the Union Building to watch it.

The game was a close one, thrilling to watch, and getting pumped up and excited made me feel alive. Calvin played almost the entire game. As I watched his magnificent body moving powerfully up and down the court, I became increasingly enthralled.

I was sitting in the stands next to a girl I didn't know. "Calvin Zook sure is a good-looking guy," she commented after he made a half-court shot that had all the screaming fans on their feet.

"Well, I think so," I replied. Then I proudly added, "He's my boyfriend."

The girl stared at me in awe, as if my dating a demigod had elevated me to the status of goddess in her eyes.

I turned my attention back to the court, watching Calvin through a filter of magic and enchantment. I felt tingly and stirred-up inside. *I'm going to start being a real girlfriend to you,* I promised him in my mind. *I think I'm ready to have sex with you again. We'll finally be a real couple.*

The buzzer announced the end of the game. Goshen had won by two points, and the crowd was on their feet, cheering wildly. As the players trotted off to the locker room, I waved frantically at Calvin, trying to get his attention. But he still hadn't noticed that I was there. "Calvin!" I called out.

Then, like an echo of my own voice, a female voice above me in the stands yelled, "Calvin!" I watched his face light up, his eyes traveling past me and up toward the object of his interest. I turned around to see who it was. And there was Bonnie Springer, bouncing up and down in excitement, beaming at my boyfriend. "Hey, handsome," she called, blowing him a kiss.

I swung my gaze back toward Calvin. As if in slow motion, my horrified mind captured every detail of what happened next. I watched a smile spread across Calvin's flushed, sweaty face. I watched his open hand rise into the air, then close as he pretended to catch the kiss. Then he mouthed the words, "See you later." And I suddenly knew that while I'd been distant and unavailable to my boyfriend, he'd gotten what he wanted from someone else. I knew full well that this had been going on for quite some time.

As Calvin turned to head off to the locker room with his teammates, he suddenly saw me. For a few seconds, he looked stunned, his mouth dropped open in an ungainly expression that distorted the lines of his handsome face.

While the rest of the crowd filed noisily out of the gymnasium, I remained glued to my seat, too stunned to move. The minutes passed. Finally, a kindly custodian approached to tell me that I needed to leave, as he was ready to turn off the lights.

Feeling numb, I got up and walked out of the gym. Just as I passed the entrance to the locker room, Calvin came out, his hair wet from the shower. I imagined him scrubbing the sweat from his body in preparation for his late-night rendezvous with Bonnie Springer.

We stood mutely staring at each other. "How long?" I finally asked him.

"What do you mean?" he said, feigning innocence.

"How long have you been sleeping with Bonnie Springer?"

He hung his head. After a few moments, he raised his eyes. They flashed with accusing anger. "Well, you didn't want anything to do with me."

"Calvin!" I hissed. "My mother just died! You know I've been through a rough time."

"I know," he said. "That's why I decided to wait to break up with you. I didn't want to be an ass."

"You are an ass!" I could feel sobs welling up inside me, but I pushed them down, as I didn't want to give Calvin the satisfaction of knowing how badly he'd hurt me. As I ran out of the building, I turned and yelled over my shoulder, "Go screw your new girlfriend! She's waiting for you."

I stumbled blindly across the campus, my flimsy tennis shoes encountering patches of slushy snow on the sidewalks. Within minutes, my feet were soaked and cold. I balled my gloveless hands into angry fists, trying to keep them warm. When I'd gotten ready for the basketball game earlier that evening, I hadn't bothered to don much winter protection for the short trek between my dorm and the Union Building.

I had no idea what to do, or where I was going. Suddenly, I found myself crossing College Avenue and heading down Eighth Street. I could hear a faint echo of my mother's stern voice in my head, scolding me for behaving like a foolish child. But I didn't care.

When I reached the intersection of Eighth and Reynolds Streets, I turned left and cut over to Seventh Street, where I continued to walk north, away from the campus. Away from the school where selfish boys betrayed their unsuspecting girlfriends. I wondered how many of my friends had known about Calvin's cheating, but had been afraid to tell me.

For almost an hour, I wandered in the dark like a mad woman, up and down Sixth, Seventh, Eighth, and Ninth Streets. I had no tissues with me, so I wiped my weeping eyes and runny nose on the sleeve of my jacket. The moisture froze, stiffening my sleeve.

The bleak winter night felt so much like the May evening almost three years earlier, when, after learning the secret my family had hidden from me, I ran out of the house, stole my sister's bicycle, and rode around the county roads on the west side of Goshen. I'd ended up spending the night on a picnic table in Shanklin Park. It seemed as if no time had passed between the two nights, except for the fact that my mother's death was somehow sandwiched between them. All three events melded together, rendering me a bereft soul in a permanent state of emptiness and confusion, destined for a life of hopeless wandering.

"Why?" I whimpered again and again. "Why does all this happen to me? What have I done to deserve this?"

Finally, the intensity of my emotion began to subside. My agitation gave way to exhaustion, and my walking slowed to a shuffle. As my legs were on the verge of giving out, I leaned against a sturdy maple tree for support, shivering in the frigid night air. *Enough of this nonsense, Victoria,* my mother's voice scolded me. *Go back to your dorm and go to bed. You can figure this out in the morning.*

I looked around, trying to get my bearings. The nearby streetlight illuminated signs that told me I was at the intersection of Ninth and Pearl Streets. Wiping my nose on my frozen sleeve, I headed south on Ninth Street, back toward the college.

My roommate woke up when I walked into our dorm room. "Where have you been, Victoria?" she asked. "I thought you went home for the night."

Her inquiring words told me what I needed to do. "I'm going home right now," I said. Grabbing my car keys from my desk, I headed back out into the cold, crossing the campus toward the student parking lot where my mother's faithful old car awaited me.

Ten minutes later, I opened the front door of the farmhouse. Despite my efforts to be quiet, my dad heard me enter. "Who's there?" he called from his bedroom. "Is that you, Vickie?"

A moment later, he came padding out into the living room in rumpled, mismatched pajamas, the curly fringe of hair around his bald head matted and askew. I noticed how long it had gotten. My mother was not there to remind him that he needed a haircut, and he didn't think of those things on his own.

He held out his arms, as if knowing why I'd come home at that late hour of the night. "You're so cold, Vickie," he said as I nestled up against his massive chest. And with his strong arms around me, we cried together.

He smelled sweaty, and I wondered how many days had passed since he'd taken a shower. I knew that, despite his insistence that he'd be okay, he still needed me to stick close to him.

The next day at noon, I walked into the cafeteria, hoping I wouldn't have to deal with the awkwardness of running into Calvin. Thankfully, my former boyfriend was nowhere in sight.

I looked around for a group of friends I could join. And then I spotted Charlie Hess and Stephen Wenger at their usual table in the corner of the room, deep in conversation, exercising the muscles of their genius intellects. On impulse, I headed in their direction.

As I set my tray on the table, both boys stared up at me in surprise. Then they glanced around, as if expecting Calvin to join me.

"Well, hello there, Miss Unruh," Stephen said. "It's nice to see you again. Are you on your own today?"

I nodded, willing myself not to cry.

"Have a seat," Charlie said.

I sat down, fumbling with my napkin and silverware, avoiding the questioning gazes across the table from me. After an awkward silence, Stephen cleared his throat and said, "So ... did you dump the hunk?"

I shook my head. "No. He dumped me."

The two guys exchanged puzzled looks, as if wondering how that could be. Then Stephen turned to me. "My buddy and I knew you'd eventually come back to us."

"How did you know that?" I asked.

He took a bite of his sandwich, chewing slowly, smacking his lips in his usual irritating manner. Then his eyes twinkled wickedly as he spoke in a furtive voice. "Mr. Zook might be a pretty boy, but the man is dim-witted."

For the first time since the day I'd learned of my mother's terminal illness, I laughed. Not a chuckle or giggle. I joined my old friends in a hearty guffaw.

"So what else is new with you, Miss Unruh?" Stephen said after we'd all settled down.

I exhaled deeply. "A lot is new. My mother died."

I watched the humor on Charlie and Stephen's faces transmute into compassion and concern. After a few moments of stunned silence, Charlie asked, "When did this happen?"

"Two days before Christmas," I replied.

He reached across the table and took my hand. The warmth of his touch triggered the tears I'd been warding off.

"Victoria," he said, "you're a remarkable woman to keep carrying on in the face of all this."

And so, for the rest of that school year, I found a lunchtime home in the corner of the cafeteria with my old friends. Their sharp wits and intellectual discourses kept me entertained, their welcoming presence making me feel secure. I found warmth and safety in the company of Charlie Hess and Stephen Wenger for the next two months, until they both graduated in the spring.

PART III: SUMMER 1980-SPRING 1981

CHAPTER 29

Although I could have returned to my job at the restaurant the summer after my sophomore year of college, I decided not to. I was quite sure Calvin would be there. He'd maintained his employment at Taste of Home throughout the school year, picking up three or four shifts a week. The last thing I wanted was to deal with the inevitable tension that would simmer between us and spill over onto our relationships with coworkers.

However, I had a more compelling reason for taking time off that summer. I wanted to be at home with my dad, just the two of us. I needed time to come to terms with the fact that Mom was no longer with us, and to find a rhythm of life without her. I needed to make sure my dad was taking care of himself. For at least a few months, I wanted to provide him with companionship and a well-kept home.

When I told Reverend Hahn that I planned to take the summer off, he readily agreed with the idea.

"I feel a little guilty," I said. "I should be earning money for school."

"Don't worry about it," he replied. "Take all the time you need to get back on your feet. I'd like to see you fully rested when you go back to school in the fall. Your freshman year, you had to contend with the problems of adjustment. Your sophomore year, you had to deal with your mother's illness and death. I want your junior year to be different. I want you to enjoy everything about college life that you couldn't these past two years."

So, at the end of the spring trimester, I packed up the things in my dorm room and moved back home, ready to take on my self-assigned domestic role. The next morning, after my dad had left for work, I sat at the table eating a bowl of cereal, trying to work out a strategy for getting the house back into some semblance of cleanliness and order.

I'd come to realize that my dad possessed few housekeeping skills. The most he'd done since his wife's death was to run the vacuum cleaner over the middle of the living room floor and sweep up the crumbs under the kitchen table. When I'd come home from school on weekends, I'd had little time to do anything more than throw in a few loads of laundry and wash the dishes that had piled up in the sink.

I could almost feel my mother sitting across from me in her usual spot at the table, her hands wrapped around her mug of coffee, her eyes lowered as she contemplated her duties for the day. She had always maintained a routine, an efficient system for checking off every item on her mental list of things to do. No one had ever criticized Ada Unruh for shirking her responsibilities.

"Where should I start, Mom?" I whispered.

In the kitchen, I could almost hear her say. *That's the hardest job. If you can get the kitchen in order, then the rest of the house will be easier.*

Sighing, I got up, carried my bowl to the sink, and then set about washing all the dishes my dad had neglected the previous week. I scrubbed layers of grease and grime off the table, the countertops, and the stove.

The more I worked, the more energized I felt. Completing one task led me to the next thing I needed to do. I turned to the refrigerator, pulling out containers of moldy leftovers, some of which had undoubtedly been there since the day of my mother's funeral. "Oh, my God, Dad!" I scolded. "You need to clean up your act. Mom would be all over your case for this."

By early afternoon, I was ready to tackle the cupboards. But when I started pulling things out, I realized the job was going to be more difficult than I'd anticipated. My dad had apparently stuffed everything into the cupboards that he didn't know what to do with.

I pulled out an empty, unwashed pickle jar that smelled of brine, along with several containers from the deli caked with remnants of dried food. Two empty cereal boxes had been returned to the cupboard instead of being tossed into the trash. When I tried to lift out a box of old donuts, I found it was glued to the shelf by a sugary smear.

Disgusted, I pulled the overflowing trash can from under the kitchen sink, replaced the bag, and then began filling it with everything in the cupboards that needed to be thrown out. Then I scrubbed down all the shelves and put the dishes back in order: coffee mugs with handles all pointed in the same direction; flowered plates and blue-rimmed plates sorted into separate stacks; drinking glasses lined up in perfect rows. All the while, I felt smug, telling myself that if my mother knew what I was doing, she'd be pleased with my efforts.

In the corner of one cupboard, I found seed packets for lettuce and radishes. The tops had been carefully cut open, then folded down and taped into place. "Mom," I said aloud. "Did you save these from last summer? You were going to plant them this year, weren't you?" I laid the packets on the table, then turned back to my project.

While I was working on the last cupboard, I heard heavy footsteps on the porch. I realized I'd lost track of time, and that it was already late afternoon. A moment later, my dad walked into the kitchen. He stopped short when he saw the pots and pans spread out on the table.

"What on earth are you doing, Vickie?" His voice sounded sharp.

"Cleaning." I wagged a finger at him. "You let things get out of hand." Holding up a cereal box, I said, "This doesn't belong in the cupboard with the dishes. Food goes in the pantry."

My dad contorted his face into a childish pout. "You know we'll never be able to keep up with things the way your mother did."

Yes, we can, I thought stubbornly. *We're not going to dishonor her memory by allowing her home to go downhill.*

I picked up the seed packets. "Can we plant these, Dad?"

"I suppose so," he sighed.

"We could get some tomato plants. And maybe some squash and cucumber seeds."

"If you think that's what you need to do, Vickie, then you go right ahead."

The next day, I attacked the bathroom, scrubbing the floor and the grimy fixtures with my mother's trusty solution of bleach and water.

In the living room, I threw out stacks of old newspapers that had accumulated on the sofa, the coffee table, and the top of the television set. I picked up the drinking glasses sitting on the floor next to my dad's chair and carried them to the kitchen. Then I hauled out my mother's ancient vacuum cleaner and tackled the carpet, moving the sofa and chair so I could sweep under them. Using the attachment, I swept around the edges of the room, where a half-inch layer of dust and debris had accumulated. I noted the spots on the rug that wouldn't come clean, and realized that, per my mother's time-table, the carpet was due for a shampoo.

"See, Dad?" I said when he walked through the door that afternoon. "I cleaned up the living room. We need to do a better job of keeping it in order."

"Vickie, Vickie, Vickie," he muttered as he settled into his chair.

An hour later, I stood at the stove, trying in vain to replicate my mother's technique for frying chicken. My dad trudged into the kitchen. I grimaced when I spotted a chunk of dirt that had fallen from the treads of his work shoes onto my freshly mopped floor.

"You don't need to do this, Vickie," he said, his voice rising in irritation. "If you wanted chicken, you should've let me know. I would've picked some up at Kentucky Fried Chicken."

And then it hit me. My dad had no need to maintain my mother's ways of doing things. Truthfully, he was relieved to be out from under her regimen of duty and order. He was relaxing, breathing freely in the clutter accumulating around him.

For the first time in my life, I felt a moment of contempt for my dear, sweet father. Looking through my mother's eyes, I despised him for being satisfied with a life of mediocrity. But as quickly as the feeling came, it passed. I told myself that any future cleaning efforts would be for my sake, not his.

CHAPTER 30

My third day at home, I tackled the upstairs room where my brothers had slept during my mother's illness. When I discovered that Michael had left behind a sweatshirt, a wristwatch, and a bottle of shampoo, I dutifully packed up the items, carried the parcel to the post office, and shipped it off to Virginia. Afterwards, I congratulated myself for behaving like a responsible adult.

After giving my own room a thorough cleaning, there was only one space in the house left to deal with: my parents' room. And that project included sorting through my mother's belongings.

I knew my dad would never take on that task. Until someone else removed Mom's clothing from his closet, he would simply push her dresses aside when he hung up his work shirts and trousers. He would avoid triggering painful memories by refusing to open the dresser drawers that held her personal items.

"I'm not even going to talk to Dad about Mom's things," I muttered as I stood with my hand on the knob of his closed bedroom door. "He doesn't care what happens to it."

When I heard my own words, I realized how angry I was with my dad for not honoring memories of his wife in the way I thought he should. More than angry—I was furious.

My brothers weren't around to help with the sorting and decision-making. I wasn't about to involve my sister. Lucy would only rifle through stuff while talking nonsense, impeding my progress. The job was mine, and mine alone.

I opened the door and walked into the room. Wrinkling my nose in disgust, I surveyed the untidy surroundings: the unmade bed, the flannel shirt slung across the headboard, the inside-out socks my dad had tossed aside after pulling them off his feet, the pajamas lying on the floor where he'd stepped out of them. My mother never would have deigned to live in such an environment.

I'm not picking this crap up, I told myself. *If he wants to live like a slob in his own room, then I'll let him.*

I opened the closet door and peered inside. As I suspected, my mother's dresses had been squeezed to one side, no longer allowed their rightful share of the small space. Angrily, I shoved my dad's things aside and brought the dresses to the center so that I could look at them. I realized I'd need to use the bed as a surface for sorting, so I resentfully straightened the covers to create a smooth platform.

One by one, I pulled out the dresses and laid them carefully across the bed. As far back as I could remember, every item in my mother's wardrobe had been handmade. I'd never known her to shop for a dress in a department store. She had never owned more than four or five good outfits at a time, dresses or skirts and jackets. She had always turned a dress that had become too shabby for church or work into a housedress.

I examined her newest dress, a long-sleeved navy-blue knit she'd finished shortly before her illness claimed all her strength. She'd only worn it three or four times. I marveled at how expertly she'd set in the sleeves and collar, how perfectly she'd executed the lines of stitching along each side of the zipper. My mother had never done anything haphazardly.

Someone could get a lot of good wear out of this, I thought. *I'll take it to Goodwill.* My mother had always donated my outgrown clothing to Goodwill, and I knew she'd approve of my decision.

I put all of the better outfits in the Goodwill pile. I wasn't sure what to do with the older dresses, some of which she'd worn around the house for seven or eight years. They were too shabby for anyone else to wear.

When I pulled out the old patchwork skirt that had always reminded me of a quilt, an idea occurred to me. I could donate Mom's older garments to the women's sewing circle at church. They could cut them up and use them for quilt blocks. That seemed to be perfectly in line with who my mother was, and I felt satisfied with my decision.

As I placed the empty hangers back into the closet, I spotted Mom's terrycloth robe and cotton nightgown hanging on nails on one side of the door. She hadn't worn them the last few months of her life. To provide her with more efficient care, the hospice nurses had put her in hospital gowns.

My mother had typically cut up her worn-out nightwear to make cleaning rags. But I couldn't bear the thought of dusting furniture with her nightgown, or scrubbing the tub with the last bathrobe she'd ever worn. I buried my face in the gown. It hadn't been laundered since she'd last worn it, and it still smelled like her. I knew I couldn't part with this sensory reminder of my mother, so I set it aside, along with the robe, to take upstairs to my room.

I picked up her shoes from the closet floor. She'd always owned exactly three pairs of footwear. Her plain, low-heeled pumps were for work and church. She wore the flat lace-up shoes around the house. At the end of the day, she'd allow her feet some freedom in terrycloth scuffs.

The pumps were about a year old. I figured someone with tiny feet like my mother's might get some wear out of them, so I put them in the Goodwill pile. Her house shoes and slippers were too worn to donate, so I put them in a pile to throw away.

Then I turned to her dresser, a space more personal than her closet. My dad had always used the top two drawers, while my mother had used the bottom three. Her first drawer held her bras, panties, slips, and nylons, none suitable for donation, so they went into the throw-away pile.

At the bottom of the drawer was a neatly folded yellow flannel nightgown. I vaguely recalled my mother sewing it the summer before she died. Tears sprang to my eyes when I remembered her portable *Singer* sewing machine set up on the kitchen table. She'd stashed the gown away for the upcoming winter months, not knowing that she'd never have the opportunity to wear it.

I admired the flat-felled seams running down the sides of the garment, and the perfect little buttonholes she'd crafted. I held the gown up to my body. At five feet, eleven inches, I was nine inches taller than my petite mother, and a garment meant to be ankle-length on her hit me just past my knees. But I decided I would make the nightgown mine, even if it looked ridiculous on me.

Her second dresser drawer was stuffed full of quilting fabric, some of which had already been cut into blocks. This would go to the church sewing circle, along with her old housedresses.

When I opened the third drawer, my heart skipped a beat. There was Mom's stack of white head coverings, starched and ironed. Even though many Mennonite women had stopped the practice of wearing coverings to church, Mom had faithfully worn hers until the end.

I thought about the contradictions in my mother's personality. She firmly believed in a woman's right to learn, to grow, and to express her full potential. The last few years of her life, she'd delved deeply into her college courses. But at the same time, she'd clung to her plain, modest clothing and her old-fashioned head coverings, her symbols of devotion to the Mennonite church. Without hesitation, I put the coverings with the other items I planned to take upstairs to keep in my own dresser drawers.

Next to the coverings were Mom's Bible and a spiral notebook. When I opened the notebook, I saw that she'd kept a journal, her thoughts about the scripture she'd read that day. As I thumbed through the pages, I saw several verses listed under a heading of "Forgiveness."

I John 1: 9 "If we confess our sins, He is faithful and just to forgive us our sins, and to cleanse us from all unrighteousness."

Psalm 103:12 "As far as the east is from the west, so far hath He removed our transgressions from us."

I stopped reading. This glimpse into Mom's inner world was too much for me to handle at the moment. I put the Bible and notebook on the stack of things I was planning to keep.

When my dad came home that evening, I informed him that I'd cleaned out Mom's dresser drawers and her side of the closet.

"Good," he said. "I hadn't gotten around to doing that. Thanks for helping out, Vickie."

Six weeks later, our pastor's wife showed up at our front door, carrying a thick comforter the sewing circle had made out of the fabric from my mother's dresses. While my dad graciously thanked her for her kindness, he expressed little interest in the gift after she'd gone.

"I think this should be for you, Vickie," he said, handing me the folded blanket. "It'll be something to remind you of your mother."

I sensed he had no intention of doing what the sewing circle ladies had in mind for him, shrouding his bed in a comforter made from his late wife's dresses. He had moved on.

CHAPTER 31

One afternoon in late May, my dad came home from work to find me wielding a shovel in the weedy patch that had been my mother's vegetable garden. He looked irritated. "Now what are you up to, Vickie?"

"I'm trying to get this all dug up," I said. "I told you I wanted to plant some stuff. Don't you remember?"

He looked at the small amount of dirt I'd managed to turn over, then bent down to break up a clod with his hand. "It's a little late for planting. You should've started all this a month ago."

"It'll still grow," I protested.

"Well," he grunted as he stood up, "you're never going to get anywhere with that shovel. If you're really set on doing this, then I'll get Wendell to come over with his roto-tiller."

The following morning, while our kindly neighbor tilled my garden, I drove into town to the Troyer Seed Company. I thought about the times I'd accompanied my mother to that store when I was a tiny child. I'd rifle through the colorful packets of vegetable and flower seeds, pulling out whatever struck my fancy, and she'd repeatedly have to tell me to keep my hands off things.

With that same childish delight, I picked out seeds for peas, squash, cucumbers, lettuce, and radishes. As I looked at the tomato plants, I thought about the jars of tomato juice my mother had canned in years past. I could see her pulling them out of the pressure cooker, then lining them up on the kitchen counter to cool. I wasn't about to tackle a canning project, but I told myself I'd plant the tomatoes anyway.

On the way home, I felt enthusiastic about my venture. But when I carried my seeds and tomato plants to the garden plot, I was suddenly overwhelmed. Now I had to figure out how to arrange the garden. I wracked my brain to remember how my mother had organized her planting.

Around 5:00, I was sitting on the ground by the garden when my dad pulled into the driveway. The past few weeks, I'd noticed a change in his pattern. He'd been coming home at 5:00 or 5:30, instead of 3:30 or 4:00. I hadn't yet asked what was keeping him at work so late.

"Whatcha doing, Vickie?" he called as he ambled toward the garden.

"Just trying to figure this out," I said. "I think I have all the stuff I need. But I can't decide how to lay things out."

My dad picked up the seed packets lying on the ground beside me. "Put the sweet corn in the back row, so it doesn't block the sunlight for the other plants." He gestured toward the far end of the garden. "Put the cucumbers and squash over there. Plant a couple of rows of peas in front of the corn. Then the radishes and lettuce here in the front. That's pretty much how your mom used to do it."

By sunset, I had the corn, squash, and cucumbers planted. I finished the rest of the planting the following morning. After giving everything a good watering, I felt exhausted. I'd always thought of my mother's gardening as her hobby. I hadn't known how hard she'd worked to provide the family with fresh produce every summer.

Around the middle of July, Judy Prentiss called me. "Just checking up on my friend," she said. "Just wanting to see how you're getting along. What've you been up to all summer?"

"Not much," I told her. "Except for working in my vegetable garden. That keeps me busy."

"You're doing that for your mom's sake, aren't you?" She spoke with her usual gentle perception.

"Yeah. But this is probably the only year I'll be able to do it. It's a lot more work than I thought it would be."

"If you want to get out of the house and do something," she said, "come over some time. I get home from work around 4:00. We could go out and grab a bite to eat."

"Sounds good," I said. "When do you want me to come?"

"Any time. Tomorrow, or the day after that. Doesn't matter to me."

The following afternoon, I drove to Twin Pines mobile home park in Goshen, where Judy shared a trailer with her mother. I parked along the curb behind a dark sedan.

Barbara Prentiss answered the door to my knock. I'd grown rather fond of Judy's kind-hearted mother. Never a pretty woman, her thin frame seemed to have sagged under the burdens she'd carried for so many years. Her wispy brown hair, streaked with gray, was styled in a kinky perm that always seemed to be halfway grown out. She had a penchant for wearing shapeless baggy trousers, along with blouses that looked like they came from the 1940s.

When I stepped into the living room, I recoiled in shock. There sat my dad on Barbara's shabby couch, looking as if he felt perfectly at home.

My mind raced through a multitude of thoughts. That black car parked in front of the trailer belonged to my dad. Just the previous Saturday, he'd traded in the old white Chevy that he'd driven on his mail route for the past ten years, and had bought the Pontiac sedan. I'd been used to the old Chevy, and hadn't yet grown accustomed to seeing the Pontiac.

And what about those evenings he'd been coming home late? Had he been stopping by the Prentiss home? Why on earth would he be doing that?

My dad's face reddened when he saw me. "Well, I suppose I should get going," he said to Barbara.

Just then, Judy came into the living room. We both watched as my dad stood up, put his arm around Barbara's waist, and gave her an affectionate squeeze. Barbara gazed up at him with adoring eyes. "See you later," he said. Then he walked out of the trailer without saying a word to me.

"You girls have fun," Barbara called as Judy and I headed out the door.

"I'll drive," Judy offered. I followed her to her car, and we both got in.

Before she even had the chance to turn her key in the ignition, I blurted out, "What the heck was going on in there?"

"What do you mean?" Judy asked.

"Has my dad been coming over here to see your mom?"

Judy nodded. "Yup. He's been coming here a couple of times a week."

"For how long?"

"Two or three months, I'd say."

"Are they dating?"

"I'm not real sure." A mile-wide grin spread across her face. "I know they like each other a lot."

I sat there stunned, my mouth hanging open in disbelief.

"They'd make a good couple, don't you think?" Judy said.

No! I wanted to scream. *Absolutely not!*

I tried to carry on a pleasant conversation with Judy while we ate our sandwiches at Penguin Point. I plied her with questions about her job at Goshen Rubber, just to keep her talking about something other than our parents. I was afraid that if she said anything more about my dad and her mother making a good couple, I'd lunge across the table and slap her face.

"Want to see if there's a ballgame down at Roger's Park?" she asked after we'd finished our meal.

"I'm pretty tired," I lied. "I should get home."

Truthfully, I was anything but tired. I was keyed up, every nerve in my body pulsing with the urge to pounce on my dad and demand to know what the heck he thought he was doing. On my drive home, I mentally berated him for his foolishness.

When I walked into the living room, my dad was sitting in his armchair watching *The Dukes of Hazzard* on T.V. "Turn that off," I barked at him. "You and I need to talk."

He looked up at me in surprise before obligingly clicking the power button on the remote control. "What is it now, Vickie?" He sounded impatient.

Like a parent confronting a teenager who'd stepped out of line, I looked him accusingly in the eye. "Dad, are you dating Barbara Prentiss?"

He shifted uncomfortably in his chair. "I've been keeping her company."

"What exactly does that mean?"

"Just what I said. There's nothing wrong with a man going to see a woman every now and then."

I realized that I was standing over him, my hands on my hips, looking exactly like Mom had looked every time she was displeased with him. I backed away and sat down on the sofa.

"It's more than every now and then, isn't it?" I said. "It's three or four times a week. That's why you've been coming home so late. You're stopping off at Barbara's house."

"So, what?" he retorted.

I took a deep breath, trying to bring my anger under control. "Dad, this isn't right. Your wife just died."

"It's been seven months, Vickie."

"Six and a half," I corrected him.

"What's the difference? At my age, I don't have time to wait around."

I leaned back on the sofa, biting my lip to keep from screaming at him, my angry breath heaving in my chest.

After a few minutes of stony silence between us, my dad cleared his throat. "Listen, Vickie. I wasn't going to bring this subject up just yet, but since we're laying all our cards on the table, I might as well tell you now. Barbara and I are talking about getting married."

"What the hell?" I jumped up again. "Are you out of your mind, Dad?"

He said nothing, but the smug look on his broad, rugged face made me want to pound him.

"Are you bringing her here?"

He reached down for the glass sitting on the floor beside his chair, taking a long drink of iced tea before answering my question. "Of course. Where else would we live?"

"What about me?" I yelled. "Don't I get a say in anything?" Before he could reply, I turned and ran through the kitchen and out the back door, slamming it behind me.

I paced around the backyard, seething. Here I'd taken the summer off just to be with my dad, to keep him company and to help him adjust to the loss my mother. Clearly, he didn't need me there. He wasn't thinking about my mother, because he was already involved with the woman who was going to be his second wife. I felt like a fool.

How could he do this to me? I fumed. *How could he be so selfish? How could my steady, reliable dad suddenly do something so foolish?*

I stopped to stare at my garden. In spite of my late start with the planting, it was coming along nicely. The row of sweet corn was already as high as my knees. The pea plants were laden with plump pods, and tiny flowers had appeared on the squash and cucumber plants. I'd already harvested most of the lettuce.

This will never happen again, I told myself. *Barbara Prentiss won't know how to raise vegetables. She won't know anything about stepping into my mother's shoes here at the farmhouse.*

I couldn't imagine living with another woman under my mother's roof. Another woman sleeping next to my dad in my mother's bed. The thought of that made me want to vomit.

I sat down on the grass, my head in my hands. I could feel myself being squeezed out of the home that had been mine since the day I was born. Two months earlier, I'd turned twenty. Maybe it was time for me to leave the nest. The thought filled me with terror. I had no idea where I'd go, or how I'd take care of myself.

I heard the back door open. "It's time to come in, Vickie," my dad called from the steps. Obligingly, I got up and followed him into the house, through the mudroom, and into the kitchen.

"A woman on my route baked me a cherry pie," he said. "Want some?"

"I guess so," I mumbled.

He opened the freezer door. "I think we have some ice cream in here."

We sat at the table across from each other, our heads bowed over our slices of pie a la mode, as if neither of us had anything more significant on our minds than eating dessert.

I took my last bite and laid down my fork. "So when are you and Barbara getting married?"

"We were thinking September," my dad said. "We would've done it this summer, but we both thought it would be best to wait until you go back to college."

His answer stunned me. It was worse than I thought. I'd imagined the two of them getting married in a year. Not in a matter of weeks.

"Dad!" I protested. "Don't you think you should slow things down a little bit? Take some time to get to know each other?"

"Vickie...." His voice sounded impatient, as if he was scolding a young child who refused to listen to reason. "I've known Barbara Prentiss for more than twenty years. We've been good friends all that time."

I bit down hard on my lip, trying to keep myself from blurting out unfair accusations. My dad seemed to sense where my mind had gone. "And all that time, we never did anything improper. I was one hundred percent true to my marriage vows."

Of course, I thought petulantly. *Mom was the one that cheated, and you were the nice guy who got stuck with raising her kid.*

"You should try to date a variety of women," I said, grasping at any way to derail him from his plan. "You shouldn't marry the first one that comes along."

"Why should I do that?" he said. "I've already found the one that suits me."

Frustrated, I resorted to playing a card that I never imagined I would use. "Dad, Barbara Prentiss is divorced. Our church teaches that it's wrong to marry someone who's been divorced."

He snorted in derision. "You're not fooling me, Vickie. I know you're not so coldhearted as to reject a person just because she's been divorced. And I'm telling you right now, you're not going to win this argument. It's time for Herman Unruh to live his life the way he wants to live it."

With that, he pushed back his chair and stalked out of the house to the porch. I immediately felt bad for my insensitive words, and followed him out the door. "I'm sorry," I said as I sat down beside him on the swing. "This is a just hard thing for me to get used to."

In the fading light, I could see the jut of his chin, the determination in his eyes. I'd never seen my mild-mannered dad look so defiant. I'd always known him to accept, with gentle resignation, whatever card life dealt him. As the darkness settled around us, he began to talk.

You're not a child anymore, Vickie. You've dated a few boys. You know something about what goes on between men and women. So, I'm going to talk to you like an adult.

You're a pretty girl, like your mother was. You get all the attention you want from boys. Me, I never was much to look at. I was just a clod. A dumb old farm boy that didn't know anything about anything, except for growing wheat and taking care of animals. In high school, I was the fellow that everybody took for granted. People used to say that Herman Unruh would do whatever you wanted him to, and they took advantage of that. Everyone thought I was a good-hearted guy. But none of the girls wanted anything to do with me in a romantic way.

When my parents lost their farm in the depression, I was shipped off to Indiana to live with my uncle for a while. I never had any say in that. What I thought didn't matter. I just kept my head down and did what I was told to do.

I tried making something of myself, Vickie. Because I was good with animals, I thought I could go to veterinary school. But I didn't get very far with that. I wasn't sharp enough to pick up what was being taught in the classroom.

Your mother was the first woman who ever paid any attention to me. Even though the first time we met, she turned up her nose at me. She'd come to a youth gathering at my uncle's farm. I offered to walk her out to her car, but she didn't want anything to do with me.

A couple of years later, we ran into each other again. I'd gone over to the college to sign up for seminary classes. Your mother was a secretary in the office. When she started smiling and making eyes at me, I thought it was too good to be true. Come to find out, it was. I should've known I wasn't suited for a woman like her. Later, I came to realize that she'd had her heart set on marrying a preacher, and that was the only reason she was interested in me.

When I found out I wasn't cut out for seminary, your mother was mighty disappointed. Downright bitter, I'd say. I don't think she ever forgave me for letting her down. But we'd already gotten married and had a baby on the way. The only thing we could do was to make the best of what we'd done.

Vickie, I had to live with your mom's bitterness for almost forty years. Every day when I woke up and saw my wife lying beside me, I was reminded of the fact that I wasn't good enough for her. She was smart, she was beautiful, and she could've had her pick of men. Somehow, she ended up with me. It seemed like a terrible mistake.

I tried to do the best I could for her. But every time she got on my case about something I'd done wrong, I'd feel about two inches high. It's hard on a man when he has to live like that. It wears him down to almost nothing.

If I had any doubts about the way your mother felt about me, she proved her point when she had her fling with Reverend Hahn. And I never got much credit for sticking by her. Not until the very end, when she was putting everything into perspective.

Lucky for me, I did have some people who thought highly of me. Folks on my mail route appreciated what I did for them. Barbara Prentiss was one of those people. She was married to a no-good drunk, and I always tried to help her out in any way I could. Her eyes were always so full of sadness. But she'd smile when she thanked me, and I'd feel like a hero.

Barbara has struggled so hard her whole life. She deserves a break. I'd like to be the man that gives it to her.

I know Barbara isn't a pretty woman like your mother was. But when she looks at me like I'm the man of her dreams, it stirs something inside me. Something that's never been stirred before. Barbara thinks the world of me. She puts dumb old Herman Unruh on a pedestal. A man has a right to have the feeling of a woman looking up to him. I don't care what anybody says, I'm stepping up to claim that right. Nobody's going to take that away from me.

"You understand all this, Vickie?" he concluded.

"Yes, Dad," I said. "I know where you're coming from." But even though I now understood his desire to marry Barbara, I could feel a flood of tears coming on.

Abruptly, I got up and went into the house and up the stairs to my room. Curling up on my bed, I hugged my pillow, sobbing like a little girl.

My mother had seldom been the one to comfort me when I was in distress. That had been my dad's role. But right now, she was the one I needed.

"Mom," I whispered. "Mom."

CHAPTER 32

Throughout that summer, I maintained weekly visits with my birth father. Each time we met, he'd inquire as to how I was doing in various aspects of my life, as if checking on my emotional adjustment in the aftermath of my mother's death.

"How've you been sleeping?" he'd ask. "How's your appetite? Are you getting out of the house?" I had to wonder what he'd do if he thought I was slipping into depression. I pictured him picking up the phone and calling for an emergency intervention.

He always listened intently as I recounted the details of my weekly activities: cleaning the house, sorting through my mother's things, working in the garden. "And what have you been doing for fun?" he asked one day. "Are you spending any time with friends?"

"Not much," I admitted. "I've just wanted to be alone."

"Solitude can be healing," he said. "Up to a point. If you find yourself falling into unproductive brooding, then it's time to seek some good company."

Several days after learning of my dad's marriage plans, I went to see Reverend Hahn, ready to report my unfortunate news. Not waiting for his usual inquiries into my wellbeing, I blurted out, "This week has been terrible. My dad and I have been upset with each other."

Reverend Hahn cocked his head, looking at me curiously. "Is that so? I've never known you to say such a thing. The two of you have always gotten along so well."

"I know. But not this week." I leaned forward on the sofa, eager to unburden myself. "You won't believe this. I can't believe it myself. It's ... it's absolutely ridiculous."

He furrowed his brow in concern. "What happened to upset you like this?"

"My dad told me he's getting married."

Reverend Hahn gripped the arms of his wheelchair, as if to steady himself after hearing such unsettling news. "Well," he said. "I surely didn't expect to hear that. Who's the bride-to-be?"

"Barbara Prentiss. A woman he's known a long time. She's actually the mother of one of my friends."

He nodded slowly. "I see. And how are you feeling about this? Not good, I suspect."

"Not good at all." I chuckled self-consciously. "I've been a brat about it, actually. I've yelled at my dad. We've argued. But he tells me he has the right to live his life the way he wants to."

"He certainly does have that right."

"But what about his kids?" I protested. "What about me?"

As the last three words popped out of my mouth, I was hit by a powerful realization. When it came to looking after me, Herman Unruh had already gone beyond the call of duty. I was not biologically his. I belonged to his deceased wife. Furthermore, I was now a legal adult. He had no further obligation toward me, and I had no right to hold him back from what he wanted to do with his life.

The contemplative look on Reverend Hahn's face told me he was thinking along the same lines. "I know this is hard for you to take," he said. "You've just lost your mother, and now it feels like you're losing your dad as well."

"Yeah," I replied. "But I shouldn't be dependent on him anymore. It's time for me to grow up and look after myself."

"Victoria, you still need a father." Reverend Hahn's words rang out, clear and authoritative. "Just remember, for as long as I'm alive, you'll have me. And if I have any say in the matter, I'll still be looking out for you when I'm on the other side."

I felt a rush of gratitude toward my birth father, the arrogant, maddening, controlling man who'd been so difficult for me to learn to trust. The father who, despite his legacy of dishonorable behavior, loved me genuinely and abundantly. "Thank you," I said. "That means a lot to me."

I didn't recognize it then, but it was at that exact moment when, in my mind's eye, the balance of responsibility between my two fathers shifted. I saw Herman Unruh step back from the obligation he'd assumed the day I was born, moving on with his own life. At the same time, Harry Hahn leaped forward, taking over the role he'd always wanted to fulfill.

"So," my birth father said, "getting back to the topic at hand. Are Herman and Barbara getting married at Westside Mennonite Church?"

I shook my head. "Nope. Dad said they're going down to the courthouse. Just the two of them. They don't want any fuss." I hesitated before adding, "Dad hardly goes to church anymore. After my mom died, he started changing. It's like I don't even know him now."

"Interesting," Reverend Hahn mused. But he offered no theory as to why this was happening.

"I know I should be nicer about him getting married," I admitted. "I don't want to stand in the way of his happiness. And I don't want to make things difficult for Barbara."

"I'm sure you won't. You'll be gracious to her."

"I should do something special for them. Maybe get them a wedding gift. Something to mark the occasion."

"If money were no object," Reverend Hahn asked, "what would you get for your dad and his new wife?"

At that point, I assumed my birth father was initiating the *What would you do?* game he often played with me when there was nothing pressing for us to talk about. He'd ask me hypothetical questions that would make me look deep within myself, questions that would make me think about my preferences, values, and motivations. "If you could travel anywhere in the world, where would you go?" "If you were to write a best seller, what would it be about?" "If you had a million dollars to donate to charity, what organization would you give it to?" And there would always be a *why* that followed my response.

So I assumed the question about my hypothetical wedding gift was along the same lines. I thought for a moment. "I'd give them chairs. Matching recliners."

"Why?" Reverend Hahn asked.

"Because my dad has been sitting in the same broken-down armchair for as long as I can remember. It's falling apart. It needs to be hauled out with the trash. He and Barbara have both spent their lives taking care of everybody else, and not themselves. They're getting old and tired. They should be able to sit together in comfort."

Reverend Hahn leaned forward in his wheelchair, his eyes sparkling with excitement. "Go down to Westside Furniture and see what they have in stock."

I stared at him, incredulous. "I can't buy them chairs. I don't have any money."

"Go down there and pick out what you want. I'll write the check."

"That's too much!" I protested. "You don't have to do that for me."

"That's what fathers do." His face registered his pleasure in staking his claim. "And let's just say that I'm doing this for Herman Unruh, too. I caused problems in his first marriage. I'd like to make it up to him by helping him get off to a good start in his second marriage."

He looked at me intently, as if wanting to make sure I was taking in what he was trying to convey. "I have no hard feelings toward you dad, Victoria. None at all. I wish him the very best. I know he and your mother weren't happy in their relationship. I sincerely hope he gets all the love he deserves from the new Mrs. Unruh."

I knew there was no point in declining his generous offer. My birth father had made up his mind. "I need to ask you something," I blurted out.

"Yes?"

"Where do you get all your money?"

He lowered his eyes, chuckling. "Good question, Victoria. That's something you should probably know. I told you my parents ran a profitable restaurant and bakery business in Pennsylvania. By the time they retired, they were operating out of six different sites. They sold the businesses and distributed the funds to their three children. I've invested my share wisely."

The next afternoon, I walked into Westside Furniture carrying a blank check signed by Reverend Hahn. Overwhelmed by the large collection of elegant furniture, I stood in the front of the store trying to get my bearings.

A salesman asked if he could help me. "I'm looking for recliners," I said in a timid voice.

I followed him around the store as he showed me one chair after another. I had no idea which one to choose, and my confusion only served to escalate my anxiety. I pictured myself returning the blank check to Reverend Hahn, confessing to him that I was too clueless and immature to make a selection.

But when I spotted a massive honey-colored leather chair, I knew I'd found what I wanted. I could easily picture my dad reclining in it at the end of his work day. "I like that one," I said, pointing.

The salesman smiled. "That's one of our most popular recliners. Why don't you try it out?"

I sank into the luxurious leather, instantly knowing I'd never sat in anything so comfortable. "This is perfect," I said. "Could I have two of these delivered to my house?"

"Absolutely." The salesman happily wrote up the order, and I walked out of the store feeling like a full-fledged grownup.

I was hoping to be home when the chairs arrived, so that I could supervise the setup in the living room. The afternoon before their scheduled delivery date, I ran into town for groceries. To my dismay, there was a Westside Furniture truck in the driveway when I got home. My dad, red-faced and agitated, appeared to be engaged in a heated argument with the driver. I jumped out of my car and ran over to them.

"I'm telling you, I didn't order these chairs," my dad insisted. "You've got the wrong address."

The delivery man checked his invoice. "No, I'm sure they're supposed to be dropped off here."

My dad raised his voice. "Get them out of here! I'm not going to be stuck with this bill!"

"They're already paid for," the delivery man said, shrugging. "You don't owe anything on them. But if you insist, I'll take them back to the store."

"No!" I said. "Leave them here!" I turned to my dad. "I was the one who bought them. I wanted to surprise you. They're a wedding gift for you and Barbara."

My dad stared at me, dumfounded.

"Take them on inside," I instructed the delivery man. He and his assistant promptly picked up the first chair and carried it into the house.

"What on earth have you done, Vickie?" my dad asked after the men had left. "You don't have this kind of money."

"Reverend Hahn helped me," I said sheepishly.

"I don't want these damn chairs," he growled as he stomped off into the kitchen. "I've humbled myself enough by taking money from that man. I don't want anything else from him."

Devastated by my dad's belligerent response to my gift, I sank down on the sofa, mentally berating Reverend Hahn for his offer to pay for such extravagance, kicking myself for foolishly taking him up on that offer. I could hear my dad banging around in the cupboard for a glass, then yanking open the refrigerator and pouring himself something to drink.

I was about to go upstairs to mope in my bedroom when my dad came back into the living room. "I'm sorry, Vickie," he said. "Your gift will mean the world to Barbara. She's got a bad back, and she'll really appreciate having something decent to sit in."

He ran his rough hand over the leather arm of the recliner nearest him. Then, reluctantly, he eased himself into the chair. I smiled to myself as I watched a look of bliss overtake the anger on his face.

Later that evening, I persuaded my dad to haul his old chair out to the garage. Then I rearranged the rest of the living room furniture to accommodate the new chairs.

The next day after work, my dad brought his bride-to-be to the house to see my wedding gift to them. When Barbara saw the matching honey-colored recliners, she burst into tears. Throwing her arms around me, she said, "Oh, sweetheart, I never thought I'd ever have something half this nice. I feel so lucky to be marrying into such a loving family."

Her heartfelt words softened the stony resentment I'd been harboring toward her. I knew there would be challenges to come. But my dad was determined to marry Barbara Prentiss, and I truly wanted the two of them to be happy.

CHAPTER 33

The first weekend in September, my dad helped me move my belongings back into my Westlawn dormitory room. After carrying three loads up the stairs, he sat down on my bed to rest.

"All set, Vickie?" he asked, glancing around the room.

"I guess so," I said.

"Hard to believe this is already your third year of college. Are you rooming with the same girl this year?"

"Yes. Rhonda and I got along really well as roommates last year, so we decided to do it again."

"Good." My dad stared absentmindedly out the dorm room window. "That's real good. Glad it's working out for you."

I began hanging my clothes in my closet, my back to him. "Sweetheart," he said, sounding strangely nervous. "There's something I need to tell you before I go."

I held my breath, my body stiffened with dread. *Oh, no! What is it now? Everything he tells me these days is something I don't want to hear.*

"I wanted you to know that I'm planning on getting rid of the animals."

"What?" I swung around to face him. "You love them! Why would you get rid of them?"

"Barbara doesn't care much for animals."

I could hardly believe he was allowing his new wife's preferences to influence such an important decision. "Mom didn't like the animals, either. But you kept them all the years you were married to her."

"Yeah," he sighed, "I guess that's true. But a man's got to know when it's time to let go of something. I talked to Wendell, and he'll be taking the ducks and chickens. After everything he's done for me over the years, I'm not asking anything for them. And a fellow on my route says he's interested in buying the goats."

His voice softened and his eyes grew tender. "Maybe we'll keep the rabbits around for a little while, Vickie. For your sake. I know how much you loved those critters when you were a little girl."

I knew he was trying to appease me. "If you want to get rid of the rabbits," I said, "then go ahead. I'm not going to be home that much, anyway." My last sentence sounded bitter, but my dad made no reply.

He heaved his hefty body off the bed and wrapped an arm around my shoulders. "You take good care of yourself, sweetheart."

As I listened to his heavy footsteps descend the dormitory stairs, I suddenly knew why he was letting go of the animals. He no longer needed them. During all the cold, empty years he shared with my mother, he'd turned to the animals for companionship. Now, he was getting all the love he needed from the new woman in his life.

The following Friday, my dad and Barbara went down to the courthouse in Goshen and got married. Then, over the weekend, they moved Barbara's things into the farmhouse, leaving Judy to live on her own in the mobile home.

I was out. The animals were out. Barbara was in.

Nearly two months passed before I went home for a visit. While I sometimes indulged in pouting about being pushed out of the house, I secretly welcomed the opportunity to distance myself from family life. The crisis of my mother's illness and death had bound me to the family my entire sophomore year, so I was grateful for the space to focus on myself. As Reverend Hahn had hoped, I was determined to make my junior year one of the best of my life.

Now, the only person I turned to when I felt the need for family support was my birth father. I increased my visits with Reverend Hahn to twice weekly, which, of course, delighted him.

As a junior, my scholastic life was now taking shape around my English major. Reverend Hahn listened, enraptured, as I described my courses in writing, literature, and teaching English as a second language. When he'd learn that one of my reading assignments for my literature class was among the classics he owned, he'd wheel his chair to the bookshelves, reach up a long arm, pull down a volume, and lay it on his coffee table. The next time I'd come for a visit, he would have read the assignment, and would be eager to discuss it with me.

Sometimes, I'd bring a textbook with me, and would curl up on his sofa and read for an hour. Reverend Hahn would pass the time with me by reading something himself.

One day, I brought along my textbook for a class entitled, *Books and Ideas.* "What do you have there?" he asked me.

I held up the textbook. "This is the best class I've ever taken. A lot of students complain about it. They think it's a waste of time. I can't believe they say that. I love it."

"What's it about?"

I paused, thinking how to describe the course. "It's about our cultural roots. Religion, philosophy, the arts, literature."

"May I see the book?"

I placed the book in his lap. With trembling hands, he rifled through the pages. "I can see why you love this class, Victoria," he said. "I'd love it, too. It's right in line with my interests."

Suddenly, I thought of a delightful way to surprise my birth father. When I left his apartment, I went straight to the college bookstore and bought a second copy of my textbook.

Several days later, I presented the book to him. "For you," I said. "So you can be a student along with me."

I thought his smile would crack his wrinkled face into a thousand pieces. Thereafter, he read my *Books and Ideas* assignments along with me, offering me his thoughts about the material. In turn, I shared the details of my professor's lectures and our class discussions.

I'd tell Reverend Hahn about my rehearsals with the college chorale, and the performances we gave at local venues. "How I wish I could get out to one of your concerts!" he said. "But even if I can't be there, I'm so glad you're having this experience."

He laughed along with me as I described my mishaps on the girls' field hockey team. Once, I walked into his apartment wearing my field hockey uniform. He chuckled at the knee socks and short plaid skirt.

"I always thought I was an athlete," I told him. "But this definitely isn't the sport for me. I'll finish out the season. Next year, I'm going to try out for volleyball again."

Even though Reverend Hahn was now too weak to get out for church, I went back to attending College Mennonite, knowing that he was at home listening to the radio broadcast of the same service. I had given up the idea of driving all the way across town to Westside Mennonite. Every time I'd attended my home church during the summer, I had been inundated with concerned questions about my absent dad. I'd grown tired of that experience.

On an evening in late October, one of my dorm mates stuck her head in my room and said, "Victoria, you have a phone call."

I put down my textbook and went to the phone in our hallway. The caller was my dad.

"Vickie!" he exclaimed. "How are you? I haven't seen you in ages. Barbara and I were expecting you to come home for the weekend every now and then."

"I've been super busy," I told him. "Anyway, I thought I should give you and Barbara a little privacy."

"We've enjoyed our time together," he said. "But we miss having family around. Barbara wants to have all you girls over for dinner this weekend."

All you girls. I knew my dad was referring to Judy, Lucy, and me, the members of our blended family.

"Would it suit you to come home Saturday night?" he asked.

I grimaced. "Sure."

Early that Saturday evening, I pulled my mom's old car into Dad and Barbara's driveway. I hadn't seen my childhood home in almost two months. The old farmhouse looked smaller and shabbier than I'd remembered it to be.

My mother had always scolded the rest of us about letting clutter accumulate on the porch. "It makes the house look trashy," she'd say. Now, there were items on the porch I'd never seen before: a broken-down lawn chair, several plastic storage containers, and an old space heater.

When I stepped through the front door, I glanced around in dismay. After the new chairs had been delivered, I'd arranged the furniture in the living room to create an attractive, inviting space. But that arrangement had been completely undone.

I quickly realized that when Barbara had moved in, she'd brought along some of the furniture from her trailer. A third chair, upholstered in a garish plaid fabric, had been squeezed into the small living room. A hutch with doors that no longer closed properly sat against one wall, crammed full of dishes I didn't recognize. The living room carpet hadn't been shampooed in ages, and it now appeared worn and matted. A few throw rugs had been laid down to cover the worst spots.

Barbara's crocheting project lay in a pile on her recliner, and a plastic bag stuffed full of yarn lay on the floor. A lamp with a cracked shade sat on a small table next to her chair. Newspapers and magazines had once again accumulated on the floor, the coffee table, and the top of the television set.

I could tell that Dad and Barbara felt at home with each other in that cluttered space. But the scene made me so sad that my insides ached. Everything I'd accomplished over the summer had been undone. All traces of my mother's ways of doing things were now gone from the house.

"Is that you, Vickie?" my dad called from the kitchen. "Come on in."

"Supper will be ready in a few minutes," Barbara chimed in.

When I walked into the kitchen, I saw my dad and Barbara moving around the room, working together as if they'd done so for years. I could hardly believe my eyes. My dad had never worked alongside my mother in the kitchen, except for when he'd heave himself out of his chair in response to her frustrated calls for help.

Lucy was sitting at the table, chatting contentedly with Dad and Barbara while they worked. "Lucy, honey," Barbara said, "would you mind getting the plates out of the hutch for me?"

Lucy promptly jumped up. "Which ones?"

"The blue ones, I think," Barbara replied.

With a compliance I'd never witnessed before, Lucy marched into the living room, pulled a stack of plates from the hutch, and carried them to the kitchen. Her familiarity with the contents of the hutch told me that she'd already spent a great deal of time with Dad and Barbara, and that she felt comfortable in their household.

Throughout the meal preparation, Barbara frequently asked for Lucy's help. The requests were always prefaced by, "Lucy, honey," and followed by, "Thanks, sweetie." I'd never heard anyone address my belligerent sister with such terms of endearment. But I could see that Barbara's expressions of affection had gone a long way in smoothing off Lucy's rough edges. In her stepmother's presence, Lucy was as docile as a lap dog.

Lucy has a mother! I thought. *My poor sister, who has never known maternal affection, finally has a mother who loves her without reservation.* Even though I felt no daughterly fondness for Barbara Prentiss, I was glad that Lucy did.

The meal Barbara and Dad were fixing consisted of spaghetti with store-bought sauce, garlic bread from the deli, and iced tea made from instant powder and copious amounts of sugar. As I watched their preparations, I couldn't silence my judgmental inner voice. *Mom never would've served spaghetti sauce from a jar. She would've made her own sauce from scratch. And she would've fixed a green salad to go with the pasta. Mom would never prepare a meal without a proper serving of vegetables.*

Judy came to the house a few minutes after I arrived, joining the rest of us in the kitchen. "Why don't you girls go sit in the living room and visit?" Barbara suggested. "It'll be a few minutes until the spaghetti is done." Judy and I obliged, while Lucy stayed behind with Dad and Barbara.

"Cool chairs," Judy observed as she moved aside her mother's crocheting project and plopped down in the recliner. "This was a great gift for my mom. She's got a bad back. Every time I come over here, she comments on how great this chair has been for her back. She says it's so comfortable that she can hardly make herself get up."

So, Judy's been making herself at home here, too, I noted. *I lived here all my life, and now I'm the odd one out.*

When Barbara called us to the table, I watched my dad lift the heavy pot of boiling water from the stove and pour the pasta into a strainer in the sink. No doubt, he was sparing Barbara's back. I'd never seen him look out for my mother in such a way.

I ate my unremarkable meal in silence, listening while the rest of the family carried on a lively conversation. My dad chatted about the people on his mail route. Barbara talked about how much she was looking forward to retiring at the end of the year. She smiled fondly at my dad, patting his arm. "I never could've done it if this good man hadn't come into my life."

Judy talked about playing on the city's women's softball league. Lucy talked about her outings with her caseworker. There was no room in the conversation for any discussion of college life.

When I heard Lucy address Barbara as 'Mom,' I wasn't surprised, although I cringed every time the word popped out of her mouth. But when Judy said, "Dad, would you pass me the parmesan cheese," I was floored. She uttered the word as naturally as if she'd been calling him that all her life.

Since our childhood, I'd known that Judy, the daughter of an abusive alcoholic, envied my good fortune in having Herman Unruh as my father. Now, he was hers as much as mine, and she was claiming him without hesitation. In the new family configuration, my longtime friend was now my sister. I definitely wasn't ready for that.

After we finished our meal, Lucy turned to Barbara and said, "That was really good, Mom. When I move back home, I want you to teach me how to cook."

"What?" I exclaimed. "You're moving back home?"

Lucy looked at me, surprised. "Yeah. Didn't you know that?"

While I sat there trying to absorb the shocking news, the conversation flowed on around me. Everyone else seemed to have known about this development. And everyone was fine with it, except for me.

I stood up and carried my empty plate to the counter. "You girls go sit in the living room," Barbara said. "Herman and I will take care of the dishes."

My sister and stepsister each claimed one of the recliners. I sat on the sofa tuning out their chatter, with only one thing on my mind. I had to get my dad alone. I had to talk him out of this crazy notion about Lucy moving back home. After waiting for twenty minutes, I got up to see how he and Barbara were coming along with the dishes.

Barbara was standing at the sink in her shapeless baggy trousers, a far different figure from my mother in her tidy housedress. Dad was drying the dishes his new wife was washing, something he'd never done for my mother. Or even for me.

I watched him coil up his dishtowel and playfully flick Barbara on the bottom. Barbara shot him a coy look. "Now, Herman, don't you get started."

"Why not?" my dad said. He put down his towel and took Barbara in his arms. Tenderly brushing aside her frizzy hair, he kissed her neck.

The scene revolted me. I moved away from the doorway to the kitchen and went back to sit on the sofa, my mind reeling. *Oh, my God! My dad is sexually active! I'd bet anything that he and Mom never had sex the last twenty years of their marriage. And now he's doing it with Barbara!*

After I succeeded in calming my racing thoughts, I called out, "Dad, I need to get going."

Both he and Barbara came out of the kitchen. "Victoria, I thought maybe you were going to spend the night," Barbara said, sounding disappointed. "I put a few boxes in your room, but your dad can move them out. It'll just take a few minutes."

Now the one room in the house that been my private haven was no longer sacrosanct. My mother never would have violated my personal space by using my bedroom as a storage unit. Nothing in this house was mine anymore. For a minute, I wondered whether Barbara had gone through my room, whether she'd found my mother's things tucked away in my dresser drawer. The thought infuriated me, and I forced myself to put it out of my mind.

"No, I'm not staying," I said, trying to keep the irritation out of my voice. "I need to get back to the college."

My dad walked me out to the porch, as if sensing that I needed a minute alone with him. As soon as the front door closed behind us, I pounced on him. "Dad, why in the world are you letting Lucy move back home? It took you so long to get her out of here. Don't you remember what it was like when she was living with us?"

My dad shrugged. "Things are different now, Vickie. Barbara and I have been meeting with the people from Oaklawn. Lucy's been real cooperative with them. And she's been as good as gold around Barbara. It seems like Barbara's exactly what Lucy needs in her life."

"But it's not going to last," I warned him. "Once Lucy's living here fulltime, she'll start showing Barbara her true colors."

My dad shook his head. "I don't think so, Vickie. We've had her here for an entire weekend. A couple of weekends, actually. Everything went fine. The people from Oaklawn think it's going to work out okay."

"But why, Dad? Why not just leave her where she is? Why not leave well enough alone?"

"Well, for one thing, Barbara has been in a lot of pain. She gets tired out so easily. Lucy can help her with some of the heavy chores. And Barbara can help Lucy stay on track with her medication. Seems like a win-win situation to me."

I snorted. "All my years of growing up with Lucy, I never saw her do anything to help out Mom. And you know she doesn't even keep her own apartment clean. She's not going to do any work around here."

"But she's different with Barbara." I could hear the fondness in my dad's voice. "I can't quite figure it out, but Barbara has the magic touch with Lucy. I'm so grateful for what she does for my daughter. It makes me love my wife more and more every day."

His insinuation slapped me in the face. My mother never had been able to handle Lucy. Their relationship had been doomed from the day Lucy was born. Apparently, this maternal failure had rendered Mom unworthy of the devotion my dad was now offering his second wife.

Without another word, I walked out into the darkness to my waiting car. I did not look back. As of that evening, the farmhouse ceased to be my home. It belonged to Herman, Barbara, and Lucy Unruh. Even to Judy Prentiss. At least she could claim a biological parent in the household. She'd probably move in, too, and for all I cared, she could take up residence in my old room.

CHAPTER 34

"I don't even want to go home anymore," I complained to Reverend Hahn several days later. "I'm not comfortable there."

He raised an eyebrow. "Is that so?"

I nodded emphatically. "You know how hard I worked over the summer. I cleaned up the house. I tried to keep up with all the chores, the way Mom did. I thought my dad would appreciate that. But he didn't give a hoot about anything I was doing. It just got on his nerves. And now, Barbara's stuff is all over the house. Everything's messed up again."

"So your stepmother is creating a different ambiance in the home," Reverend Hahn mused.

"If you can call clutter an ambiance," I scoffed. "Barbara fits right in with my dad. They're both clutter-bugs." Then, petulantly, I added, "And I don't consider her to be my stepmother. I'm too old for that. My mom raised me, she's gone, and no one is going to replace her."

"Of course not," came the calm reply.

Having gotten my childish rant out of the way, I glanced around the apartment. I'd formed the habit of doing that, as at almost every visit, I'd spot something new in my birth father's living quarters: a fresh floral arrangement on the dining table, a tin of cookies on the counter, a new book lying on the coffee table, a scented candle perched on a bookshelf. I'd always ask, "Who brought you that?" And Reverend Hahn would launch into a story about the person who'd given him the gift, and the reason for their particular offering. The size of his social circle astounded me.

I picked up a decorative throw pillow sitting beside me on the sofa, running my fingers over the embroidered design. "This is new. It's pretty."

"Yes, isn't it?" Reverend Hahn replied. "One of the elderly women from the church made it for me. She lives on a fixed income. She needed new eyeglasses, but couldn't afford them. When I heard about her plight, I sent her a check, and she was able to get her glasses. Now, she can see well enough to do her needlework again, and she made this pillow for me. She chose exactly the right colors to fit with my décor. Don't you think so?"

"Yes, she did." I carefully set the pillow back in its place. "Your apartment always looks so nice. I love it here."

I hadn't intended to make such a bold declaration, but when I saw how much my words pleased my birth father, I couldn't regret my impulsivity. "I'm so glad," he said. "I've always wanted you to feel at home here. Especially now that your childhood home no longer feels comfortable to you."

And so, for the next two months, I made Reverend Hahn's living quarters my home away from home. If I felt the need to get away from the chaos of dorm life, I'd show up at his apartment, where I'd curl up on the sofa to study or stretch out for an hour-long nap. Upon my birth father's insistence, I stocked his refrigerator and cupboards with food, so that I could make myself a sandwich or heat up a can of soup if I missed a meal in the cafeteria. I felt free to use his bathroom to wash my face or touch up my makeup.

The relationship between the two of us became less formal. We no longer felt the need to give each other undivided attention while I was at the apartment. I moved about freely while he attended to his personal business. Several times, I stayed alone in his apartment while he wheeled his chair down the hall to the dining room.

I noticed that Reverend Hahn spent considerable time going through his paperwork and talking on the phone. But while engaging in a lengthy phone conversation, he'd occasionally glance at me and smile.

I became one of the battalion of people who ran errands for him, picking up his favorite brand of shaving cream, a card he wanted to send to a friend, or high-quality paper for his typewriter. I became a bit jealous when other people did favors for him, as I thought that I, his only child, should be the primary person he relied on. It began to seem as if I'd known my birth father forever, and I'd sometimes forget that he'd been in my life for less than three years.

"When's the best time for me to come over?" I asked early on in our new arrangement.

He responded without hesitation. "Monday through Friday. Late morning through the afternoon. That way, we're less likely to be interrupted. Most of my visitors come during the evening and on weekends."

"Sounds good," I said. I knew we shared a thought that neither of us wanted to speak aloud. If Reverend Hahn's visitors repeatedly found a young woman hanging out in his apartment, they would naturally inquire as to the relationship between us. It was best to avoid that awkward scenario.

When I enrolled at Goshen College my freshman year, I'd taken it for granted that I would participate in SST, the school's study-service program. That would mean spending one trimester in a foreign country, providing services to the local people while learning about their culture.

I had, in fact, planned my curriculum with my faculty advisor to allow for doing my study-service program the second trimester of my junior year. I had set my sights on going to China.

However, as the first trimester of my junior year rolled by, I realized those plans were no longer viable. Studying abroad would require funds above the normal cost of tuition, money I didn't have. There was no way I could ask my dad to shoulder that extra expense. Because of Barbara's impending retirement, the two of them would soon be living on one income. Over and over, I kicked myself for not having worked and saved money the previous summer.

I knew there was only one source of money for international traveling, and that was my birth father. I was surprised that he hadn't already brought up the subject of SST. As a world traveler himself, I figured he'd want the same experiences for me. But I didn't want to be so audacious as to ask him for the money outright.

While eating my turkey dinner in his apartment several days before Thanksgiving, I hesitantly brought up the subject. "I was thinking about doing my SST next trimester. But I don't know if I should. What do you think?"

Reverend Hahn's face blanched. With only a moment's hesitation, he said, "I'm not sure I like that idea, Victoria."

His response deflated me. I set down my fork, too upset to eat another bite. "Why not?"

"I can't bear the thought of you being in harm's way."

I knew what he was talking about. The previous year, a student had been assaulted and seriously injured while on SST. Reverend Hahn had been aware of that fact, as he kept abreast of all significant events related to the college. However, I was still surprised that he wasn't enthusiastic about me taking advantage of such a life-changing opportunity as the study-service program.

As if reading my mind, he said, "There will be plenty of time for international travel a few years from now. When you're a little older."

I didn't press the point. Arguing about the matter wouldn't do any good, because when Reverend Hahn made up his mind, he was not to be swayed. I felt profoundly disappointed, even though I knew I had no right to demand anything more from the man who'd been so generous to me.

I picked up my fork, stabbed a bite of turkey, then laid it down again. "I'm too full to eat anymore," I said. Angry thoughts churned in my mind. *He doesn't want me to travel because he wants to keep me close to him. It's not fair. He's holding me hostage.*

I took several deep breaths, trying to settle myself down. And then, I realized that I felt more relieved than angry. If I left the country for three or four months, I might come home to find that another parent had died. That was not the way I wanted to handle my birth father's passing. The disease was marching on, and I doubted he could last much longer than a year. Until then, I'd stay close to him.

The following week, I met with my faculty advisor. We changed my plans for the next trimester, scheduling me to take the required courses that would substitute for my SST experience.

CHAPTER 35

On an evening in early December, the Goshen College chorale, along with the orchestra and chamber choir, presented a Christmas concert in the campus's newly built Umble Center. Clad in my dark choir robe, I stood on the stage with the other forty-nine members of the chorale, feeling both important and incredibly insignificant.

We'd been rehearsing all trimester for this event. Even though I'd grown accustomed to performing with the chorale, my mouth felt dry that evening, my palms sweaty. This was no ordinary venue. It was the first time I was participating in a performance that was being recorded for a later broadcast on our local public television station.

I glanced at the cameras that would be recording my every move, and wondered how I was going to keep from vomiting. I was glad I was several rows back instead of standing in front, so that if I did something out of kilter, it might go unnoticed.

As our director Dr. Metzler walked out on stage, a hush fell over the audience. In those few seconds of quiet, I thought I was going to jump out of my skin.

We sang the *Coventry Carol, O Little One Sweet,* and *Rise Up Shepherds and Follow.* During rehearsals, I'd been envious when soprano Maria Klopfenstein had been chosen for the solo in *Once in Royal David's City.* But that evening, I was enormously relieved that I wasn't the one in the spotlight.

Throughout the concert, I thought about Reverend Hahn, wishing he'd had the strength to get out one last time, to be there watching me. He would have been so proud.

After I finished the trimester's final exams, I was not eager to go back home to spend my three-week holiday break with my dad and his new wife. So I stayed in the dorm for as long as I could. During that time, I ran out to the Concord

Mall to do my Christmas shopping. And one afternoon, I passed the hours by helping my birth father decorate his apartment for the holidays.

Under his direction, I brought out his collection of holiday decorations, and we collaborated in finding places in the living room that would highlight each piece. I set out the fresh candles I'd bought for the table centerpiece. I strung the tree with colorful lights, and then sorted through the boxes of fine ornaments for the perfect final touches.

"Beautiful!" I exclaimed when I was finished. I spun around, taking in every detail of the room.

"Indeed. This is the loveliest this apartment has ever been at Christmastime. Thank you, Victoria." But Reverend Hahn's smile was bleak.

"Is something wrong?" I asked. "You don't seem like yourself today. Aren't you feeling well?"

I immediately chided myself for my insensitive question. *Of course he's not feeling well. He's been sick ever since you've known him.*

He sighed, his emaciated chest heaving with the effort. "Truthfully, I'm not feeling my best." He hesitated, as if deciding whether he should continue. "My child, I need to talk with you about something important. I was going to wait until after the holidays to bring it up. But the matter has been weighing heavily on me, and I think it's best if I tell you now. Otherwise, I'll be so preoccupied that I won't be able to enjoy the season with you."

A wave of fear drained the strength from my body, and I sank down on the sofa. "What is it?"

"As you might've suspected, Victoria, my days in this lovely apartment are coming to an end. When I met with my doctor earlier this week, he said it's time for me to transfer to the skilled nursing care unit here at Greencroft. That way, the staff can provide me with more comprehensive care."

I suddenly felt dizzy, and the beautiful decorations surrounding me seemed blurry and surreal. Part of me had known this day would come. But all the months I'd witnessed his slow decline, I'd gone on pretending that my birth father and I would carry on our relationship in his charming little apartment until the end of his time.

"When?" I whispered. "When is this going to happen?"

"Right after the holidays. I told my doctor that I wanted to celebrate one last Christmas in my apartment, and he agreed."

"We'll make this the best Christmas ever," I promised.

"Indeed, we will," he said. "Then I'll need to get down to the business of getting everything in order for the move." A tear trickled down his cheek.

This outward sign of his sorrow was more than I could bear, and my own tears began to flow. I jumped up, ran to the bathroom for tissues, and then knelt on the floor next to my birth father's wheelchair. I tucked a tissue into his hand, and we cried together.

"It's been so difficult to let go of my independence," he told me. "In my younger years, I was so healthy. Traveling all over the world was easy for me. I never envisioned myself being in this state. I'm not yet seventy years old. I'd always imagined that I'd be going strong until ninety."

He stopped to blow his nose. "But what hurts me most is that you and I have developed a comfortable relationship in this lovely apartment. By leaving here, I'm depriving my daughter of her home away from home. I feel as if I'm letting you down."

I flung my arms around him, sobbing against his bony shoulder, my tears soaking the sleeve of his sweater. "No," I choked out. "No, this isn't your fault. You're not letting me down."

He leaned his cheek against the top of my head, resting an awkward hand on my back. To the extent that his wheelchair would allow, my birth father and I held each other. I could sense the fragility of his sorrow mingled with the strength of his spirit, the spirit so akin to my own.

After a few minutes, I got up and went back to the bathroom for more tissues. When I looked into the mirror, I was reminded of my uncanny resemblance to the man whose life was rapidly running out, and my sobbing renewed. I blew my nose and wiped my eyes, only to start crying again. After several repetitions of this cycle, I finally succeeded in composing myself, and I went out to sit on the sofa.

"Wherever you are, Father," I said, "that will be my home."

Never before had I called him *Father*. The more casual term *Dad* would always be reserved for Herman Unruh, the man who'd raised me. When addressing my birth father, I'd always called him Reverend Hahn. He'd never asked me to call him anything else. It seemed as if he knew I'd have to come to that point on my own.

When he met my gaze, the blissful look in his eyes told me that the word *Father* had penetrated all the way to the center of his heart.

"I want to help," I said. "What can I do to make this move easier for you?"

Reverend Hahn took on his usual dignified bearing. "First, we'll have a wonderful Christmas together." He sounded confident and in charge. "Then, there will be things to pack. Books, pictures, keepsakes I've picked up from my travels."

"We'll tackle this together," I assured him. I glanced out the patio door and saw that it was already dark outside. It was evening, and I was still in his apartment. His church friends might come for a visit, and we'd have to deal with the awkward introductions. But I didn't care. I couldn't bear to leave him just yet.

I looked at my watch. It was time for the surprise I'd planned for him. "Let's do something different," I said. "Let's watch TV."

Reverend Hahn looked a bit bewildered, but didn't object. I scooted over to the end of the sofa, and he wheeled his chair around so that he could sit next to me. Picking up the TV remote control, I turned the channel to the public broadcasting station. Then, sitting side by side, we watched the Christmas concert that had been recorded several weeks earlier.

"See?" I said when the chorale came onto the screen. "That's me. Third row back, second from the end."

"Indeed it is," he chuckled.

We sat together in the room illuminated only by the lights of the Christmas tree. My birth father spoke little during the performance. From time to time, I glanced over at his enraptured face. I could tell he was savoring the experience, hanging onto the cherished moments that were rapidly running out.

CHAPTER 36

When I finally made it home a week before Christmas, my stepmother was all smiles. "Victoria!" she exclaimed. "Lucy and I could hardly wait for you to get here!"

Coaching myself to be pleasant, I submitted to her eager embrace before trudging up the stairs, lugging the suitcases Reverend Hahn had given me the previous Christmas. Upon entering my bedroom, I surveyed every inch of the space, looking for signs of intrusion. The room was dusty, the mattress bare. *Mom would've cleaned before I came home,* I thought. *And she would've had the bed made up for me.*

But at least there were no strange fingerprints on the dusty furniture, and nothing appeared to be out of place. Whatever Barbara had been storing in the room had long since been moved out.

I flung my suitcases on the bed and unpacked the clothing I'd brought home, stashing all the garments away in my closet and dresser drawers. Then I went back downstairs to get linens for my bed. I found the linen closet stuffed full of blankets Barbara had brought with her. Sorting angrily through the stack, I pulled out sheets and an old quilt that belonged to the era of my mother's housekeeping.

After making up my bed, I lay down on top of the quilt, staring at the familiar cracks in the ceiling plaster, trying to take in the changes that had pervaded the house while I was gone. But for now, the room felt like it still belonged to Victoria Unruh.

That evening, my dad pulled into the driveway with a scraggly pine tied to the top of his car. Excited as six-year-olds, Lucy and Barbara moved the furniture so the first Christmas tree that ever graced our farmhouse could be squeezed into the corner of the living room.

Minutes later, Judy arrived, and she, her mother, and Lucy proceeded to drape the tree with the lights and ornaments Barbara had brought with her from the trailer. My dad and I sat in the kitchen, watching the merriment from a distance.

Holding up an ornament for her mother's inspection, Judy said, "Didn't Grandma give this to me when I was little?" And I realized that the Prentiss family traditions had found their way into our household. The thought was disconcerting.

I glanced at my dad, who was wearing a contented smile. *Mom never would have allowed all this,* I wanted to remind him. But uttering such words would have been unreasonable and mean-spirited. Mom had been gone for a year. Whether I liked it or not, her imprint on the home was slowly fading.

Lucy came into the kitchen, overheated from her exertion, her forehead beaded with sweat. Opening the refrigerator door, she grabbed a two-liter bottle of *Pepsi,* something that had never been there when my mother was in charge. "Can you believe it, Tori Grace?" she chortled as she poured herself a drink. "We finally get to have a Christmas tree!"

She brushed her red curls off the back of her sweaty neck, and they bounced when they settled back into place. I noticed that her hair, which had been cut short for years, now reached the top of her shoulders. It looked clean and shiny, as if she'd shampooed it that morning.

"Are you growing your hair out, Lucy?" I asked.

She took a long gulp of her *Pepsi,* then nodded. "Yup. Barbara says it's too pretty to keep short. She says she's jealous, because my hair is naturally curly, and I'll never have to get it permed like hers. So, I'm going to grow it long again." She turned around and pointed to a spot on her lower back. "Way down to here, like it used to be."

She lifted her glass, eyeing the contents. "And maybe if I stop drinking this stuff, I'll lose some weight, too."

I slept in late the following morning, waking around 11:00 AM to a sweet smell wafting into my room. When I came down the stairs, I saw that the entire kitchen had been turned into a cookie-baking factory. Barbara was busy rolling out sugar cookie dough, and Lucy stood beside her, wielding the cookie cutters. I figured the set of cutters was one more thing that had come to the farmhouse with Barbara. My mother had never bothered with such nonsense. Her sugar cookies had always been round, cut with a jar lid.

"If I flip the cookie cutter this way and then that way," I heard Lucy say to Barbara, "then I can get more snowmen out of this space."

"I guess there's a science to it, huh?" Barbara said. They both laughed, at ease in each other's presence.

Lucy looked up and saw me standing in the doorway to the kitchen. "Look, Tori Grace!" She gestured toward the table laden with rows of cookies in the shapes of Christmas trees, stars, bells, and snowmen. They were all iced and topped with various kinds of sprinkles.

"Wow!" I said. "You've been working hard."

"Well, we did it the easy way." Lucy held up a tube of store-bought cookie dough.

I thought about the countless hours my mother used to spend in the kitchen baking her Christmas goodies: date pinwheel cookies, spritz cookies, seven-layer bars, fudge nut bars, and of course, fruitcake. She'd taken no shortcuts—everything was made from scratch. Everything perfectly executed. Never a batch that flopped.

I closed my eyes for a moment, remembering myself as a tiny child making sugar cookies with my mom. Under her coaching, I'd mixed sugar with drops of red food coloring, then had sprinkled it on the cookies after she'd spread them with white icing. Lucy had never been part of that scene. Somehow, Barbara was taking my sister back to revisit parts of childhood she'd missed. I wondered if my stepmother knew how crucial her role was in Lucy's life.

On Christmas Eve, I went with Dad, Barbara, Lucy, and Judy to the service at Westside Mennonite Church. Although the other congregants greeted them warmly, I could tell Dad and Barbara felt uncomfortable in the church that Herman and Ada Unruh had attended for almost four decades. My mom and dad had always sat on the right-hand side of the church, three or four pews from the front. Dad and Barbara chose to sit in a back pew, as if unsure of themselves in that environment.

Unsurprisingly, Lucy edged Judy out and claimed the spot next to Barbara. "Lucy's really taken to Mom," Judy observed as we filed out of the church after the service.

"Yeah," I said. "She hogs all her attention, doesn't she?"

"That's okay," Judy replied. "I think your sister needs that."

On Christmas morning, Barbara could hardly wait for all of us to gather around the tree to open gifts. I could tell she'd taken great delight in buying presents for us three girls. Her warmth and enthusiasm touched me. Even though my heart ached for my own mother, I didn't have it in me to spoil the day by being standoffish.

Lucy and I received nearly identical gifts, different only in color, pattern, and scent: multicolored knit gloves with socks to match, inexpensive charm bracelets, and a set of cologne and body lotion.

Always the tomboy, Judy was thrilled with her new blue jeans and her sweatshirt emblazoned with the *Chicago Cubs* logo. "My mom knows me," she laughed. "She's probably glad to have stepdaughters who are real girls."

Lucy sat next to me on the sofa with her gifts in her lap, looking misty-eyed. She pulled on her gloves, turning her hands to inspect them on both sides before carefully pulling them off and laying them on one knee. Then she picked up the bracelet, examining each charm.

"Look," she whispered, nudging me. She pointed to one of the charms, a heart engraved with the word *daughter.*

"That's really nice," I said. "Barbara got us some great gifts, didn't she?"

Lucy nodded. "Mom wouldn't have done this."

That's true, I thought. *Mom never would've bought us such frivolous things, just for the sake of seeing our eyes light up.*

My gifts to the family were a hit as well. A trio of sturdy flannel shirts for my dad, to replace the threadbare ones he'd worn for too many years. Soft skeins of yarn for Barbara, for her never-ending crocheting projects. A sweater for Lucy in a shade of blue that matched her eyes. And a gift certificate for Judy, to the Super Steer Steakhouse.

"Lucky you," Lucy said when she saw Judy's gift. "I love that place."

"I'll take you with me," Judy promised.

I smiled, happy that my sister had found so much love in her new family. I was almost envious of her.

I glanced over at my dad reclining in his new chair. He was gazing blissfully on the scene of his wife and three daughters happily chatting with one another. And I had to admit to myself that in all of my twenty years, I'd never had such a good time on Christmas morning.

Christmas dinner was palatable: canned ham, instant mashed potatoes, store-bought green beans, brown-and-serve rolls. For dessert, Lucy proudly served the cookies she and Barbara had baked. Nothing was as tasty as what my mother would have made. But Judy and Lucy ate with gusto, as if a delectable feast had been spread before them.

Having behaved myself like a true member of the family, I decided I had the right to sneak out of the house early that evening. Dad and Barbara were both dozing in their recliners. They barely nodded when I said, "I'm going out for a while."

I no longer informed my dad about my visits with Reverend Hahn. There was no reason to bring that reality into his new life. He deserved a break from the pain he'd lived with the last twenty years of his marriage to my mother.

At my birth father's apartment, I obligingly consumed a mug of hot chocolate and Christmas cookies brought by visitors from his church. Then, with Christmas tree lights twinkly festively, we exchanged gifts.

Mindful of his impending move to the skilled nursing unit, I'd given careful thought to what he might be able to use there. I'd ended up buying him a plush velour bathrobe in a rich shade of maroon.

He lifted it up with shaking hands, his lips smiling even though his eyes looked sad. "This is exactly what I'll need for the next chapter of my life. Thank you for your thoughtfulness, Victoria."

My gift from him was an expensive set of leather-bound books, the complete works of Shakespeare. "For my English major," he said.

"I'll cherish these for life," I assured him.

I knew that Reverend Hahn's nurse would soon arrive to help with his bedtime care. I was getting ready to leave when we heard the sound of Christmas carolers. The singers moved down the hallway, their voices coming closer and closer, until they stopped in front of Reverend Hahn's doorway.

"Well, isn't this a lovely surprise," he chuckled. "Carolers from church. I should invite them in."

As he moved toward the door in his wheelchair, I had a few moments of panic. *What will Reverend Hahn's church friends think about the strange young woman in his apartment on Christmas Day?* I thought about making a dash for the bathroom and locking myself inside, where I could press my ear to the door and eavesdrop on my birth father's conversation with his visitors.

But I didn't. As the eight carolers streamed into the living room, I moved back into the kitchenette, standing in the shadows while Reverend Hahn engaged his friends in lively conversation.

However, he didn't allow me to be overlooked. "This young lady is my dear friend Victoria," he said to his guests. "She's a student at Goshen College. I've known her and her family for a long time. She kindly took time out of her busy holiday to keep me company for a few hours."

Once again, I marveled at my birth father's way of skillfully avoiding the truth without telling a lie. I wasn't sure whether I admired or despised that ability. His unsuspecting visitors smiled at me. One woman said, "I think I've seen you at College Mennonite Church."

"Yes," I replied. "I've been attending there."

And then, the carolers broke into a four-part harmony rendition of *Silent Night,* before offering Reverend Hahn their holiday wishes and moving on down the hallway with their songs.

CHAPTER 37

Three days later, I returned to Reverend Hahn's apartment toting a stack of large storage containers he'd instructed me to buy at the hardware store. When I arrived, the door was open. Several men were in the process of carrying out the dining table and chairs.

The sight unnerved me. "Where are they taking your furniture?" I asked Reverend Hahn, who was supervising the project from his wheelchair.

"I've rented a storage unit on the west side of town, near Peddler's Village," he replied. "That's where I'll keep my things for now. We'll have to see what the future holds."

He seemed to have the move carefully planned, as he immediately instructed me as to my role in the process. "Why don't you begin by dismantling the Christmas tree? Then the movers can carry it out. That will give them more room to maneuver the sofa."

Slowly and carefully, I began removing Reverend Hahn's treasured ornaments from the tree, turning them over in my hands, savoring their beauty one last time. But halfway through the process, I realized that two of the movers were standing behind me with their arms folded, impatiently waiting for me to finish my task. So, I picked up my pace, hastily placing the ornaments in their boxes. The moment I pulled off the last string of lights, the men grabbed the tree and bustled it out of the apartment.

Throughout the afternoon, as the men carried out the sofa, recliner, coffee table, television set, and bookshelves, I worked nonstop at packing up books, dishes, and keepsakes. At times, I wanted to pause to inspect an item I hadn't seen before, to ask my birth father to tell me a story about it. But I knew now wasn't the time. I had to stay on task. As soon as I filled and labeled a storage container, the movers whisked it away to the truck.

At five o'clock, I looked around at the stripped-down

living room and kitchenette, a hollow feeling in my stomach. *I'll never see that beautifully furnished apartment again,* I thought. *I'll never be able to walk over here from the college and stretch out on the sofa for a nap. I'll never again be able to open the cupboard and fix myself a cup of tea or hot chocolate. I'll never decorate another Christmas tree in the living room.*

I wished I had arrived an hour earlier, to take in the sight of the intact apartment one last time, to say a proper goodbye before the movers came to strip it down.

As if sensing my melancholy mood, Reverend Hahn said, "Victoria, I think you've done enough for the day. You look worn out."

"What about your bedroom?" I asked him. "We haven't packed up your clothing."

"My nurse Cynthia will help me with my personal items," he quickly assured me.

Then he reached into the pocket of his sweater and pulled out a key. "This is the key to my storage unit." He pressed it into my hand. "I'll leave you in charge of it. I've tried to sort out everything that I'll need in my new living quarters. But in case I want something that's been packed up, perhaps you'll be so kind as to fetch it for me."

Then, suddenly solemn, he said, "The next time you see me, I'll be in the skilled nursing unit. You know where that is, don't you?"

I nodded.

"Just check in at the nurse's station, and they'll point you to my room."

I looked at the elderly man in his wheelchair, his body hunched from exhaustion. He suddenly seemed small and vulnerable.

"What are you going to do now?" I asked him.

"Cynthia will we here in a few minutes," he said. "We'll get everything wrapped up here. I'll be spending the night in my new room."

I couldn't bear the thought of leaving him alone. "I'll stay with you until she comes," I blurted out. "I'll help her take you over to your new place."

"No." Despite his exhaustion, Reverend Hahn's word was strong and emphatic. "I need to spend a few minutes alone now, to adjust to the change."

"Okay." I understood that he wanted privacy for handling the strong emotions that were threatening to overwhelm him. I also knew he didn't want me to witness any indignity associated with the nurse packing up his personal effects and wheeling him to his new destination.

I bent down and kissed his cheek before heading toward the door. Then I stopped to glance back at him. He looked so forlorn, so pitiful in the empty apartment. My mind traveled back in time, imagining the youth in his parents' bakery, eager to break out and see the big world. The young man in Hollywood, surrounded by starlets, dreaming of fame and fortune. The newly wedded man embarking on his career in the ministry.

Then I recalled my earliest memories of him, the middle-aged evangelist who'd brought such excitement to our humble rural church, whose charisma and stunning good looks made all the ladies a little dizzy. He'd been strong back then, invulnerable.

How does it come to this? I wondered. *How does it ever come to this?*

"Will you be all right?" I said aloud.

Reverend Hahn lifted his head and flashed me his dazzling smile. "Of course. Don't worry about me, Victoria. I'll be receiving the best of care."

But as I was about to close the door behind me, I heard him call out in a tremulous voice, "My child, will you be with me through all of this?"

I stopped and turned to face him. "Yes, Father. I'll be there with you. Every step of the way."

Tears blinded my eyes as I headed out to my car. I thought about the enormity of the commitment I'd just made, wondering whether I had the stamina to deal with this heart-wrenching journey so soon after my mother's death. But I knew I needed to. More than that, I wanted to.

CHAPTER 38

I dreaded my first visit to Greencroft's skilled nursing unit. I pictured Reverend Hahn lying in bed in an ugly hospital gown, all his dapper slacks, shirts, and sweaters packed away as relics of the past.

So, I focused my attention on settling back into my dorm room and registering for my second trimester's classes. On the night before classes were to begin, I lay in bed, my anxious mind going over the next day's schedule. Then my worrying expanded to include uneasy thoughts about my birth father that I'd been trying to keep at bay. Counting on my fingers, I realized it had been ten days since I'd seen him, ten days since he'd transferred to his new unit.

I felt profoundly ashamed of my neglect. "I'll go see him right after the chapel service tomorrow," I whispered into the darkness.

The next morning, I resolutely drove the brief mile from the college to the Greencroft complex. Without thinking, I pulled into the lot adjacent to the manor where Reverend Hahn had lived in his apartment. I had just opened my car door when I realized my mistake. I closed my door and sat there for a few minutes, blinking back my tears. After I succeeded in composing myself, I started my car again and drove the short distance to the new parking lot.

With trepidation, I entered the unfamiliar building, anxiously surveying my surroundings. "I'm here to see Reverend Harry Hahn," I announced to the woman at the nurse's station.

Barely glancing up from the chart she was writing in, the nurse rattled off the number of my birth father's room.

I was afraid she'd inquire about the reason for my visit, that she might put me in a difficult position by asking whether I was a relative. So, imitating my birth father's style, I searched for an innocuous explanation that would ward off any line of questioning. "I've known Reverend

Hahn since I was a little girl," I informed her. "He used to preach at my church. We've become good friends. So I'll probably be here a lot."

The nurse nodded, disinterested. "That's nice. Our residents get lonely, so visitors are always welcome."

Feeling disoriented and uncertain, I walked down the hallway and through the open door of Reverend Hahn's room. To my profound relief, I found him sitting in his wheelchair next to his neatly made bed, fully dressed in black slacks, a striped dress shirt, and a blue cardigan. He looked up from the *Christian Living* magazine he was reading and greeted me with a broad smile. "Victoria! I'm so delighted to see you!"

He didn't say a word about my not having visited him sooner, but immediately launched into questions about my new school term, just as he'd done when he lived in his apartment. And I realized that nothing about him had changed, except for his environment.

"How do you like it here?" I asked him.

"Oh, I'm getting wonderful care," he gushed. "The nurses are all so kind. They watch my nutrition very closely. They insist that I eat, whether I want to or not. They're constantly plying me with nutritional shakes." He chuckled, patting his concave abdomen. "I guess they want to see me fattened up a bit."

"You seem stronger," I told him. "More energetic."

"Yes," he replied. "I believe I am. And I am so grateful."

When I understood that I was not about to witness a rapid decline in my birth father's condition, visits to the skilled nursing care unit became easier. I developed the habit of stopping by three afternoons a week. I grew used to sitting in the chair beside Reverend Hahn's bed, rather than on his sofa. Even though the new room wasn't nearly as attractive as his apartment had been, he had still managed to add decorative touches with his favorite pictures and art objects. Each time I visited, there was a bouquet of fresh flowers on his bedside stand.

The round-the-clock care seemed to be exactly what my birth father needed. He put on a little weight, which made him look less gaunt and debilitated. He appeared to thrive in an environment where healthcare workers bustled around him.

When I arrived for a visit one afternoon in February, I saw a nurse's aide coming out of Reverend Hahn's room, giggling, her cheeks flushed with an embarrassment she was clearly enjoying.

"What's going on?" I asked her.

She put her finger to her lips. "Shhh." Then she took my arm and propelled me a few steps down the hall. "I don't want to talk where he can hear me."

She glanced around covertly, as if to make sure there were no eavesdroppers in sight. "I probably shouldn't be saying this. But I know you come here a lot, so you know him pretty well. Reverend Hahn can be ... a little naughty."

When she saw my shocked expression, she hurried to add, "He really is a very nice man. Always so cheerful. He never complains. And he's so smart. Sharp as a tack. We all enjoy having him here."

She cocked her head, looking coy. "All of us aides fight over who gets to take care of him. He makes us all feel special. I tell the other girls that I can come to work feeling fat and bloated or having a bad hair day, and after I take care of Reverend Hahn, I feel like the most beautiful woman in the world. He has a way of making all of us feel like that."

She giggled again. "He's fun. Like I said, he can be a little naughty. You probably know what I mean." She glanced at my face, then added, "But I don't supposed he talks that way with girls as young as you."

"No," I said emphatically. "He never talks that way with me."

As the nurse's aide moved on down the hall, I leaned against the wall outside my birth father's room, trying to collect myself before going inside to greet him.

Sometimes when I'd arrive at the unit, I'd find Reverend Hahn's room empty. "He's down the hall in Mr. Schrock's room," a nurse would inform me. Or it might be Mr. Cole's, Mrs. Thompson's, or Mrs. Covington's room.

I often overheard his conversations as I approached the other patient's room, and would listen outside the door for a minute or two. I marveled at his uncanny ability to enter another person's world. He could talk intimately with an elderly woman about her grandchildren, even though he had none himself. He could carry on a well-informed discussion about World War II with an army veteran, even though he'd never had military experience.

Once, I heard another patient question Reverend Hahn about his children. "My wife and I were never able to have children," came his smooth reply. "Myrna had to have surgery at a young age, which took away her possibility of ever bearing a child."

Abruptly, I turned and walked out of the building. I sat in my car, letting ten minutes pass before I went back inside, so that my birth father would never know I'd overheard what he'd said about the childless state of his marriage.

Whenever I'd walk into the room of the patient he was visiting, Reverend Hahn would beam with pleasure at the sight of me. He'd introduce me to his companion as "my dear young friend Victoria Unruh." Then I'd walk with him as he wheeled himself back to his own room, where he'd inevitably tell me an interesting story about the new friend he'd just made. He always seemed to be meeting someone new, learning something new.

Reverend Hahn came to know a great deal about the personal lives of the staff as well. "How's your husband doing after his knee surgery, Rose?" he once asked a nurse who entered the room while I was with him. "Is he up and around yet?"

Other times, it was, "Linda, I heard your son's team won the game last night." "How's Tiffany getting along with her new braces, Marie?" "It's good to have you back, Suzanne. I missed you. Did you have a good time in Florida? You look like you got a little sun while you were on vacation."

Time and again, I heard the staff singing his praises. "He's our resident chaplain," one nurse told me. "He knows which of our patients never receive visitors, and he makes a point to go see them. He'll take the ladies a flower from the vase beside his bed. Even if the patient is unresponsive, he'll sit and talk to them. Last week, one of our residents passed away. When the family came in, Reverend Hahn wheeled himself down to the room to pray with them."

Her eyes misted with tears of tenderness. "He's so sick himself, but he still wants to take care of other people. It's touching. He's an inspiration to all of us."

"I'd like to change things around in this room," Reverend Hahn said to me one day in March. He pointed to a picture hanging on the wall across from his bed. "I think that would look better on the wall next to the window. There's something else I want to hang in that spot."

"What?" I asked.

"The painting I brought back from the Holy Land. Remember it? The one with the lake and the beautiful hills? It's in my storage unit."

"Yes," I said, remembering exactly which box I'd packed it in. "Do you want me to get it for you?"

He smiled sweetly, and then lowered his voice to a near whisper. "If you'd be so kind, my dear child."

After our visit, I drove across town to the storage facility. When I unlocked Reverend Hahn's unit and lifted the heavy door, I was aghast at the state of his belongings. The movers had done the job he'd paid them to do, but they certainly hadn't gone beyond the call of duty. It looked as if they'd rushed through the unloading of the truck, haphazardly dumping the contents into the storage unit.

The sofa sat diagonally across the middle of the space, with the coffee table turned upside down on top of it. Several lamps lay on their sides on the overturned coffee table. Sections of the bookshelves were scattered around in different parts of the unit, with one section lying on the dining table. The boxes I'd packed so carefully were randomly shoved into any available space.

It looked as if a bomb had gone off in my birth father's apartment, utterly destroying the beautiful arrangement. The sight hit me so hard that I couldn't breathe for a few seconds. I was furious, while at the same time glad Reverend Hahn would never see the disarray. The careless treatment of his possessions would have hurt him.

I poked around in the mess until I located the box I wanted, then removed the painting and carried it out to my car. Returning to the storage unit, I set about organizing the space. I moved aside boxes so that I could shove the sofa against the wall, where it sat beside the console television set. I placed the coffee table in front of the sofa, and the end tables on each side, just how they'd been arranged in the apartment. I set the lamps upright on the end tables. I managed to heave all the bulky sections of the book shelves over to the other side of the unit. I couldn't begin to assemble them the way they'd been in the apartment, but at least they were now stored together. I moved the dining table and chairs next to the bookshelves. Then, in the center of the space, I carefully stacked the storage containers. I worked for a full hour, until I was satisfied that I'd done my best in putting Reverend Hahn's belongings in order.

Why am I so invested in this? I wondered. *Why am I taking this so personally?*

Because I care about him, came the answer. *Because he's my father. Because it's a child's responsibility to look out for an aging parent.*

On an afternoon in late April, Reverend Hahn and I sat together in his room, discussing my upcoming final exams. "Victoria, what are you going to do this summer?" he asked. "Are you moving back home?"

"No, I'm not." I smiled as I thought about the plans I'd worked out.

I'd called my old boss Bob from Taste of Home, to see if he had any waitress positions open for the summer. "I'd be more than happy to have you back," he'd told me.

I knew I wouldn't have to worry about Calvin being there at the restaurant. He was graduating and moving back to Nebraska. Bonnie Springer was dropping out of school and going with him. She'd broadcasted the news of their engagement all over campus, flashing around her modest diamond like it was the most important rock in the world, while I thanked my lucky stars that it was on her finger, not mine.

My roommate Rhonda and I had arranged to rent a house on Sixth Street, sharing it with two other girls. I figured the money I made as a waitress would be enough to feed me and cover one quarter of the rent. We'd all agreed to continue our off-campus living arrangement during our senior year.

"Good for you," Reverend Hahn said after I informed him of my plans. "My daughter is becoming self-sufficient." Then he quickly added, "But if you need anything, don't hesitate to let me know."

"I will, Father," I promised.

PART IV: SUMMER 1981-SPRING 1982

CHAPTER 39

The third week in May, I finished the last classes of my junior year. I felt sentimental as I packed up the things in my dorm room, knowing that I was moving out of Westlawn for the last time. My roommate Rhonda and I, along with our friends Tamara and Charity, would be taking possession of our new apartment on the first of June. Until then, I would need to stay with my dad and Barbara for ten days.

I felt impatient about this imposed interlude. As I lugged my bags and boxes to my car, I wished that I was driving them the few blocks to my new apartment on Sixth Street, rather than hauling them across town to my childhood home.

When I pulled into the driveway, my dad and Barbara were sitting on the porch swing. She was nestled up to his bulky frame, his arm around her narrow, stooped shoulders. Relaxed and sleepy-eyed, they looked like a contented older couple who had nothing more pressing to do than to gaze out over their front yard and watch the traffic pass by on their county road.

"Vickie!" my dad called as I approached the house carrying my suitcases. "You're home!"

As I climbed the steps to the porch, Barbara eased her body off the swing, wincing in pain. She kissed my cheek, then attempted to take one of the suitcases from my hand. "Let me help you, honey."

I shook my head. "No. I'm fine. I don't want you to hurt yourself."

"Let me help her," my dad said. "You sit down, Barbara." He headed to the car and began carrying boxes into the house and up the stairs to my room.

That evening, while Dad, Barbara, Lucy, and I were eating a simple supper of store-bought pot pies and applesauce, Barbara made an announcement. "Guess what, Victoria!" Her eyes sparkled. "Your brothers are coming to visit next month."

"Oh, really?" I said, surprised. My brothers hadn't been back home since my mother's funeral.

"Yes," Barbara said. "Isn't that something? They're driving out here right after the kids are done with school. They said they're all coming in one big van." She clasped her hands together, as if trying to contain her excitement. "Your brothers are such fine young men. I'm looking forward to getting to know them better. And it will be wonderful to have the grandchildren around."

Her enthusiastic words threw me off balance. I'd never seen my mother acting this excited about the boys coming home. She'd always been glad to see them. But their visits were inevitably marked by tension, and afterwards, gloom would linger in the household for days.

And my mother had been hesitant in relating to her grandchildren, never able to reach out to them with confidence. She'd known that, in her sons' eyes, her image was tainted. No doubt, she feared that their wives and children shared the same impression of her.

But here was Barbara, ready to pick up a role that my mother never had the opportunity to play.

I glanced at my dad. His face was impassive. I was quite sure that he'd recounted nothing of our family's dark history to his new wife, and I was glad. Telling her about my mother's affair and my illegitimate birth would serve no purpose.

"We'll certainly have a houseful," Barbara prattled on. "I have no idea where we'll put everyone." Her face lit up with a sudden idea. "Maybe I'll send you two girls over to the trailer to spend the night with Judy while your brothers are here. Judy would get a kick out of that."

I reminded Barbara that by the time my brothers arrived, I'd be living in my own apartment. "You can put one of the families in my old room," I told her.

Barbara's smile vanished, and she lowered her eyes. "I keep forgetting that you're moving out, sweetie. Maybe I just don't want to accept that it's true. You've been away at school, and I haven't had any time with you."

Then she looked up, and her voice brightened. "Well, you'll just have to come back home to visit while your brothers are here."

"Of course," I said.

After supper, I went upstairs to the solitude of my room, still troubled by Barbara's eagerness to form a relationship with the grandchildren my own mother barely had the chance to know. It seemed so unfair.

But I forced myself to shrug off those unhappy thoughts and turn my attention to my own future. I had a lot of work to do to get ready for living on my own.

Deep inside, I knew this was going to be a permanent move. I'd come back to visit for a few days every now and then. But I would never live in the old farmhouse again.

The significance of the move weighed heavily on me, saddened me. But I felt I had no other choice. While I no longer resented Barbara, I had no desire to live in the household she was now in charge of. I couldn't imagine adapting to a myriad of habits that were so different from those of Ada Unruh.

I was determined to leave nothing of mine behind in the bedroom, nothing that would act as a link to my childhood years. I had to sort out what I would take and dispose of the rest, carrying nothing with me that no longer served a purpose in my life.

The sorting task seemed overwhelming. I looked around the room, thinking about how my well-organized mother would have tackled the project.

I decided to start with my closet, and began pulling out items I hadn't taken with me to college. Clothing I'd worn in high school, and even middle school. Jeans that were too short. Out-of-style tops. Worn-out shoes. I smiled to myself as I piled the discarded clothing on my bed, wondering how my mother had refrained from hounding me about getting rid of those things years ago.

When the closet was finally empty, I went downstairs to find trash bags for hauling the clothing to Goodwill. I found Barbara at the kitchen sink washing the last of the supper dishes. She turned her head to look at me, and her eyes filled with tears.

I was getting used to the fact that it took very little to bring Barbara to tears. I never saw her cry from anger or self-pity. Her tears flowed for sentimental reasons. Unlike my mother, Barbara wore all her tender feelings on her sleeve.

"Victoria, sweetie," she said, "I apologize for overstepping my bounds at supper. I know this house doesn't feel like home to you anymore, not since your mother passed away. I know you miss your mom. I know I can't take her place. I just hope you don't hold anything against me."

I walked over and put my arm around her shoulders. "I don't hold anything against you, Barbara. You make my dad happy." Then I spoke words that I'd never been able to say before. "And I love you for that."

She looked up at me, her sentimental tears streaming down her wrinkled face. "Honey, I love your dad more than anything in the world. I want him to be happy. And I want his children to be happy."

I headed back up the stairs, trash bags in hand, passing by my dad who was watching TV in the darkened living room. "Vickie," he called out, his voice tentative.

I stopped on the third step. "What do you want, Dad?"

"Come sit down so we can talk for a minute."

Changing my course, I went back down the stairs and into the living room, where I pushed aside Barbara's crocheting project and sat down in her chair. The flickering light of the television screen illuminated the sadness on my dad's face. I wondered if he, too, had been remembering bygone days.

I recalled the simple, tidy arrangement of the living room during the era of my mother's frugal housekeeping: the shabby sofa, the worn-out armchair, the TV, the lamps, the coffee table, the desk, the small set of bookshelves. Back then, when I wanted to talk with my dad, I'd flop down on the sofa while he sat in his chair. Now, I felt ill-at-ease in the cluttered living room, overcrowded with Barbara's furniture and the chairs I'd bought.

My dad picked up the remote control on the arm of his chair and switched off the TV. "Are you sure you want to do this?"

"Do what?" I asked.

"Move out. Live out there on your own. You could be living here for free."

"I'm going to start work in a few days," I reminded him. "I'll have money to live on."

"I know. But you could stay here and save up for your future."

"I'll be okay, Dad." I didn't tell him what he undoubtedly suspected, that my birth father was providing a financial safety-net for this new venture.

He sighed heavily. "I guess I'm just not ready to let my little girl go."

I stood up. "I know, Dad. But things are different now." Before heading back up the stairs, I bent down to hug him, pressing my cheek against his, feeling the familiar prickle of his day-old growth of beard.

The next few days, I occupied myself with preparing for my move. I did the backlog of laundry I'd brought home with me, washing all my clothing, sheets, and towels. With Barbara's permission, I collected extra sheets and towels from the linen closet, making a stack in the corner of my room.

When Barbara asked if I needed dishes, I panicked. Oddly, I hadn't given much thought to supplying my new kitchen.

"We have more than enough," she said, "with everything I brought over from the trailer." Then her voice softened to a whisper. "Sweetie, why don't you take some of your mother's things with you? I think she'd like that."

So, I gathered up plates, bowls, cups, glasses, and silverware, along with several pots and a skillet, carrying everything upstairs to the growing stash in my room.

I paused in my preparations long enough to celebrate my birthday with my family. Under Barbara's supervision, Lucy baked a chocolate layer cake from a mix. Then, on her own, she decorated it with an assortment of colorful candies, creating a scalloped edge around the cake and a floral design in the center.

She beamed with pleasure when I complemented her on her work. "Barbara says I'm artistic."

Before cutting the cake, Lucy led a rousing rendition of *Happy Birthday* in her lovely soprano voice. Dad and Barbara chimed in, both decidedly off-key.

The morning after my birthday, I donned my waitress uniform, a black skirt and white blouse, and headed off to work. When I pulled into the city parking lot behind the Taste of Home restaurant, I completely gave way to the anxiety that had been plaguing me the past few hours. "There's nothing to worry about," I chided myself as I switched off the ignition. "You know how to do the job."

As I walked through the back door and into the kitchen, I realized it had been almost two years since I'd set foot in the restaurant. I surveyed my surroundings, taking in the new equipment, the new people bustling about their work.

The first familiar person I spotted was Allen, the former dishwasher. "Hey, Stretch," he said when he saw me. I noticed that he'd grown a few inches since I'd last seen him. The extra height only added to his cocky attitude.

"Where's Edna?" I asked him.

"Edna?" he said, as if he barely remembered her. "That old bag retired a year ago." He pointed to a heavy-set young man wearing a chef's coat. "Elliot's the head cook now."

After several hours of working with Elliot, I grew so sick of him that I could hardly stand to look at his smug face. He wasn't hesitant to spout out all his credentials for the job of head cook, as if to remind me of my lowly position as a waitress. Because he'd worked as a line cook at a upscale restaurant in South Bend, he seemed to think his skills were on par with someone who'd graduated from culinary school. Clearly, he believed his talents were wasted on a small family restaurant.

I learned that Allen had been promoted from his dishwashing job to Elliot's assistant. He proudly referred to himself as the sous-chef. I'd been primed and ready to ward off my former admirer's advances, but discovered that his amorous attention was now turned to Jamie, a new waitress who couldn't have been over seventeen.

Mindy still worked as a waitress, and I was relieved to see her familiar face. Bradley the busboy was no longer there. Mindy told me that after his high school graduation, he'd moved out of town. So, with the exception of Mindy and Allen, all the employees of Taste of Home were new to me.

By the end of my first day, I knew I had no desire to form friendships with my new coworkers. While several people made efforts to pull me into the workplace banter, I found the teasing and joking to be childish and annoying. I remembered my own silly behavior the first two summers that I worked at the restaurant, and wondered at my foolishness in choosing to date a coworker.

Just mind your own business, I repeatedly told myself when my irritation rose to levels I could hardly contain. *Just do your work and get out of here at the end of your shift.*

CHAPTER 40

On the morning of June 1, Wendell Hooley pulled his pickup truck into our driveway. My dad had asked our neighbor to help move my bedroom furniture to my new apartment. I was surprised, and a little flustered, when I saw that Daniel was with his father.

After the men carried my furniture down the stairs and loaded it into the back of the truck, my dad and Wendell rested on the porch for a few minutes, drinking the iced tea Barbara had brought out for them. Daniel and I stood beside the truck, talking.

As always, being near Daniel stirred up a swarm of sensual feelings in me. Two nights ago, I'd had another one of my erotic dreams about him. I'd woken up feeling ashamed of my dreamtime improprieties with a man who was engaged to marry someone else.

"So, what's new with you?" I asked, hoping he wouldn't sense my guilt.

"Well, I just graduated from Purdue," he replied.

"Congratulations!" I said. "You're lucky. I've got one more year to go."

He looked down at the ground, rubbing the toe of his shoe over a patch of gravel. "Deanna and I will be getting married at the end of the month."

Jealousy welled up in me, but I forced myself to speak cheerfully. "Wow! That's awesome! Are you excited?"

He looked up and nodded, breaking into a wide grin.

"Where's the wedding?"

"At Deanna's church. Waterford Mennonite."

He didn't say anything about me being invited. I knew it would be best for everyone if Daniel's former girlfriend wasn't present at the ceremony.

"Where will you be living?" I asked him.

"For now," he said, "we'll be renting an apartment on the west side of town, in the Silverwood complex. We're looking for a house to buy somewhere around here. My dad's in the process of buying a few more acres, and I'll be helping him farm."

"Good for you," I said. Things were working out in Daniel's life just the way I'd expected they would. I thought about my erotic dream again, wondering if my subconscious mind would ever allow me to let go of Daniel.

Diverting the conversation off his own life, he said, "It looks like you're moving on, too. You and I have lived our whole lives as neighbors on this county road, and now we're both moving away in the same month. Crazy, huh?"

Wendell came walking toward us, interrupting our conversation. "We should get going," he said to Daniel. The two burly men got into the truck and drove away, carrying my furniture to my new address.

Feeling sad and nostalgic, I walked back into the house and up the stairs to make sure I'd packed up everything. The sight of the empty room made my stomach clench. The patches of dust that had accumulated under the furniture, a large one under the bed, smaller ones under the dresser and bedside stand, remained behind as tell-tale signs of an era now past. All three pieces had been in those exact spots ever since I could remember. I felt as if I'd robbed the room of furnishings that rightfully belonged to it.

As I stuffed the last of my clothing into the luggage Reverend Hahn had given me, I heard my dad's footsteps on the stairs. "All set then, Vickie?" he said as he entered the room.

He picked up one of the suitcases, looking puzzled. Even though I'd carried my luggage in and out of the house several times, he acted as if he hadn't seen it before. Then a dark look crossed his face, and I figured he'd guessed where the suitcase had come from. But he made no comment.

A moment later, a tearful Barbara came into the room. "I hate to see you go, Victoria," she said, dabbing at her eyes.

"It feels like I'm losing my own child." Reaching for me, she squeezed me tightly. "I want you to know that if things don't work out, you can always come back. You're always welcome here."

"Thanks," I said, kissing her cheek.

"Let's go, Vickie," my dad said, his voice resolute. "The guys will be waiting for us."

Thankfully, my new landlord had cleaned up the squalor left behind by the previous tenants, Calvin Zook and his friends. When I carried my belongings into my new bedroom, it was as clean as if Ada Unruh had done the job.

I'd claimed one of the downstairs bedrooms. I certainly hadn't wanted to take up residence in Calvin's old room, where I'd had my one and only intimate encounter with him. Rhonda took the other downstairs bedroom, while Tamara and Charity happily moved into the upstairs rooms. Both of them had boyfriends, and I was glad I'd be some distance away from any private activity.

Rhonda, always organized and efficient, ended up being the leader of our little group. That first afternoon, she sat us all down at the kitchen table to come up with a list of household rules. We were each assigned a section of the kitchen cupboard for storing our groceries, and we agreed to refrain from invading each other's stashes of food. We also agreed to promptly wash our own dishes after eating a meal.

We brainstormed a list of chores that included cleaning the bathroom, mopping the kitchen floor, vacuuming the living room, and taking out the garbage. Then we set up a schedule that specified who would be responsible for what chores each week. All of us expressed optimism that our household would run smoothly and peacefully.

Several hours later, when my empty stomach started grumbling for my attention, it occurred to me that my first order of business was to stock up on groceries. I suddenly realized how much I'd taken for granted during all my years of living at home. My mother, and now my stepmother, unfailingly set meals on the kitchen table at the expected times. At the college, all I had to do was walk down a flight of stairs, enter a cafeteria, and choose whatever food struck my fancy. I had a moment of panic, doubting whether I had the ability to keep myself fed.

"Does anyone else need to go to the grocery store?" I called to my roommates.

"I do," Tamara said.

The two of us drove across town to the Kroger store. Foolishly, I'd come without a list. The mental strain of trying to envision what groceries I'd need over the coming week exhausted me. Instead of cooking that evening, Tamara and I opted to stop for burgers at McDonald's.

The next morning, which was Sunday, I felt so disoriented in my new home that I had to mentally rehearse the steps for getting myself ready for church. I went to the bathroom to take a shower, but found it to be occupied by one of my roommates. I waited five minutes, then ten, and when twenty minutes passed without the bathroom door opening, I gave up on the idea of making it to church. "Rhonda needs to sit us all down to discuss bathroom schedules," I muttered as I walked away.

With no other agenda for the morning, I milled around my room, arranging my things one way and then another. I had no idea what to do next. I decided I needed to write out a schedule, a blueprint for the adult life I'd been so eager to embrace, but which now felt overwhelming to me.

Then I realized I didn't even have paper on which to write such a list. At home, there had always been paper, along with pens and pencils, in the desk in the living room. My frugal mother had kept a stash of scrap paper—the empty side of junk mail letters, the backs of used envelopes—and barked at the rest of us to use the scraps instead of wasting good paper. But while I had a pen in my purse, I had no such stash of paper in my room.

Frustrated beyond reason, I remembered that during our roommate meeting the previous day, Rhonda had been writing on a pad of lined paper.

When I went to her room and informed her of my plight, she grimaced, as if to chastise me for being unprepared. "How much do you need?" she asked.

"Just two sheets," I said apologetically.

Back in my own room, I used one piece of paper to write down the items I still needed to buy. At the top of the list was *paper.*

On the other sheet, I wrote down my work schedule. Then I puzzled over how to fit in other activities of daily living. Shopping for groceries. Going to the laundromat. Cleaning my room. Doing my weekly household chores.

I suddenly realized that, in the flurry of activity surrounding my move, I'd gone more than a week without visiting my birth father. Under *Wednesday Afternoon,* I penned in, *Go to Greencroft.* I promised myself to visit more often, if I could.

On the back side of my shopping list, I tried to brainstorm a list of meals I knew how to prepare. *What was I thinking, moving away from home already?* I asked myself as I chewed on the cap of my ink pen.

I was astounded at what a huge bite one trip to the grocery store took out of my meager paycheck. Thankfully, I was allotted one free meal for each shift I worked at the restaurant, which took care of some of my nutritional needs. Our new cook Elliot insisted that all food left over at the end of the day had to be thrown into the garbage. "I'm not going to be responsible for any of you getting sick from spoiled food," he'd bark whenever he'd catch someone trying to circumvent his rule.

Of course, throwing out good food seemed like a waste to the rest of us. In spite of Elliot's watchful eye, we all managed to rescue the occasional chunk of meatloaf or batch of fried fish from the fate of the dumpster. I sneaked home as much leftover food as I could, providing meals for myself, and sometimes for my roommates as well.

When I shamefacedly walked into Reverend Hahn's room four days after my move, I apologized for my absence. He immediately inquired as to how I was doing with my new living arrangement.

I sighed heavily. "It's hard. There's so much to get used to." And in response to his probing questions, I spilled out the details of my frustrations.

He listened intently, nodding his approval. "I'd say you're getting the hang of living on your own. You're learning a lot through trial and error."

Then, smiling broadly, he held out his arms for a hug. "My child, I am so proud of you."

CHAPTER 41

Three days before my brothers and their families were due to arrive in Goshen, my roommate Rhonda informed me that I'd received a message on the household answering machine. When I pressed the play button, I was surprised to hear my sister's plaintive voice. "Tori Grace, Barbara's getting really nervous. She doesn't know what to fix when the boys get here. I don't know what to tell her. Can you come over and help?"

I immediately called the house. Barbara answered the phone. "Lucy says you need some help," I said. "Do you want me to stop by the house tomorrow?"

"Oh, sweetie, I'd appreciate that!" Barbara gushed. "If you're not too busy. If it's not too much trouble."

The following afternoon, I drove over to the house and sat with Barbara and Lucy at the kitchen table. Barbara seemed to be at her wit's end. Her hands were aflutter with nervous habits, twisting the ends of her frizzy hair, fingering the buttons on her old-fashioned blouse.

"I don't know where to start," she fretted. "I'm used to fixing meals for my own kids. They're not picky. They'll eat anything. But I don't know what your brothers like."

"Why don't we make a list?" I suggested. Lucy jumped up, went to the desk in the living room, and brought back a pad of paper and a pencil.

"So," I asked Barbara, "what ideas do you have for breakfast?"

"Mom always made scrambled eggs and sausage when the boys came," Lucy chimed in. I shot her a dirty look, and she clamped her hand over her mouth.

Tears pooled in Barbara's eyes. "I know I'm not the cook your mother was. But I'll give it a try. Lucy, honey, would you start writing down a grocery list? Put down eggs and sausage."

I suggested that she buy several packages of sweet rolls to go with the eggs and sausage, discreetly omitting the fact that my mother always made her own rolls.

We fumbled our way through the rest of the menu planning. Just when we'd exhausted our store of ideas, my dad called from the living room, "Don't worry about supper on Saturday night. I'll take everyone out to eat at Peddler's Village."

Barbara sighed with relief. "Herman, you're so good to me."

I was not at the house on Friday when the boys arrived with their families, as I was scheduled to work both the lunch and the dinner shifts that day. I'd thought about asking my boss for the day off. But I knew that if I missed an entire day of work, my depleted paycheck would fail to cover my share when next month's rent came due.

I could ask Reverend Hahn for help, I thought. *He told me to come to him if I ran short on money. He'd understand that I need a day off to visit with family.* But I couldn't bring myself to do it. I had been on my own for less than a month, and I didn't want to admit inadequacy so early in my quest for independence. So I worked my scheduled shifts that day.

I worked the lunch shift on Saturday as well, but was able to meet the family at the Peddler's Village restaurant for dinner. Judging by the way the evening went, I didn't regret missing out on family time the previous day.

We loaded our plates with sumptuous food from the buffet: ham, fried chicken, Swiss steak, potatoes, and a variety of vegetables. Then we seated ourselves at a table large enough to accommodate all of us: Dad, Barbara, Lucy, and me; Michael and his wife Cheryl, along with their daughters Laramie and Mallory; Robert and his wife Deborah, and their two sons, Jeffrey and Jeremy.

As I'd always known them to be, my sisters-in-law were quiet and guarded in the family circle. Deborah kept glancing at her watch, as if wondering how long it would take to get the insufferable meal over with. If Cheryl was attempting to hide her misery, she failed at that task. I could tell that traveling to Indiana to visit with her husband's relatives wasn't her idea of a fun vacation.

The table conversation consisted of a desultory exchange between my brothers and my dad. The boys teased my dad about the poor showing of his favorite major league baseball team, the Chicago Cubs, while singing the praises of their own team, the Baltimore Orioles. They talked about Wendell's crops, and my brothers feigned interest when my dad announced that our neighbor had recently purchased another hundred acres of farmland. They reminisced about the animals that no longer inhabited our old barn, chuckling about the ornery goats of bygone days.

"Have you been thinking about retirement, Dad?" Michael asked. "How many years have you been doing your mail route?"

"Almost forty," my dad replied. "I'm thinking I'll work through the end of the year. I'll do one more Christmas season, and then I'll be done. That's pretty much all I got left in me."

Reaching over to pat Barbara's arm, he added, "It's time for me and the missus to slow down." I saw my brothers exchange covert glances, as if discomfited by my dad's reference to his marital status.

Ten-year-old Jeremy became increasingly restless as the evening progressed, resorting to entertaining himself by elbowing and poking his fourteen-year-old brother Jeffrey. Irritated, Jeffrey repeatedly pushed him away, and the poking and shoving turned into a full-blown tussle. When Jeffrey pushed his brother so hard that Jeremy fell off his chair, their mother emerged from her cocoon of silence and barked at them to settle down. But the scuffle didn't end until Robert jumped in and added the weight of fatherly authority.

Seventeen-year-old Mallory and fifteen-year-old Laramie made no attempt to hide their contempt for the company they were forced to keep. Sour looks marred the prettiness of their young faces. Adding not a word to the group conversation, they rifled through their purses and whispered to each other. Periodically, they stifled giggles.

I looked across the table at Barbara, who was sitting next to my dad. But her chair was pulled back from the table a little farther than his, as if she thought she didn't belong with the rest of the family. She looked exhausted. Intimidated. Hurt.

Lucy had been sitting on the other side of Barbara, but now that chair was empty. Twenty minutes earlier, my sister had gotten up, whispering as she passed me that she was heading to the bathroom. Since she hadn't returned promptly, I figured she'd wandered off to the part of the building where the craft and artist booths were set up. That kind of thing always caught her attention.

I was sitting next to Laramie, who was fidgeting in her chair, sighing in exasperation. On impulse, I leaned toward her, and pointing to Barbara, I said to my niece, "Why don't you go over there and talk to your grandmother for a minute? She'd like that."

Laramie looked at me with disdain. "She'd not my grandmother."

Taken aback by her impertinence, I must have stared at her in a way that she interpreted as a dirty look. She emitted a testy little grunt, rolling her eyes to communicate her total contempt for not only my suggestion, but for me as well. I clenched my hands in my lap, digging my nails in my palms to keep from slapping her.

Then Laramie turned to her sister and said, "I'm bored. Let's go walk around and look at stuff." And the two girls flounced away.

In that moment, I knew that even if Michael hadn't told his daughters about my illegitimate birth, they had, over the years, adopted his attitude that visiting their family in Indiana was a repugnant obligation.

I got up and went back to the buffet for dessert, hoping that a piece of sweet cheesecake would rid me of the bitter taste the evening had left in my mouth. I had wanted to believe that, after the intimacy surrounding my mother's passing, the rift in the family would be mended. And I had foolishly hoped that my brothers would start taking an interest in me. In light of the conversation we'd had on the porch shortly before my mother's death, I had expected a bit of warmth from Michael. He had apologized for not having treated me like a sister.

But the only personal thing he'd said to me that evening was, "So, I hear you're out on your own now." And before I could even respond, he'd turned back to join Robert and my dad on the topics of crops and tractors.

The rift between the Virginia family and the Indiana family was still there, now widened by my dad's decision to marry Barbara. Long ago, an insidious poison had been injected into our family system, infiltrating the generation that had followed. That poisonous process had started the moment Reverend Hahn's sperm had joined my mother's egg, creating the embryo that was to become me. I had no idea what the antidote to that poison would be.

I sat at the table stabbing at the cheesecake with my fork, the pain in my chest so thick and heavy that it almost choked the breath out of me. I knew my existence was a blight on the family. All I could think to do was to extricate my troublesome presence from the gathering so that the Unruh family could be whole again.

Abandoning my cheesecake, I stood up, mumbling my goodbyes. Then I turned and walked out of the restaurant. It was time to let go of old hopes and expectations. Time to slough off the pain from the past and move on with my life.

As I walked through the restaurant door, Lucy came rushing up to me. "Tori Grace, you've got to see all the booths they've set up on the other side of the building. Artists and woodworkers and jewelry makers—they've got everything."

She stopped talking when she saw the look on my face. "What's wrong?"

"Nothing," I said. "I've got to go, Lucy."

She took a few steps back, looking hurt. On impulse, I stepped forward, closing the distance between us, then wrapped my arms around her and hugged her tightly. *My sweet, troubled sister,* I thought. *You're still my family.*

"I love you, Lucy," I said aloud.

"Oh, I love you, too, Tori Grace," she crooned, returning my embrace. She rocked my body from side to side, soothing me. Then, as if with an uncanny sixth sense, she uttered the exact words I needed to hear in that moment. "I'll always love you, baby sister. No matter what happened in the past. No matter what happens in the future. I'll love you forever and ever, and even longer than that."

CHAPTER 42

Within a few weeks of moving into my new apartment, I could tell things weren't going to run as smoothly as I'd hoped they would. My roommate Charity was proving herself to be a challenge to live with.

She was a cute girl, barely over five feet tall, with a mane of fluffy blonde hair and a voluptuous figure that turned male heads. When I'd first met Charity, I'd been charmed by her bubbly personality.

However, sharing a house with her was a different matter. She talked nonstop, jumping from one inane topic to another, getting on everyone's nerves. Learning to tune her out became a survival skill for the rest of us household members.

One evening when Tamara and I were in the kitchen preparing our evening meal, Charity walked in, having just completed her first day on the job at Kmart in Elkhart. "Whew!" she exclaimed. "Glad that's over with! I was so nervous. My insides felt like *Jello* all day long."

Sparked by her own reference, she began prattling about *Jello*. "My mom makes the best *Jello* parfait. She always puts the red *Jello* in the bottom of the glass. Then the yellow *Jello*. That's funny, it rhymes. Yellow *Jello*, yellow *Jello*. Then the green *Jello*. Sometimes, she puts fruit it in. Like bananas or mandarin oranges. I love it when she uses marshmallows. Marshmallows are awesome."

Then, carried on the wings of her marshmallow reference, her chaotic thought processes flew on, alighting on the topic of making s'mores around a fire on her family's camping trips.

Tamara and I looked at each other and shook our heads, while Charity babbled on, oblivious to our irritation.

Charity was erratic in completing her chores, and Rhonda had to issue her daily reminders to check the chore list posted on the refrigerator.

"I'll do it later," Charity would promise when it was her turn to clean the bathroom. "When I get home this evening." Or, "I'm really tired now. I'll do it first thing tomorrow morning." Of course, such promises were never kept. Rhonda would sigh in exasperation, and end up scrubbing the sink and shower stall herself.

Charity was the youngest in the household, the last of the four of us to turn twenty-one. As her milestone birthday approached in early July, she announced to the rest of us that she would soon be of drinking age, and that she wanted us to celebrate her birthday by taking her out to a bar.

Rhonda and Tamara turned deaf ears to her clamoring. When Charity failed to get their attention, she focused her efforts on me. One evening, she cornered me while I was watching TV in the living room, pleading with me to get on board with her plans.

"Why don't you have your boyfriend take you out?" I asked, hoping to spark a different idea in her chaotic brain.

Charity contorted her pretty face into an expression of disgust. "Nah. David's too uptight. He doesn't believe in drinking. Besides, I don't want him tagging along and spoiling my fun. I want it to be a girls' night out. Please? Come with me?"

When I declined, she persisted. "You just turned twenty-one, didn't you, Victoria?"

I nodded. "Yup. In May."

"How did you celebrate?"

"With my family. My sister made me a cake."

"That's pathetic!" she sputtered. "You and I need to go out and do this right!"

Then a wicked little voice inside my head whispered, *Why not?*

I should have known better. This was the same little voice that had urged me to have sex with Calvin. I should have remembered where that decision had gotten me, the pain and regret it had caused.

Instead, my thoughts honed in on the sheltered life I'd lived for the past twenty-one years. The most excitement I'd ever had was at church youth group parties, where we'd drank fruit punch and played innocent games. The worldliest thing I'd ever done was to go to the movies. I told myself that I'd been overly responsible, and that it was time to cut loose and do something outside the bounds of my narrow range of experiences.

"Okay," I said. "I'll go with you."

Charity clapped her hands. "Oh, goody! We're going to have so much fun!" Gleefully, she jumped up and ran up the stairs to her room.

As soon as Charity was gone, Rhonda walked into the living room. "Don't do this, Victoria," she cautioned.

The scolding tone in her voice and her hands-on-the-hips stance aroused my anger. "Why not?" I said defensively. "Don't a lot of people go out drinking when they turn twenty-one?"

"Maybe," Rhonda said. "But you know what Charity's like. She doesn't have any self-control. I don't think you know what you're getting into."

"I'll be okay," I snapped.

So on a Tuesday night in early July, Charity and I walked the few blocks from our home on Sixth Street to a bar in downtown Goshen. Charity had tried to convince me to drive her to Elkhart, to a club she'd heard about. But a sliver of reason had prevailed in my mind, and I'd reminded her that neither of us would likely be in a condition to drive the ten miles back home.

The minute I walked into that seedy bar on Main Street, I knew it was not the place for a girl to celebrate her twenty-first birthday. The room was dark and dank. The stale, smoke-filled air and the stench of alcohol hit me hard, nearly propelling me backwards through the door.

I quickly surveyed my surroundings, registering the fact

that there were only two other females in the establishment, a pair of women smoking cigarettes in one of the three booths along one wall. Their haggard, unkempt appearances made it difficult for me to determine their ages. They eyed Charity and me suspiciously. Then one whispered something that elicited a spine-chilling cackle from her companion.

The row of men hunkered down at the bar looked tragically at home there, more comfortable than in their own living rooms. Most of them were of the geezer variety, flush-faced and vacant-eyed. Noticeably absent were the cool young guys Charity had been hoping to meet.

There was one fellow, however, who appeared to be in his forties, youthful in comparison to his companions. When Charity and I walked in, he swung around on his bar stool to check us out, running his hungry eyes up and down the lengths of our bodies. He was a slender man of medium height, not bad-looking, the kind of guy who would have cleaned up well. But cleaned up he wasn't. He wore a grungy tee shirt and ragged jeans, and his long, matted hair straggled out from under his baseball cap. He held a smoldering cigarette between two stained fingers.

Turning back to the older man sitting next to him, he nudged him and said something. The older man turned to look at us, breaking into a gap-toothed grin. I knew that, in the mind of the two leering men, the evening had just taken a turn for the better.

Afraid that Charity would head straight to the bar, I gestured toward the booth nearest the door. "Let's sit here."

A sullen waiter in a grease-stained shirt approached to take our drink orders. I'd never had more than the occasional sip of alcohol, and didn't like the taste of it. So, I ordered a mixed drink, rum and *Coke,* hoping the *Coke* would drown out the unpleasant taste of the rum. With the giddy excitement of an animal being released from a cage, Charity ordered a beer.

I suddenly knew Charity would be ordering beer after beer, and the thought alarmed me. "Let's get something to eat," I suggested, hoping food would slow down the mad rush of alcohol into her bloodstream. She shook her head, but I insisted, so we each ordered a burger and fries.

Charity gawked around the room, wide-eyed, like a child on her first trip to the circus. Every few minutes, she'd catch the eye of the forty-something fellow at the bar and smile at him.

I watched the man glance at Charity, grin, and then lean in to say something to the bartender. Half a minute later, we heard country rock music blasting over a PA system.

The man stood up, ambled over to our booth, and extended his hand to Charity. "Young lady, would you like to dance?"

I glared at Charity, shaking my head. But she put down her burger, and giggling, took the man's hand, allowing him to escort her to the tiny dance floor at the back of the room.

Facing each other, they awkwardly gyrated their bodies to the beat of the up-tempo music. Then a slower song came on, and the man pulled Charity into his arms. My stomach heaved, both from the unaccustomed alcohol I was drinking and from the revolting scene I was watching.

When Charity returned to the table, she was flushed with excitement. The waiter approached us again. Even though I'd barely choked down my first drink, I agreed to a second rum and *Coke,* telling myself that would be it for the night. One of us needed to keep her wits about her.

As I'd feared, Charity ordered one beer after another, leaving her food untouched. She alternated her drinking with the man at the bar and with me in the booth. Periodically, she and her new friend, whom she informed me was named Larry, got out on the dance floor. As her buzz progress into full-blown intoxication, she hung onto Larry in a seductive manner.

The women in the booth seemed to resent the fact that Larry's attention was focused entirely on Charity. They weren't hesitant to voice their opinions of her. "We don't need no little sluts hangin' all over the men in here," one of them called out. "You're gonna get yourself in trouble, little girl," her companion chimed in. "You better go home to your mama."

"What are you doing?" I hissed at Charity when she came back to the booth. "You've got a boyfriend. Besides, that guy's twice your age. And those women are about ready to kick your butt." But she waved a dismissive hand at me and order another beer.

My misery increased with every minute that passed in that stinking bar. I sat alone in the filthy booth, fuming, wondering how I'd ever allowed Charity to dupe me into coming there. After two hours, when Charity once again came stumbling back to the booth, I stood up, grabbed her arm, and said, "We need to go."

"Why?" she protested.

"Because you're drunk and making a fool out of yourself."

"You're no fun!" she wailed.

I guided her toward the back exit of the bar, knowing it would open into the ally. That would be the quickest way to get her home. "Let me say goodbye to Larry," she slurred.

I glanced around, but the man was nowhere in sight.

When we stepped out the back door, I gasped with relief, inhaling the fresh summer night air. But then I heard a rough male voice call out, "Hey!"

I turned toward the sound and saw a man standing in the shadows several feet away from the door, smoking a cigarette. The dim lighting made him appear sinister.

"Where're you girls going?" he asked. I recognized the ugly voice. It belonged to Larry.

"Home," I stated emphatically.

"Oh, come on," he crooned. "The night is still young."

"We've got to get to bed," I said. "We both have to work tomorrow."

He dropped his cigarette butt on the ground, crushing it with the toe of his heavy boot. "Want me to give you a lift?"

"No," I said. "We'll be fine."

"We'll be okay," Charity sang out. "We live just over there." She pointed awkwardly to the east. "Over there on Sixth Street."

I tightened my grip on her arm. "Shut up!" I hissed in her ear.

But she kept blathering on, her unbridled tongue completely loosened by alcohol. "There's four of us girls all living together in one house. Isn't that something? We have a lot of fun. We're all college students. You should come visit us sometime. What's our address, Victoria? I can't remember."

"Maybe I should walk you home," Larry said.

"No!" I shouted at him. "I said we're fine!"

"She says we're fine," Charity echoed in her sing-song voice. I could tell she'd completely lost her grip on reality.

A car passed by in the alley. The headlights illuminated Larry's face for a few seconds, and I saw the evil in his eyes. Pointing a condemning finger at Charity, he snarled, "You've been hangin' on me all night, you little cunt. Don't think you're gonna cut me off now."

Terrified, I propelled Charity across the ally, then across an empty city parking lot. I didn't glance back until we reached Fifth Street. To my dismay, I saw that Larry was twenty paces behind us. "He's following us," I whispered to Charity. "Come on! Hurry!"

I broke into a run, but my inebriated friend collapsed and fell to the ground. Frantic, I turned around to face our pursuer, standing like a bodyguard over my fallen companion. Pointing a finger at him, I screamed, "Get away from us, you creep! If you come any closer, I'll kick you in the balls and scratch your eyes out!"

A nearby porch light flashed on, and a man stepped out his front door. "What's going on out here?" he called.

Screeching the ugliest obscenities I'd ever heard, our pursuer turned and headed back in the direction of the bar.

I yanked Charity to her feet, perhaps a little too roughly, and she started to cry. I tried to put my arm around her waist to brace her, but that proved to be difficult, as she was nearly a foot shorter than me. I attempted to pick her up, but she was a solidly built girl, heavier than she looked. So I ended up half-carrying, half-dragging her the last block to our house, where she collapsed on our front steps.

Helpless and frustrated, I pounded on our door. Rhonda promptly opened it, as if she'd been dutifully awaiting the return of her errant housemates. When she saw Charity lying on the steps, she gasped and put her hand over her mouth. "What ...?"

"Don't say a thing," I growled at her. "Don't say I told you so. Just help me get her into the house."

Rhonda and I each grabbed an arm, rousing Charity enough to get her to stumble through the door. The minute we got her safely into the house, she topped off her night by vomiting all over the living room carpet.

Normally even-tempered Rhonda was seething with anger. "Take her upstairs to bed," she ordered. She turned away, gagging from the stench of the vomit. "Just get her away from me. I can't stand the sight of her."

Pointing to the puddle on the carpet, she said, "I'm not cleaning up her puke. I've cleaned up enough of her messes."

I managed to drag Charity up the stairs and heave her onto her bed. Then, feeling more contrite than I'd ever felt in my life, I went to the kitchen, filled a bucket with water and detergent, and tackled the mess on the carpet.

I suspected that sometime in the next couple of days, Rhonda was going to set us all down to review and revise the roommate agreement. I knew she needed to.

The next morning, I woke up feeling horrible, queasy from the unaccustomed alcohol in my system, ashamed of my foolhardy behavior, and shaken by the encounter with the predator from the bar.

I longed for a normal, uneventful day, to get back into the humdrum routine of my life. I took my time in straightening my room and washing my breakfast dishes, making sure that I wasn't guilty of any further infractions. Then I headed off for a four-hour lunch shift at work, where I completed my responsibilities with extra diligence.

That afternoon was my scheduled time to see Reverend Hahn. Visiting him was the last thing I felt like doing. But I'd promised him the week before that I would be coming, and he'd written the time in the appointment book he kept on the stand beside his bed.

More than that, I couldn't bear the guilt of canceling a visit with a sick and aging parent just because I'd been out drinking the night before. So I drove straight from work to the Greencroft complex.

As I'd feared, it took Reverend Hahn no time at all to detect the fact that I was feeling off-balance. "Victoria, you don't seem like yourself today," he said, his dark eyes searching my face.

I tried to evade his probing questions, but within two minutes of my arrival, I found myself pouring out the story of the previous night's misguided adventure. Reverend Hahn listened intently, taking in every detail, skewering me on the beam of his laser gaze.

At the end of the story, I felt so ashamed that I bent over in my chair, covering my face with my hands. A long silence passed before Reverend Hahn spoke. "Victoria, I sense that you've learned your lesson from this unfortunate experience. I suspect you'll think twice before doing such a thing again. But I must add my thoughts."

He paused, and when he resumed speaking, his tone reminded me of years earlier when he'd preach at Westside

Mennonite Church. "Victoria, you are a young woman with exceptional endowments. As you stand on the brink of your adult life, your potential is unlimited. But if you happen to be at the wrong place at the wrong time with the wrong people, it could all be gone, just like that."

He raised his hand in the air, giving a dramatic snap with his gnarled fingers. "Just that quick."

Then he leaned toward me, speaking gently. "I understand the urge to experiment. God knows I had more than my share of foolish adventures. But I just can't bear the thought of my daughter ..." His voice caught. "... my only child putting herself in harm's way."

His voice took on a pleading tone. "Promise me, Victoria. Promise me that you'll never allow yourself to give way to such habits."

"I promise," I assured him. "I don't even like alcohol, really. And I'll never go into that kind of bar again."

I almost expected Reverend Hahn to tell me that I was grounded. I almost wanted him to impose a punishment for the poor choice I'd made. I'd never before experienced a father's discipline. During my childhood, my dad had played the role of nurturer, while my mother had been the taskmaster, the rule enforcer, the deliverer of consequences. In a strange way, it felt good to have my birth father respond to my infraction with paternal displeasure.

CHAPTER 43

In August, Lucy left another message for me on our answering machine. Her voice was excited this time. "Tori Grace, Barbara wants to have a birthday party for Dad. Judy's going to come. You'll come, too, won't you? We want the whole family here."

The words *whole family* resounded in my mind. Lucy had happily redefined family as the new configuration of important people in her life: Dad, Barbara, Judy, and me. Biological relationships were now irrelevant. Love connections mattered.

I knew that I couldn't pass up Lucy's invitation. Despite having petulantly extricated myself from the family gathering at the time of my brothers' visit, I felt a rush of warmth about being included in my sister's new circle.

Three days later, when I walked through the front door of the farmhouse, I was surprised to encounter something I'd never seen before. Crepe paper streamers were strung from one end of the ceiling to the other, transforming the subdued tones of the living room into an explosion of color.

My first indignant thought was, *Mom would've been disgusted by this mess. She never would've condoned such foolishness.* In my critical eyes, the decorations only added to the clutter in the room. But the longer I stood there taking in the scene, the more I appreciated the festive ambiance created by the party co-conspirators, Lucy and Barbara.

A small pile of wrapped gifts lay on the coffee table. I immediately felt guilty, chastising myself for having come empty-handed. Birthdays had never been big occasions in our household when I was a child. While my mother had been faithful in marking her children's birthdays with a cake, my parents' birthdays had passed without celebration. I'd never remembered anyone giving my dad a birthday gift.

Taped on the wall above my dad's recliner was a poster-board with the words *Happy Birthday, Herman* printed in ornate letters. Gold and silver glitter added the final decorative touches to the giant greeting card. I figured it was Lucy's handiwork.

My dad was sitting in his chair staring up at the streamers, looking both pleased and confounded. Seconds after I stepped through the door, Lucy came prancing into the room, her cascade of red curls bouncing. "There," she chortled as she perched a cone-shaped party hat on top of my dad's bald head. She secured the elastic strap under his double chin. "Happy Birthday, Dad!"

He looked so comical that I doubled over with laughter. After enduring a minute of me poking fun at him, he calmly removed the hat. "I don't think I need this," he said as he set it on the arm of his chair.

Barbara came into the room to give me a hug. "We're having pizza," she announced. "Judy went to pick it up. She should be back any minute now."

After gorging ourselves on pizza, we all agreed that we were too full to eat birthday cake right away. My dad retired to his chair in the living room, while Judy helped her mother clean up the kitchen.

"Come upstairs with me, Tori Grace," Lucy said. "I've got something to show you."

As if we were two little playmates, she grabbed my hand, pulling me along with her. She seemed surprisingly light on her feet as she climbed the stairs, and I noticed that her body was less bulky.

"You've lost some weight, haven't you, Lucy," I commented when we reached the top.

"Yes, I think I have." She grabbed the front of her tee shirt, showing me the excess fabric. "My doctor changed my medication. He lowered the dose because I've been doing so well. Now I'm not so hungry all the time."

We stood in front of the closed door of my old room, Lucy's eyes sparkling with excitement. "Tori Grace, you're not going to believe what I'm going to show you."

With a flourish, she flung the door open. I stared into the room, bewildered by what I saw. A long table stood in the middle of the room, spread with an array of beads. A chair was pulled up to the table, as if it was someone's workspace.

"What's all this?" I asked.

Lucy looked sheepish. "I hope you don't mind, Tori Grace, us using your old room like this. Barbara got me started on making jewelry. She said I needed a creative outlet. We got all this stuff from the craft store in Goshen. But Barbara said we could start ordering supplies out of a catalog. We'll have more choices that way."

"No," I said. "I don't mind, not at all. This isn't my room anymore." I moved closer to the table to examine the beads. Half a dozen pairs of earrings, two bracelets, and a necklace were laid out at one end of the table. Apparently, Lucy had recently completed those projects. It looked as if she was currently working on another necklace.

"I just love it," she said with a sweeping gesture of her hand. "I love it more than I've ever loved anything." She looked at me questioningly, as if eager for my approval.

If I'd been told that Lucy was involved with stringing beads, I would have pictured a very simple process, perhaps a kindergartener's alternation of red and white plastic beads on a thread. But here, she'd been working with beads of different sizes, colors, and textures, and had combined them in astonishing ways. I was amazed by the originality and beauty of her work. Clearly, my sister had talent.

"Lucy, these are awesome!" I exclaimed. "They're gorgeous! Where did you get all these ideas?"

"Out of my head." Grinning, Lucy tapped her skull with her forefinger. "I guess something good can come out of this noggin." She picked up the partially completed necklace, fingering the beads lovingly. "I'm not totally crazy, Tori Grace."

"No, Lucy," I said. "You're not crazy. You're talented."

At that moment, I not only loved my sister, I admired her. A year earlier, I'd viewed Lucy's life as hopeless. She'd been living in squalor, valuing nothing about herself. But she had risen above the limitations of her mental illness, and had begun to express the unique gift she'd been endowed with.

I thought about how I'd berated my dad for his decision to marry Barbara so soon after my mother's death. I saw how wrong I'd been, and how my dad had instinctively known he was making the right choice. Here was Barbara, an ordinary little woman worn out from a lifetime of factory work, who possessed an extraordinary gift for bringing out the best in her husband's troubled daughter. I'd seen Lucy with psychiatrists and therapists and caseworkers, and none of them had been able to ignite the spark of confidence and motivation that Barbara had lit in her. As far as I was concerned, Barbara Prentiss Unruh was a genius.

Lucy moved over to a chest sitting on a card table. "Come look, Tori Grace. This is where I keep all my supplies." Opening one small drawer after another, she showed me stashes of beads, special cord used for stringing, hoops for earrings, and clasps for necklaces. I was surprised at how adeptly she'd organized her belongings.

She closed the last drawer, and then rested her hand on the top of the chest. "Barbara says I should start selling my jewelry. She says that after I build up enough inventory, I could maybe get a booth at Peddler's Village. She's going to look into it."

She raised a hand to brush the hair away from my face, examining my ears. "Tori Grace, we need to get your ears pierced. Then you can wear some of my earrings."

CHAPTER 44

The first two weeks of September rushed past me in a blur. In addition to starting my senior year classes, I had to attend meetings regarding working on the *Maple Leaf,* the college yearbook, and the *Record,* the campus newspaper. We English majors were encouraged to get involved in those extracurricular activities to practice our writing and editing skills.

And I was still working at the restaurant, something I'd committed to do throughout the school year. The prospect of juggling the responsibilities of work and school terrified me. Bob had agreed to reduce my hours from fulltime to halftime. But my first two weeks of school, he was shorthanded, and insisted that I come in for extra shifts.

I had intended to visit Reverend Hahn on Wednesday afternoon of that first week. However, a meeting with my academic advisor on Tuesday was canceled and rescheduled for Wednesday afternoon. Following the meeting, I had to rush off for an evening shift at the restaurant. The rest of the week zoomed by, and before I knew it, my visit with my birth father had been squeezed out of my schedule.

Late Friday morning of the second week, I finally found a few minutes to drive over to the Greencroft complex. I hurried into the building, but as I headed toward Reverend Hahn's room, a nurse stopped me. Her face looked grim.

"I know you haven't been here for a while," she said.

Her words added to the load of guilt I was carrying. "No, I haven't," I admitted.

"Well, I thought I should let you know that Reverend Hahn has taken a turn for the worse. I didn't want you to be shocked when you saw him."

"What?" I gasped. "What happened?"

She shrugged, lifting her hands, palms up, in a gesture of helplessness. "The ALS finally caught up with him. He fought a good fight. But in the end, the disease always wins." Her voice quavered with emotion. "It's amazing that he stayed as healthy as he did for as long as he did. I think it had to do with his strong will to live. I've never seen a patient with as much determination as Reverend Hahn had. No matter how bad he felt, he'd be up in his wheelchair trying to do something for somebody else."

She walked on down the hallway, leaving me standing alone, feeling stunned. A rush of thoughts came to me. Over the summer months, I'd witnessed the insidious progression of my birth father's symptoms: his increasing fatigue, the weakness in his arms and hands, his sonorous voice growing fainter, the occasional slurring of his words. But I had refused to acknowledge the implication of those changes.

"What should I do?" I called to the nurse just as she was about to enter the room next to Reverend Hahn's.

She stopped, allowing me to catch up with her. "Just go on in and see him," she said in a hushed voice. "Try to stay calm. Don't let on that you're upset. He still enjoys visitors. He needs them more than ever now, because he spends most of his time in bed. Don't expect him to talk to you. He's having a hard time breathing, and it's difficult for him to speak. His doctor said he'll have to put him on a ventilator in a week or two."

When I hesitated, she fluttered an impatient hand at me. "Go on in. Talk to him like you normally do. He's fully aware. There's nothing wrong with his mind. It's just trapped in a body that doesn't work for him anymore."

Overcome with a sickening dread, I walked the short distance to Reverend Hahn's room. I found him lying in his bed with his eyes closed. The heaving of his thin chest bore witness to his struggle with breathing. Approaching the bed, I laid a hand on his arm. His eyes flickered open, and he smiled as much as his stiffened facial muscles would allow.

"I'm so sorry," I said, "for not coming to see you last week. It was the first week of school, and I got so busy. But I still should've found time to come."

With considerable effort, he turned his arm so that his hand was lying palm up on the bed. I knew this was an invitation for me to hold his hand. When I took it in mine, it felt cold and dry, almost lifeless.

His lips moved, and his voice came out in a raspy whisper. "It's okay."

I pulled the nearby chair up to the bed so that I could continue to hold his hand while sitting. I suddenly understood that touch was now going to be a primary form of communication between us.

After a few minutes of this silent connection, Reverend Hahn whispered again. "Tell me everything."

I realized that he wanted our visits to continue as normally as they possibly could. Even though his response would be limited, he still wanted updates on every aspect of my life.

"I'm taking my upper-level English classes," I told him. "It makes me feel like one of the big kids now. I can't believe I'm old enough to be a senior. College has flown by so fast."

I knew that his slight nod conveyed an interest far beyond what he could express, so I continued. "I'm going to be working on the *Maple Leaf* and the *Record* this year. And I'll be in the chorale again. I've decided not to do any sports. I wanted to play volleyball, but I just don't have any room in my schedule."

He gave another slight nod. "Busy," he whispered.

"But I'm not too busy to come see you," I said. "I'm never going to wait so long between visits again. I feel really bad." I clasped his hand with both of mine. "Will you forgive me?"

"Of course." His voice had faded to almost nothing, and I had to bend close to hear the rest of what he had to say. "Look in the nightstand."

"Do you need something?" I asked. "Should I call a nurse?"

He shook his head slightly. "Just look."

I opened the top drawer of his stand and found a long white envelope. On it was written *Victoria Unruh* in a shaky script. I knew he'd prepared the envelope and its contents before his downhill turn.

"This is for me?" I asked, holding up the envelope.

"Yes," he whispered. "Open it."

I did as he instructed, and pulled out a handful of money. "Oh, no!" I protested. "I can't take this!"

"Yes!" The whispered syllable carried authority. Then his voice weakened again. "Last time ... I can ... do this."

I counted the money. Ten one-hundred-dollar bills. Just when I had started to wonder how I was going to make it through the trimester, my birth father had come through one last time. Tears welled in my eyes.

"This will help so much," I said. "You always know how to help. I'm so lucky. You're a wonderful father."

I saw a tear leak from the corner of one of his eyes. I took a tissue from his bedside stand and dabbed it.

Then, in a whisper that seemed to take the last of his strength, he repeated the question he'd asked me the day he'd moved out of his apartment. "My child, will you ... stay with me ... until the end?"

"Yes," I said, tenderly but emphatically. "I'll be with you, Father."

His eyes closed, and he looked as if he was drifting into sleep. I held his hand for a few more minutes before gently extricating my fingers from his and tiptoeing out the room.

As I walked down the hallway, I felt guilty about the one-thousand dollars I was carrying in my purse, hoping no one would stop me and accuse me of stealing from a patient. However, I still took the risk of pausing at the desk to consult with the nurse again.

"It's so sad, isn't it?" she said.

I nodded. "Who's looking out for him now? Who's taking care of all his business?"

"That's an interesting question," she replied. "All this time, he's been his own legal guardian. Just a week ago, his sister in Pennsylvania took over the role of guardian. It's up to her to make all the medical decisions now."

A puzzled look crossed her face. "His sister wanted to transfer him to a facility in Pennsylvania so he could be close to family out there. But he insisted that he wanted to stay here. We all thought that was strange, because he has no family here. His wife is dead, and they didn't have any children. But he does have a good support system with his church. Maybe he feels more comfortable in a community where things are familiar to him."

The nurse's words further added to the emotional load I was carrying. I knew full well why Reverend Hahn had chosen to stay in Goshen instead of being transported to Pennsylvania. He wanted to be present in my life for as long as he possibly could.

I had an obligation. While I had no legal matters to take care of, no medical or financial decisions to make, it was my job to let my birth father know that he was loved. Until the end of his days, he needed to experience the deep bond between parent and child, the joining of our two hearts.

At that moment, I made a commitment to myself. No matter how busy I got with work, school, and extracurricular activities, I would visit Reverend Hahn at least three times a week. More often, if possible. Every day, if I could, even if I only stayed in his room long enough to kiss his forehead and tell him I loved him. Without a shadow of a doubt, I knew what my priority needed to be. And I knew that I could never live with myself if I didn't honor that priority.

CHAPTER 45

As I lived so close to the school, it didn't make sense to take my meals in the college cafeteria. I always ate breakfast at home, and, more often than not, had my dinner during my evening shift at the restaurant. Sometimes, I ran back home to grab a quick lunch between classes.

On other days, I ate lunch in the snack shop in the Union Building. The typical snack shop crowd consisted of professors, staff, and students who commuted to the campus.

One day in mid-September, as I waited in line at the snack shop counter, I spotted a young man standing several places ahead of me. I couldn't see his face, but something about him caught my attention. He was tall and slim, with wavy brown hair flowing slightly over the crisp white collar of his shirt. He was wearing a dark sweater and dress trousers, attire a little too formal for the average student. I wondered whether he was a new professor.

When the man picked up his tray of food and turned away from the counter, my heart did a strange little flip in my chest. He was handsome in an understated sort of way, with a neatly groomed beard and mustache and wire-rimmed glasses. His deep-set blue eyes reflected keen intelligence. He looked distracted, as if puzzling on some intellectual conundrum.

I couldn't stop myself from staring at him. He didn't have the striking good looks and muscular build of Daniel Hooley or Calvin Zook. But his chiseled features, combined with his dignified bearing and obvious intelligence, made me a little dizzy. I felt a powerful pull of physical attraction toward him, which embarrassed me, and I prayed that my face didn't reflect my inner experience. I wondered who on earth the man could be, and what he was doing there at Goshen College.

Then, to my surprise, he looked at me and broke into a wide smile. "Victoria Unruh!" he exclaimed.

And I thought I was going to faint right there in the snack shop line. The man was my old friend Charlie Hess.

I was astounded by the transformation in him, wondering how it had come about. It seemed as if he'd left behind the socially clueless, tousle-haired boy, and had become a handsome man with a newfound social confidence.

I stood there with my mouth hanging open in shock while Charlie continued to talk. "I almost forgot that you'd still be here. What a pleasant surprise to see you! You'll be graduating this year, right?"

Nodding, I managed to get a few words out of my mouth. "What are you doing here, Charlie?"

He pointed toward an empty booth. "Why don't you join me after you get your food? We can catch up with each other."

"I'd love to," I said.

Several minutes later, with a pounding heart and shaking hands, I carried my tuna fish sandwich and soft drink to Charlie's table. "Are you back on campus now?" I asked as I slid into the booth.

"Yes, I am." He took a bite of his cheeseburger, chewing slowly. "I'm here for the academic year. I completed a year of grad school at Massachusetts Institute of Technology. Then I got a call from Dr. Liechty in the physics department here, asking if I'd like to do a year of assistant teaching. It seemed like the right thing to do, not only for the experience, but to help me get ahead financially. As you can imagine, MIT can be a little pricey."

I was so astonished by this news that I couldn't think of what to say next. I felt like a star-struck schoolgirl sitting across from a celebrity. "So, what ... what are you studying at MIT?" I stammered.

"Physics," he replied. "Specifically, astrophysics."

"I have no idea what you'd do with an advanced degree in physics."

Charlie emptied a packet of sugar into his coffee, then stirred it with his spoon. "There are a lot of things a person could do. I like the idea of teaching physics, along with working in the research department of a university. But what I really have my sights set on is working for NASA someday."

"Wow!" I exclaimed. "I'm impressed."

Charlie shrugged, as if casting off an unwarranted compliment. "And you? What major did you end up choosing? I never did find that out."

"English," I replied. "With a minor in writing. And I'm working on getting my certification in TESOL. Teaching English to Speakers of Other Languages."

"Wonderful," he said. "That sounds perfect for you. Are you still living in the Westlawn dormitory?"

"No," I replied. "I'm living off campus this year, with three other girls. We're renting a house on Sixth Street." I suddenly found myself divulging more information than he'd asked for. "A lot has changed in my life. My dad got remarried a year ago. My stepmom's a nice person, but I don't feel comfortable living at home with the two of them anymore. So I moved out this past summer."

Charlie gazed at me, sympathy in his deep-set blue eyes. "I can understand that. It has to be hard to get used to such big changes in your family life. Are you enjoying being on your own?"

"Sort of," I told him. "But it's hard. I worked all summer, and I'm still working about twenty hours a week. I have to. I need the money."

"Doing what?" he asked.

"Waitressing. In the evenings and on weekends." I smiled sheepishly. "Pretty prosaic job, huh?"

Charlie smiled back. "The quintessential job for the young American woman. It offers invaluable life experience, I'm sure. Do you have plans for what you're going to do after graduation?"

I winced, not wanting to address the anxiety-inducing subject I'd been trying not to think about. "Truthfully," I admitted, "I have no idea what I'm going to do after graduation. The idea scares me to death. We'll be talking about employment options in my senior seminar."

"Have you thought about going on for your master's degree?"

Charlie's question triggered an inexplicable feeling of hopelessness that had been plaguing me at odd moments the past few months. I lowered my head, staring down at my half-eaten food. "Graduate school sounds nice. But right now, I don't know how that would be possible. I don't know how it will ever be possible."

"I hope you consider it at some point," he said softly. "You certainly have the intellect for it."

Feeling uncomfortable with his compliment, I diverted the focus away from myself and back onto him. "So where are you living now?"

"Nowhere fancy, that's for sure." He chuckled. "Dr. Liechty and his wife have an efficiency apartment in their basement. They're letting me live there for next to nothing. That way, I can save a little money for my second year of grad school."

We ate in silence for a few minutes. I sensed he didn't know what else to say to me. So, to break the awkwardness between us, I asked, "What's Stephen Wenger doing now?"

"He and I went out to MIT together," Charlie replied. "We shared an apartment. Then Stephen met a girl. They got married last month."

"Huh?" I set down my sandwich and stared at him. "Stephen Wenger got married?"

Pain flickered in Charlie's eyes, and I immediately regretted my incredulous tone. "Yes," he said, an edge of defensiveness in his voice. "He found the right woman. She's a graduate student, too. Someone who appreciates him for who he is. He's a good guy, and he deserves that."

My face burned with shame at my insensitivity. "I think that's wonderful," I said quickly. "I'm really glad for him."

Then I impulsively blurted out a bold question. "And you? Have you found your right woman?"

Charlie took the last bite of his sandwich, then wiped his mouth with his napkin and pushed his tray aside. For a few seconds, I thought my nosey question had offended him, and that he wasn't going to answer me. "No, I haven't," he finally said. "Although I trust that I will, in time." He looked at me pointedly. "How about you? Have you found your right man?"

"Nope. I don't have a minute of spare time to date." I thought for a moment before edging closer to the real truth. "I have a philosophy at this point in my life. I don't want to waste my time with casual dating. The next guy I date needs to be the right guy. Someone I can really trust. Someone I can have a future with."

Charlie nodded. "That makes sense."

It seemed as if he was as uncomfortable as I was in the aftermath of our shared confidences, and we steered the conversation toward less intimate topics. I told him about my classes, and he outlined his duties in the physics department.

"I tutor students over my lunch hour on Tuesdays and Thursdays," he informed me. "But I eat lunch here in the snack shop on Monday, Wednesday, and Friday." I wondered whether he was letting me know where I could find him if I wanted to see him again.

Then he glanced at his watch. "I need to get going." He flashed me a smile that left me a little breathless. "It's been great catching up with you, Victoria. I hope to see you around."

"Yes," I said. "I hope so, too."

He picked up his tray, and with a nod, turned and walked away. Wistfully, I watched as he returned his tray to the counter, then strode out of the snack shop.

I didn't lay eyes on Charlie Hess for another week. As I walked across campus to my classes, I wondered whether I'd cross paths with him. I hoped that I would.

But I also felt terrified at the prospect of seeing him again. Something inside me was stirred up and excited, making me feel weird and vulnerable. I didn't know how to interpret that strange emotion. So for that reason, I avoided the snack shop, where I knew Charlie would be eating lunch, opting instead to run over to Greencroft to see Reverend Hahn on my lunch hour.

Tragically, my birth father's ravaging illness continued to advance, overtaking his frail body a little more each day, the changes happening so quickly that I couldn't fathom what was going on. I watched helplessly as the disease carried him farther and farther away from me.

I had no legal right to ask for information about his medical status. But from the bits and pieces I gleaned from the nursing staff, I came to understand that most of Reverend Hahn's muscles had become paralyzed. In no time at all, he lost his ability to speak, to swallow any food or drink, and to breathe on his own. Sadly, I had to get used to the sight of the ventilator parked alongside his bed, its plastic tubing inserted through the tracheostomy in his neck. The whooshing of the machine's respiration sounded ominous to me, a harbinger of impending death.

"They call it locked-in syndrome," a nurse said to me one day. "It sometimes happens with ALS patients. Reverend Hahn's mind is fully aware, but he's unable to express himself." She shuddered. "I feel so bad for him. It must be a horrible way to live."

She then informed me that the staff had established a means of communication with him that involved his one remaining ability, blinking. "If you want to ask him a question," she said, "make sure it's a *yes* or *no* question. He'll blink once for *no* and twice for *yes.*"

I was hardly ready for that new style of communication. As I stood at his bedside that day, I felt at a complete loss. I could think of nothing to do but to hold his stiffened hand for a few minutes and say, "I love you, Father."

Arriving at the nursing care center during lunchtime proved to be less than optimal. The passing of food trays to the patients created congestion in the hallway. And the privacy curtain would be drawn around Reverend Hahn's bed, as one of the nurses was inevitably in the process of administering liquid nutrition through the feeding tube in his stomach. I'd stand in the hallway outside his door, waiting nervously, feeling like an intruder.

"The lunch hour isn't a good time for you to visit," an ill-tempered nurse barked at me one day. Shame-facedly, I walked out of the building, realizing it was time to abandon my silly strategy for avoiding Charlie Hess.

So at noon the following Monday, I once again ventured into the snack shop. I glanced around the room, both hoping and afraid to spot Charlie. Sure enough, he was there as he'd told me he would be, sitting alone in a booth along one wall. He was eating a sandwich while reading a document spread out on the table in front of him.

As if sensing that someone was looking at him, he glanced up and met my gaze. Smiling, he gestured toward the empty seat across from him.

While my lunch order was being prepared, I watched Charlie out of the corner of my eye. I saw a man stop at the booth, as if asking whether he could join Charlie at his table. I heard Charlie say something that sounded like, "I have a friend coming." And the man moved on.

A minute later, I stood at the booth with my tray. Looking at the document he was reading, I asked, "Am I interrupting something?"

With long-fingered hands, Charlie slid the papers into a neat stack and tucked them into the briefcase propped against his chair. "Absolutely not. I prefer human company over reading a research paper."

For the first minute after seating myself, I was too nervous to maintain eye contact with my companion. I sneaked glances at him between bites of my soup. *God, he's attractive,* I thought as I took in his thick wavy hair, his well-balanced features, his dignified mannerisms, and the depth of intelligence in his sky-blue eyes. *How did I not notice this when he was a student here?*

I wondered if the other females on campus were whispering about the handsome young teaching assistant in the physics department. I wanted to grab a stick and beat them all away.

"I haven't seen you for a while," Charlie said. "Where have you been?"

I've been busy avoiding you, I thought. *You've shaken me up so bad that I can't handle myself around you.*

When I opened my mouth to speak, my nerves were so on edge that I couldn't censor the flow of my words. "Last week, I went over to Greencroft on my lunch hour."

"Oh?" Charlie sounded concerned. "Do you have a relative over there?"

Inwardly, I winced, desperately wishing that I could tell him the truth. But that wasn't possible. I couldn't blurt out my convoluted life story to this man I was just getting to know again. Not right there in the middle of the snack shop, with a hundred listening ears surrounding us.

Instead, I once again resorted to my birth father's technique of offering a half-truth. "I've been visiting Reverend Harry Hahn. He's someone I've known since I was a little girl. He was an evangelist who preached at my church from time to time."

Charlie chewed on his lip, thinking. "The name sounds vaguely familiar. I wonder if I've met him."

"He was a tall man. Dark complexion, black hair. He was a dynamic speaker, and people loved to hear him preach.

Especially the women." I laughed self-consciously. "Because he was really handsome."

A look of recognition crossed Charlie's face. "Oh, yes, I do remember him. He preached at my church in Eureka, Illinois, several times. Having him there was quite an event for the congregation. Wasn't he from California, or someplace out west?"

Anxiety gripped my stomach, twisting it into a hard knot. Giving up on my efforts to finish my soup, I put down my spoon. "Yes, he was from Bakersfield, California. But then he moved to Indiana and became the pastor of the First Mennonite Church in Warsaw. Not that far from here."

"Interesting," Charlie mused. "So he ended up at Greencroft?"

"Yes. He's really sick. He has ALS."

Charlie grimaced. "That's a rough disease."

His sympathetic words stirred the reservoir of grief in my heart. I closed my eyes for a moment, trying to compose myself. "Yes," I finally said. "It's horrible. "

Taking a deep breath, I continued. "For a few years, Reverend Hahn lived there at Greencroft in his own apartment, and he managed okay. Then, around Christmas of last year, he had to move into the skilled nursing unit. The past few months, he's gone downhill really fast."

"It sounds like you know him pretty well," Charlie observed.

"Yes. I've been visiting him the past four years or so. We've gotten close, I'd say. We've become good friends."

Charlie looked puzzled. "Does he have family around here?"

"No." The lies coming out of my mouth tasted so bitter that I paused to take a sip of my sweet drink to wash away the acridness. "His wife died several years ago. They never had children. He has a lot of visitors from his church. But I still feel like I need to see him. Especially now that he's so bad off. I don't want to abandon him."

"That's kind of you," Charlie said. "Being young and healthy and focused on my goals, I don't often take time to think about the difficulties that come at the end of life. It's thoughtful of you to be concerned about his needs."

I felt myself blushing at the compliment I knew I didn't deserve. "He has something called locked-in syndrome," I said. "His mind is alert. He knows everything that's going on around him. But all the muscles in his body are paralyzed. He can't move, and he can't speak. He communicates through blinking."

My eyes welled, and a tear escaped, trickling down one cheek. As I wiped it with my napkin, I hoped Charlie wouldn't think I was weird for weeping over a man who was nothing more than a friend. "I'd like to do something for him," I said, speaking my heart's full truth. "But I have no idea how to help him."

"Here's a thought." Charlie pushed aside his tray and leaned toward me. "Why don't you read to him? Take a book, pull up a chair, and read for twenty minutes or so."

Of course, I thought, feeling a little foolish. *Like I did for my mother.*

"That's what I used to do for my grandfather at the end of his life." Charlie leaned back again, a wistful look on his face. "My grandpa died when I was a senior in high school. He was a farmer, but a scientist at heart. The family always said I took after him. When chronic lung problems slowed him down at the end of his life, he didn't take it well. He could be pretty cranky, a handful for my grandmother. I'd take my chemistry and physics textbooks over to their house and read to him. That would settle him down. I figured that if I read my assignments aloud to him, I was killing two birds with one stone. I was getting my own reading done while spending quality time with Grandpa."

He chuckled. "Grandma used to tell people that she always breathed a sigh of relief when she saw little Charlie coming with his physics book."

"Little Charlie?" I teased.

"Yeah," he said. "I was a shrimp in high school. I got my growth spurt late."

I smiled to myself, picturing the gawky, skinny adolescent Charlie lugging around a textbook almost as big as himself. "I've always been tall," I told him. "From the day I was born, I think. I used to hate being taller than the rest of the kids my age. But I don't mind it so much now."

I saw tenderness in Charlie's eyes. He looked as if he wanted to tell me something he couldn't quite bring himself to say. Evading the awkwardness of the moment, he steered us back to the subject we'd been discussing. "Do you know what kind of literature Reverend Hahn used to enjoy?"

Wading back into the murky waters of partial truth, I said, "When I used to visit him in his apartment, I saw a lot of literary classics on his bookshelves."

"There you go," Charlie said. "You're an English major. A perfect match. You'll know exactly what to do."

"Yes," I said, "I think I do. Thanks for the suggestion, Charlie."

CHAPTER 46

The next afternoon, I walked into Greencroft's skilled nursing unit carrying my British Literature textbook. When I entered Reverend Hahn's room, it was deathly quiet, except for the rhythmic whisper of the ventilator. My resounding footsteps shattered the stillness as I walked over to stand beside his bed.

"Hello, Father," I said.

Even though I hadn't asked him a question, he blinked twice, affirming his gratitude for my presence.

Hesitantly, I reached out a hand to caress his gaunt cheek. The skin on his face was flaccid and pallid. "How are you?" I asked.

Another two blinks, letting me know, as always, that he was fine.

"I brought along my literature book. Would you like for me to read you some poetry?"

He responded with another two blinks. I wondered whether he was eager to hear me read, or whether he was just humoring me. I had no way of telling.

"Okay." I sat down on the chair beside his bed, thumbing through the pages of my book to find the passages I'd selected. I read Elizabeth Barrett Browning's *How Do I Love Thee?*, John Keats' *Ode to a Nightingale,* William Blake's *Jerusalem,* and Lord Byron's *She walks in Beauty.* All the while, his eyes were closed, but I sensed he was listening intently.

"How did you like that?" I asked him after I was finished. He blinked twice.

I closed the book and stood up. As I bent down to kiss his forehead, I saw the imploring look in his eyes, and I realized I had forgotten something. I hadn't updated him on what was happening in my life.

I sat down again. "You probably want to know what's going on with me."

He blinked twice.

"I'm really busy, but everything's going pretty well. I'm taking my senior English classes. I have to do a lot of writing, and I love that. I'm still working at the restaurant. I'm glad for the money, and the free food helps a lot. It cuts down on my grocery bill." I stopped, hoping he'd smile, then remembering that he couldn't.

"I met a new friend," I continued. "Actually he's an old friend. I knew him when he was a student here. He graduated two years ahead of me, and then went off to grad school at MIT. But now he's back as a teaching assistant in the physics department. I've had lunch with him a couple of times."

I knew Reverend Hahn would be eager to know the nature of this relationship, and I imagined the questions he'd asked if he could speak. "I like him a lot," I said. "But we're just friends. Good friends. I really enjoy talking with him."

The following weeks flew by. With barely any time to catch my breath, I attended classes, completed my assignments, worked on the *Maple Leaf* and the *Record,* attended chorale rehearsals, worked my shifts at the restaurant, and completed my chores in the apartment. But I made sure to visit my birth father at least three times a week, even though I rarely stayed for more than thirty minutes at a time.

Sometimes, I did as Charlie had done with his grandfather, reading my assignments to Reverend Hahn. Sometimes, I'd take the Bible out of his bedside stand and read a few verses. Utilizing his blinking responses, I'd determine what passages he wanted to hear. "Do you want me to read from the New Testament?" I'd ask. If he'd blink only once, I'd know he wanted something from the Old Testament, and I'd go down the list of the books until I hit upon the right one. I soon realized that he preferred to hear me read from the Psalms.

Later in the trimester, I read him pieces I'd written for my poetry class. Every time I did this, he gave me three sets of double blinks. *Yes, yes, yes.* A powerful affirmation of my creativity.

And this became our new mode of interacting with each other. I told myself that it was okay, that I could do this for the remainder of his life. I had no idea how long that would be. I didn't want to know.

If my ailing birth father held the distinction of being the most important man in my life that first trimester of my senior year, Charlie Hess ran a close second. We developed a pattern of eating lunch together in the snack shop every Monday, Wednesday, and Friday. Those hours with Charlie seemed to be the only time in the week where I could slow down and catch my breath. Just as in the days when I ate with him and Stephen in the cafeteria, he and I never made a formal arrangement about spending time together. Neither of us ever said, "Would you like to have lunch with me on Monday?" We shared an unspoken understanding.

On a Wednesday in early November, Charlie said, "I wanted you to know that I won't be here Friday. I'll be attending a seminar in Chicago."

Upon hearing this news, I was overtaken by such a powerful sense of loss that I could hardly finish my sandwich. I hoped that the change in my demeanor wasn't obvious to him. But he must have sensed my distress. When he stood up to leave, his tone was warm and reassuring. "I'll see you next week, Victoria."

I often thought about the two brilliant men who were so temporarily present in my life. My birth father, his keen intellect trapped in the prison of his unmoving body, would soon be moving on to the next world. Charlie Hess would be going back to graduate school in less than a year. But for now, I had them both.

I never knew what was going to come up in my conversations with Charlie. Our topic of discussion always emerged as a pleasant surprise. One day, we delved into the subject of religion.

"I don't know if I'll always be a Mennonite," I confessed to him. "But I don't know what else I'd be. I guess I'm scared not to be a Mennonite."

"I've had those same thoughts," Charlie said. "I value my Mennonite upbringing a great deal. The church has provided me with a strong moral structure. But that isn't all I believe in."

Intrigued, I sat forward, my arms folded on the table top. "So tell me, Charlie. What else do you believe in?"

He took a sip of his coffee, then furrowed his brow, pondering. "That's a huge question, Victoria. I hardly know where to start. When I was out in Massachusetts, there were no Mennonite churches in the area. So I tried out several other denominations, the Episcopal Church and the Quaker Church. Each of them had their attractions. I especially liked the Quaker idea of listening in silence to the voice of God."

I nodded, captivated by his words.

"This might surprise you," he continued. "Even though I was a physics major, one of my favorite classes here at Goshen College was World Religions. I was both amazed and delighted to discover a core of truth in each religion we studied."

"I'm taking that class next trimester," I told him. "Now I'm really looking forward to it."

"I think you'll love it," he said. "I'll enjoy hearing your thoughts about the course. But don't get me wrong. I'm not turning my back on the Mennonite tradition. It provided a powerful formative experience during my growing up years. Even if I move on to a different denomination, or stop attending church altogether, I'll never lose my identity as a Mennonite."

Knowing that I continued to visit Reverend Hahn several times a week, Charlie never failed to ask me about the state of his health. We'd talk about the passages I was reading to him. One day, I told Charlie about reading one of my own poems to Reverend Hahn. "He seemed to like it," I said.

"Oh, really?" A strange look crossed Charlie's face. His reaction surprised me, and I didn't know how to interpret it. *Is he jealous?* I wondered. *Because I shared something so intimate with Reverend Hahn that I never shared with him? Surely not.*

"Would you like to see it?" I ventured.

"Certainly," he replied.

The next moment, I remembered the subject matter of the poem, and immediately regretted my offer. But I dug it out of my notebook and slid the paper across the table to him. I held my breath as he read it.

He looked up at me. "This is a sonnet, isn't it?"

"Yes," I replied. "A fourteen-line poem with a specific rhyme scheme. This was an assignment for my poetry class."

"It's about a father's love."

I willed my face not to redden. "It could also be referring to the love of God the Father," I said quickly.

Charlie turned his eyes back to the poem, re-reading it. "Yes. It works on both levels. Very well, I should say." He shook his head in wonder. "As a scientist, I've always approached life from a rational, analytical viewpoint. I'm in awe of people who are talented in the arts. Victoria, your creativity astonishes me."

One day, Charlie and I waded into the uncomfortable topic of our dating histories. "I never had a single date until I went to graduate school," he confided. "I went out with a couple of women there at MIT. But I never developed feelings for them."

Although his revelation didn't entirely surprise me, I still asked the question that had been on my mind for weeks. "How is it possible that a guy like you would never have a girlfriend?"

My words seemed to throw Charlie off balance. He blushed and looked away for a few seconds. "I was called a nerd in high school," he said when he finally responded. "Even in college. Nerds don't get dates. I guess I still am a nerd, and probably always will be."

The pain in his eyes contradicted his smile. "In high school, I was well aware of the fact that I was a social outcast. I didn't understand my classmates' interests, and they didn't understand mine. Trends and popular culture seemed frivolous to me, when there was so much else to explore in life. Such as math and physics. The wonders of space and astronomy. I couldn't understand why everyone wouldn't be fascinated by such topics."

"Did you get picked on?" I asked.

He shook his head. "Not much. I was just the brainy freak that everybody left alone. Thankfully, being well-loved by my family made up for the lack of acceptance by my peers."

An uncomfortable silence hung between us, while I recalled my brazen confidence as a child, my tendency to dominate other kids who were unable to stand up to me. I knew that if Charlie and I had been classmates, I would have treated him unkindly.

Charlie shifted his eyes, as if he couldn't bear the intimacy of looking at me when feeling so vulnerable. Gazing out over the snack shop crowd, he said, "It took me until graduate school to recognize the fact that adopting more socially acceptable habits would benefit me."

So, that's how the transformation in his appearance came about, I thought. *He realized that paying attention to his clothing and grooming would make him more attractive to others, and would contribute to his success.* I felt incredibly proud of my friend, while at the same time strangely protective. No one would ever again get away with making fun of Charlie Hess in my presence.

"I'm sure you were never a social outcast like I was," he said, forcing a smile. "I imagine you were popular in high school."

"I was," I admitted, "for my first three years, anyway. But when I was a senior, I pulled back from all that social stuff. That year, I was kind of like you. I studied all the time."

He looked at me curiously. "Why the change?"

Suddenly, it was my turn to feel vulnerable. Rifling through my stockpile of half-truths for an appropriate response, I said, "I guess I just grew up."

"When I first saw you during your freshman year here at the college," Charlie said, "I thought you'd be a social butterfly. But when I got to know you, I realized there was a lot more to you than that."

"Thank you," I said. "That's one of the nicest things anyone has ever said about me."

I sometimes asked myself whether these lunchtime encounters with Charlie were dates. Were he and I a couple of sorts? The confusion about our relationship agitated me, and I often wished he'd clarify his intentions toward me. But I also knew that trying to move the relationship to another level would pose a risk. We could lose a much-valued friendship if romance didn't work out between us. So, when feeling impatient with Charlie, I'd comfort myself with the knowledge that our current arrangement carried no risks.

But no matter how hard I tried to minimize my feelings, I had to admit to myself that I found my friend physically attractive, intellectually stimulating, and emotionally comforting. Being with him felt like coming home. I trusted him deeply. As far as I could tell, Charlie Hess was a good man in every regard.

On the last day of the trimester in mid-December, Charlie asked, "What are you planning to do over the Christmas break?"

His words sent a shiver of excitement through me. *Does he want to know whether I'm free to spend time with him over the holidays? Are we going to have a real date during our three weeks off from classes?*

Trying not to reveal my eagerness, I shrugged nonchalantly. "Nothing very interesting. I'll be working extra shifts at the restaurant. I need the money. Then, of course, I'll be spending Christmas Day at my dad's house." I took a deep breath before asking, "What are you planning on doing?"

"I'll be staying at my parents' house in Eureka, Illinois," he replied. "I haven't had a lot of time to spend with them recently. It'll be good to see the whole family again."

His announcement exploded my fantasy into smithereens, instantly deflating my mood. I wondered how I'd manage to get by without seeing him for three weeks. A fragment of hope held out for the possibility that he'd say, "I'm coming back a few days early. Maybe we could get together and do something then." But he said nothing of that nature.

As we got up to leave our booth, I blurted out, "I'll miss you." Immediately, I felt mortified. I desperately wished I could reach out and grab the words I'd just said and stuff them back down my throat.

Charlie's initial response was a look of surprise. Then a slow smile spread across his face. "I'll miss you too, Victoria. I enjoy our conversations very much. There certainly will be an emptiness in my life every Monday, Wednesday, and Friday at noon."

That night, I had another one of my erotic dreams. Up to that point, they'd always been about my old boyfriend Daniel Hooley, the first guy I'd ever loved.

But that night, my lover wasn't Daniel. It was Charlie Hess's eyes that looked back at me in my dream, so lovingly, so sincerely, that it felt as if he was gazing into the depths of my soul. And then he kissed me.

At the moment of the kiss, I was jolted wide awake. A current of powerful energy was sizzling through my body, from my head to my toes. For a few seconds, I couldn't move. I didn't want to move, for fear of breaking the ecstatic spell.

When the energy subsided, I slowly sat up. "I'm in love with Charlie Hess," I whispered into the darkness. My heart felt wide open, unguarded, allowing strange, sweet feelings to flood in. And I knew that whether or not Charlie reciprocated my affections, I could no longer deny how I felt about him.

Several days later, I went to see Reverend Hahn. "I didn't bring anything to read," I said as I bent down to kiss his cheek, "because I wanted to talk to you about something."

He blinked his eyes twice, as if to say, *go ahead.*

"I'm in love," I said.

A pause, then two blinks of affirmation.

I knew that if he could, my birth father would ask me a series of important, well-crafted questions. No doubt, they were formulating in his mind. So, I imagined what he would say, and then answered the question.

Who is this fellow?

"His name is Charlie Hess. He's the guy I told you about several months ago, the one I've been talking to at lunch. He's the teaching assistant in the physics department."

What is it that attracts you to this man?

"I like everything about him. He's kind. He's trustworthy. He's brilliant. And he's good-looking."

Does he feel the same way about you?

"I'm not sure how he feels about me. But I think maybe he's developing feelings. He hasn't said anything yet. He's a cautious person, not one to rush things."

I'm so happy for you. But I want you to take your time. I want you to be sure this is really what you want.

"You don't need to worry. I'm being careful. I haven't said anything to him about my feelings. Right now, we're just talking and getting to know each other, and I'm enjoying that. I don't want to do anything to mess things up between us."

My birth father gave three sets of affirmative blinks, as if offering me his blessing. In my mind's eye, I pictured the charming smile he would have given me six months earlier. Then he closed his eyes, as if exhausted.

"I love you," I whispered before tiptoeing out of the room.

CHAPTER 47

On a blustery Monday in January, the first day of the second trimester classes, I walked into the busy snack shop at noon. It seemed like ages since I'd had lunch with Charlie. I glanced around, nervously scanning the crowd for my friend.

When I failed to spot him, I panicked. *Maybe his schedule is different this trimester. Maybe he has some other obligation at noon.* As I continued to search for him, my mind raced on to more drastic scenarios. *Maybe he didn't come back to the college. Maybe his position was cut for some reason. Maybe he decided to go back to grad school in Massachusetts.*

Feeling dejected, I was just about to turn around and leave the snack shop, when, out of the corner of my eye, I saw a man standing beside a booth at the far end of the room, waving. I turned in that direction and saw that it was Charlie. We locked eyes, and he smiled at me. I almost collapsed with relief.

Minutes later, I made my way to the booth with my tray of food. Charlie jumped up to help me out of my heavy coat. Then, in an uncharacteristic gesture, he hugged me.

His warm greeting was profoundly reassuring. In the three weeks Charlie and I had spent apart, I'd begun to wonder whether I was imagining his fond feelings for me.

"Were you hiding from me way back here in the corner?" I teased as I scooted into the booth.

"Absolutely not," he said quickly. "I got here a little later than I usually do, and our favorite booth was already taken. I worried that you wouldn't be able to find me, so I was watching for you."

He searched my face with hungry eyes, as if taking in everything about me. "It's so good to see you again."

"You, too," I said, trying to keep my overwhelming emotions from gushing out. "How were your holidays?"

His voice took on a more even tone. "Oh, pretty routine. I had a nice time with my family. And plenty of free time to catch up on the reading I wanted to do before I go back to MIT this fall. How about you?"

I tried not to let the mention of his upcoming departure deflate my mood. "I was busy," I told him. "I had chorale concerts. Some of the employees at the restaurant took time off over the holidays, so I was able to work a lot of extra shifts. My boss Bob had a holiday party for all of us. And my roommates and I had a little party at our house."

"Wow," Charlie said, "you certainly were busy."

"On Christmas Eve," I continued, "I went caroling with a group of people from College Mennonite Church. We went to Greencroft and stopped by Reverend Hahn's room. I was glad we did that."

I didn't tell Charlie about watching the tears leak from Reverend Hahn's eyes while we sang, and how my own eyes teared up in response.

"And, of course, I went home on Christmas Day, to spend time with my dad, my stepmother, my sister, and my stepsister."

Charlie and I had already told each other about our family configurations. I'd learned that he had a brother and a sister, and he knew that I was the youngest of four. He was aware of Lucy's mental illness, and the fact that she'd shown improvement since living at home with my dad and Barbara. But he knew nothing about the strained relationships between my brothers and the rest of the family.

"Didn't your brothers come home for Christmas?" he asked.

"No," I said, suddenly uneasy. "They don't come home very often. They were here for a few days last summer. We probably won't see them for another year."

Charlie must have sensed my discomfort, as he diverted the conversation to a lighter topic. "Tell me about your family's holiday tradition."

"During my childhood, my parents never made much of a fuss about Christmas," I told him. "My mother was really strict. She didn't believe in the secular traditions. She never even allowed us to have a Christmas tree. But now that my stepmother is in the home, things are different. Barbara really gets into the Christmas spirit. She enjoys making the holiday special for us. This was the second year we had a Christmas tree. My sister loves that. She gets excited, like a little kid. It's kind of like she's making up for what she missed out on during her childhood."

Charlie's smile encouraged me to continue. I almost started to tell him about my first Christmas with Reverend Hahn, and what it was like to decorate my first tree. But I caught myself just in time. I knew he'd find such family-like activity with a man who was no more than a friend to be a little odd.

And I did not tell him about the fact that I'd spent an hour with Reverend Hahn on this most recent Christmas Day, and that I'd done everything I could to bring some joy to his nursing home room. I'd read him the Christmas story from the Bible. I'd played him a tape of our chorale singing carols. I'd described in detail the snowy scene outside his window. And I'd read him another poem I'd written as a Christmas gift.

"How about you, Charlie?" I asked. "Does your family put up a Christmas tree?"

"Yes," he said, "we always have, as far back as I can remember. Relative to other Mennonites, my parents weren't particularly strict. But they didn't go overboard with Christmas. They weren't inclined to get caught up in the silliness of the season."

He chuckled. "So, my mother never took me to sit on Santa's lap. And I bet yours didn't either."

"Not a chance!" I laughed at the thought. "My mother never allowed Santa Claus, his elves, or his reindeer to enter my life. She made sure I kept my eyes on the Baby Jesus."

My association with Charlie quickly settled back into the routine of the previous trimester. Admittedly, I was disappointed in the lack of forward movement in our relationship. I had to repeatedly remind myself how fortunate I was to have him as a friend.

But while things stayed the same with Charlie and me, my birth father's condition continued to decline, slowly and insidiously robbing him of everything he had. His body became cadaverous, completely useless, and his spirit seemed to be hovering somewhere between life and death. I knew full well that if his ventilator would ever be unplugged, he'd be gone within minutes. It became difficult for him to keep his eyes open for more than a few seconds at a time. Blinking in response to my questions seemed to take more strength than he could muster.

So I kept my visits short. I'd tell him about my day, then read a passage from the Psalms, something that would be a source of comfort to him. I was never sure he heard me, as he always appeared to sleep throughout most of my stay.

One day in late February, I stepped out of Reverend Hahn's room just as a nurse was coming in. "He's going to die soon, isn't he?" I whispered so that he couldn't hear.

The nurse looked startled by my question. She hesitated, then nodded. I followed her a few steps down the hallway so we could talk. "We don't expect him to be around much longer," she confided. "The poor man. It'll be a blessing for him when his time comes."

"Yes," I said. "It will be. He's suffered long enough."

"Reverend Hahn is dying," I told Charlie the next day at lunch. Against my will, tears flowed down my cheeks.

Charlie reached across the table and placed his hand over mine. "This is hard for you, isn't it?"

"Yes."

"Let me know when it happens. Call me." Releasing my hand, he reached into his briefcase and pulled out a pad of paper. He jotted down his number, then tore off the sheet and handed it to me. "Here's the number at my apartment. You can call me any time. If I'm not there, leave a message, and I'll call you back as soon as I can."

On a Monday in early March, I passed the nurse's station as I headed toward Reverend Hahn's room. It was 3:00 PM, and the afternoon shift of nurses had just come in. I overheard a nurse from the morning shift passing along information to her replacement. "The doctor said he has pneumonia. He's too weak to pull through this."

My heart sank. I knew who they were talking about. I paused, pretending to examine a painting hanging on the wall, waiting to hear more.

"We called his sister in Pennsylvania this morning," the nurse continued. "It'll be up to her to decide when to stop the feedings and take him off the ventilator. The news took her by surprise. She said she needs a few days to think it through."

Of course, I thought. *Reverend Hahn's sister, my biological aunt, has to shoulder that responsibility. The decision is up to her.*

I felt powerless, drained of all strength. I could do nothing to ward off the end that was rapidly approaching. I could barely lift my feet to walk down the hallway to Reverend Hahn's room.

When I touched his arm and said, "I'm here, Father," his eyes barely flickered. His body had all but lost the fight.

CHAPTER 48

The next few days, whenever I wasn't in class or at work, I sat in Reverend Hahn's room, my chair pulled close to his bed. I brought my textbooks with me, reading my assignments while keeping vigil. Every few minutes, I'd reach out to caress my father's arm or hold his hand, reminding him of my presence. Sometimes, I'd lean over to whisper loving words in his ear.

He no longer responded in any way, and I wasn't sure he was even aware of what was going on around him. Still, I wanted to believe that his spirit knew I was there for him, that I was doing as I had promised, remaining with him until the very end.

Many grief-stricken visitors passed in and out of the room. Whenever someone came in, I'd set aside my books and step out into the hallway, allowing them to visit with Reverend Hahn in private. For the most part, the visitors were too focused on their friend's imminent death to be curious about my presence.

My vigil took its toll on me. I got little sleep at night, and that, combined with the emotional strain, left me feeling weak, dazed, and unable to think straight.

Late Friday afternoon, I sat in the chair next to Reverend Hahn's bed, attempting to read an assignment for my World Religions class. I didn't realize I'd drifted off to sleep until I was jolted awake by the sound of footsteps and a murmured conversation. When I opened my eyes, I saw two women enter the room. Embarrassed, I sat up straight, adjusting my rumpled clothing and running my fingers through my tousled hair.

These new visitors were people I'd never seen before. One of the women appeared to be quite elderly, in her eighties. She was wearing a white head covering tied under her chin, and the modest cape dress typical of the most conservative factions of the Mennonite denomination. Her tall, thin frame was hunched, and her haggard expression, unkempt hair, and tottering gait suggested that she was worn out from recent travels.

Her companion looked to be her junior by thirty years. While her long hair was wound into a bun, she wore contemporary clothing, a dark skirt reaching to her mid-calf and a cardigan sweater over a white blouse. She held the elderly woman by the arm, steadying her as they made their way into the room.

I jumped up, offering the older woman my seat. The younger woman thanked me as she guided her charge to the chair. Still, it seemed as if neither of them really noticed me.

Then the younger woman leaned over the bed, putting her mouth close to Reverend Hahn's ear. "Uncle Harry, this is Violet. I brought your sister Emma here to see you." And I suddenly knew exactly who the women were.

Leave the room, a scolding inner voice instructed me. *Let them visit with their brother and uncle in private.* But my overwhelming curiosity about these unknown relatives kept my feet glued to the floor. I stood in the corner of the room, trying to be unobtrusive.

"I need to find a restroom," Violet said to Emma. "Will you be okay for a few minutes while I'm gone?" The elderly woman closed her eyes, nodding wearily.

A moment after Violet left, Emma opened her eyes and glanced around the room, as if trying to get her bearings. Then her gaze fell on me, and she looked puzzled. "Who are you?" she asked in a quavering voice.

Perhaps my dazed brain was too exhausted to filter my response. Or perhaps some part of me knew the time had come for complete honesty. Before I could think, words tumbled out of my mouth. "I'm his daughter."

Emma's eyes grew wide, and her body swayed slightly in her chair. She grabbed the railing of Reverend Hahn's hospital bed to brace herself. I immediately recognized my mistake. *Oh my God, oh my God,* I thought, horrified. *What have I done?*

"But Harry and Myrna never ...." Emma stared at me, her eyes searching my face for a full minute, as if trying to fit the pieces of a puzzle together. I watched her expression change from questioning to knowing. As if realization had dawned. As if she'd already known her brother for who he was.

"I'm sorry," I said, gathering up my books. "I'm so sorry. I shouldn't be here."

As I headed toward the door, Emma called out, "Don't leave, dear. Please."

I froze, waiting for what she was going to say next. A long silence ensued before she spoke again. "I know you're telling me the truth, although I don't know how this all came to be. I can see just by looking at you that you're Harry's daughter. He was a good man, but he had his weaknesses. I've known he dallied with women over the years."

I turned to face her, and she scrutinized my appearance again, taking in the totality of me, her gaze flickering from my head to my feet. "And what is your name, dear?"

"Victoria," I replied.

"Victoria," she breathed, as if the name brought her pleasure. With a trembling hand, she attempted to smooth back the wisps of unruly white hair that had sprung out on either side of her face. Then her expression darkened, and she seemed to be struggling with inner turmoil. "Thank you for telling me who you are, Victoria. Now I'm going to tell you who I am. And I trust you to never repeat this to another soul."

She cleared her throat noisily, as if preparing for the passage of words that would be difficult to utter. "I am your grandmother."

I stared at her, wondering if I'd become completely confused about my birth father's family configuration. "But I thought you were Harry's sister."

"That is true," she said. "But it is also true that I am his mother."

Her announcement sent my mind reeling. But before Emma could say anything else, Violet walked back into the room. "Are you doing okay, Aunt Emma?" she asked, still disinterested in my presence. "You look like you're running on the last ounce of your strength. I think we should get you something to eat."

"Give me just a few more minutes to rest here," Emma said. "How about if you get us checked in at the Holiday Inn?"

"That sounds like a good idea," Violet replied. "I'll be back in half an hour or so." She left the room again.

Then Emma turned back to me. "Stay with me, Victoria. I want to talk with you. Please tell me how you came to be in Harry's life."

Knowing that our time together was limited, I tried to condense my life story into a few sentences. "Reverend Hahn met my mother when they were working together at a mission in Mexico. He got her pregnant."

Emma lowered her eyes, clucking her tongue and shaking her head. "Oh, Harry. Harry."

"I was raised by my mother and her husband," I continued. "I didn't know Reverend Hahn was my father until five years ago. Then, four years ago, we got to know each other, and we've become close. I'm a student at Goshen College, so I've been visiting him on a regular basis."

Emma nodded as she took in my story, as if it was beginning to make sense to her. "Now let me tell you how Harry came into my life."

Reaching out to Reverend Hahn, she ran an affectionate finger over his flaccid cheek. "If you can hear me, Harry darling," she crooned, "listen carefully. I'm not going to scold you for your indiscretions, because I am no saint myself. I know you've always wondered about your birth parents. So I'm going to tell you now. Perhaps the truth will be a comfort to you as you move on to the next world."

I pulled around a chair from the other side of the room so that I could sit near Emma. My mind felt as if it was entering an entirely different realm, ready to receive the remarkable story that was about to come.

I grew up in Lancaster, Pennsylvania, in a quiet Mennonite community. I've lived there all my life, except for one year. My parents owned a restaurant, and from the time we were small children, my younger sister Rose and I worked for them. That was the only life I knew.

However, when I was fifteen, everything changed. A couple from our church were serving as missionaries in Romania. They sent word to our congregation that the mission was struggling, and pleaded for help.

My parents felt moved by their plight. They put their restaurant in the charge of a manager, and they, along with Rose and me, set sail for Romania. They planned to stay at the mission for two years.

Of course, this was a great disruption in our family life. Rose, who was timid and shy, didn't want to go. But after living fifteen years of an uneventful life in Lancaster, I was eager for something new.

The long ship ride across the ocean was grueling. When we landed, we took a train to Bucharest, and from there, we traveled by horse and wagon to the mission. Back then, traveling was more difficult than it is now. But I loved every minute of the adventure.

The mission was located in a tiny village several hours north of Bucharest. It consisted of a small church, a makeshift medical clinic, and a half-built schoolhouse, along with several acres of farmland that helped to feed mission workers and impoverished villagers.

My family arrived in early summer. We stayed in an old farmhouse near the mission. It felt small and cramped compared to our spacious two-story home in Lancaster. But we were surrounded by beautiful forested hills that made up for the shabbiness of our living conditions.

The day after our arrival, my father turned his attention to the school construction project, supervising a group of workers from the village. Although she had no formal training, my mother worked as a nurse in the clinic.

My sister Rose and I were assigned the task of cooking. It was our responsibility to carry food and drinking water to the farmhands in the fields, and to the workers at the construction site. Shy as she was, Rose preferred to stay back in the kitchen while I delivered the food and water to the men.

During my free time, I loved to roam the forested hills surrounding our home. My parents repeatedly cautioned me to be careful, to stay close to the house. Ignoring their concern, I ventured farther into the woods on each excursion.

One week after our arrival, I was carrying a jug of water to the construction site when I spotted a young man I hadn't seen before. The sight of him took my breath away. He was the most strikingly handsome fellow I'd ever laid eyes on, tall and muscular with black hair and an olive complexion. When he glanced my way, I saw that his dark eyes flashed with intelligence. It seemed as if he possessed some secret knowledge that the rest of us knew nothing about.

I couldn't stop staring at the young man. He returned my gaze with a nod and a slight smile. When he accepted a cup of water from my hand, his fingers brushed mine, and a thrill shot through my body.

I'd never had such an experience before. Back in Pennsylvania, I hadn't yet developed an interest in the Mennonite boys in my community. So, I was unprepared for the impact this young man had on me.

My father noticed that I was lingering a little too long at the construction site, and he ordered me back to my work in the house. I walked away, but when my father wasn't looking, I hid behind tree for a few minutes so that I could watch the young man undetected.

I discovered that this young man worked in different capacities at the mission. Sometimes when I'd carry food and water to the farmhands, he'd be out in the field. At other times, he'd be in the stable tending the horses. On occasion, he'd drive to Bucharest with his horse and wagon to bring supplies back to the mission.

I never asked questions about him, because I didn't want to betray the fact that I was captivated by him. It was as if he'd cast a spell on me. I could hardly breathe in his presence. If my parents would've known of my infatuation, they would've done everything they could to discourage it.

So, I watched and listened, trying to find out everything I could about this young man. I soon learned that his name was Constantin. Although he seemed to have the bearing and the ability of a grown man, he was only seventeen, just two years older than me. I learned that he'd been orphaned as a child, and had been raised by a kindly couple who lived near the mission. But they had long since died, and he now lived on his own in the small house they'd left him.

People would remark about his unusual complexion, saying he was so dark because he was a gypsy. While Constantin was always treated with respect at the mission, in the village, the word "gypsy" was spoken with contempt.

One day, Constantin showed up to work at the mission with a swollen eye and a cut on his cheek. At supper that evening, my father sadly informed us that Constantin had been attacked by several men in the village. He explained that in Romania, gypsies were often treated unkindly. Reiterating the teaching of our church, he told Rose and me that we should never treat Constantin with disrespect.

"All people are the children of God," he said. "No one should be treated harshly because of the color of their skin."

Of course, I never felt inclined to look down on

Constantin. In my mind, he was someone special, better than an ordinary person like me.

After that unfortunate incident, my father kept a protective eye on Constantin. He thought so highly of the young man, and considered him to be an asset at the mission. When he'd ponder over some difficult task that needed to be done, I'd often hear him say, "I'll have Constantin take care of this."

My first three weeks at the mission, Constantin and I never spoke a word to each other. We'd exchange smiles when I carried food and water to his worksite. Sometimes when I walked away, I'd sense his eyes following me. But I'd tell myself this was only my imagination.

One Sunday afternoon, I was out roaming the hills, feeling happy and free. Suddenly, a man stepped out from behind a tree, startling me. I screamed and was about to run. But then I saw that it was Constantin.

"Don't be afraid," he said to me in his broken English. "I won't hurt you. I wanted to meet you here." And I realized that Constantin had indeed been watching me, taking note of my habits, waiting for a time when he could speak with me alone.

We stood there staring at each other. My heart was pounding so hard that it echoed in my ears.

"Emma," he said, letting me know that he knew my name. He reached out to touch my cheek. "So beautiful."

His touch both terrified and thrilled me. I was unable to speak, unable to move.

"Walk with me," he said.

As if given a command I didn't dare to disobey, I followed his lead, going deeper and deeper into the forest with him. He pointed out various trees, the oak, the poplar, and the beech. He told me about the bears, the lynx, and the wolves that used to inhabit the forest. When he saw me shudder in fear, he laughed and said, "You are safe with me."

He picked a bouquet of wildflowers and handed them to me. I spoke my first words to him. "Thank you."

Constantin knew his way around those woods. He was at home there, as if he was one of the creatures of the forest. At the end of our walk, I realized he'd led me in a full circle, delivering me back to the point where I'd started my trek.

Before we parted ways, he took my hand. Gazing at me with his dark, soulful eyes, he said, "Walk with me again, Emma."

I nodded.

"Next Sunday," he said.

I nodded again.

And so, Constantin and I began to meet secretly in the forest. He seemed to know that any open involvement with me would never be tolerated, neither in the village nor at the mission. Sadly, I knew the same.

At first, we met every Sunday afternoon. Then we began stealing time during the lovely summer evenings, when both of us were finished with our day's work.

A bond quickly grew between us. We'd walk through the forest holding hands, in an enchanted world that only the two of us shared. My love for Constantin overwhelmed me, consuming me every minute of every day. While I completed my daily chores, I'd think of nothing but meeting him in the forest that evening.

By that time, my parents had become less anxious about my excursions into the woods. They had no idea what was happening.

I was still so young, hardly more than a child, and my mother had not yet talked with me about the private relationship between a man and a woman. So, I knew nothing about such matters when my relationship with Constantin became more intimate. But he taught me, gently and sweetly.

I knew what I was doing was wrong. But I was powerless to stop my yearning for Constantin. When we were alone together in the forest, our intimacy seemed right and beautiful.

Emma suddenly stopped speaking. She dropped her head, slumping against the arm of her chair.

"Are you okay?" I asked, alarmed. "Can I get you something?"

She shook her head, then reached for her handbag sitting on the floor beside her chair. She fumbled awkwardly in the bag and pulled out a tissue. Dabbing at her eyes, she said, "Victoria, I've never spoken of these things before. I hope you'll forgive me. This is difficult."

"Of course," I said. "You don't need to tell me any more if it's too hard for you." But I was so drawn into her story that I couldn't stand the thought of having the narrative cut off.

"I need to tell it," she said. "I've carried it alone all these years." She looked down, wringing her gnarled hands in her lap. Then she began speaking in an impassive voice, as if trying to separate herself from the wrenching emotion embedded in her story.

One Sunday afternoon in autumn, when the trees were ablaze with color, Constantin and I were walking hand in hand in the forest. Then we lay down on a bed of leaves, and he held me in his arms, kissing me passionately.

Suddenly, we heard a loud shout, followed by cursing. I couldn't understand everything the man was saying, but I made out the words, "filthy gypsy."

Constantin jumped up and took off running. I sat up, calling out for him. Then the shouting man came into view, and I saw that he was a hunter. I watched him lift his rifle, take aim, and fire. I saw Constantin's body lurch from the impact of the bullet. I heard his cry, then I watched him stumble and fall to the ground. I saw the blood gushing from the wound in his back.

I jumped up in dismay, wanting to rush to my fallen lover. But I stopped short when the hunter approached me with concern on his face. "Are you okay?" he asked.

In that moment, I realized that the hunter thought I had been attacked, and that he had come to my rescue.

Victoria, I cannot begin to describe what a state I was in. "Stunned" and "shocked" fall short of conveying my distress. I couldn't fathom what had happened. Leaving Constantin's body behind in the forest, the hunter took me by the arm and escorted me home. There, he explained to my surprised parents that he'd come upon the dirty gypsy boy in the act of raping me, and that he'd shot him.

My parents were horrified. "Tell us how this happened, Emma," they said. But I was too frightened and too traumatized to respond to their questions.

The entire mission soon learned about the tragic event. Everyone sorrowed over the attack on an innocent girl. They mourned Constantin's death, grieving over the fact that the young man they'd trusted had taken such a wrong turn.

People kept saying I'd been raped. I didn't know what that word meant. My mother explained to me that a rape occurs when a man overpowers a woman and takes advantage of her.

All my life, I've carried a burden of shame about the lie I perpetrated. I never corrected my parents' misperception of what happened to me. I was terrified of confessing my own wrongdoing. I was afraid I would be punished severely, and that everyone at the mission would look upon me with judgment. And I couldn't even allow myself to think about the role I played in a young man's death. The story of Constantin's attack on me became fixed in everyone's mind, and it seemed best to leave it that way.

The day after the shooting, several men from the mission retrieved Constantin's body from the woods. He was buried without a funeral. The hunter who shot him was not even charged with a crime.

For weeks, I remained in a state of shock. My parents assumed I was suffering from the trauma of the attack. At night, my mother would come to my room to console me. "Just let this go, Emma," she'd say as she stroked my hair and rubbed my back. "Just put this terrible thing out of your mind."

She had no idea I was mourning the death of my lover, that I was dealing with the horror of watching him die. I couldn't get the sights and sounds out of my mind: his cry, his fall to the ground, the blood. Every day, I berated myself for the fact that I hadn't rushed to his side to comfort him while he lay dying.

Every evening, my father would sit with his head in his hands, sorrowing. "Grace," he'd say to my mother, "I deeply regret bringing my family to this foreign country, only to have such a terrible thing happen to one of my children. Let's make arrangements to return home before another misfortune befalls us."

When my belly began to swell in a strange way, I didn't know what was happening to me. I started feeling nauseas, and couldn't keep down food. I wondered if I'd contracted some deadly illness. I fantasized about dying, because I wanted to be with Constantin.

At that point in my young life, I didn't understand the association between intimacy with a man and becoming pregnant. The day my mother first noticed my swollen belly, she sat down and wept. Then she explained to me how Constantin had impregnated me when he'd raped me. "Emma," she said, "you're going to have a baby."

I didn't tell my mother that Constantin and I had been intimate many times before the day he was killed. On the day of the supposed rape, we were actually interrupted by the hunter before intimacy occurred. The baby would have been conceived at a previous encounter.

That evening, I eavesdropped as my mother and father had a long talk about how to deal with the impending birth of my child. Together, they knelt beside their bed, their faces buried in their folded arms. My mother sobbed as my father pleaded with God to provide them with wisdom and guidance.

"We cannot return home yet," my father said to my mother. "Not until after the birth of Emma's child."

Night after night, they prayed fervently. During the day, their faces looked grim, heavy with the weight of the burden they were carrying. I felt so guilty, and so sorry for them. They were honest, upright people who'd come to Romania to do God's work. They'd had no idea that they would find themselves in such a dilemma.

Of course, my sister Rose had been deeply shaken by what had happened to me. "I hate this place," she said to my parents. "Let's go home."

So, when another couple working at the mission made plans to return America, my parents arranged to send Rose back with them. She was to stay with our grandparents until the rest of us came home. My sister went gladly. She never knew that the true reason my parents sent her home was to spare her the knowledge of what was about to happen.

As my figure continued to change, my mother cautioned me to stay inside the house. My absence in the activities of mission life didn't seem strange to the other workers, as I'd kept myself out of sight since the day of Constantin's death. Everyone assumed I was still shaken by the attack.

After weeks of anguished prayer, my parents sat me down to tell me of their plans. "We must give this child up for adoption," my father said. "There's an orphanage in Bucharest. After the baby is born, we will put it in their charge. Then we will immediately return to America."

I had been in such a state of grief and confusion that I hadn't been able to think clearly about giving birth, or about what would happen to my child. But upon hearing my father's words, I protested. "Please let me keep the baby," I pleaded.

"That isn't possible, Emma," my father said. "You can't live with the shame of having a child out of wedlock. And the child can't live with the knowledge that it is the product of a heinous crime. That would be a burden it would carry for life."

I wanted to tell my parents that the baby was not a product of rape, that it had been conceived in love. But all I could do was weep over the prospect of losing my child.

"Please let me keep the baby," I begged them again and again. Of course, they couldn't understand why. How could I tell them that this child was the only piece of Constantin I had left?

Every night, I cried myself to sleep, while my parents continued to pray. Then, when I was a month away from delivering the baby, they sat me down for another talk.

"God has put another plan in our minds," my father told me. "Here is what we've decided to do. After the child is born, we will place it in the care of the orphanage in Bucharest. We will do this in secret, so that no one will know the identity of its mother. We will allow a few weeks to pass. Then your mother and I will return to the orphanage to adopt the baby as our own.

"By following this plan, we will take responsibility for the baby, who is, after all, our own flesh and blood. It will not be consigned to an unfortunate life of growing up in an orphanage. But the child must never know of the tragic circumstances around its birth. As it grows up, it will simply be told that it was adopted from an orphanage in Romania. In telling the child this, we will not be uttering a lie."

My father looked at me sternly. "Your sister Rose must never know that you are the mother of the child we will be adopting. You must tell no one. When we return to America with this infant, it will be the adopted child of your mother and me."

"Do you agree to this plan, Emma?" my mother asked. "Can you give us your word that you will never let anyone

know that you gave birth to the child we adopted? Can you promise to never tell the child about its unfortunate conception?"

"Yes," I said as relief washed over me. "I promise."

For the first time since Constantin's death, I felt a flicker of hope. I would not lose my baby after all.

My father must have sensed my joy, because he spoke with caution in his voice. "Emma, you must understand that when this child returns to our family, you will no longer be the mother. You will have no authority over the child. You will confine yourself to the role of sister."

Victoria, there was nothing I could do but to agree to this plan. As a young teenage girl, I had no means of raising a child on my own. The best I could do was to be a loving sister.

Four weeks later, I felt my first birth pangs. As my parents wanted no one else to know about the pregnancy, it was up to my mother to deliver the baby. She tended to me in my bedroom, while my father paced outside the door, praying for the safety of both the baby and me. Despite my terror and pain, my baby boy arrived safely.

At the mention of her baby, Emma's face took on an expression of tenderness. Turning to Reverend Hahn, she reached over and stroked his arm. "Harry, dear," she murmured, "after you were born, I didn't let you out of my arms for three days. I nursed you at my breast. You were the most beautiful baby I had ever seen. I could tell you looked just like your father, and that pleased me so much. I thought my heart would burst from all the love I felt for you."

Turning back to me, she continued her story.

When little Harry was only three days old, my father announced that it was time to deliver him to the orphanage. I didn't want to let him go, but I knew I had to. That night, we bundled him up warmly, and under the cover of darkness, we made the two-hour trip to the orphanage in our horse-drawn wagon. My mother had prepared a little basket for Harry, but I insisted on holding him in my arms, nursing him for the last time.

My father stopped the team of horses about a quarter of a mile away from the orphanage, while my mother took little Harry from my arms and placed him in the basket. Then she and I waited in the darkness while my father set out on foot, carrying the basket. All the while he was gone, I cried and prayed that everything would go well.

Half an hour later, my father returned, empty-handed. "I set the basket on the doorstep of the orphanage," he told my mother and me. "I pounded on the door, and then ran to hide behind some nearby bushes. I kept watch while a woman opened the door and looked around. Then she looked down and saw the basket at her feet. She hesitated only a moment before picking it up, carrying it inside, and closing the door behind her."

I wept quietly on the drive home, while my mother held me close. The next few weeks were difficult for me. My breasts were engorged with milk for the baby I could no longer suckle. But within a month, my body was back to its normal state, and I once again resumed my part of the work at the mission. Everyone assumed that I had finally recovered from the shock of being raped by the gypsy boy.

About that time, my parents told me they were ready to return to Bucharest to adopt the baby. I'm not sure why they waited so long. Perhaps they wanted to make sure that no one at the orphanage would associate them with the appearance of the baby on the doorstep. Or maybe they wanted to wait until I'd regained my full physical and mental strength.

I was excited by their news and wanted to go with them. But they wouldn't allow me to make the trip. They told me not to get my hopes up, reminding me there was a possibility that the baby would no longer be at the orphanage. "He was a beautiful child," my mother said. "Someone else may have been eager to adopt him."

My parents were gone for three days. When they returned home, I was overjoyed to see that they'd brought little Harry with them. I rushed out to their wagon, ready to take my child into my arms. But my mother refused, cuddling him in her own arms. He had become her child.

Several weeks later, my mother, my father, and I left Romania to return to America, taking little Harry with us. When we arrived back in Lancaster, I remained silent while people congratulated my parents on the adoption of their baby boy. "God led you all the way to Romania to find your son," they'd say.

"If they only knew," I'd whisper to myself. But no one would never know.

The years passed, and Harry was raised as my little brother. Our family life solidified around the story of Harry's adoption, hiding the secret known only to my mother, my father, and me. And inside that secret lay another secret, one known only to me.

Harry was a handful for my parents. He was a restless, inquisitive child, who always pushed against the limits they set for him. At the time of their greatest struggles with him, I'd feel guilty, knowing that I was the one who'd brought this challenge into their lives.

As your father might have told you, Victoria, I have never married. Doing so would have required being honest with my husband. I could not be close to a man without divulging my secret. And back in that day, no man wanted a woman who'd given birth to a child out of wedlock.

Harry has known me only as his doting older sister. He's never had the slightest inkling that I brought him into this world. And I never thought I'd see the day when he would leave this world. I never imagined that he would go before me. It doesn't seem like the proper order of things for a child to pass before the parent.

Emma looked as if she was prepared to say more. But she stopped short at the sound of approaching footsteps clicking on the tile floor in the hallway. Violet bustled into the room, ready to resume her mission of caring for her elderly charge.

"We're all set, Aunt Emma," she said cheerfully. "I've checked us into the Holiday Inn, and our luggage is already in the room. Let's go to the cafeteria and get you something to eat. Then we'll come back and spend a few more minutes with Harry before I take you to the hotel."

Still disinterested in my presence, she took her aunt's arm and helped her to her feet. "We need to get you to bed early tonight, Emma. You're exhausted."

As the two women made their way out of the room, Violet holding onto her aunt to steady her, Emma turned her head and shot me a plaintive look. I could tell she wanted to reach out to me, to maintain some type of connection.

But I also knew I would never come face-to-face with my grandmother again. She was feeble, dependent. No doubt, her family oversaw her every move. If she tried to establish communication with me, she would be forced to reveal the secret she'd hidden for seventy years, along with the one her son had hidden for more than twenty years. She was not prepared to sort out this messy business with her family members, to deal with their shock and dismay.

I lifted a hand in a farewell gesture, then placed it over my heart. Emma smiled sadly, and then almost lost her balance.

"You need to watch where you're going, Aunt Emma," Violet scolded. "We can't have you falling."

After the women left, I moved to the chair next to Reverend Hahn's bed. Throughout the coming and going of his family members, he'd shown not the slightest response. "Did you hear everything Emma told us?" I asked the inert form. "She fought to keep you. She loves you dearly."

I sat back in the chair, forcing myself to think about what was coming. The next day, Emma and Violet would be consulting with Reverend Hahn's doctor. Emma would give her permission to discontinue life support. And within minutes after the ventilator was removed, my father would be gone.

This was it. This was the last time I would see my father alive. It was time for a final goodbye. Pulling my chair as close to the bed as possible, I spoke softly into his ear.

"Goodbye, my dear father. These past four years with you have been wonderful. I'm so grateful that I had the chance to know you. Thank you for everything you've done for me. Thank you for everything you've taught me. Thank you for encouraging me and believing in me. I love you. You'll always be in my heart. And someday, we'll see each other again."

I saw his eyelids flicker ever so slightly. Twice. He was acknowledging my goodbye. I stood up, then bent down to kiss his forehead one last time. "I love you," I whispered again before turning away from the bed and leaving the room.

CHAPTER 49

I slept fitfully that night. My brain felt as if it had been blown out of my skull, the cells whirling crazily in the air. I wanted desperately to sort things out and establish some measure of order in my world again. But I couldn't.

I kept thinking about my father hovering on the brink of death, wondering whether he was still in this world, or whether he'd passed on to the next.

My father had spent his whole life wondering who he was, while all along the answer to his question had been so near at hand. It felt strange to be in possession of a piece of his history that he'd never known himself. I wondered whether he'd been conscious enough to take in Emma's story, whether hearing it had comforted his soul as it prepared to leave his body.

In the dead of the night, I didn't think I could possibly carry the weight of Emma's secret on my own. Not in addition to the one I'd already been carrying. It occurred to me that, on my father's side of the family, secrets had been lurking in the shadows for three generations.

How is it that Emma's story ever reached my ears? I asked myself repeatedly. Our meeting had been completely random. If I hadn't been in that room when she and Violet arrived, we never would have crossed paths. If they hadn't caught me dozing, I would've been more mentally alert, and would've left the room immediately. If I'd gone to the restroom or to the cafeteria for a cup of coffee, and then returned to find Emma and Violet in the room, I would've stayed in the hallway, allowing them their privacy. If only one aspect of the bizarre circumstances had been different, I never would have known who my birth father really was. Who I really was.

When Emma had recounted the story of the hunter interrupting her and Constantin during their intimacy, horrifying pictures had formed in my mind, images that refused to leave. My grandfather running for his life, then stumbling, falling to the ground. The blood gushing from the bullet wound in his back. My grandmother, a mere child, sitting bolt upright on the pile of leaves, screaming, her eyes wide with terror.

My grandfather, the boy of seventeen. How could someone who never had the chance to reach adulthood ever become a grandfather? Yet, here I was, his descendant, carrying his olive skin, his black hair, his dark eyes.

The next morning, I fought the urge to drive over to Greencroft to see what was going on. But I knew I had no right to be there, no right to disrupt Emma and Violet as they made their decisions, said their goodbyes, and took care of business.

Thankfully, I had to work both the lunch and dinner shifts at the restaurant. Although my mind and body had reached a state beyond exhaustion, I was glad to have something to distract me from my ruminations. I knew that if I stayed home, I'd do nothing more than lie in bed, staring at the ceiling, my mind racing in circles.

The next morning, despite feeling drained and depleted, I forced myself out of bed and into the shower. I sensed that I needed to be at College Mennonite Church to hear the sad news I'd been waiting for. And I wasn't surprised when, during the announcement time, the pastor informed the congregation that Reverend Harry Hahn had passed away the previous afternoon.

"We all know that Reverend Hahn struggled with a challenging illness for years," he said. "He fought a valiant fight, serving the Lord until the very end. But God has finally relieved him of his suffering."

I could hear the gasps and murmurs of the people around me. To keep from crying out, I dug my nails into my palms and bit my lip so hard that I tasted blood.

As soon as the service was over, I rushed out of the

church and back to my apartment. There was only one thing I could think to do. I had to call Charlie.

His phone rang six times before the answering machine kicked on. "You have reached the residence of Charles Hess," his pleasant voice said. "Please leave a message, and I'll call you back as soon as possible."

Caught off guard, I stumbled over my words. "Charlie, I just wanted to let you know that Reverend Hahn passed away yesterday. I found out this morning in church." Not knowing what else to say, I hung up the phone.

Then it occurred to me that I hadn't asked Charlie to call me back. Maybe he would register the information I'd given him and assume that we would talk about it at lunch tomorrow. While my noisy roommates milled around in the kitchen and traipsed up and down the stairs, I sat by the phone in the living room, nervously leafing through magazines while I waited for it to ring.

"Victoria," Charity called out, "Rhonda fixed lasagna. Want some? If you don't come soon, it'll be gone."

"No, thanks," I replied. My throat was constricted, my stomach clenched in a tight knot. I knew it would be impossible to choke down any food.

I went to my room to lie down, but felt too restless to stay there. So, I got up and left the house, pacing around our small yard, then wandering up and down the nearby streets, my thoughts clouded by grief. The world around me seemed hazy and surreal.

When I came back into the house twenty minutes later, Rhonda said, "Someone called for you." She pointed to the notepad beside the phone. "I wrote down the message."

Rushing over to the phone, I snatched up the note written in my roommate's fastidious script. *Charlie called. He's going to be home for a while. Call him back if you want to talk.*

My fingers shook so badly that I had to make repeated attempts before I dialed Charlie's number correctly. He answered on the first ring, as if he'd been anticipating my return call. "Charlie," I said.

"Victoria?"

"Yes. You got my message. I just wanted you to know."

"How are you doing?"

"Not very well. I'm pretty shook up."

Charlie paused for a few seconds. "Would you like to get together to talk?"

"Yes," I said, "I'd love that. If you have the time."

"I don't have anything going on for the rest of the afternoon and evening. So my time is yours. Would you like for me to come over?"

I glanced at my roommates, who were all chatting noisily in the kitchen. "We wouldn't have any privacy here."

"How about if you meet me on campus? At the Union Building. We can decide where to go from there."

"I'll be there in ten minutes," I told him.

"Great," he said, "I'll see you then."

As I set out for the campus, I felt more disoriented than ever. Just an hour earlier, I'd received the news that Reverend Hahn had died. I could hardly fathom that my daily schedule would no longer include a trip to Greencroft to see him. And now, Charlie and I were about to step outside the bounds of our circumscribed friendship, doing something other than eating lunch in the snack shop three times a week. The routine of my daily life had suddenly been thrown off track, leaving me feeling frightened and bewildered.

Charlie was waiting at the Union Building when I arrived, standing beside the bicycle he'd ridden there. The cloud cover present earlier in the day had cleared, leaving the March afternoon sunny and unseasonably mild. "It's so nice," Charlie said, tilting back his head to take in the expanse of the sky. "Are you up for a walk?"

"That sounds good," I replied. "Where to?"

"How about going down to the dam?"

I nodded in assent, waiting while Charlie chained his bike to the bicycle rack. Then we crossed Main Street and headed down GraRoy Drive toward the dam at the Millrace Park.

We walked in silence for the first five minutes. Every few seconds, Charlie would turn his head to look at me, as if to make sure I was okay. "So how are you doing?" he asked as we neared the park.

"I'm feeling pretty rough," I admitted.

"Tell me about it," he said.

And my words began tumbling out. "Charlie, do you remember when I used to eat lunch with you and Stephen Wenger in the cafeteria?"

"Of course."

"Remember the day when you drove me over to my parents' house? And the next day at lunch, when the two of you teased me about my criminal activity?"

I glanced over at him. He was grinning. "How could I forget that?"

"You probably won't remember this," I said. "But I do, because it hit me kind of hard, even if it was a joke. Stephen said, 'What else don't we know about Miss Unruh?'"

I drew a long breath, then exhaled forcefully. "Well, Charlie, there's a lot you don't know about Victoria Unruh."

I looked sideways at his face, trying to gage his reaction. He was listening intently, but seemed unperturbed.

We'd reached the park, which was swarming with people who'd come out to enjoy the early spring afternoon. "It seems like everyone else had the same idea," Charlie said, chuckling.

With his hand on my back, he guided me to the rocks overlooking the dam, where we stood gazing down at the rushing water. "This is nice," I said, breathing in the refreshing air. "Let's stay here for a while."

"Want to sit down?" Charlie asked. He held my arm to steady me as we settled ourselves onto a large, flat rock. For a few minutes, we sat side by side in silence, our shoulders barely touching. I wanted to speak, to let the pent-up words come rushing out. But they remained a ball of tangled thoughts, heavy as a rock in the pit of my stomach.

"I was here five years ago," I finally said. "Sitting in this exact spot. I sat here for hours. And then I spent the night on a picnic table in Shanklin Park. I stayed there until the police came the next morning and took me home."

"Huh," Charlie said. "There must be an interesting story behind that."

"There is. It's something I need to tell you, Charlie. I'm not supposed to tell anyone. But I have to. I can't take this anymore. I'll go crazy if I don't talk with someone."

"I'm here to listen." Charlie reached over and took my hand. "You can tell me whatever it is you need to talk about. I'm not a gossip. I can promise you that I won't repeat a word that you say to me."

A long moment passed, with only the mesmerizing sound of the rushing water filling the silence. Then I took another deep breath, and on my exhale, I blurted out the words I'd never spoken to anyone else. "Charlie, Reverend Hahn wasn't just my friend. He was my father."

I held my breath, waiting for him to recoil. But he didn't flinch. Putting his arm around my shoulders, he pulled me closer to him. "Whenever we talked about Reverend Hahn over lunch," he said, "I sensed there was more to the story than what you were telling me. But I didn't want to pry. I figured you'd tell me when you were ready. It seems like now is the right time."

So I began my story, gaining confidence as I talked. Charlie listened sympathetically, occasionally asking questions. I told him about my early childhood of being nurtured by my dad, blissfully unaware of the dark side of our family life. I told him about the strange absence of my brothers in our lives. The mysterious sums of money that came into the household, which I later learned was Reverend Hahn's child support. Being informed at sixteen that Reverend Hahn was my biological father. My anguish and terrible disorientation as I tried to adjust to this information. The long talks with my parents, during which I learned the circumstances around my birth: my mother's affair with Reverend Hahn while doing mission work in Mexico, and the decision that I would be raised as her husband's child.

I told Charlie about my first face-to-face meeting with Reverend Hahn five years earlier, how I'd despised him at first. How he'd manipulated me into a relationship with him. And how, over time, I'd grown to appreciate him, to depend on him, to love him. I told Charlie about the uncanny similarities between my birth father and me, how facing some of the unattractive aspects of Reverend Hahn's personality made me question myself.

"Wow," Charlie said when I finally paused for breath. "This is mind-blowing."

"But there's more," I said. "Something I found out just two days ago." And then I told him about my encounter with Reverend Hahn's sister in the nursing home, and her story about my father's birth.

"That's absolutely incredible," Charlie said when I was finished. "Victoria, I don't think meeting your grandmother was an accident. It almost seems providential."

"That's kind of what I thought," I said. "It's so strange to know something about my father that he never knew about himself. It's such a huge thing. I don't know what to do with it. I don't think I can handle it. My mind feels like it's going to explode."

Charlie removed his arm from around my shoulders and took my hand in his. "I'm a scientist," he said. "I'm not an expert in matters of the heart. But I know that your story has moved my heart in a way that it has never been moved before. You've gone through far more than your share of challenges these past five years. Learning about your birth father. Dealing with his death. And, of course, losing your mother in the middle of all this. In spite of everything, you've made it through four years of college. In fine form, I'd say. Your strength amazes me."

"I'm not strong," I protested. "Not at all." And then I began to sob. It seemed as if everything I'd held in for the past five years came bursting out of me.

Charlie readjusted his position on the rock, using an adjacent rock as a backrest. Then he pulled me into the cradle of his arms. I snuggled deep into his embrace, feeling his hands caress my back, his cheek pressed against mine.

"I'm sorry," I whispered when my sobs finally subsided. "I didn't mean to lose control like that."

"Don't be sorry, Victoria." His voice was husky. "I feel honored that you shared your secret with me."

"Thank you for listening to it," I said. "Thank you so much. I don't deserve to have a friend like you."

Releasing his embrace, he took my chin in his hand and raised my face to look into his. "Yes, you do. If anyone is undeserving, it's me. I'm awed by the fact that a woman like you has consented to be my friend."

As we gazed at each other, I saw all the feelings in Charlie's eyes that I'd ever hoped to see. "I want very badly to kiss you, Victoria," he said. "But I won't right now. You're in a fragile state emotionally, and I don't want to take advantage of that."

He put his arms around me again. I lay my head on his shoulder, and we rested quietly together. Finally, we separated and sat side by side, looking out over the rushing water. Charlie took my hand, running his thumb across the back of it. The sensual feeling sent shivers of ecstasy through my body.

"I like the fact that you have gypsy blood in you," he said, humor in his voice. "It's pretty cool. In my family, we're all descendants of Swiss and German Anabaptists. The gene pool is limited, and my ancestors were terribly inbred. Your diverse gene pool strengthens you biologically. It makes you a fine specimen of a human being."

We both laughed, and the mood suddenly lightened between us. I felt a strange joy, a buoyancy in my being that I hadn't known in years. I looked down at our hands, Charlie's long fingers intertwined with mine. *I never want to part ways with this man*, I thought. *He and I belong together.*

"When's Reverend Hahn's funeral?" Charlie asked.

"Next Saturday afternoon," I told him. "This morning in church, the minister said it would be just a memorial service. His body will be cremated tomorrow, with only immediate family present at that service. Of course, I can't go."

"Would you like for me to attend the memorial service with you?"

"I'd love that," I said.

CHAPTER 50

That week, my lunches with Charlie were quiet. I had little energy for talking. He seemed to understand this, and sat with me in supportive silence. At the end of our meal, he'd reach across the table to hold my hand before we parted ways.

On Saturday afternoon, we met outside the College Mennonite Church for Reverend Hahn's memorial service. When Charlie escorted me inside, I was not surprised to see that the sanctuary was packed. We climbed the stairs to the upper level and found seats in the front row of the balcony.

Peering down at the main floor, I scanned the center front row where Reverend Hahn's loved-ones were sitting. "See the white-haired woman in the covering and cape dress?" I whispered to Charlie. "That's my grandmother Emma. The woman next to her is my aunt Violet."

A man and two women were sitting in the pew with Emma and Violet. I presumed they were Rose's children, Reverend Hahn's nephew and nieces. My cousins. I imagined what it would be like to sit there with the immediate family, to be openly identified as one of the bereaved. But here I was, way up in the balcony with the people who knew Reverend Hahn only marginally.

The service opened with a prayer, followed by the congregation singing, *How Firm a Foundation.* Next, the minister spoke about Reverend Hahn's life, beginning with the account of his adoption from a Romanian orphanage by a missionary couple. I could hear gasps of surprise throughout the audience. "Really?" the woman sitting next to me whispered to her husband. "I never would've guessed that."

As the minister continued with Reverend Hahn's life story, he listed a long litany of projects and accomplishments that amazed even me, holding him up as an example of someone who'd dedicated his life to the service of God and his fellow men. He included Reverend Hahn's years of Civilian Public Service during World War II, but, unsurprisingly, made no mention of his three years in Hollywood.

When the minister described the mission project that Reverend Hahn had headed up in Mexico in 1959, I winced. Charlie squeezed my hand, then whispered in my ear, so softly that I could barely hear him. "His most important work was making you."

After the sermon, the woman sitting next to Violet, whom the minister introduced as Reverend Hahn's niece, sang a solo, *Precious Lord, Take My Hand*. Then Violet stood up and walked to the podium, announcing that she was going to read the thoughts written by Reverend Hahn's older sister Emma. In a tearful voice, she began.

I will never forget the day at the mission in Romania when my parents came home from their trip to the orphanage in Bucharest. My mother was cradling their new baby boy in her arms. When I looked at him, I knew he was the most beautiful child I'd ever laid eyes on. The day Harry became part of our family was one of the best days of my life.

I adored my baby brother. He was intelligent and inquisitive, adding such brightness and liveliness to our family. Little did I know that he'd grow up to do so many great works and touch the lives of so many people. Harry, I'm so proud of the man you became. I love you, and I look forward to the day when we will be reunited in Heaven.

As I listened, I knew that only Charlie, me, and Emma herself understood that she was eulogizing, not her brother, but her son. Her words had come from the depths of her heart, expressing all the love and tenderness she possibly could without revealing her secret.

Sobs welled up from my stomach, threatening to escape noisily from my throat. Charlie put his arm around my shoulders and drew me close. His presence gave me the strength to keep from completely breaking down, which would have caused those around me to wonder about my relationship with the deceased.

The congregation then sang, *Children of the Heavenly Father.* Tears streamed down my face as I pictured my suffering father now resting in a divine embrace.

Before the closing prayer, the pastor announced that a funeral luncheon would be served immediately after the service. Charlie looked at me questioningly. I shook my head. "I need to get out of here," I whispered.

I had no time off from my busy schedule to mourn the passing of my father. Immediately after the memorial service, I had to go home, change clothing, and report for my evening shift at the restaurant.

The next day, I confined myself to my room, attempting to work on a term paper. But I couldn't concentrate. My mind seemed to be running in a hundred different directions.

I wondered if Charlie would call me. I hoped he would. At the memorial service, I'd felt so close to him. I was sure that we were now more than just friends. We were a couple. But I didn't hear from him, and I spent the afternoon and evening feeling neglected.

However, at lunch the next day, he seemed delighted to see me. "How are you feeling, my friend?" he asked.

His obvious concern for my wellbeing instantly melted the resentment that had been building inside me. *Don't be petty,* I scolded myself. *You know he cares about you.*

"I'm still feeling a bit out of it," I told him. "I really need to get focused. Graduation is less than four weeks away. I have papers to write, and exams are coming up. I got behind these past few weeks."

"That's understandable," he said. "It's pretty amazing that you've held up the way you have."

I was silent for a minute, reviewing in my mind what

needed to be completed in each of my classes. My insides churned with anxiety. "I feel like I need a break," I said. "But I'm not going to get one now. I just have to get through the next month. Then I'll probably collapse and stay in bed for a week."

"Have you thought about what you're going to do after graduation?" Charlie asked.

My anxiety escalated into panic at the thought of future plans. I remembered Charlie asking me the same question in September, the first time we'd met in the snack shop. And now, six months later, I had no more of an idea about my future than I'd had back then. I felt my face redden with embarrassment.

Charlie seemed to sense my distress. "I'm sorry. It's not fair to ask that question right now. You've been preoccupied with your father's illness and death this entire year. You haven't had time to think about the future."

"You've got that right," I said, grateful for his understanding. "I haven't had time to think about anything. I have no idea what I'll be doing. I guess I'll just keep on working at the restaurant until I figure something out. Maybe I'll look into teaching English to the Latin American immigrants here in Goshen."

"Don't rush yourself," Charlie said. "After all you've been through, you'll need some time to clear your head."

The talk of future plans seemed to make both of us morose. I would be done with all my classes by the third week in April. But Charlie was going to be working throughout the third trimester, which would end in late May. I could hardly stand to think about what would happen after that.

"And you?" I said, braving the dreaded topic. "What are you going to do after you're done with your assistant teaching?"

He looked down at his food, absentmindedly stabbing his salad with his fork. "I might stick around here for a few weeks. Then I suppose I'll run back to Illinois for a week or two before I head out for Massachusetts."

"I'm going to hate that," I said.

"I know," he said. "Me, too."

It felt strange not to make trips to the Greencroft Center six or seven times a week. Sometimes, I fought the urge to go to the skilled nursing care unit, just to walk into Reverend Hahn's old room and revisit the place where he and I had spent our time together the last year of his life. But I knew there would be another patient in that hospital bed. My business at Greencroft was done.

One week after the funeral, I got into my car to head off to my Saturday evening shift at work. I was about to start the car when I noticed that the key to Reverend Hahn's storage unit was still on my keyring.

I fingered the key thoughtfully, remembering the single visit I'd made to the storage unit. I'd retrieved a painting my father had asked for, and had then spent an hour tidying up the space.

What am I supposed to do with this key? I wondered. *It will probably be up to Emma and Violet to take care of Reverend Hahn's personal belongings. Should I try to get hold of them? Mail the key to them? No, that would be silly. Anyway, if I did that, I'd create complications for Emma. Her family would want to know why Reverend Hahn had given the key to some strange girl in Goshen. I'm sure the manager of the facility will have another key for them.*

Should I just run out to the storage unit and give the key back to the manager? That's probably the best thing to do.

I turned my car key in the ignition. "Well, I don't have time to deal with that right now," I said aloud.

CHAPTER 51

On a Monday morning in early April, I lay in bed exhausted after yet another night of troubled sleep. "Please God," I prayed. "My life's been so intense recently. I'm so tired from everything that's been going on. Can you give me a break? Can I have just one week where nothing happens?"

But as I rolled my weary body out of bed, I somehow knew that was not going to be the case.

As usual, Charlie and I met for lunch that day. We'd had no contact with each other outside the snack shop since Reverend Hahn's memorial service. I wished he would say something to let me know where we stood as a couple. If we even were a couple. Maybe in his mind, we were nothing more than friends.

Where's that kiss he wanted to give me? I fretted as I picked at my French fries. *Does he still think I'm too fragile to handle it?* But even as I asked myself that question, I knew that one kiss from the man I loved would overload my precarious emotional state, spinning me completely out of control.

As I looked at the silent man sitting across from me in the booth, his eyes downcast, I wondered whether he was pulling back emotionally, preparing himself for our impending separation. But when he raised his eyes to look at me, I saw tenderness in them. Then he reached across the table to hold my hand, his touch communicating what his words weren't saying.

Oh, Charlie, I thought, *why don't you explain to me what's going on? I can't read your signals.*

That evening, my dad called me. "Vickie," he said, "something came in the mail for you today."

"What is it?" I asked.

"It's a letter from a lawyer's office. Attorney Edward Landis, on Washington Street in Goshen."

His words sent my heart racing. I'd never in my life had any dealings with an attorney. Was I in trouble? Was somebody suing me? Had I unknowingly broken the law? Perhaps I'd committed some kind of traffic violation that I wasn't aware of. But I couldn't imagine an attorney writing to inform me of that.

"This is making me nervous," I said. "Would you open the letter and read it to me? I need to know if it's something urgent I need to take care of."

"Sure." I could hear a crackling sound as my dad opened the envelope and unfolded the letter. "It says ..." He spoke slowly, as if perusing its contents. "It says that he needs to meet with you regarding the contents of Harry Hahn's will."

"What?" I exclaimed.

My dad sounded as bewildered as I felt. "Well, Vickie, Reverend Hahn must've left you something. I guess you need to call Mr. Landis to find out. Do you want me to come by your place and drop off the letter?"

"No," I said. "Just give me the phone number, and I'll call tomorrow." I tore a sheet of paper off the notepad by the phone and jotted down the number as he read it to me.

With the scrap of paper in hand, I rushed to my room and closed the door. I sat on the bed, barely able to breathe, trying to make sense of this new thing that had just shown up in my overloaded life. I hadn't given a single thought to the possibility that I would inherit anything from Reverend Hahn. I'd assumed that his lavish generosity had ended the day he instructed me to take the one thousand dollars from his bedside stand.

Don't get carried away now, Victoria, I cautioned myself. *Maybe this isn't a big deal. Maybe it isn't even about money.*

Before I set off for the campus the next morning, I called Attorney Landis's office. I spoke to his secretary, who informed me I needed to schedule an appointment with him.

"What's all this about?" I asked her.

"Mr. Landis will have to tell you that." She sounded unconcerned about my anxiety. "Can you come in at four o'clock Friday afternoon?"

"Sure," I said.

Over the next few days, fretting about the appointment added one more thing to my list of worries: my upcoming exams, papers I needed to write, pressure from my boss to work extra shifts, and Charlie's unrelenting silence.

Late Friday afternoon, I pulled into a city parking lot in downtown Goshen, then walked half a block to the office of Attorney Edward Landis. The building was ancient, at least a hundred years old, with sagging hardwood floors and heavy woodwork surrounding the doors and windows. As I seated myself in a waiting room that looked as if it belonged to a bygone era, I felt like an actress in a 1930s movie, playing the role of a sad divorcee seeking legal help to protect her assets from her scoundrel of an ex-husband.

I sat there for a full thirty minutes past my appointment time, my anxiety rising with every second that ticked by. I began to wonder whether there had been a mistake, whether I'd come on the wrong day, or to the wrong place. I was staring out the window at the traffic passing by on Washington Street, thinking that I should get up and leave, when I heard a deep male voice call out, "Miss Unruh?"

I turned to see a tall elderly man with a shock of unruly gray hair standing in the doorway to his office. His appearance was in keeping with my fantasy of an old movie, as he was wearing a bright red bowtie and a dark pinstripe suit that looked as ancient as the building he worked in.

I stood up and walked toward him. He extended his hand. "Ed Landis."

I followed him into his office, where he seated himself behind an enormous wooden desk covered with countless stacks of messy files. He gestured for me to sit in the chair across from him. Muttering to himself, he rummaged through the files on his desk. "Harry Hahn. Harry Hahn. Now where did I put that folder?"

Just as I was beginning to worry that he'd lost my birth father's vital information, Attorney Landis turned to the shelves behind him, rummaging through more stacks. A minute later, he retrieved the file he was looking for, waving it in triumph.

Reaching into his desk drawer for a pair of reading glasses, he scanned the contents of the file. "Miss Unruh," he intoned. "It seems as if you are the sole beneficiary of Reverend Harry Hahn's will." He looked at me over the top of his glasses. "You're his daughter, right? His only child?"

His eyes reflected little curiosity. I could tell that, for him, my relationship to Reverend Hahn was only a legal matter, not a subject for gossip or intrigue. "Yes," I said.

"Okay, then." He handed me a stack of papers filled with legal jargon I couldn't make sense of.

"I don't know what any of this means," I told him.

Reaching a long arm across his desk, he pointed to the document on the top of the stack. "You are the beneficiary of Harry Hahn's life insurance policy. The amount is listed there at the bottom of the page."

I gasped when I saw the number. "Is this for real?"

"It is," he said, ignoring my astonishment. Then he flipped a few pages over to show me a second document. "And these numbers are what you will be receiving from his various investments."

He chuckled as he flipped over to a third document. "You've also inherited the contents of your father's storage unit. I guess you'll have some sorting out to do. Children always get stuck with that kind of mess after a parent dies."

The unbelievable news rendered me speechless. Attorney Landis folded his arms on his desk, his half-smile failing to mask his readiness to be done with our meeting. "Any questions?" he asked.

"Would you ... would you tell me everything again?" I said in a weak voice.

Obligingly, he separated the three documents, spreading them out in front of me. "Here's the amount from his life insurance, and here are the amounts from his investments," he said, pointing to the first and second documents in turn. Then, slapping his palm on the third document, he said, "This one pertains to the personal property in his storage unit. The location of the unit is listed in the document."

Handing me a pen, he pointed to a blank line on the first document. "You need to sign here."

I scrawled a shaky *Victoria Unruh* on the designated line. Then Attorney Landis had me flip through the pages of all three documents, showing me where my signature was needed in other places. When we were finished with the signing, he took all the pages and secured them together with a paperclip.

"That's it," he said. "I'll have my secretary make copies for you, and you'll be all set. This will take a while to process. So, don't expect to have any checks in hand for a few more months."

"That's okay," I said. I knew I wasn't ready to have that amount of money in my possession any time soon.

Attorney Landis reached into a drawer, pulled out a key, and slid it across the desk to me. "You can go ahead and dispose of the items in the storage unit. Good luck!"

"I already have a key," I mumbled, but took the one he offered anyway.

A few minutes later, I walked out of Attorney Landis's office carrying a large envelope containing copies of the documents I'd just signed. I sat behind the wheel of my car for ten minutes before I started it, as my hand was too shaky to turn the key in the ignition.

When I succeeded in calming myself enough to drive, I didn't head back to my apartment. Instead, I drove west through town, then down the county roads until I reached my dad's house.

Not wanting to startle anyone by my unexpected visit, I knocked on the door instead of walking in unannounced.

I could hear my dad's slow, heavy footsteps crossing the living room floor. "Vickie!" he exclaimed as he opened the door. "You don't need to knock. This is your home. You can always come right in."

I stepped into the house, giving him a quick hug. He appeared to be alone, which relieved me. "Where's Barbara?" I asked him.

"Judy took her out shopping," he replied as he settled back into his chair. "She should be home any minute now. She's bringing supper with her."

"And Lucy?"

"She's upstairs working on her beads." He shook his head, chuckling. "When that girl gets going on her jewelry, she's in her own little world. The house could be burning down around her, and she'd never notice. But I'm glad she has something to do."

Pushing aside a pile of newspapers, I sat down on the sofa. My dad shifted in his chair, angling his body toward me. "So, what brings you here, sweetheart?"

I took a long breath, then exhaled deeply. "Dad, I went to see Mr. Landis today."

He looked puzzled. "Mr. Landis?"

"Edward Landis, the attorney. Remember the letter he sent me?"

"Oh, yes. So, what did he have to say?"

"You're not going to believe this." Speaking my news aloud made me feel a little dizzy. "I can't believe it myself. Reverend Hahn left me money."

My dad's body lurched backward in his chair, as if my words had hit him hard. "How much money?"

"I don't know the exact amount. I haven't totaled it up. But it's a lot."

"Whew!" he whistled. "I didn't see this coming, and I bet you didn't, either."

We sat together in a stunned silence, both of us trying to comprehend this new reality in my life. "Dad," I finally said, "what am I going to do with all that money?"

"Well ..." He scratched his chin, squinting one eye. "I guess you'll use it to get started in your life. I'm sure that's what Reverend Hahn meant for you to do."

My eyes roamed around the cluttered living room, with its worn carpet and shabby furniture. I got up and went into the kitchen, taking in the battered cupboards, the ancient refrigerator, the electric stove with only three working burners, the old chrome and laminate table my parents had purchased when my brothers were little. This was the lifestyle I was accustomed to.

"I'll give you some of the money, Dad," I said as I walked back into the living room and stood beside his chair. "After everything you've done for me, I owe you something."

He shook his head emphatically. "Nope. You don't owe me a penny, Vickie. It didn't cost me anything to raise you. Reverend Hahn gave us more than his share of child support money."

"Maybe you could remodel the house. Buy some new furniture. Fix up the kitchen for Barbara."

My dad waved a dismissive hand. "Nah. We're doing okay. Now that I'm retired, I have time to putter around the house a little bit. We'll get things in shape. Matter of fact, we're going out to look at kitchen stoves this weekend."

"Maybe you and Barbara would like to do something special. Like go on a trip."

"Nah. Barbara and I don't need to go anywhere. There's no place we'd rather be than right here. You just keep that money, Vickie. The next few years, you'll have places you want to go and things you want to do, and it's going to come in mighty handy."

His voice softened. "See, Vickie, this was Reverend Hahn's way of taking care of his child. He was looking out for your future. He knew that was his job to do."

Reaching over to squeeze my hand, he said, "This is kind of hard for me to admit, sweetheart, but I'm glad you and he got to know each other. Even though I never cared for the man myself, I had to come to terms with the fact that you needed him. I don't think you could've put all the pieces of your life together without having some time with him."

Sighing, I flopped down on the sofa again. "You're the only parent I have left now, Dad. Mom's gone. Reverend Hahn's gone. You can't leave me. You can't ever die."

He threw back his head, laughing. "Well, I can't promise you that I won't go when the good Lord calls my name. But don't you worry, sweetheart. I don't plan to kick off any time soon. I just had a checkup. Dr. Miller says my old ticker is beating along just fine. My blood pressure's good." He patted his ample belly. "Dr. Miller always tells me I need to lose weight. He's been singing that song for years. So, Barbara's trying to cook a little healthier. All of us here could stand to drop a few pounds."

He pulled the lever on the side of his chair to move it into the reclining position. "Nope, Vickie, I'm not going anywhere anytime soon. You're gonna be stuck with your old man for a good long while."

I heard the crunch of car tires on the gravel driveway. "That's probably Judy and Barbara," he said.

"Dad, don't tell anyone about the money," I pleaded. "Don't tell Barbara or Lucy. I don't want anyone to feel bad about it."

"I won't tell a soul." He yawned, deeply relaxed. "That money is entirely your business. I don't aim to be poking my nose in it or stirring up any trouble over it. Tonight, I plan on laying my head on the pillow and going to sleep, putting it all out of my mind. And when I wake up in the morning, I won't be thinking about it anymore."

The front door opened and Judy came in, carrying a load of groceries for her mother. "Hey, sis," she called when she saw me. "Whatcha been up to?"

After she deposited her bags in the kitchen, I followed her back out to the car, where I filled my own arms with groceries and carried them into the house.

"Oh, thank you, sweetie," Barbara gushed as she began putting the groceries away.

"I'm going to say hi to Lucy," I called to my dad as I ran up the stairs.

Lucy beamed when she saw me walk into her work room. She pointed to the rows of necklaces, bracelets, and earrings she'd carefully laid out on one end of her table. "I'm building up my inventory," she said proudly. "Pick something out, Tori Grace. It'll be my gift to you. I think the earth tones would look good with your complexion."

I shook my head. "No, Lucy. The next time I come over, I'll bring some money with me, and I'll buy something from you."

As I descended the stairs, I could see my dad and Barbara sitting in the matching recliners I'd bought them. I could hear their slow, desultory conversation. Mostly, they were just breathing freely in each other's presence, at ease with their shared life. I knew that, truly, they had everything they could possibly want.

"Judy left," Barbara said when she saw me. "She has softball practice this evening. The city leagues are starting up again. She said to tell you goodbye."

I went over to the chairs, bending down to give Barbara a hug. She kissed me on the cheek. "I love you, Victoria."

"I love you, too," I said. "I love both of you."

Then I went to my dad, and he wrapped his burly arms around me. "Vickie, Vickie, Vickie," he crooned as he'd done when I was a little girl. "You take good care of yourself now, sweetheart."

CHAPTER 52

Four days before my college graduation, I rushed into the snack shop at noon. Charlie was sitting in our usual booth, engrossed in the journal article he was reading. Too impatient to stand in line to order lunch, I went straight to the booth and dropped down on the seat across from him.

"I did it!" I exclaimed. "I just finished my last exam. I'm completely done!"

Charlie looked up, smiling at me. "Congratulations! Now you're just one ceremony away from being a college graduate."

"I'm not going to end up with the GPA I wanted," I admitted. "I was hoping to do a lot better. But at least I got through."

Charlie put his journal away and let me prattle on for a while, about the exams I'd just taken and the papers I'd turned in at the last minute. "Thank God I don't have to work tonight," I sighed. "I'm ready to crash."

When I finally stopped babbling, it occurred to me that there was one thing I was still holding back from Charlie. He now knew almost everything about me, not only the secrets of my past, but the details of my current life. However, I hadn't brought myself to tell him about my trip to the attorney's office and the news I'd received there. I wasn't sure why I'd kept that secret from him.

Maybe it's because I haven't been able to wrap my own head around it, I thought. *I still can't imagine myself as a person with a lot of money.*

Charlie must have noticed a change in my demeanor. "You look worried, Victoria. Is something on your mind?"

I shrugged, trying to sound nonchalant. "Pretty much everything is on my mind. My thoughts are going ninety miles an hour."

He looked at me intently, an inscrutable expression on his face. "Victoria, I need to talk with you."

Although spoken in a pleasant tone, his words sounded ominous to me. "About what?" I asked.

He glanced at his watch. "I can't tell you right now. Not here."

"Okay. So, when do you want to talk?"

"Since you're free tonight, how about then?"

As I stared at him, bewildered, he quickly added, "I know you're tired, and you probably want to turn in early tonight. Let's meet right after dinner. Maybe around seven?"

"That's fine," I said. "Where?"

"At my apartment?"

His response surprised me. Although Charlie and I lived only two blocks apart, me on Sixth Street, him on Eighth Street, we had never entered each other's apartments. That had been a line we'd never ventured to cross.

"Okay," I said. "I can do that."

He glanced at his watch again. "I've got to get going." We both stood up to exchange the hug that was now customary between us.

"See you tonight," he said. He shot me another inscrutable look, then picked up his briefcase and hurried out of the snack shop.

After Charlie left, I sat alone for a few minutes, feeling abandoned and a little hurt by his abrupt departure. Then I slid out of the booth, went to the snack shop counter, and ordered a cup of coffee. Returning to the booth, I sipped my coffee, trying to collect my thoughts.

I can't believe it! My four years of college are over. I have no assignments looming over me. I have nothing to do this afternoon. I have nowhere to go but home.

I tried to enjoy those relaxing thoughts, but troublesome concerns bubbled to the surface. *What am I going to do with my life now? What am I going to do tomorrow, next week? A month from now? A year from now?*

What the heck am I supposed to do with the money I

inherited? Reverend Hahn would want me to use it wisely, to invest it in something that would move my life forward. I wish he was here to give me advice. I want to do something that would make him proud. Would he want me to go to graduate school? We never talked about that. I have no idea where I'd go, or what degree I'd pursue.

I need to talk to Bob tomorrow, to tell him I want to increase my hours at the restaurant as soon as possible. Otherwise, I'll be sitting around with nothing to do. Maybe now that I'll have a little bit of free time, Charlie and I can spend more time together. Of course, he'll be busy with teaching for another four weeks. But surely, he'll be available on weekends.

What about our lunches? I won't be here on campus to eat with him. That will be strange. Will he miss me? The thought of Charlie eating lunch with anyone else, even a male colleague, filled me with jealousy.

But maybe Charlie wants to cut things off between us now. Is that what he's going to tell me this evening? He's leaving for Massachusetts at the end of the summer. Maybe he doesn't want us to get more serious, and then have to part ways.

Suddenly, I felt so ill at ease that I couldn't stay in the snack shop for another minute. I got up, returned my cup to the counter, and headed out the door.

The spring day was beautiful, the blue sky dotted with fluffy white clouds. As I walked back to my apartment, I noticed that new leaves were coming out on the maple trees, enveloping the dark, sturdy branches in a pale-green haze. Despite my worries, I couldn't help but think about the promise of a new beginning in my own life.

After fixing lunch for myself, I tried lying down for a nap, but found myself too keyed up to relax. So, I got up, collected the dirty clothes from my overflowing hamper, and drove to the laundromat. Afterwards, I bought groceries to stock my section of the kitchen cupboards. Back at the apartment, I gave my room a thorough cleaning, setting my belongings in order, wishing my entire life could be that easily managed.

At ten minutes before seven that evening, I started on my short walk to Charlie's house. Anxious thoughts flooded my mind. *He's been acting so odd recently. Is he getting ready to break up with me? How can we break up, when we haven't actually dated? But he might tell me there's no point in us seeing each other anymore, that we shouldn't develop a deeper relationship because he'll be leaving soon.*

"Dear God, don't let it be that," I whispered. "Don't let Charlie leave me yet. I can't deal with another loss right now. Let me have just a few more months with him."

When I arrived at Professor Liechty's large, two story home, I saw Charlie standing out front waiting for me, jacketless, rubbing his arms to ward off the evening chill. In the waning light, I could see the eagerness on his face, which eased my anxiety a bit.

"Victoria!" he exclaimed. Taking my hand, he led me to the side entrance of the house, which opened to a set of stairs leading to his efficiency apartment in the basement.

I glanced around the single room, not surprised by what I saw. Charlie's living quarters matched his persona, clean and tidy, but unpretentious. A narrow bed covered in a dark bedspread was pushed up against one wall. The opposite side of the room held a stove, a dorm-sized refrigerator, a sink, and a single row of cupboards. A small table with two chairs stood in the center of the tiny space.

The dominant piece of furniture in the room was Charlie's massive desk, covered with neat stacks of papers and scientific journals. The shelves beside the desk were loaded with books.

"I'm sorry," he said. "I don't have anywhere for us to sit, except for here at the table." He pulled out one of the chairs for me, clearly nervous about playing the role of host. "Can I get you something to drink?"

I shook my head, my anxiety rising again, wondering what was about to come.

We sat at the table facing each other, the only lighting in the room coming from the floor lamp beside his desk. "I've been thinking a lot," Charlie said.

Oh, no, I thought, my stomach sick with dread. *Here it comes.*

"I've been thinking about you and me. I've had a hard time thinking about anything else." He slid his hand across the table, palm up. I responded to the invitation by placing my hand in his.

"Victoria." His voice caught, and he took a moment to clear his throat. "Last September when we met in the snack shop, you asked me if I'd found the right woman. I told you that I hadn't. But by the end of that hour, I had an inkling that she was sitting right there across from me. Now, seven months later, I know that to be true."

He looked at me imploringly. "I just hope you feel the same way about me."

I stared at him, wide-eyed. All I could do was nod.

"As a scientist," he said, "I used to question the concept of being in love. The idea seemed irrational. The term didn't refer to anything tangible or measurable. But here I am, so in love with a woman that I sometimes think I've lost all reason."

"Oh," I whispered.

"Over the months that we've been talking," he continued, "my feelings for you have been growing steadily. But ever since our afternoon out by the dam, my love for you has been overwhelming. It's been making me a little crazy, actually. If I've been quiet and distant recently, it's because I've had no idea what to do or what to say. And when I think about leaving at the end of the summer, the thought of losing you sends me into a panic."

His outpouring of feeling stunned me. I'd always known Charlie to be a level-headed man with well-modulated emotions. "I love you, too, Charlie," I said softly. "I've been crazy about you for a long time. For months."

He sighed deeply, his shoulders sagging in relief. Then he looked down at the table for a few seconds before meeting my gaze again. "In September, I'll be heading back to Massachusetts. I want you to come with me, Victoria."

Overcome with emotion, he jumped up from the table and stood with his back to me. "For God's sake, Victoria, tell me that you'll come with me. I can't stand the thought of going back without you."

Suddenly, it seemed as if I was outside myself, observing the momentous event that was unfolding between the two of us. I watched myself stand up, walk over to Charlie, and place a hand on his shoulder. "Of course, I'll go with you, Charlie," I heard myself whisper. "I can't stand the thought of you going without me."

He swung around and pulled me into his arms, holding me tightly. "Did you say yes? Did I hear you say yes?"

"Yes, yes, yes!" I said.

As he held me, I could feel the beating of his heart against my chest, a sensation that lulled me into a state of deep peace. Then he pulled back, taking my chin in his hand. "I should have done this a long time ago. If a man is going to ask for a commitment from a woman, he should kiss her first."

And then he did. The kiss was timid at first, questioning. Then it became more passionate, each of us exploring the depths of the other, losing ourselves in each other. Charlie lips would momentarily leave mine to kiss my forehead, my cheeks, my neck, his hands caressing my back and entangling themselves in my hair. Then his lips would find mine again, hungry to reconnect.

Finally, we reluctantly released our embrace and sat down at the table again. Reaching for my hand, Charlie said,

"I wanted very much to tell you about my feelings earlier. But I didn't want to cause you any turmoil when you already had so much upheaval in your life. That's why I waited until you were completely finished with your exams. I didn't want to distract you when you were facing your finals."

I laughed. "That was good thinking. Because right now, I'm completely mind-blown. I wouldn't have been able to concentrate at all."

Charlie turned my hand over, running his finger over the lines in my palm, caressing each of my fingers in turn. Then his brow furrowed with concern. "There's something that troubles me, though, Victoria. I've looked at every aspect of our relationship, and I am one hundred percent sure of my feelings for you. I know you're the right woman for me. But you've just come through some of the roughest years of your life. I've had to wonder whether you need more time to figure out what you want. I care about you too much to stand in the way of your doing what you need to do for yourself."

"Charlie," I said, "I've known for the past six months that I want to be with you. Five years ago, I vowed that I would never get serious about a man unless I could trust him enough to tell him who I really was. That day at the Millrace Park, I told you my story because I was sure about you. And when you responded with so much sensitivity, I knew we belonged together. I couldn't stand the thought of us parting ways. So, whatever we need to figure out about our future, we'll do it together."

Charlie looked at me with such tenderness that I thought I was going to cry. "I hope you understand, Victoria," he said, "that I'm asking you to marry me."

"I thought you were proposing," I replied. "I wasn't sure. But my answer is still yes."

"We have plenty of time," he said. "We don't need to rush into anything. If you're not ready to go to Massachusetts when I leave here at the end of the summer, that's fine. You might want to spend time with your family, or even be alone for a while to clear your head. We could manage a long-distance relationship for a while."

I laced my fingers through his. "I appreciate you giving me some time. But I'll probably be ready sooner than you think."

Charlie released my hand, then sat with folded arms on the table, as if ready to talk business. "I'm not saying this is going to be easy. Even though I have money put back, we'll still have to live on a tight budget. But I'd like to think that being together will make up for our frugal lifestyle."

"I'll help out," I promised. "I'll do my part."

Should I tell him about my inheritance? I wondered. *Should I erase all his concerns by telling him we'll have a substantial sum of money to draw on?*

But I knew the timing wasn't right. Charlie had planned carefully for our immediate future, and I deeply respected him for that. I didn't want to wound his pride by undermining those plans. I couldn't bring myself to spoil the beautiful moment by bringing up the complicated subject of my newfound wealth.

"I know you want to do your part," he said. "And I appreciate that. But I understand that it might take a while for you to find suitable employment, although your TESOL credentials could be quite marketable. You might even find work there at MIT with international students and their families. But I don't want to put you under any pressure. I want you to know that I'm prepared to carry most of the financial load."

He hesitated. "And, of course, there's the matter of you furthering your own education. If you want to start graduate school, we'll make that happen."

Standing up, I went around the table to give him a hug, and he pulled me onto his lap. "I have confidence in you," I said as he held me tightly. "I have confidence in us. Things will work out for us."

"I've never believed in miracles," he said softly. "I've never even believed much in divine providence. But I have to think back on the day Dr. Liechty called me about the teaching assistant position. My first thought was to decline, because I didn't want to interrupt my schooling. I was ready to move full speed ahead into my future career. But something inside me urged me to consider his offer. I had a strange sense that I needed to return to Goshen for a reason. And now, I know the reason."

Tenderly, he caressed my back, which relaxed me so deeply that I thought I might fall asleep in his arms. Laying my head on his shoulder, I murmured, "I'm so glad you came back."

He must have sensed my weariness, because he said, "You've had a big day. You're tired. We'll talk more tomorrow. I need to get you home."

He held my jacket while I slipped my arms into the sleeves. Then he grabbed his own, and we headed out the door together. As we walked hand in hand the two blocks to my house, I sensed a new protectiveness in him. I loved it.

We stood outside my front door, our bodies pressed together for our last embrace of the night. "I'm so happy, Victoria," he whispered in my ear. "Happier than I've ever been in my entire life. I didn't think it was possible to be this happy."

I could feel a powerful current passing between our bodies, foretelling the physical pleasure that we would soon share. I knew that intimacy with Charlie would be vastly different from the awkward, immature fumbling I'd experienced with Calvin.

Despite my exhaustion, I couldn't fall asleep when I collapsed into bed that night. I lay awake until four o'clock in the morning. But I didn't mind my sleeplessness. My insomnia didn't feel torturous.

My mind felt quiet and peaceful as I considered

everything that had happened to me over the past five years. Things I'd been unable to fully absorb now seemed to sort themselves out and fall into place, becoming coherent chapters of my life story.

My body felt light and airy. For the moment, I was free of any heavy responsibility and all sense of impending loss. My college career was over. All that was left for me to do was to collect my diploma at my graduation ceremony. I had no worries about my birth father, as he'd been released from his suffering and had made his transition to the next world. And, most importantly, I no longer needed to face the prospect of losing Charlie.

My thoughts drifted to my family. My dad and Barbara were supremely content with their life at the farmhouse. They both seemed to sense that I'd soon be moving on. They wouldn't be surprised or dismayed by my decision to leave the state. And my sister Lucy was just fine, snug and secure in the care of her father and stepmother.

I thought about my mother and my birth father on the other side. Somehow, they didn't seem far away. In the stillness, I could almost feel their spirits hovering nearby, loving me, supporting me.

And when my thoughts turned to Charlie, I felt my heart expand to infinite proportions, until my love for him filled the entire room, the entire world, the entire universe. I'd never been as sure of anything as when I'd agreed to spend the rest of my life with him. Our future stretched before us, filled with unknown blessings that we'd share, unknown challenges that we'd face together.

"Tomorrow," I whispered aloud, "I'll tell Charlie about my inheritance. We'll have plenty of time to figure things out."

As I grew drowsy, hovering on the verge of deep sleep, everything in my life seemed unified, perfectly choreographed, like the strains of a magnificent orchestra. One harmonious whole.

AUTHOR'S NOTE

As in this novel's prequel, *Blessed Transgression,* I have referred to a number of businesses and organizations that currently exist or have existed in the city of Goshen, Indiana, and the surrounding communities. I have used them fictitiously, and it is not my intention to accurately portray any activities, events, or people associated with these businesses and organizations. Westside Mennonite Church, First Mennonite Church of Warsaw, and Conrad Grebel Christian High School are entirely products of my imagination.

It is not my intention to imply that any activities or practices associated with the Mennonite Church in this story are typical of the Mennonite Church in general.

I have given many of my characters surnames common in the Mennonite community. I have not used the full name of any person whom I have ever known. If any of my characters share your name or the name of someone you know, please understand that this in unintentional on my part, and purely coincidental.

OTHER BOOKS BY LOIS JEAN THOMAS
www.loisjeanthomas.com

Me and You—We Are Who? (The Sambodh Society, Inc., 2006)

All the Happiness There Is (The Sambodh Society, Inc., 2006)

Johnny and Kris (The Sambodh Society, Inc., 2013)

Daughters of Seferina (Seventh Child Publishing/ CreateSpace, 2013)

Days of Daze: My Journey Through the World of Traumatic Brain Injury (Seventh Child Publishing/ CreateSpace, 2014)

Rachel's Song (Seventh Child Publishing/CreateSpace, 2014)

A.K.A. Suzette (Seventh Child Publishing/CreateSpace, 2014)

Blessed Transgression (Seventh Child Publishing/ CreateSpace, 2015)

A Weekend with Frances (Seventh Child Publishing/ CreateSpace, 2016)

www.ingramcontent.com/pod-product-compliance
Lightning Source LLC
Chambersburg PA
CBHW060142260626
47160CB00001B/89